THE THIRD HOUR
Richard Devin

D1637221

13Thirty Books

ISBN: 0692218661
978-0692218662

The Third Hour is a work of fiction. Names, places, characters, and incidents are the products of the author's imagination or are used fictitiously. Any resemblance to actual events, locales, or persons, living or dead, is entirely coincidental.

Acknowledgements

To the class of 1977 Fairport High: Your youth and enthusiasm remain with me each day and the memories of our times together in the multi-colored halls of FHS inspire me always.

Especially to: Leslie Mannix (Plucknette), Mike Stolt, Debbie Jerome (Alderson), Mike Celent and Bill DaRin. The character within each of you, has inspired the characters within each of these pages.

And to Annabelle and Joseph DePew.

In Memory

Nonna, Antonia (Antoinette) Rienzi and Nonno, Rocco G. LaFica,

Thank you for braving the cold stormy seas in 1920 aboard the SS Patria, coming to port at Ellis Island - and giving me life.

La famiglia ricorda, ama e ti manca.

PROLOGUE

June, 1943
Philadelphia Naval Yard
Philadelphia, Pennsylvania USA

The second of two massive 75-kilovolt generators was being carefully lowered to the deck of the U.S.S. Eldridge, a 1,240 ton destroyer escort, by the land based crane. The first generator had been set in place without incident earlier this morning and was now being secured to the deck of the Eldridge by a crew of eight seamen, who scurried around and over the generator, bolting it to the ship's deck. The weight of the generator set on the port side of the deck caused the ship to list a few degrees. Now, with only a few feet remaining before the second generator touched down onto the starboard deck of the destroyer escort, all hands were silent.

The entire 306 foot length of the Eldridge had already been braided with thousands of feet of copper wire during its construction. Three Radio Frequency transmitters and three thousand 6L6 power vacuum tubes had been installed into a lead coated panel mounted to the super structure of the destroyer escort.

Four enormous coils of copper wire that would take the electricity produced by the generators, convert it from direct current to alternating current, and step up the power, were secured ahead of the generators delivery. In theory, the steady current of electricity produced via the generators, spun through the cooper coils and then stepped up, would create a harmonic magnetic field that here-to-fore had been unknown.

"Easy down," the seaman shouted to another crewman, who repeated the order to another, until the chain of voice commands reached the crane operator. "Easy. Easy," he repeated, and the entire command chain followed.

The crane's motor revved and strained as the generator was slowly moved into place, hovering above the steel reinforced and cross-braced deck pad, where, once in place, it would be bolted and then welded to become one with the Eldridge.

"Eighteen inches...twelve inches...six inches. Easy now," the seaman shouted, as he quickly laid himself down onto the deck of the ship. He raised his body up slightly, supporting himself by his toes and fingers, as he eyed the distance between the pad and the generator.

Several other seamen, in sweat soaked and greased stained t-shirts, took hold of the cables and guided the generator over the seven-inch bolts protruding from the hull of the ship's superstructure. They pushed and turned the massive machine slowly, until the holes in the base of the generator aligned with the bolts in the ship.

"We're there," a seaman said, waving his hands flat against the deck. An echo of the command continued for several seconds until it reached the crane operator.

The ship tilted slightly to the starboard side as it absorbed the weight of the second generator, then slowly righted. The tilting and then leveling of the ship created a small wake that crashed into the sea wall, splashing white foaming water onto concrete walls and rocks. Most on deck took no notice of the movement of the ship as it continued a slight sway from side to side.

Albert did.

He steadied himself, placing one foot to the side of the other, spreading his legs, and reached for an iron ladder rung. He had not been on a ship for many years; the last time was a great crossing over the Atlantic. He wasn't fond of the ship's movements then, and he was even less fond of them now. He took a firmer grip on the rung of the ladder running up the side of the ship's tower.

The crane powered down and the cable relaxed as a crew of seamen, electricians, and midshipmen swarmed the machinery, securing it in place.

The Third Hour

"Are you holding up?" Lieutenant Hamilton asked, noting that Albert was still supporting himself with the ladder.

"Yes. Yes, just fine," Albert said, his German accent punctuating each word.

"We'll be on our way by nightfall," Lieutenant Hamilton said and checked his watch, silently calculating. "Your quarters are ready for you below."

"Very good. I should like to go there now and prepare for the experiment." Albert took his hands from the ladder, pausing momentarily, then took a step, his sea legs returning.

"Corporal Jennings?" Lieutenant Hamilton called out to the young man.

"Yes sir, Lieutenant?"

"Kindly show our guest to his quarters."

"Yes, sir."

"If there is anything you need, do not hesitate to ask," Lieutenant Hamilton said, giving an informal salute. "And, Mister Einstein? It is an honor to have you aboard."

Legend: A tale told when truth is too dangerous.

ONE

Spring, 2006
Rome
3:00 A.M.

The thought that he should be more careful on the slippery ancient stones had no sooner crossed the mind of Dominic Renzi, when he found himself lying flat on his face on those same cobblestones.

The light drizzle that fell throughout the city and surrounding Roman countryside all through the day had continued into the early morning hours. It brought with it both a chilling air that seeped into Dominic's bones—despite his Armani Exchange leather jacket—and a dampness that made for dangerous walking on wet, ancient stonework.

Dominic saved himself from serious injury, by throwing his arms out at the last second before hitting the stones, but the palms of his hands took the brunt of the fall and they were stinging. He landed, face to the stones, arms under him. His hands molded around the curves and ridges of the stones, that had been carried from the fields that once surrounded the city and the river bed, then laid out all along the Roman city some two thousand years ago. He could feel the wetness seeping into his clothes.

Of course I landed in a puddle. The thought was both self-effacing and sarcastic.

Slowly, Dominic began to push himself up. His hands slipped slightly on the sticky wetness of the foul smelling puddle he had landed in, and he struggled for a moment to regain his balance.

His apartment was just up the road, not more than ten yards. *This was not the brightest idea,* he chided silently, *walking at this early hour with the rain still falling.*

He eased himself up from the roadway and continued to make his way along the few remaining feet with a slight limp to his gait, but without further incident. He leaned against the doorframe to his apartment putting pressure on his left leg. It hurt. He pushed the door open and stepped inside. *I didn't lock it?* He shook his head at his own thoughtlessness and justified his lack of action by the lateness of the night and the fact that no one else was out at this time, at least none that he saw. Still, clear thoughts seemed to be a thing of the past. He sighed heavily. *I couldn't even remember to lock my door, what else have I forgotten?* He didn't know and he didn't care. He couldn't think about it now. His thoughts were too clouded, filled with indecision. He hated indecision in others and now that's all his thoughts were, one indecision after another. Taking long late night walks and sleeping until the sun was high, did not make thinking or decision making any easier. It did nothing to clear up his mind. In fact, it might be making everything worse.

A sudden image materialized in his mind; a lone lamb in an expansive field, baying to an unseen and unresponsive flock. He was that lamb without a flock and certainly no herder. He pondered the biblical reference then closed the door to his apartment. He turned and walked the few steps down the main hallway toward the living room. His left knee ached. Old uneven bricks were just as hard and unforgiving to human skin and bones today as they were when first pried from the earth and laid to form the old Roman streets.

He leaned against the wall with an outstretched hand, while using the other hand to check his knee. His pants weren't torn. *That's good.* Not that he was a clotheshorse, but he had just purchased these pants, some shirts and the jacket he was wearing, about a week ago—and he didn't want to have them ruined already. Funds were tight and even shopping at the exchange got to be expensive.

His left knee took more of the fall than he had previously realized. There was blood soaking through the pants at the knee. Then, glancing to his right knee Dominic noticed that blood covered his pants there, too. He was bleeding from both knees. His eyes skimmed the fabric of the pants from the knee to the hem. They too were stained with the rain-diluted blood.

He reached out to touch the hem of the pants and noticed that his hand was covered in the thick red liquid. As he pulled his other hand away from the wall, blood, like a watercolor painting, smeared the wall with a reddened handprint, reminding him of the Anasazi Indian rock art he had seen in deserts of Arizona. He had spent two years after high school finding himself, as well as ancient petroglyphs and pictographs, in the mountains of Nevada and Arizona. He didn't fare very well at finding himself, but he did manage to stumble upon a previously unrecorded trove of pictographs in Sloan Canyon in the Black Mountains of southern Nevada, and he'd received some acclaim for the find. He still had the pictures that appeared with an article on the find in the Las Vegas Review Journal, somewhere.

After finding the intellect in himself, he decided to find the man and joined the military for a short stint. Dominic never saw any action, save a few exercises in the New Mexico deserts. But he did find a calling—at least he found what he had thought to be a calling.

His knees were bleeding and so were his palms. He must have hit the roadway harder than he had originally thought. Attempting to avoid contact with any other surface, he made his way to the hallway bath. It wasn't anything more than a room with a sink and toilet, but being the American he was, he still referred to it as a bathroom, just as he refused to call the apartment a "flat." Something his onetime housekeeper, a local woman from his church, could never understand. "Toletta, non una stanza del bagno," she kept telling him.

"I know it's a toilet," he would respond. Then he'd call it a bathroom again, just to get her going. He couldn't afford the housekeeper anymore, so now he was free to call the room whatever he wanted, without outside commentary.

Tapping at the faucet handle with his elbows, he got the water to pour out. A little too cold, but he couldn't make an adjustment with bloodied hands, so he just let the numbing cold flow over his flesh.

The water ran red, then clear. He dried his hands gingerly on the terrycloth towel that hung from a hook in the wall, taking care not to exacerbate the injury any further. On closer inspection, he saw clearly that his palms were scratched, but not cut. He pulled his hands closer to his face. There was nothing more than a minor scratch. He turned his hands over slowly, one at a time, checking the top of each. He checked his knees, rolling up the legs of his pants as far as he could. Then, looking into the mirror, he checked his face. Dark brown hair, now looking black from the rain, hung, weighted down with tiny drops of water over his forehead. His cheeks were flushed with color from the cold, and the slight creases around his black eyes showed signs of age slightly ahead of his years. But there was not one cut on his hands, knees or face. And yet, there was clearly blood on his pants, his hands, and the wall. He paused in his thoughts as the question rose up. *If not mine?* And begged the answer. *Whose?*

A crash from the hallway startled him from his self-examination and he rushed from the bath, out into the hall that lead from the main entrance down toward the living room of the apartment. The door, the same door that Dominic had just entered through a few moments ago, smacked hard against the wall, pushed by a heavy wind that gusted from outside and now cylconed through the apartment.

Dominic closed the door, this time remembering to lock it. Then, turning in the opposite direction, he began to make his way toward the main living quarters of the apartment. He saw them a second before his mind admitted what he was looking at.

Footsteps.

Bloodied footsteps.

Confused, he hesitated. Then, bracing himself against the rough plaster walls, he checked the bottom of his left and then his right shoe. There was a touch of blood on the sole of the right shoe and an uneven thin line of it around the ankle, but not near enough blood to mark his own footstep. He studied the tracks for a moment, squinting his eyes at them to make out the detail. And then, the thought hit him hard enough to cause him to suck in his breath. He had stepped into the bloodied tracks...not made them.

A cool sweat broke out under his arms and quickly began to trickle down his sides. He began to breathe heavily, an unconscious response to the now growing fear. *Run. Get out!* His conscious thoughts screamed in his brain in response. But he paid no attention.

Dominic stepped around the crimson footsteps, walking alongside the bloodied path into the living room. There, they faded into the dark room. The lights were off. He damned himself for being so conscientious about wasting power and turning the lights off when he left a room. He decided that he would leave the lights on in every room from now on. So what if he wasted power?

Commanding one hand to do what he wanted it to and not to act on its own, as the deepening fear willed it to, he slid the hand around the corner of the wall. He fingered it slowly along the rough stucco. Finding the light switch, he let out a gasp of breath. Did it come from the greater fear of being able to see, once he switched the lights on, or from a sense of relief that he would soon have light? He wasn't sure.

He wasn't sure what to do next either. His fingers paused on the button of the electrical switch; the bottom button was extended out, the top button in. That's all he needed to do was push in the bottom button, popping out the top button and the lights would be on. He thought about what he'd do after the lights came on, and came to the quick conclusion that...he had no fucking conclusion. He didn't know what he was doing or what he was looking for, and he didn't know what the hell he was doing still in this apartment? More indecision, of course, he cursed. He was growing angry with himself and his inability to make a decision in life, in love, and in this damned moment. Before he could consciously decide what action to take, his fingers took control and pushed the bottom button in.

There was just a second's hesitation before the lights came on—flickered really. The tattered electrical wiring in the old apartments of this Rome neighborhood was held together with masking tape and rat spit. He prayed that the lights wouldn't flicker back out as they tended to do. The faint glow from the dust-covered, glass bulbs nearly illuminated the room. It was better than nothing. He nodded his head slightly in self-agreement.

He scanned the room, began to take a step in, and then hesitated. A few seconds later, he had a plan. Make it to the phone. Call the police. Of course, he knew damn well that the Italian polizia were notoriously slow, unless, of course, there was a beautiful actress, a socialite, or the Pope on the other end of the line calling for help. He dismissed the plan as quickly as he had come up with it. *I'd be long dead before they got here,* he reasoned.

Surveying the room, he noted that nothing looked out of place. His half-eaten dinner of a peanut butter, honey and banana sandwich, now stale, sat on a plate on the scratched end table. A pair of dress shoes—recently purchased—were tossed carelessly in a corner. Magazines—partially read—and newspapers—completely read—lie in assorted stacks. *I gotta' clean this place up.* Then he frowned as he considered that to be an odd thought given the circumstances. *But true nonetheless,* he admitted.

Convinced that the room was clear of...well, he wasn't really sure of what. But it was clear, he noted, and stepped into the room.

Off to one side was the kitchen, to the other side the bedroom and another bathroom. This one was really a bathroom. He decided to go for the kitchen. He was sweating more now, under his arms, in the crevice of his back and on his upper lip. He had gotten his breath under control, and outwardly, was quite composed.

The light in the kitchen was off. Of course! He shook his head at the thought of his mother, yelling in Italian, "Chiuda la luce." And his response to her in English,

"Mom, we do not close lights in America—we turn them off!" The kitchen in his apartment was like most other kitchens in the apartments in this section of Rome—narrow with an old looking and acting stove and a refrigerator that matched the stove's style and inability to operate. A farm-style sink—complete with a leaking faucet—was attached to the wall. One small window at the far end of the narrow room barely let any light in during the brightest hours of the day. Now, at something after three in the morning, it was almost invisible.

Dominic took a step closer, peering into the darkness.

Waiting.

Watching for something to move.

Nothing did.

In the kitchen, there was only darkness upon more darkness. The faint light from old, dust-covered bulbs in the living room did not make a dent into the shadows that engulfed the small kitchen. The switch to the overhead kitchen light was on the wall about halfway into the room. If someone—or something—was in there, it would have him long before he made it to the switch and the comfort of light. He held his breath and strained to hear. He could differentiate between the sounds of the refrigerator motor whirling away, the drip of the faucet, and the wind still gusting outside. Then, there was something else. Something more. There. He heard it again. Some unexpected sound that was mixed in with the other sounds: the fan motor on the refrigerator, the wind seeping in through the cracked window seal, and a drip of water from the faucet falling into the still unwashed coffee cup. There again. The strange wheezing noise crept in as if it were trying to disguise itself among the other sounds, yet didn't quite fit in. Dominic leaned into the kitchen slightly, cupping one ear with a hand.

Then, again, but this time more prominent.

And then the darkness moved.

Dominic yelled.

It fell upon him.

Instinctively—instead of jumping back—Dominic grabbed at the form ready to protect himself against the unknown assailant as best that he could. He steadied himself for whatever was to come and was completely unprepared when the form slowly slid through his hands and down onto the floor.

An old man lay there, gasping for breath. His black coat and the black shirt underneath were wet. Dominic quickly pulled his hands away from the body and brought them close to his face. The smell of the liquid was metallic and it ran thick through his fingers. Blood. "Imploratio Adiumentum. Ue Bonfjote." The old man's lips moved and a gurgling whisper escaped, "Tazor Li." The old man's speech was barely audible.

The Third Hour

The words the old man spoke were somehow familiar, yet Dominic could not immediately place them. His heart pounded as adrenaline coursed through him, pulling him in the two instinctual directions of fight or flight.

The old man's voice was so weak Dominic had to lean in closer, his ear just touching the old man's lips. "Ancora. Dirlo ancora," Dominic begged. And then thinking about it, added in, "Again. Say it again."

The old man's breath grew weaker, short shallow breaths quickening. He reached out with his right hand, grasping weakly at Dominic's arm. "Father, forgive them; for they know not what they do," he said with a voice that was momentarily strong. Then his body fell limp, puddling on the floor where he had fallen.

Dominic ran for the telephone and dialed.

TWO

"Where is he?" Tonita Clifford said as she pushed open the door to Dominic's apart and hurried past him.

"He's in the kitchen."

She paused in the hallway. "What? Was it your cooking?

"Don't be a smart ass," Dominic said, leading her to the old man still lying on the floor just at the kitchen doorway. "I think I stopped the bleeding."

Tonita put her fingers to the side of the old man's neck.

"I don't think he's dead?" Dominic said as more of a question than a statement.

"He's not. He's got a pulse. Weak, but still there."

Dominic pulled back the old man's coat and shirt slightly. "It looks like there's a gash in his chest. I don't know if there are any other injuries. I was afraid to move him until you got here.

"Dom? Why didn't you call the police, or an ambulance, or a doctor?" Tonita felt around the old man's chest and stomach, sliding her hands as far as she could around the back of his rib cage.

"I called you." Dominic stood, moving to the other side of the old man.

"I know. That's why I asked. Why me? Why not some authority?"

Dominic hesitated looking from the limp body of the old man to the expectant gaze of green eyes. Even now, having been shocked awake from a deep sleep, hurriedly dressing, and looking disheveled, Tonita Clifford was striking. "I knew you had medical training and that you'd be able to help him," Dominic said, his voice only just above a whisper.

"I was a candy striper! That does not make me a doctor." Tonita stood, brushing loose strands of hair from her eyes. "We've got to get him to the hospital." She picked up the telephone and began to dial.

Dominic jumped up grabbing the phone from her. "We can't." He felt as though he was near panic and was sure Tonita could read him.

"Dom?" Tonita paused, looking directly at Dominic, "You didn't have anything to do with this?" She motioned toward the old man. "I mean...did you?" She did read him.

He didn't let her continue. "Are you nuts?"

"No. Concerned." She eyed him quizzically.

"I couldn't do anything like this."

Tonita's eyes shot down to the telephone still in Dominic's hand and then back to his eyes.

Dominic glanced away from her and tightened his grip around the telephone handset.

"Then why don't you want me to call a doctor?"

Dominic sensed the slightest hint of fear in her voice. It was the last thing that he wanted to do. Scare her? *Hell, I'm petrified!* He couldn't lose her. He needed her too much. The instant they had met, some ten weeks ago—wait, he hesitated. *Ten weeks? Is that all it's been?* It seemed longer.

"Well?" She interrupted his thoughts, then held out her hand.

For the longest moment he remained silent as he contemplated a barrage of questions that all demanded answers at once. Did he trust her? Did she trust him? He didn't really know her. It had only been ten weeks. Their relationship had happened so quickly. He was in the middle of sorting out his own life crises and suddenly there she was. He wanted to believe it was divine intervention. But dismissed that idea and just went with pure coincidence.

Did she believe him? Why should she? His thoughts of self-doubt shouted internally. Why should she trust him? He hadn't given her any reason to. He handed the telephone to her.

She immediately began to dial.

She doesn't trust me. He placed his hand on hers. He was cautious, aware of the touch of his hand to her skin. "Hear me out. Then if you want to, call a doctor or the police, whatever. I won't care."

Tonita cocked her head and looked at him, her fingers still poised to dial. Then, she replaced the telephone to its cradle "First, we take care of him." She nodded in the direction of the old man. "Then you talk." She moved back to the injured old man.

Dominic remained, frozen.

"You're going to have to help me," she said, removing one shoe from the old man's foot.

"Thank you for trusting me." Dominic moved to help her with the old man's clothing. "I don't know why he's here or what happened to him. He was just here."

"Dom?" She looked at him pulling the worn shoe from the old man's other foot "I don't have time for games. I don't know if I trust you." She noticed a sudden grimace on Dominic's face, then added, "I don't know what to believe, I don't know what to think. I only know that this man is not going to live if we don't help him. So shut up and help me." She continued to undress the man, pulling off his socks and then his pants.

Dominic had the old man's overcoat nearly off when he noticed a glint of light from some shining object on the man's chest. He continued to remove the coat as carefully as possible, peeling it away from the man's body. Then he unbuttoned the remaining buttons of the old man's shirt. "Oh my God!" He pulled the shirt, soaked with blood, back away from the object imbedded into the old man's chest.

The Third Hour

"What the hell is that?" Tonita wiped some of the blood away with her hand. "Get me some wet cloths—clean ones if you've got any?"

Dominic jumped up, retrieved the dishtowel from the sink and several others from a nearby drawer. He turned on the tap, soaking the towels in the hottest water that his own hands could take.

"Here," he said tossing, one to Tonita.

She caught it without hesitation and brushed it gently over the wound. The fabric of the towel caught on the object and pulled it up partially away from the old man's chest.

"Oh shit." Dominic's voice rose. "Careful. Careful!"

"Would you stop?" Tonita shook her head. "As if I'm trying to hurt him." She pulled the twisted and frayed pieces of cloth slowly away from the object that was now protruding from the wound.

"What the hell?" Dominic didn't intend the irony.

Tonita, raised her eyebrow, then carefully wiped the dried blood away from the object.

A crucifix.

"Why would anyone do that?" Dominic asked, not really hoping for her to answer.

"I should be asking you that." Tonita pulled up on the crucifix. It slid up easily.

"Should you be doing that?" Dominic grimaced as he asked.

"Probably not," Tonita said as the long, ice pick like stake that had been attached to back side of the crucifix slid completely out of the old man's chest.

The old man heaved and choked.

"Quick. Turn his head to the side, he's choking," Tonita spat the words out as she applied pressure to the chest wound.

The old man choked again, his gag reflex taking over. He vomited. His body convulsed.

"Hold him still," she yelled.

"I'm trying," Dominic said, leaning into the man.

The old man's body convulsed again, his legs kicking widely, his arms flailing, twisting. A gasping sound emanated from his throat. He gagged, arched his neck up off the floor, and gagged again.

Dominic held the man's head to the side.

The old man spat out blood and vomit, then fell silent.

Dominic stared at the body, then quickly drew back his hands and sucked in a quick breath. The raw stench of blood and vomit mixed together and he could taste it in the air. He gagged. "Is he dead?"

Tonita held up the small crucifix with the four-inch spike welded in place to the smooth metal on the back of it, looked to the old man and then to Dominic. "Now, can we call the police?"

THREE

Trepuzzi, Lecce, Italy.

The now seldom used church of Maria Assunta stood crumbling and decaying at the end of Via Assunta in the old village of Trepuzzi. The streets surrounding the small square church were now empty, broken streetlights and falling fencing hinted that the area had been abandoned years ago. The once bustling markets and stores were now silent, boarded up and in ruin.

Brother Salvatore had parked his car on Via Leonardo Da Vinci, about a kilometer away from the Church of Maria Assunta. He walked down to Via Galileo Galilei and then to Via Assunta, where the streets came together to form the small plaza.

The plaza was empty. Nearly forgotten. Silent.

He crossed the square and stopped in front of the rotting structure of the church. The single working street lamp behind the church cast a faint halo-like glow around the building. Brother Salvatore made the sign of the cross and quickly headed to the side of the building.

Just as the Jesuit had said it would be, the lock to the decomposing side door of the church, hung open on the hook of the lock plate. Brother Salvatore removed the lock, noting with some surprise at the relative newness of it, given that the door and the church itself had not been used in years. He carefully replaced the lock, hanging it on the lock plate and then pushed on the door. Remarkably, the door swung open without a sound, gliding as though the hinges had been oiled often. The interior of the small church was dark, despite the stained glass windows that were placed high up on each of the four walls that should have let in some light from the street lamp. Dust whirled up as the door completed the arc and swung fully open.

The night air that hung about Trepuzzi was heavy with the salty smell of the nearby Adriatic Sea. It mixed in swirls with the dank, dusty air of the old church caught in momentary glimpses by the faint light. Brother Salvatore hadn't brought a flashlight. He assumed the lights in the church would be on and working. If there were working lights, they weren't on and he didn't know where the switch was to rectify that. He slid his hand over the carved stone surround of the door and then off to the side, where he thought a light switch might be. Nothing.

"Superior?" Brother Salvatore spoke softly, by way of habit. The years that he had spent in the church were evident in his demeanor and reverence, even for a church that had not seen a mass in decades. "Superior, are you here?" He waited. After a moment with no response Brother Salvatore stepped through the door and into the church, instinctively, his right hand reached out to the carved marble vessel that would have contained Holy Water when the church had been in use. He expected the vessel to be dry, filled only with dust and debris, instead, his fingers dipped into cool water. Startled he pulled his hand away, then, paused momentarily, before continuing with the tradition, of putting a finger of the right hand into the holy water, then raising them to his forehead. "In the name of the Father." Brother Salvatore lowered his hand to his chest. "And the Son." Then crossed his hand to his left shoulder. "And the Holy." Then brought his hand to the right shoulder. "Sprit." He ended the ritual by brushing his lips with his moist fingers and finished, "Amen."

A match burst into flame at the far end of the church. Brother Salvatore's heartbeat quickened as he watched the flame move, briefly floating on air, before touching down, and bringing life to a single candle.

"You may not proceed farther," The Superior's deep baritone voice echoed in the emptiness of the church.

"I will stand where I am."

"The task is complete?"

"Superior," Brother Salvatore said. "It is not."

Brother Salvatore heard a long breath being sucked in, followed by several long minutes of silence. He twice considered speaking out, asking if The Superior was all right, saying something, just to speak, but caught himself in time and remained silent.

A movement passed quickly in front of the candle, hiding the flame briefly.

The Superior finally spoke. "What has become of the Key?"

"I'm afraid, Your Eminence, that it has been lost."

"Where?"

Brother Salvatore felt the air around him move. He glanced around the darkness unable to pierce it. He began to sweat, wondering. Worried.

Aside from the small circle of light surrounding the candle, the blackness filling the church grew darker. Had The Superior moved? Was The Superior close? Brother Salvatore quickly dismissed the thought as pure imagination and answered, "On the streets of Rome, Your Eminence."

"You will find it."

"We have tried, but it is gone...lost...Your Eminence, among the old streets and alleys." Brother Salvatore's voice trembled slightly and he fought to keep his composure.

"For this son of mine was dead and is alive again; he was lost and is found." The Superior's hand grabbed Brother Salvatore's arm.

Brother Salvatore jumped back hitting the wall hard. He hit something hanging from the wall and it fell to the floor. "Your Eminence, I do not know where the Key has gone," he said, all control of his voice lost.

Richard Devin

The Superior's face moved from the darkness in close, nearly touching Brother Salvatore's.

Brother Salvatore tried to focus his eyes and make out the features of The Superior's face.

"You will find the Key or you will suffer." The Superior tightened his grip around the Brother's arm. "This is what the Sovereign Lord says: My anger and my wrath will be poured out on this place, on man and beast, on the trees of the field and on the fruit of the ground, and it will burn and not be quenched."

The hand that tightly gripped Brother Salvatore's arm released and he could feel the blood rush once again to his forearm, wrist and hand. He breathed in quick gulps of air and unable to support himself any longer, his knees weakened and he slid down the wall, crumpling to the floor.

Then darkness once again consumed the room as the flame at the far end of the church flickered out.

Brother Salvatore lay back against the wall letting the coolness of the carved stonework seep into his skin and squelch his fear. He sat there through many hours of silence, until daylight eased across the sky and took his fear with it.

FOUR

"Dominic, exactly what do you mean we can't call the police?" Tonita didn't wait for an answer. "Just watch me." She grabbed for the telephone.

"Tonita, no!" Dominic reached the telephone before she did. He pulled it away, placing it behind his back.

"Oh, that's nice. Do you think we're playing a game of hide and seek now?"

"Don't be a smart ass."

"Don't be a dumb shit." Her lips pouted and her entire body took on attitude.

An attitude that sent Dominic's senses reeling. "If only I had lived a different life, Tonita."

"What the hell are you talking about? You know, you don't make any sense to me? No wonder you're so screwed up." She put her hand out. "Are you going to give me that phone?"

He was screwed up. She was right. He couldn't help but to agree with her, at least silently. They had only met about ten weeks ago and she already knew him.

Could I be that transparent?

He thought about it for moment and concluded that he could and probably was.

"I can't."

"Then, I'm leaving," she said, taking up her coat from the floor and heading toward the door.

"No, no, no." He took a step in her direction, then stopped. "You don't understand."

She turned. "Try me," she said, placing her hands on her hips, giving him more of that attitude.

Dominic bit on the inside of his cheek, a bad habit that he was trying to break. "He knew me."

"He?" Tonita raised an eyebrow. "Who? Who knew you?"

Dominic glanced to the body lying near the kitchen.

Her eyes widened. "He knew you? The dead guy?" Tonita dropped her coat to the floor and made her way into the living room. She paced between the sofa and the chair, sitting on the arm of the chair then getting up again. "I thought that you had no idea why this guy was in your apartment?"

"I didn't." Dominic brushed his hand through his hair, trying to keep it out of his face. "I still don't."

She stared at him for a long moment. "Look, you're either trying to make this difficult or you're trying to cover something up? Be honest with me, Dom."

Dominic sat down sinking into the worn leather chair, he pushed his hair back from his face—a nervous habit that he internally added to the list of tics and vices he was trying to break—*I'm trying to change too much too soon. And not changing a damn thing.* He sighed letting the breath flow from him. "I went out for a walk. You know the usual thing. Late night, alone..." He gave her a nod. "I slipped on the street and landed pretty hard. Luckily, I caught myself and I thought that I was all right. But when I got back, I noticed blood on my hands and pants."

"You cut yourself?"

"No, that's just it. I checked and I wasn't cut. I wasn't bleeding anywhere." He looked up at Tonita, showing her his hands. "Nothing." He turned his hands over inspecting them once again as though he may have missed something. "It was his blood." He glanced at the body. "He was waiting for me."

"Why do you say that? Maybe you just happened along." Tonita took a few steps toward the body. "He was injured, stabbed by that cross ice pick thing, and then you came along and he followed you in."

"That's what I thought at first. I didn't see anyone when I was walking. Sometimes, I see a few people, but not tonight. No one was out."

"He could have been hiding."

"True." He let out long sigh. "If he was, he was hiding in here. Waiting for me."

"And that's why you think he knew you?"

"That, and then he said, 'help me.'"

Tonita walked back to him. "Dom, the old man was dying. Of course he asked for your help."

"It's not just that he said, 'help me'. It's the way that he said it. Three times." He paused, looking directly into her eyes. "Once in Latin, once in Greek, and once in Hebrew."

"So, he didn't know what language you spoke and he was just covering all the bases."

"Then why not Italian? We're in Rome for God's sake. At least Italian would have made sense. But instead he uses three languages. And one of them Latin? A language that almost no one uses."

"All right, I give up. Why?" She crossed her arms and focused on him.

"Because. Well, I think because," he paused thinking it through, then continued, "they are the three languages used on the plaque placed on Christ's crucifix."

"Okay, you've lost me." She dropped her arms and shook her head.

"You've seen it abbreviated as I.N.R.I. on a board just above Jesus' head in paintings. Pontius Pilate placed the titlum on the cross..."

"The what?"

The titlum. The plaque. The piece of wood."

"Okay. Continue."

Dominic sighed, "Pilate placed the titlum to identify the crime that Jesus was being crucified for. Jesus the Nazorean, the King of the Jews." Dominic stood up and walked the few steps to a bookshelf in the corner of the room, "It was a common practice by the Romans to place a plaque above the head of the crucified, letting everyone that saw the dying man know what crime he had committed. Let me show you." He pulled a book out from under several others and handed it to Tonita. "Here's a good example from Nicolas Tournier. He painted it about 1635."

She glanced at the cover of the oversized art book. The scene was of the crucifixion of Christ on the cross, surrounded by an old man, two women and another person that Tonita could not decide if it was a man or a woman.

"See the titlum is above Christ's head." Dominic pointed to the place on the painting.

"I see it, but I don't understand how you get from this plaque on a cross to the conclusion that the man over there knew you."

They both could not help but glance quickly to the body.

"It wasn't just that he spoke those languages, it was in the order he used them. Latin first, then Greek, then Hebrew. In the bible, John says that the titlum was written in Hebrew first, then Greek, and the Latin was last. That's the common belief and if you asked anyone that's what they would say."

"I doubt that."

"No, really."

Tonita smiled. "You missed the sarcasm. I don't think that almost anyone would know that."

"You've got a point," he said, then continued with his own point, "Theological historians will tell you that the titlum was actually written in Latin first, then Greek and then Hebrew. The language of official Rome, the government, was Latin. However, because of all the lands that the Romans conquered many people spoke Greek. Pilate was Roman, and he was the Governor of Judea. So protocol would have mandated that the titlum be written in Latin first, since that was the official language of the Roman government. And the act of crucifying Christ was a government act."

"That's a great little history lesson, but I don't get anywhere near—that man on the floor of your kitchen knowing you—from the title thing on the cross." Tonita turned a page in the book to a painting entitled the "Denial of Saint Peter." She noted the caption and closed the book quickly, handing it back to Dominic.

"There's more."

Tonita looked at him. Waiting.

"He said one more thing. And this is why I am certain that he knew me."

"Well?" Tonita crossed her arms in front of her. "What did he say?"

"Father, forgive them; for they know not what they do." Dominic waited a moment as he watched the expression on Tonita's face change to complete recognition. "He knew that I'm a priest."

FIVE

"So, you expect me to believe that the dead body just walked into your flat and you have no idea of who he is?" Inspector Carrola spoke adding the hard 'eh' endings to the English words as so many Italians do.

"Signore," Dominic began.

"Excuse me, Father," Inspector Carrola interrupted. "English, please. I wish to rehearse my English."

"Fine, Inspector. English it is."

"And, I am so sorry to again interrupt you, but please, if I make the mistake in English, you make it correct."

"Yes, Inspector." Dominic's tone was impatient.

"Va Bene," Inspector Carrola said smiling, then remembering, "I mean, all is good."

Dominic's apartment was packed to capacity with policemen, inspectors and detectives. The local station captain had, it seemed to Dominic, sent every available officer, those on duty and those off. Most of the plentitude of polizia gathered in groups in corners of the apartment. Some busied themselves skimming through books. Two relaxed on the sofa, one smoking, and another on the chair, head tilted back, eyes closed.

The body of the old man was now wrapped in a body bag, having been photographed from every possible angle and examined by everyone who came through the door. Dominic half expected a cop to draw a chalk line around the body, as he had seen done in so many old movies.

Tonita had been separated from Dominic by several other inspectors. Dominic watched her animatedly explain to the Roman police her story. She gesticulated wildly at one point, arms at her chest, her face bent over as though she was vomiting, legs kicking in a reenactment of the old man's final moments. A good little actress, Dominic noted.

"So, now please, Father, you tell me the story." Inspector Carrola blinked several times, an odd expression of disbelief to a story he hadn't yet heard, evident on his face.

"I have told the other inspectors what happened and they all took notes Inspector. Perhaps we could save some time and you could simply ask them," Dominic spoke each word clearly and slowly.

"You are not a priest anymore, Father?" Inspector Carrola cocked his head to the side.

"I'm on a leave."

"Why? Why do you leave?"

"I haven't left the priesthood, Inspector. You misunderstand the meaning of the word. I'm still a priest. I just needed some time away to get my head straight."

"So then, I can ask you?" Inspector Carrola asked not waiting for an answer. "You no believe in God now?"

"Yes, I still believe in God. That hasn't changed. It's not that at all"

"It is what then?"

"Like I said, Inspector, I needed some time away."

"Ah." Inspector Carrola clicked his tongue. "For your sake, Father, I hope that God does not need some time away from you." He looked to the black vinyl body bag stuffed with the corpse of the old man and shrugged.

Dominic let out a long sigh. The last thing he wanted now was for a cop to give him advice on his calling. What he really wanted, was everyone out of his apartment, a shower, and a few hours of sleep. He had been up since the late afternoon of the day before. The adrenaline of the night's events had long since worn off and his body ached.

"Is she your girlfriend, Father?" Inspector Carrola tilted his head toward the corner of the room where Tonita was standing.

"I'm sorry." Dominic heard Inspector Carrola's question, but needed a moment to think. "Inspector?"

"The woman, she is no Italian, correct?"

"No. She's American, like me."

"I see. And she is, come dite?" He slipped back into Italian. "I am sorry, how do you say in English? A metà negro e mezzo bianco?"

"Mulatto."

"Ah yes.

"Her mother is South African, but born and raised in England. Her father is Irish.

Then, I am correct, she is your girlfriend, no?"

"No."

"No?"

"Good friends. Nothing more."

"She is very beautiful? No? Father?"

"Inspector? Call me Dominic, or Dom." Dominic thought he may have sounded too irritated. Then thought about it again and concluded, he was irritated!

"Ah that is right, you are not a priest now."

"I am still a priest. I have already explained to you that I just needed some time."

"I understand, Dominic. You need some time with the girlfriend." Inspector Carrola winked.

"She's just a good friend, Inspector. Nothing more."

"Va Bene," Inspector Carrola said, apparently forgetting again that they were conversing in English.

Long moments of silence followed as Dominic watched while Inspector Carrola looked around the room, taking—Dominic assumed—mental notes of everything that was on the floor, ceiling, and walls. *Thank god I left the crucifix up,* Dominic thought, as he watched Inspector Carrola shake his head back and forth when he caught sight of the wooden crucifix hanging near the bedroom door.

Dominic had actually taken the crucifix down several weeks ago, removing it from the rusty nail holding it in place on the wall. He had taken it down, but had only moments later replaced it. It was a few weeks earlier, as he prepared for one of his late night walks. He had caught sight of the crucifix when he'd sat down to put on his shoes. It had seemed odd to him to have that object of the church hanging on the wall as a statement of his belief when he wasn't sure what he believed, so he'd taken it down. Just before walking out the front door to the street, however, he'd returned to the living room and re-hung the cross to its place of prominence in the apartment. *He who walks without God walks alone*, he reminded himself of the modernization of the quote from Genesis.

"Why, Father, do you call your girlfriend and not the doctor or the police?" Inspector Carrola asked as he finished with his mental notes. "You want to hide something?"

"Not my girlfriend, Inspector."

"She is a girl, no?"

"Yes, she is."

"And she is your friend?" Inspector Carrola's eyebrows arched.

"Yes." Dominic knew where the inspector was going with this line of questions.

"Then why no girlfriend?"

"Because girlfriend means that there is something sexual...something more to the relationship than just a friendship," Dominic said, hoping to put an end to the discussion.

"I see." The Inspector clearly didn't. "This beautiful girl is just a friend?"

"Yes."

"But you call her and no police or doctor?"

"Yes."

"Let me ask you then, can a priest lie and still go to heaven, Father?" The Inspector punched up the last word.

He was lying. She did mean more to him than just a friend who happened to be a girl. Why not admit it? Dominic was about to respond to both his own internal questions and those of Inspector Carrola, when Tonita approached. He glanced at her and smiled. She looked tired and a bit haggard, but attempted to smile back.

"Dom, have you finished with the Inspector?" Tonita said, as she mutilated a business card left with her by the detectives. Her hair fell around her face and over her eyes. She brushed it back.

Dominic wanted to reach out and hug her, assure her that it would all be okay, apologize to her for getting her involved. Instead, he commanded his arms to remain by his side and not to make any movement toward her.

Inspector Carrola's eyes moved up and down Tonita's body, watching carefully for any sign, a hint of what really happened here, and what really was happening between this woman and priest. "I believe I have the information I need for now, Father," the Inspector said. Then, turning back to Tonita, he asked, "You will call if you have something more to say?" And looking directly at the now mutilated business card in Tonita's hand, "You have our card and number, no?"

Even through the dark coloring of Tonita's skin, her father's Irish could be seen as her cheeks reddened. "Yes, Inspector, we do."

"Va bene. Va bene."

Twenty minutes later the detectives, inspectors, photographers, technicians, and the dead body were out the door. The apartment was once again quiet.

The Third Hour

Dominic collapsed into the worn leather chair, physically and mentally exhausted. He closed his eyes. "I'm beat."

Tonita stood by the kitchen where the old man had fallen and died. She looked to Dominic "What do we do now?"

"Sleep."

"Dom, I'm serious."

"So am I."

"Listen, if all you told me was true..." Tonita didn't get a chance to finish.

Dominic's eyes snapped open. "I told you the truth. I'm a priest for God's sake."

"How convenient."

"It's the truth."

"And we all know that priests never lie."

"This one doesn't."

"Oh, yeah." Tonita crossed the room and knelt by the chair. She stared directly into Dominic's eyes. "How do you feel about me then?"

His eyes darted away from hers.

"See there?" Tonita said. "You looked away. You're going to lie to me."

"No, I was just thinking about your question."

"If you don't know the answer already, then you're lying to yourself."

Dominic was about to mount a defense, when a loud banging on the front door distracted them both. Thankful for the interruption, he pulled himself out of the chair and made his way to the door, half expecting more cops, more questions, and more time without sleep. He reached for the small handle on the deadbolt to turn the lock and unlock the door, but it was, as usual— he cursed at himself—unlocked. He pulled the door open. No cops, no photographers, and no technicians awaited him. The sidewalk was empty. Only a black Mercedes Benz Berlina was there, parked directly in front of the apartment, its motor running and back door open. The driver stared straight ahead, not once turning in Dominic's direction, giving no clue as to what was expected next. Had someone gotten out of the car and knocked at the wrong door? Dominic looked up and down the street. Not a soul, only the driver and Dominic. He was about to close the door and ignore the car and driver, when a glint of red on the Mercedes windshield caught his attention.

In a corner of the windscreen there was a small red sticker with the imprint of a shield with two crossed keys, two ribbons, two cords, and a tiara.

Dominic recognized the symbol immediately, and it sent a slight chill up his spine.

The keys in the symbol represented those given to the Apostle Peter by Christ; one silver and one gold. The cotter of the keys pointed upward and toward the sides of the shield. The grips pointed down. Two cords wrapped through the grips of each key, bonding them together. And at the top of the shield, a tiara with two ribbons flowing from it fell to each side. Each ribbon bore the imprint of a patent cross.

It was the seal of the Holy See.

The Vatican.

And the driver was clearly waiting for Dominic.

SIX

"Don't follow me," Dominic yelled down the hallway into the living room.

"Why? Where are you going?" Tonita's questions were answered by the sound of the door slamming. She hesitated, a moment's indecision, and then picked up her coat and ran down the short hall to the front door. She pulled the door open to the screech of tires and acrid smell of burnt rubber, as the black Mercedes sped away, maneuvering easily down the narrow street. Tonita watched for a moment until the car, taking Dominic with it, was out of her sight. Exasperated, she slammed the door to Dominic's apartment behind her and headed out onto the street in the opposite direction of the speeding car. She was tired, fed up, and she was going home.

With anger, frustration, and concern fueling her stride, she made the few blocks to her apartment in quick time and had arrived at her door almost without realizing it.

Once inside, she stripped off her clothes, letting them lay were they fell and headed to the bath. She turned on the water and was about to let the tub fill, when she decided she could wait no longer and pulled up the little knob on the water spout that converted her bath to a shower. She stepped in and let hot water, streaming from the showerhead, beat against her. Tonita leaned against the tiles of the shower, their cold slick feel contrasted with the heat of the water and it eased the pain of tension in her shoulders. Her arms and her back ached. She should never have tried to move the old man's body or hold him down when he was convulsing, she thought. Hell. She should've never gone to Dom's apartment in the first place. That was stupid. Helping him with the old man was stupid. Getting involved with the situation was stupid. Getting involved with him was unplanned and stupid. It was all stupid and she was unbelievably confused.

She closed her eyes and let the sound of the water bouncing off of the shower curtain and splashing in the small tub, lull her to near sleep. She thought back to the first time she had seen Dom.

He was standing by an ancient fig tree, near the old Roman baths in the hills surrounding the city. She walked by and although she did think he was very nice looking—she wasn't really interested—she said hi, just to be nice.

"My family was caretaker to most of the fig trees in ancient Rome." Dominic was matter-of-fact speaking as though they had been carrying on a conversation that he was continuing.

Tonita didn't know how to respond, so she just said, "Really?" And then regretted saying it.

"My uncle, a great uncle many times over was a senator in the early days of Rome and he oversaw the fig crops."

"Really?" she said it again without thinking and this time she wanted to slap herself.

Dominic turned to her. "You don't believe me?"

"Why wouldn't I believe you?"

"I don't know, but you keep saying 'really,' as though I'm making this up."

"No, I don't think that," Tonita said in her defense. "I believe your uncle was a Roman senator. Why wouldn't I?"

Dominic looked in her direction, brushed the hair from his forehead and smiled, "Good. You'll find that I don't make things up."

She turned the water off and stepped from the shower. Grabbed a towel and wrapped it around her.

It started to rain, she recalled with a bit of smile forming on her face, that afternoon by the fig tree at the ancient Roman baths. Dominic didn't have an umbrella, and neither did she. She wasn't prepared for the rain. He didn't seem to care if it rained. They pushed in close and huddled under the canopy of the fig tree as the rain intensified.

"You visiting?" Dominic picked a small stone up from near the trunk of the tree and turned it over, examining it.

"Sort-of. I was just visiting when I got here. But now I think I'm staying for a while."

"School?"

"Pre-med," she laughed. "Pre-everything."

"You don't seem to know."

"You're right."

"I understand," Dominic said, dropping the stone back to the now muddy ground. "It's the same for me."

"Really?" Oh God! She promised to kill herself if she said that stupid word again.

Dominic smiled. "Really?"

Tonita twisted the towel around her, folding one corner into the wrapped terrycloth securing it tightly in place. She picked up a brush and drew it through her hair. From the cabinet she took out a bottle of Avon Skin-So-Soft bath spray and applied it, pushing down on the pump top and letting the oily mist float down onto her. She loved the scent of the oil and the smoothness of it on her skin. She rubbed it over her and watched as the water beaded up on her arm.

"You must be getting cold," Dominic said peering out from under the ancient fig. The rain had slowed. "You're getting goose bumps on your arm."

"I am a little," Tonita said, rubbing her hands up and down her arms. "Should we chance it and make a run for a café?" She surprised herself a bit at being so forward with this man she had just met.

Dominic put his hand out. "Dominic Renzi," he said.

"Tonita Clifford."

Richard Devin

"Tonita Clifford? Dominic's eyebrows arched.

"My dad's Irish. My mother's black. And before you say it, I've heard it already."

"Say what?" Dominic laughed, letting a smile take shape on his face.

Tonita's gaze reflected on herself as she came out of the trance of memories and stared into her eyes in the medicine cabinet mirror. She contemplated what she had gotten herself into, thought about giving up, turning away and going back. She couldn't. It was too late.

She dropped the towel onto the bathroom floor, pulled on the pair of jeans she had thrown on earlier when Dominic had called in a panic, grabbed a clean T-shirt, and then pulled on a sweatshirt over that. She stuffed all the Euro she could find from inside the dresser drawers, purses, and on top of the dresser, into her pockets. She dug out her credit cards and passport, which were hidden under the corner of the carpet and headed out the door.

SEVEN

Dominic sat back into the plush interior of the Mercedes Benz, not because he was enjoying the feel of the car or the thick smooth leather or the deep pile carpet, but because he was terrified. The driver of the automobile had not spoken one word since Dominic had jumped into the backseat of the vehicle, slammed the door and locked it, just in case Tonita had decided to follow.

The driver took every turn as fast as he could. There were no stoplights worth stopping at, no pedestrian worth giving a right of way to, and no car that shouldn't be passed, despite the narrow roads.

Just moments ago, an early morning shopper had had to dodge the Mercedes which had been speeding around a corner. The bewildered shopper threw a basket of fruit at the car and screamed at the driver as he blurred by, pushing the auto onward. Dominic turned and looked out the back window, trying, in vain to apologize to the shopper. Instead, he had the 'bird' signaled to him and nearly got whiplash as the driver took another turn at an even faster speed than the previous corner.

"For God's sake, could you be more careful and slow down?" Dominic shouted. "I'm not going to jump out."

His answer came in the form of screeching brakes as the driver narrowly missed a lamppost, skidding to a stop. Dominic looked out of the rear passenger window, considered jumping out, even though he had just said he wouldn't, but discovered he had given it too much thought and not enough action as the driver threw the car in reverse, backed up a few feet, and then floored it into drive.

"Are you trying to kill us? Is that the plan here?" Dominic shouted again, expecting no answer. He glanced out the side window at the nearly blurred scene as the driver pressed the car on faster. He wasn't sure where they were, and although he had expected to be taken to the Vatican, he couldn't say for certain that he would end up there. As far as he could figure, the driver had intentionally taken a secure route from the apartment in an effort to disguise where they were headed. Either that, or the driver was simply insane. He hoped for the former.

The towering steeples of Saint Peter's Basilica rose above the walls of the Vatican in the distance and Dominic began to breathe easier when the driver slowed the Mercedes as it approached the outer roads to the old gates. Even with The Vatican, or the Holy See as it was referred to among Catholic society, completely surrounded by the city of Rome and located deep within the country of Italy, it was a sovereign nation, maintaining its own government, security, and police force. The old wall that was built to protect the Holy See, was little more than decorative now, and the gates to the Vatican City were a formality rather than a true defense.

Noting the Vatican seal on the front windshield, the guards passed the Mercedes through the gate without the slightest hesitation. Dominic half expected an escort from the Swiss Guard, the official police of the Vatican, as they passed the Cancello di Sant Anna—Saint Anne's Gate, but there was none.

Now, inside the gates of the Vatican, the driver became a different man. He drove carefully and slowly, allowing pedestrians to pass in front of him without the threat of death by motorcar. He became polite and courteous.

"When did you become a boy scout?" Dominic's barb went unnoticed.

The Third Hour

From Cancello di Sant Anna the driver moved up Via di Belvedere, making a quick right onto Via del Pellegrino, then past Via della Tipografia and Via della Posta. He stopped the Mercedes on Vio Pio X, turned off the ignition and opened the driver's side door. He stepped out of the car and then leaned back in and handed Dominic an envelope. Then he closed the door and calmly walked away.

Dominic flipped the envelope over. It had been sealed with black wax, which bore the imprint of the Vatican Seal. Other than the heaviness of the wax seal, the envelope felt empty. He held it up to the sunlight that filtered in through the closed windows of the Mercedes. Inside the envelope he could see the darker outline of a strip of paper. He carefully slipped the flap open and took out the small strip of paper. He flipped it over, held it up to the sun, and when it appeared to him to be nothing more than a piece of paper torn from a page of a telephone book, he read the few names that were complete:

Renner, Michael

Reno, Paulo

Renta, Antoinette

He turned the strip over and studied the other side. There in light pencil, the words *Bramante's Stairway* had been written in block text over several more names.

Dominic knew where the stairway was, just around the corner and to the right of where the driver had parked the Mercedes. That's convenient. He had used the stairs many times crossing from the Vatican post office to the Vatican Museums. Like most, Dominic had little knowledge of Donato Bramante. He was shocked when he discovered, through the extensive Vatican library, that Donato Bramante was actually chosen before Michelangelo, by Pope Julius II, to design and build Saint Peter's Basilica. Dominic just assumed that Michelangelo had always been the only master architect to work on Saint Peter's. The original design called for a church in the form of a Greek cross, with all four arms the same length, topped by a great dome. When Bramante died and after several other architects contributed to Bramante's work, Michelangelo took over. "It would be hard to imagine anyone other than Michelangelo completing Saint Peter's," he had explained to Tonita, the first day that they had met, at the old Roman Baths. The rain had stopped just long enough for them to make it to a café where they sat, and talked for hours. He told her how he felt the first time he made his way up the front steps of the building and walked through the massive doors. "The Basilica inspires, overwhelms, and makes one realize how insignificant we are," he said to her.

"Well, I'm sure glad Jesus never ventured in," Tonita said in between sips of espresso. "What would have happened if he'd left feeling insignificant?" She waived the cup in the air. "No need for a basilica, then."

Tonita's innocent observation weighed on Dominic's thoughts for a long time. How true it was, he contemplated, that the church often makes those who are most important, the common man, feel like the least important. That observation by Tonita may have been the proverbial 'straw that broke the camel's back,' and sealed his fate. After that he was certain that he would leave the church.

Dominic opened the door and stepped out of the Mercedes, then closed the door quietly in an odd reverence for the city, and started off toward the stairway. He folded the envelope in half and pushed it into his back pocket, then studied the piece of paper torn from the phonebook. He let his eyes follow each of the letters spelling out Bramante's Stairway. He searched the letters written in light pencil for some clue, some sign of...

He stopped. Despite the sun's warmth on his face and skin, a chill shot up his spine. He looked up from the scrap of paper and slowly turned his head to the side, then back in the other direction. Then he took in every window, doorway, and cranny of the old buildings surrounding the small square at the base of Bramante's Stairway. His senses reeled as sweat beaded on his lips and forehead. He stepped slowly onto the first of the stairs leading to the plaza above. He hesitated, then took another step, trying in vain to disguise his growing fear and the gnawing pain of panic.

He was sure that someone was watching him and the hairs shot up on his neck as he read the words printed on that slip of paper from the phonebook.

Names.

Dominic read the names printed under the block letters that spelled out Bramante's Stairway, saying each aloud as he took one step.

Renteria, Rocco.

He took another step.

Renzetti, Mateo.

And one more step.

He stopped. Frozen in place.

Renzi, Dominic.

EIGHT

Rome
11:00 A.M.

Brother Salvatore pushed the door to Dominic's apartment open. It was unlocked.

As he stepped inside he picked up the faint scent of disinfectant, vomit, and the coppery smell of blood all mixed together and lingering in the air. Brother Salvatore rubbed the bottom of his nose at the smell and held his hand there, covering his nostrils until his sense grew accustomed to the concoction of odors. He considered leaving the apartment door open and letting a bit of fresh air in from the street, but thought better of it and closed it quietly behind him.

He had been standing on the opposite side of the street from the apartment.

Waiting.

Watching.

No one arrived to enter, and no one exited. He had half expected that Dominic or Tonita would attempt to return. They did not.

He had hidden himself in the shadows of a doorway—carved into a building—just across from Dominic's apartment for several hours. Enough time had now passed and he felt it was safe for him to attempt to enter the apartment. He hadn't counted on the door being unlocked. At first it was a relief that he would not have to break in, but could just walk in. A second thought, however, put him on guard. Had the door been left open on purpose? Was this a trap? He cautiously stepped in, listened, and when he felt secure that the apartment was empty, he pushed in the button on the hall light switch and the lights snapped on, then dimmed slightly. He hesitated a moment, then once sure that the lights would remain on, proceeded down the hall.

The coppery smell grew stronger as he turned the corner from the hallway nearing the kitchen. It was a smell he had grown accustomed to. It was blood, and even now, the odor brought back memories of his youth and summers spent working in a slaughterhouse. At first he'd hated every minute detail of his employment. He'd hated every person that worked in that horrific place. And he'd hated what they were doing. His hatred didn't stop with the people that worked in the plant. He'd hated the animals for being so dumb and allowing their slaughter. But mostly, he had hated himself for taking part in these terrible acts of death. That was until he'd realized that the work he was performing in the slaughterhouse was his beginning, his apprenticeship. The slaughter of chickens, swine and cattle became practice for him. He had honed his craft by perfecting his art, experimenting with knives and cleavers, bolt shots and hammers, and bare hands. His experimentations and practice were a toil in perfection, so that one day, he would be able to perform the ultimate slaughter, flawlessly.

Brother Salvatore let a small whimper escape from his throat as the thought of his pleasure was imagined before him. When Dominic returned, that time would come. He giggled with the thought.

The floorboards by the kitchen, old and unsealed, were stained with blood that had streamed from the body of the old man, and had soaked into the rough wood, giving the planks a reddened varnish. This is where the protector had died, he thought as he knelt down, extending his fingers so that they touched the stained floor. He quickly brought his fingers to his forehead and said aloud, "In the name of the Father and of the Son and of the Holy Spirit. Amen." He concluded by making the sign of the cross two more times and silently repeating the movement of his hand from head to chest to shoulders. He brought his index and forefinger to his lips and kissed them. "Rest in peace, my brother," Brother Salvatore whispered and lightly touched the blood soaked floorboards. "You did what you could, my brother," he spoke aloud gazing upon the blood stained floor with reverence. "I am only sorry that your powers were too weak. Don't worry, my brother. He will prevail." Brother Salvatore stood up. "I'm sorry that you will not be here to bear witness."

He looked around the apartment, noting the blackened dust swirls on the walls and floor where the police had dusted for prints. He heard the slight dripping of water from the faucet and the hum from the refrigerator. Other than that, he was confident that the apartment was empty and quiet.

He moved to the living room and the worn, leather chair that was pushed along a side wall. He sat down, pulled a rosary from the pocket fold of the dark brown tunic he was wearing, folded his hands across his chest, and prepared to wait. The Key will return soon. And once he had the Key, he would destroy it. That is what the Jesuit wanted. No, he corrected his thoughts. Willed. This is what the Jesuit and God willed to be.

"Thy will be done," Brother Salvatore said out loud. "Thy will be done."

NINE

June 30, 1908
Tunguska River, Siberia
7:15 A.M.

The sun had risen high enough to chase away the red, orange, and purple hues of morning's first light. The sky was now clear and blue, the air still frosted from the sunless chill of the night before.

The morning started for the herdsmen and villagers as each morning had started for countless years, gathering the herds of reindeer and moving them to the river's edge where they would quench their thirst, before heading up to the flat tundra to feed on the nutrient rich grasses until dusk and then the routine of life on the Siberian tundra would prepare to repeat.

This morning began no differently from all the other mornings, until, a flash of silent white light, brighter than the sun, lit up the sky. It blinded the reindeer herdsmen at the Tunguska River's edge, who were forced to close their eyes tightly in an attempt to shield them from the searing light. Some herdsmen grabbed on to trees to steady themselves. Several reindeer in the herd, stumbled into the river, blinded, then panicked to regain their footing as the swift and cold early summer waters threatened to carry them away.

Then the air split as an explosion of searing white light filled the sky, sending rings of shock waves crashing into the forest.

In the distance a tower of flames shot up hundreds of feet. From there, a wave of super-heated air rolled out. The trees closest to the flashpoint burst into flames, and those farther out, tumbled into a concentric circle of destruction.

The currents of searing air swept into the Evenki village, scorching thatched roofs of tundra grasses and singeing the hair on herds of frightened reindeer and even more frightened woman and children.

Then a second explosion, more powerful than the first and closer to the forest floor, ripped through the river valley, the few trees that had managed to remain standing after the first explosion, now fell, unable to stand against the wall of air. The intensity of the shock wave shattered the eardrums of reindeer and herdsmen alike, sparing them from the anguished cries of their dying brethren.

A morning that had begun as a quiet June day was now in turmoil. The clouds above that were once white against the blue sky, now unleashed a rain of blackened ash and soil. The sun, that only moments before had warmed the forest, was all but gone, hidden by the veil of smoke, dust and ash.

All was chaos.

Gregori Rasputin braced himself. Even here at the Lake Baykai observatory, some one hundred miles away, the ground shook, causing the observation tower to sway. From his vantage point on the sixty-foot wooden tower, Rasputin watched as the smoke rose, the skies darkened and the forest in front of him burned.

Even at this distance the air picked up the cries and screams of the forest. Rasputin covered his ears and turned away from the distant destruction and the sight of his failure.

He quickly climbed down from the tower and stumbled as he ran toward his carriage. There, a groomsman held fast to the reins of the harness, fighting to steady the four frightened horses.

Rasputin stepped up to the carriage, and shouted to the groomsman in Russian, "Take me to Alexandra," his thick accent was barely understood by the locals, but his wild gesticulations made the point clear. The groomsman climbed up onto the carriage, slapped the reins onto the backs of the horses and galloped away.

Inside the carriage, Rasputin closed the curtains covering the windows tightly. He did not want to complicate matters any further by witnessing any more of the destruction his invention had caused. He would have much to explain to the Tsar when he returned to Saint Petersburg, and his mind was already at work on possible causes, excuses, and of course, who the Tsar should blame for the failure. Fortunately, Rasputin's relationship with Alexandra was steadfast and he took comfort that she would protect him.

She always had.

TEN

Dominic turned the piece of the page torn from the telephone book over in his hands, twisting it between his fingers, as if he were a magician on a Vegas stage and could make his name disappear from the paper in puff of smoke.

It did not.

A feeling that was at first odd was now gnawing at him and becoming increasingly more uncomfortable. He was beginning to think that all he had experienced in the last day was not just happenstance, and was not just an unfortunate event that had unfolded upon an innocent person. But was something more. Something planned.

None of it made sense.

The thought that there was more to the events of the last hours caused his stomach to lurch and the bile started to rise to his esophagus. He had to choke back the fear that threatened to spill out.

Dominic stood upon the Bramante's steps, torn paper in hand, and thought back to the circumstances of the day. He was growing surer by the minute that the old man who had died in his apartment had sought him out. He was certain that the old man knew who he was and what he was and had deliberately sought him out. That alone didn't justify the feelings that were growing and beginning to crawl up his spine. Anyone could have known that he was a priest. Many people did. It was no secret. And the fact that he was on sabbatical was also no secret. Perhaps the old man was one of his congregants or maybe he saw him at mass. After all, even now he went to mass several times a week and met up with the priest of the local parish. And he made regular trips to Saint Peter's, where he spent hours in contemplation. He wasn't hiding anything from anyone.

Except Tonita.

He pushed the guilt laden thought away and turned back to the events of the day.

When he jumped into the back seat of the Mercedes, he was calm, confident that he was being called to the Vatican to face a barrage of questions regarding the dead man in his apartment. He could almost hear the first question lobbed at him; How is it that an old man, stumbles in the apartment of a priest, dies there, and you claim not to know him? There have been far too many scandals in the church recently and the Vatican was being very proactive in an attempt to stomp out any scandal before the press got a hold of it.

Now, he wasn't sure if he was just, seeing things that weren't there, making things up, putting things together that didn't really go together, or if all wasn't just as it should be. Typical of his current state of indecision, he thought, and then reconsidered. He was sure. All was not as it should be.

Dominic casually glanced around the street. Once he was sure—well, as sure as he could be—that he wasn't being watched, he climbed up Bramante's stairway. He looked back toward the Fountain of the Gallery. No one waited there for him. He slowed his pace, taking each step carefully, expecting someone at any moment to approach him from atop the stairs. He took several steps quickly, thinking that his random pace would throw off anyone watching. He paused, looked behind him, and then up to the street at the top of the stairway.

Again no one.

At the top of the stone stairway, he turned left and continued heading in the direction of the Pio— Clementine Museum. His heart was beating harder than he would have expected from a short walk up a stairway. But then, it wasn't the walking that caused his heart to beat ever faster. He pushed the hair off his face and bit on the inside of his lip.

Fuck trying to stop bad habits now.

He could see that there were people milling around the entrance to the Vatican Museums. To the right and beyond were the gate and the walls of the Vatican. Outside lay the city of Rome proper. He continued his casual walk, even stopping to inspect a bit of the Vatican architecture. He almost laughed at himself and the absurdity of it all. He wasn't fooling anyone, but maybe himself.

"Padre," A deep voice called out. "Padre, attesa."

Dominic's heart skipped a beat and his knees started to buckle. He caught himself by grabbing onto the building and the piece of cold stone architecture that he was just inspecting.

He wanted to turn around to face the man and to discover why someone was calling out to him. To attempt to understand. Instead, a primal fear response kicked in, and without a second thought, just seconds later, Dominic was turning the corner, charging through the Vatican Museum gate and out onto the streets of Rome.

He didn't look back. He didn't know where he was going. He just ran. His only thought was that of self-preservation.

ELEVEN

July 22, 1943
U.S.S. Eldridge, Destroyer Escort 173
0900 Hours/ 9:00 A.M.
150 Miles of the Eastern Coast of the United States

"Sir, power to the generators is at near capacity," the seaman said, standing at attention.

"Thank you. Carry on." Lieutenant Hamilton dismissed the young man, as the steady and slightly increasing hum of the generators resonated in the background.

As the Eldridge steamed out of the Philadelphia Naval Yards and into the waters of the Atlantic, the current to the generators had been initiated. Magnetic power was slowly building as the ship sailed through the fresh and salt water mix of the Delaware River into the now deep salt waters of the cold Atlantic. Lieutenant Hamilton had put more than one hundred and fifty miles between the ship and the Philadelphia Navel Yards. In that time the harmonic buildup of the electrical frequency into magnetic energy was nearly complete.

"Mr. Einstein, we will be moving you to an observation ship." Lieutenant Hamilton turned to the small graying haired man as a PT boat, launched from one of the observation ships just off the Eldridge's bow, pulled up alongside.

Einstein looked away from the row of panels of tubes, fused wires, and toggle switches, "We are ready then. I have done all that I can."

Seven minutes later on the observation ship thirty five yards off the starboard bow of the U.S.S Eldgridge, Einstein and the crew aboard the observation ship Rainbow stared in horror and disbelief.

Richard Devin

It was gone.

Not just off of the radar instrumentation, but from sight as well.

A thick greenish fog had built up at the water line, and then increased, until it slowly engulfed the U.S.S. Eldridge. The dim hum from the massive generators on board the Eldridge resonated throughout the hull of the ship and into the deep waters of the Atlantic. The sound waves hit the observation ship Rainbow at the same time the fog lifted, rising up from the water line to the height of the Eldridge's super structure.

In the quarters below deck of the Rainbow, a team of seaman listened intently through hydrophones, keen to the slightest change in the sound waves emanating from the electronic hum of the generators. Despite their preparedness and efforts to foresee a problem, it happened too quickly for any of them to react. The steady wave of sound from the Eldridge was replaced in a second's time by the sound of silence.

The Eldridge was gone.

Only still water remained.

"Well, Mr. Einstein, congratulations are in order." Lieutenant Hamilton offered his hand to the scientist.

Einstein did not accept the proffered hand. Instead, he turned away, muttering in German, and rechecked the dials on the nearby instrument panel. "This is not right," he said, glancing back to the Lieutenant briefly. "No. No. Something is wrong here. We should see the ship. The ship is not supposed to disappear. It should only become invisible to our instruments." Einstein moved to the railing of the ship and stared at the place where the Eldridge was once anchored. "It should still be there."

"It seems to have worked better than we expected." Lieutenant Hamilton smiled, but this time kept his hand to his side.

The Third Hour

"This is not what we had planned." Einstein considered the Lieutenant's words, then dismissed them. "I do not know what is happening to that ship."

"Sailor, are we maintaining radio contact with the Eldridge?" Lieutenant Hamilton shouted to the young radioman.

"Sir, radio contact maintained."

"Mr. Einstein, it appears as though we still have radio contact with the Eldridge."

"Good. Then, tell them to shut it down," he said, rushing back to the instrumentation. "Order them to turn off the generators." Einstein stared at the man who commanded the ship. "Your men are on board that ship, Lieutenant."

Hamilton hesitated, then said, "Sailor, give the order to shut down the generators."

"Yes, sir," the sailor replied. "U.S.S. Eldridge this is observation ship Rainbow. You are ordered to disengage the generators. Do you read me Eldridge?"

Static.

"U.S.S. Eldridge, come in." The radioman paused for a moment. "U.S.S. Eldridge come in."

"Observation ship Rainbow. This is U.S.S Eldridge." The static was broken. "We read you. We are shutting down the generators. I repeat. Shutting down."

The thick greenish fog that had enveloped the Eldridge before its disappearance began to build again. At the exact site where the Eldridge had been anchored, the fog grew, becoming a dense swirling mass.

Below deck on the observation ship Rainbow, the hum from the generators returned, vibrating within the steel walls of the hull, and then began to diminish steadily.

As the hum of the generators wound down, the fog surrounding the site of the Eldridge began to dissipate, and with it the outline of the Eldridge began to materialize.

Fifteen minutes after the experiment had begun, the Eldridge was back.

Within minutes of the ship's return, Lieutenant Hamilton and a crew of six came alongside the ship. The ship and its crew were silent. Lieutenant Hamilton expected a crewmember to come along the side of the ship, as protocol demanded, and attend the small boat. The lack of protocol alerted his senses. He knew that something was different aboard the Eldridge, but hid his concern in his voice. "Prepare to board," Lieutenant Hamilton shouted the order to several crewmembers aboard the Eldridge that were in clear sight. His order was ignored. The crewmen never responded, and wandered off.

It took another five minutes, after coming alongside the Eldridge, to secure the PT to the ship, and board. The crew of the Eldridge, disoriented, wandering aimlessly on deck, took no notice of Lieutenant Hamilton or his crew as they climbed up the net ladder attached to the side of the Eldridge and onto the boat.

The generators were intact and now completely off and silent. The acrid smell of burning wire and insulation hung in the air about the boat. If there had been a fire, it was out now.

A gagging sound caught the attention of Lieutenant Hamilton and his crew. They turned to the bow where several crew members from the Eldridge had draped themselves over the side, heaving, over whelmed by nausea.

Lieutenant Hamilton pulled the radio from his belt. "Observation ship Rainbow. This is Lieutenant Hamilton. Prepare to bring Mr. Einstein to the Eldridge." He hesitated for a moment, choosing the correct words. "Something has gone wrong here. Very wrong."

TWELVE

Putting the Vatican behind him and the voice that called out, "Padre, attesa," Dominic took the corner quickly, turning off of the wide street into a narrow alley. Still running, he barely missed colliding into a young woman walking several small dogs. Yorkies, he thought, as he stepped, then skipped around the trio of ankle biting pups.

"Hey, scatto. Faccia attenzione," The young woman yelled after Dominic.

"I'm sorry. Sorry," Dominic said, then noted the confused look on the young woman's face. "Spiacente. Scusilo." He sucked in a gasp of air, nearly exhausted. He sprinted to the doorway of a store and dodged inside the shop.

The Deposito Del Libro was dark and dusty. He didn't mind the dark, but breathing hard from the long run, the dust collected in his nostrils and he sneezed several times in a row. Not the best move for someone trying to hide, he thought, looking around the shop quickly, then sneezing again. He glanced up from his cupped hand and noticed that he was the only person in the shop, other than a lady working a stack of books. He smiled at her.

The woman took a close look at him from behind books stacked so high that it looked as though they were about to fall to the floor at any moment. Apparently, she didn't consider Dominic to be of any concern or a likely sale; she turned her back to him and continued with whatever important matter she had been dealing with before he had entered the shop.

Dominic pushed the sweat soaked hair back from his face and bit into his lip. He was relatively sure he had not been followed. His zigzagging run even confused himself. He needed time to figure out where the hell he was and what the hell he was going to do next.

The woman, whom Dominic assumed was the shopkeeper, glanced at him again. He managed to smile back, picking up a book and examining the cover, feigning great interest. Then he slowly began to make his way to the back of the small shop, keeping a watch on the door the entire time.

A smallish man with a young boy in tow stepped into the doorway of the shop.

Dominic froze. Then relaxed.

"No. Nonno, non qui. L'altro deposito." The young boy pulled at his grandfather's arm as they stepped out of the store, the grandfather muttering something to the boy about not always doing what the boy wanted to do.

Dominic's breath was returning and he felt himself relax even more as the older man and the boy moved down the street. He flipped the pages of the book he'd picked up and paused on a page for a moment as if he were reading. Then he turned a few more pages and paused again. His mind wandered from the words printed on the worn browning page of the book back to the stairway and the voice calling out to him. Who had called to him? He chastised himself out loud, "What a fool."

The store clerk popped her head up over the same stack of books that she apparently hid behind throughout the day and glared at him. Dominic held up the book and smiled. "This is good." The shopkeeper ducked once again behind the leaning tower of books and disappeared.

Dominic shook his head recalling with embarrassment, his actions while at Bramante's Stairway. He could not believe how idiotic he had been, and that he didn't bother to turn around to see who had been calling to him. Why did he run? What if it had been someone he had known? What if? He decided to stop with the 'what ifs,' since they could and would go for quite some time. Now, there's a thought. He had been reacting without thought. Reacting to pure animal instinct. Fight or flight. Even though he didn't see who had been calling to him, his instincts told him that it wasn't safe. Instinct urged him to run.

Yeah, where was that instinct when a man bleeding all over your apartment was hiding in your kitchen? Maybe, he was learning? He considered that. Maybe he was just like the young predator that has to learn to kill and the young prey that needs to learn how to hide and outwit the predator? Could be? But that brought to mind a new question that needed to be answered: *was he the prey or the predator?*

After twenty minutes in the book store, browsing through several books—that he would have actually liked to buy—he felt confident enough that he wasn't being followed and placed the small stack of books down onto a stack of other books, being careful not to knock the whole pile tumbling to the floor. He couldn't buy the books now. He had figured out where he was, but he didn't know what he was doing. He couldn't be hampered by a bag of books, should he need to bolt again. The thought stopped him. Wasn't that thinking like prey?

He exited the store to the sound of the shopkeeper's "Tsk-tsk," but didn't turn around to acknowledge her. Turning left out of the shop, he made his way down the narrow alley, walking slowly, until he reached a main thoroughfare. He needed to find his way home. He needed time to think. And he needed to call Tonita and explain everything. The trouble was—he didn't know how to explain. Not since his days at Saint John Fisher's seminary, had he felt this confused. And it wasn't just about the last twenty-four hours, but about every day for the last four or five months.

Four or five months? He wasn't even sure how long it had been. He tried to think back to the last sermon. After a moment it came back to him, with a blast to his brain. The sermon was so apropos that it was almost as though the moment had chosen Dominic, rather than Dominic choosing the moment.

He had just finished speaking from Deuteronomy of all the blessings the Lord will grant to those who are faithful and follow His commandments. He quoted, 'If you fully obey the Lord your God and carefully follow all his commands, I give you today, the Lord your God will set you high above all the nations on earth. All these blessings will come upon you and accompany you if you obey the Lord your God.'

Dominic had gone on that day, recounting to the congregation all the blessings that the Lord will allow to those that obey and follow him. He had paused in his speech, sweeping the church with his eyes, and allowed a stern frown to form on his face. Then he began to speak of those who do not obey the Lord.

"What will become of those who do not follow the Lord?" he had asked the congregation in animated English and in Italian, his voice echoing through the small church. He hadn't expected anyone to actually reply and offer a suggestion, and so he was completely caught by surprise when a small voice from the back of the church spoke up.

"The Lord will afflict you with madness, blindness and confusion of mind," a man in the back of the church shouted.

"That is right," Dominic said. "That is indeed included with the curses in Deuteronomy." He stepped around the altar table and called out to the man hidden in the shadows of the balcony. "Why don't you come forward so that we may speak?"

"The Lord will give you an anxious mind, eyes weary with longing, and a despairing heart. You will live in constant suspense, filled with dread both night and day, never sure of your life," the voice from the balcony boomed at Dominic and the others in the church. "You will live in constant suspense, filled with dread." the command was punctuated by the slamming of a door.

Dominic hurried down the aisle to the back of the church. Whoever had been in the balcony, had made his way down the curving stairs and out the church door before Dominic could reach him.

Dominic opened the door to the church, looked in both directions and saw no one. He turned to make his way back up to the nave of the church and stopped. All eyes of the congregation were on him. They followed him like the lenses of the cameras held by a throng of paparazzi. He tried to remain calm, taking in a deep breath and forcing a smile to go with the nods of the head he was giving the congregants. Then something out of place caught his attention. He stopped.

A book had been laid out on top of the offering candles set in tiered rows near the back of the church and off to the side of the doorway. And it was smoldering. Smoke wafted up from a corner of the binding that was about to burst into flames. Dominic grabbed for the book. Picking it up he blew on the corner, putting out the small flame that had grown there.

He didn't need to turn to the title to know what the words imprinted into the old leather cover were. His mind had registered the book as The Bible, long before his conscious thoughts.

Dominic looked to the scorched pages, The Bible had been left open to Deuteronomy or more precisely to the Curses for Disobedience. The same passage of his sermon. He slammed the book closed, dowsed it into the vessel of Holy Water and walked out the front door of the church, leaving behind the congregation, the mass and his faith.

Now, just a few streets from his apartment and an hour and a half's walk from the small bookshop, Dominic came to an abrupt halt, stopping in the middle of the sidewalk, forcing others to walk around him, most with typical Italian commentary at the inconvenience.

The realization came to him so suddenly; it was as if he had just walked head on into a brick wall. No one was following him. There hadn't been anyone following him all day. He was certain of it.

He had been trying to answer this one question all along, giving it long moments and many city blocks of thought. Why would anyone go through such elaborate theatrics as to have black cars with silent drivers and a cryptic torn piece of a telephone book, and then not bother to follow him?

The answer was simple and clear. It was the perfect predator and prey scenario. No one followed because they were waiting for him at the destination. No need for the predator to follow along on the journey, when it would be so much easier to catch the prey at the destination. They were waiting for him where he would feel the most secure.

With his apartment building in view, Dominic turned around and walked in the direction that he had just come, abandoning the long trek that he had just taken.

There was only one place that he could go now. A place where he would be safe and a place where he would find help.

And he knew for certain that she would be there.

THIRTEEN

October 28, 1943
Observation Ship Rainbow,
150 yards off the starboard bow of the U.S.S. Eldridge,
Destroyer Escort 173
17:15Hours/ 5:15 P.M.
200 Miles off the coast of the Eastern United States and
the Philadelphia Navel Yard
Final Test—Project Rainbow

"Power up to all generators," Lieutenant Hamilton broadcast the order over the observation ship Rainbow's radio.

"Yes, sir," The new crewman radioed back from the radio room of the Eldridge. "Power is up."

The Eldridge had returned to port after the first experiment and a new crew had been assigned, replacing those who were now reassigned to land-based duties. The previous crew members were separated and placed in positions at bases across the United States, where they were kept under close scrutiny by the Navy's doctors. They appeared to have had no long term ill effects from the first experiments aboard the Eldridge. And although their daily activities were monitored, they were not encumbered.

The generators aboard the Eldridge had been reset. All the wiring, fuses, tubes, and the ship itself, had been tested and retested for any leaks, cracks or structural integrities. Lieutenant Hamilton and the Navy were convinced all was in order.

"Eldridge. This is Lieutenant Hamilton. We will now begin radio silence. We will contact you again at the end of the experiment."

"This is the USS Eldridge. Radio silence to begin."

"Radio silence to begin in five, four..." Lieutenant Hamilton counted down. "Three, two, one." There was, of course, no confirmation from the Eldridge.

From the observation ship Rainbow, now anchored three hundred yards from the Eldridge—considerably farther away than on the first experiment—and absent most of the crew, sailing with only a skeleton staff aboard, a seaman monitored a panel, showing the building electromagnetic field surrounding the Eldridge. Below deck, technicians listened in as the slow growing groan of the generators built, as they powered up to maximum output.

The monitoring instrumentation clearly showed a mounting magnetic field forming around the Eldridge. The slow build was right on course. "How are we doing?" Lieutenant Hamilton asked a young crewman.

"No anomalies, sir."

Lieutenant Hamilton smiled and nodded his approval to the crewman. He and the Navy were convinced that they could pull off the experiment without any of the initial scientists along. Secrecy was a key factor to the project, and as far as Einstein and the others who had worked on the first experiment in the project were concerned, the Eldridge had been refitted and was now back into regular service. Its crew had suffered no long-term ill affects from the first experiment and all were back to their original duties.

"Generators reaching half power, sir," the young crewman monotoned.

The waters surrounding the Eldridge began to smooth out. Waves that approached the ship slowed and flattened, as they neared. The electromagnetic field had already encircled the ship and the green fog seen building during the first experiment had begun to form once again at the water line of the ship.

"Very good," Lieutenant Hamilton responded with as much enthusiasm as the crewman. "Maintain a slow and steady..." Before the Lieutenant could finish the command, a blinding, bright blue light flashed from the Eldridge, lighting up the day lit sky, as though thousands of flashbulbs had popped simultaneously.

The stunned silence aboard the observation ship Rainbow was broken as the crew's eyes adjusted from the searing flash to the normal brightness of the day.

Glancing toward the Eldridge, Lieutenant Hamilton saw that the ship appeared to be fine. Nothing, at least on the surface, was out of order. "Status..."

Then a second flash. Blue, bright, and hot.

And when the eyes of all aboard the observation ship Rainbow had once again adjusted, they stared in disbelief, dumbfounded by what they saw.

Lieutenant Hamilton spoke, his voice near a whisper, "Radio the Eldridge." Before him the sky and the sea spread out. There was no fog. No outline. And no movement in the water.

The Eldridge had vanished.

FOURTEEN

The Jesuit stood tall looming above him. The Novice lay naked and shivering on the cold stone. The Jesuit's fingers wrapped tightly around the hilt of a sword, he pressed the sharp pointed end into the naked skin just above the heart of the young man, applying enough pressure to pierce the flesh. A trickle of blood first beaded then began to roll down the well-formed pectorals and over the ridges of the Novice's abdomen. The Jesuit watched as the blood flow continued trailing down the Novices upper thigh, then down his leg over the powerful calf muscle. The Jesuit was in awe of this Novice. He was a perfect specimen of a man and would be a perfect warrior for God.

The sharpened metal edges of the hilt cut into the Jesuit's hand, as he wrapped his fingers tightly around the crucifix that formed the hilt of the hammered iron sword.

It had been many months since a novice of this caliber had obtained the right to move from the lowest of classes in the Society to the Professed. Once the Novice was confirmed into the ranking of the Professed, he would take his place among those in the Society, and among those who knew the secrets and the holy power of the Society.

"My son, heretofore you have been taught to act the dissembler," The Jesuit spoke softly. "To spy even among your own brethren. To believe no man. To trust no man, so that you might be enabled to gather together all information for your Order as a faithful soldier of the Pope."

The Jesuit leaned into the hilt of the sword sending the point deeper into the Novice's chest. Blood now ran freely, puddling into the outer edges of the cross that had been chiseled into the stone floor, and above which the Novice stood.

"You have been taught to insidiously plant the seeds of jealousy and hatred. You have the power to ensure that only the Church might be the gainer and that the end justifies the means." The Jesuit pulled the sword out and slightly away from the Novice's heart, and then allowed it to slowly drag along his chest and stomach scratching a line of blood down to the Novice's genitals. He held the sword there for several minutes, the sharpened edge of the blade just touching the base of the Novice's penis, poised to slice into the organ or to cut off the sack of testicles that hung below. A slight twitch in the Jesuit's hand and the penis would be amputated.

The Novice stood absolutely still, staring directly into the eyes of the Jesuit.

The Jesuit relaxed his grip on the sword and it fell to the cold stone floor causing a spark to flare up.

"Kneel."

The Novice knelt without hesitation, his knees straddling the cross carved into the stone, so that his testicles and penis hung at the apex of the now blood-filled indentation.

"You have received your instructions and must now serve the proper time using your body and soul as both the instrument of death and the executioner. This you must do as directed by your superiors. For none can command here who has not consecrated his labors with the blood of a heretic. For without the shedding of blood, no man can be saved." The Jesuit's voice trembled. "Do you now declare and swear that his holiness, the Pope, is Christ's Vicegerent and is the true and only Head of the Church throughout the earth? And by the power of Jesus Christ, he hath the power to depose heretical kings, princes, states, commonwealths, and governments, as all are illegal without the sacred confirmation of the Lord?"

"It is my obedient obligation," the Novice said, head and eyes down.

"Do you now renounce and disown any and all allegiance?"

"It is my obedient obligation."

"Do you declare that you will assist your brethren or any agent of his Holiness in any place and for whatever reason?"

"It is my obedient obligation."

"Do you further declare that you shall have no opinion or will of your own, and that you will be submissive in all things commanded?"

"It is my obedient obligation."

The Jesuit's voice rose and echoed in the empty chamber. "To your feet Novice."

The Novice pulled himself up from the floor, his skin sticking to the cold stone by his own drying blood.

"You stand here naked before God," The Jesuit said handing a parchment to the Novice. "Take this and read it so that God and all of mankind may hear."

"In confirmation," The Novice's raspy voice grew louder with every breath, "I hereby dedicate my life, soul, and all of my powers. And with this sword, that I will now receive, I shall scribe my name, written in my blood, in testimony."

"Go ye then into all the world, and take possession of all the lands in the name of the Pope. He who will not accept him, the Lord Jesus, let him be exterminated." The Jesuit bent down, picked the sword up, and turning the blade to his own heart, and the hilt to the Novice said, "Will you do that?"

The Novice took hold of the hilt. "I will," he said, eyes closed head held high.

A breeze quickly began to make its way around the chamber, as if a door had been opened. It circled the chamber throwing a shivering chill into the air.

The Third Hour

The Novice opened his eyes and looked around the darkened chamber, expecting that someone must have entered. Instead, when his gaze returned to the spot where The Jesuit stood, found that it was empty.

The Jesuit was gone.

Only the Novice remained. He stood in the dark, sword in hand and God's commandment in his heart.

FIFTEEN

Cardinal William Celent peered out of the window from the second story Vatican flat that had been his home for more than forty years. He watched helplessly as Dominic fled through the Vatican Museum Gate and out into the maze of old Roman streets. He stood motionless, only his eyes moving to keep pace with Dominic, until Dominic rounded a corner and was out of sight.

Cardinal Celent remained at the window, staring blankly into the sky for several minutes. His eyes occasionally squinting from the bright sun, involuntarily closing then reopening.

He turned away from the window, slowly, allowing his eyes to readjust to the darkened interior of his Vatican flat. He was cautious of his step and reminded himself to be careful of quick movements and the danger of losing his balance. A fall just a week earlier had left him on the floor for nearly five hours, unable to pull himself up to his feet, until a fellow priest came to the flat with a dinner tray. After being helped back to his feet and moving as quickly as he could to the toilet, then relieving himself, he had been holding his bladder as a mind game in an attempt to keep himself alert and because he did not want the embarrassment of being found with clothing-soaked with urine. He then ate a bit of dinner and rested. The next day he was himself again, although a bit more cautious about his movements. That caution had carried over and was fast becoming habit. In his eighty plus years of life, he had experienced many broken bones and he wasn't quick to wish for any more.

His bones were growing brittle, and his skin was a little thinner and now sagging on his arms where they once covered taught muscles. But his mind remained sharp. Ever since his youth, he had been considered brilliant and described as a near genius. Always enjoying science and art, his flat above the Vatican Museums was a perfect place for him. *Why I'm almost a museum piece myself.* He was quick to point out on the rare occasions he visited with others. For almost sixty years he had lived in this flat at the Vatican. It was both his sanctuary and his prison. It was difficult to say which was which, and when, but he had learned to call it home, and the flat did offer the comforts of location and security. The Cardinal had sparsely furnished the flat with a sofa, a couple of armchairs, a desk, and several small end tables. All of the furniture had come to him from priests, nuns, and lay people who lived or worked in the Holy See. He didn't have to buy a single piece of furniture in all his years here. But he did buy books. He had the flat loaded with them. Books were piled everywhere, on tables, tucked into chairs, along the sides of chairs and tables, on windowsills and fireplace mantels, and still not one book was out of place. If anyone asked Cardinal Celent anytime, where any title was, he would tell you exactly. He had read and re-read them all. There were books of fiction and non-fiction, books of reference, books of paintings and drawings, books of photographs, books of romance, books of life, and books on death. Books had become his solace.

His days here were uneventful. He had had enough excitement and adventure in his younger days that the routine of his quite unassuming days at the Vatican were welcomed. It was only now, as he entered the last stage of his life that he had grown anxious about the inevitable events that must soon occur. Although, he had prepared for this time, all the preparation he had done would not make the transition any easier. Cardinal Celent wasn't fearful, he was hopeful. He knew the truth. And the realization that he would now be able to pass it on filled him with anxious anticipation and a sense of relief.

Richard Devin

He pulled on his coat, grabbed a walking cane, and opened the door. He sucked in a long breath as he took the first step down the set of stairs that led from his flat to the street below. He followed the street to Bramante's Stairway, navigated the stairs and made his way to the black Mercedes, which was parked where the driver had left it when Dominic had arrived. He opened the back door to the car and climbed in. Moments later the driver opened the driver's side door, slid into the seat, and waited.

SIXTEEN

February, 1945
Roosevelt Aviation School
Roosevelt Field, Naval Air Facility

"Using just one word," Bill swept the room of classmates with his eyes then continued, "please describe the following: A limited stretch or space of continued existence." He paused looking directly at each of the seventeen men in the room.

"No one?" Bill looked around hoping that someone would say something. When no one did, he said, "Okay, then. What if I added this...the interval between two successive events?"

A student in the back of the room wearing a grease covered sweater shuffled his feet, looking as though he was about to answer, when he caught a stern glance from another student. He looked away from Bill, finding interest instead in a spot on the floor.

"Come on now, gentlemen. Someone must have some idea?"

Blank faces and empty stares were their responses.

Bill glanced around a room filled with mechanics and engineers who couldn't shut up in the dining room or out on the tarmac, yet here, not one of them was willing to speak out. "Let me help you along here." Bill turned to the black chalkboard behind him and wrote one word on it.

Time.

He turned back to the classroom and waited for some response. There was, again, none. "The two definitions I just gave you...describe time." Bill looked around the room once again and realized, by more blank looks and condescending glares, that this crowd was not buying into anything a nineteen-year old kid was selling. And he hadn't even said anything! The thought caused him to let out a long sigh.

"I understand that you're supposed to be some kind of a whiz kid, a genius, I guess, but we don't have time for this." An older mechanic sitting in the front row spoke up.

"My point exactly," Bill said, happy just to have someone speak up. He walked over to the mechanic and stood by his side. "We don't have time."

"If that is your point, you're making no point," the same student said with a Texas twang. "My men and I have more important issues at hand."

"Yeah. Football and girls," another shouted out to rowdy applause and laughter.

"Let's not waste any more of our time," the older mechanic said, punching up the 'time,' "and end this."

The others responded to the pun with raucous enthusiasm.

"What if I could make you travel through time?" Bill asked. "What if you already had?"

"Yeah. Okay," shouted a scrappy little guy from the back row.

"How so?" the grease stained sweater wearing mechanic, who was reluctant to speak earlier, asked with genuine interest.

"Just like this."

The class settled down

"What's your name?" Bill called out to the reluctant student.

"Jonathan. Jonathan Kim."

"Well, Jon, do you have a watch?"

"Sure." Jon held up his left arm, displaying the inexpensive timepiece.

"Nice," the older mechanic stated. "Cracker Jack prize?"

"No. Christmas gift." Jon's tone was serious.

"That's great, Jon." Bill brought the short attention span of the group back to him.

"When I ask you to, Jon, would you please stand up and walk over to me?" Bill moved to the center of the room as close to the chalkboard as he could get.

"Okay, I can do that." Jon said, glancing around the room.

"Jon, what time is it?"

"One thirteen," Jon said, then added, "and twenty seven seconds."

"Perfect. When the second hand is at forty five seconds, I want you to walk over to me."

"Got it." Jon stood up. His lips moved as he silently counted out the seconds. "Forty five," he said out loud, and walked directly to Bill, avoiding a stray leg that shot out to trip him.

He came up beside Bill and stopped.

"What time is it now?" Bill asked.

"It's a...one thirteen and fifty three seconds."

"Congratulations, Jon," Bill said, slapping him on the back. "You've just traveled through time."

"Aw, this is stupid," the older mechanic shouted.

"Look," Bill turned to the older man, "I have a question for you. Are you game?"

The older mechanic looked to the others in the room, most of whom only offered a shrug.

"Go for it Captain," a tall slim man at the window side of the room shouted.

"Yeah, all right then. I'm game," the older mechanic said.

Bill paused for a moment and looking directly at the older mechanic asked, "Do you believe in God?"

"Sure I do."

"Would you mind standing up, please?"

The older mechanic stood, pushing the chipped wooden chair aside. "Okay?"

"Captain. I can call you Captain?"

Richard Devin

"Well, I'm not really a Captain anymore, but sure, go ahead."

"Are you standing still at this moment or are you moving?"

"I'm standing still," Captain said, with a sarcastic grin forming on his face.

"And you believe that?"

"Yes, completely. I know when my feet are moving and I can assure you, son that they are not moving." He glanced down at his feet as if to make sure that his statement was correct.

"Would you say that you have a strong belief in God, Captain?

"Yes, I do."

"Would say that you believe in God as much as you believe that you are not moving?"

"Yes." Captain raised an eyebrow. "I'm not moving. I haven't moved my feet an inch since you asked me to stand up. And I still believe in God, whatever that has to do with this?" Captain's tone grew agitated.

"Then I might suggest to the rest of us here, that you have a false belief in God." Bill hesitated a moment as the others in the class grew restless. "You see, Captain, you believe that you are standing still, that you are not moving. And you...well really I...equated that same belief to your faith in God. You, Captain, are moving. We are all moving. And we are traveling through space and time at this very moment."

"What kind of talk is this?" Captain said. "You're no genius. You're just nuts."

"That may be so, Captain. And someday I'm sure that we will find out. But for the moment, I am the only one here who understands that this Earth we are standing on is moving through time and space at more than one thousand miles per hour. And that means that you, Captain, are not standing still at all. You are spinning through space and time at more than a thousand miles an hour." Bill starred into Captain's eyes, waiting.

Captain sat down without saying another word.

"You see, we all have beliefs and perceptions based on what we think we know to be, true, just like Captain's faith. He believed that he was not moving. He had faith in his own perception. But as you have seen, we cannot believe in our perceptions." Bill turned to the chalkboard and picked up a piece of chalk. "Maybe Mister Shakespeare said it best." Bill wrote on the board. *To Be or Not To Be*. "So if we all believe that we are standing still, even though the Earth is spinning at a thousand miles per hour, does it make it so?"

"I guess not," Captain said.

"My feet are firmly planted below me and yet I know that I'm not standing still. I understand that my perceptions of movement are clouded by my understanding of movement. The same is true about time. You are trapped by your perceptions of time and therefore cannot see that we travel through time every day."

"Wait," Jon said. "How can we travel through time every day?"

"When you wake up it's one time. Then you go to work, and then you go back home. Each of those events takes place 'through time.' None of us has problems with the fact that every day we travel forward in time, yet not one of you wants to believe that we can also travel backwards in time. Why? When did we all agree that time only moves in one direction?"

"Because when we're dead, time is up and no one ever comes back," Captain's matter-of-fact tone added to his sarcasm.

"Is that so, Captain?" Bill turned to the man. "What about Jesus?"

Momentarily caught off guard, Captain hesitated, then shouted out, "That's because he's God. He can do that."

"Or maybe he was just a man, a man who died and returned because he didn't buy into your beliefs. He wasn't restricted by them, like you are." Bill glanced at the men in the room. They were young and old, mostly first generation Americans. They were thinking about getting home, and dinner, and their kids. They were certainly not thinking about time travel. "There were others who thought like you. Lord Kelvin, President of the Royal Society said in 1895 that heavier than air flying machines were impossible. Look out that window, gentlemen. I see an airfield with thirty or more of the machines that Kelvin said were impossible." Bill paused letting that bit of trivia sink into the room filled with airplane mechanics.

"Now what if you had bought into Lord Kelvin's beliefs?"

SEVENTEEN

Dominic concealed himself in a crevice made of brick and mortar—that two thousand years ago, would have held a statue of some god or other as decoration—in the ruins of the ancient Roman baths. From his vantage point, he could clearly see the majority of the hillside and the few enormous walls of the once great Roman baths that remained. Beyond that the modern city complex, all stretched out before him. He liked it here and had come on more than one occasion to sit and ponder the sight below, where ancient civilizations met the modern. It was hard for him to say which was better.

The stand of fig trees, planted long ago by Dominic's ancestors, was just to his right. He recalled the story told him by his Nonno when he was about six or seven.

"Your great, great, great uncle," Nonno emphasized each word more powerfully than the last, "was a very powerful man during the time of Caesar. He was the keeper of all the fig crops in Rome and Caesar himself made him the Senatore dei Fico—the Senator of the Figs," Nonno said this to Dominic with great reverence. His grandfather's story would be repeated many times over at every family Christmas and Easter gathering, beginning the moment his Nonna brought out plates mounded with fig filled cookies—cuscidati.

The fig trees spread out in a tangled mass of branches and roots. No longer cared for and pruned, the branches wrapped around pillars that once held up the retractable roof of the baths, but now stood concealed from the casual observer, covered in and protected from the elements by the gnarled arms of the figs. Centuries of root structures from both the fig and ancient olive trees held the hillside in place, preserving the ruins from further decay and still producing fruit in abundance.

Richard Devin

Dominic breathed in the scent of the damp crumbling stone and the rain-soaked earth. The scent of wet grass, dirt, and stone had become a comfort to him throughout the many days that he had sought refuge here. Refuge mainly from his own thoughts. He chuckled at how ironic it was that he had to get away and be by himself so that he could get away from his thoughts. It didn't make sense, but then, not too much did lately.

He closed his eyes, imagining the sights, the sounds, and the smells of the baths centuries ago. Common citizens, as well as the elite, of the Roman Empire would have mixed here. It was the place where the city's populous would come together.

Oil scented pools filled with waters pumped up from the nearby wells would have been heated through a labyrinth of fire-stoked bricks to steaming, and then pumped directly into the baths. Cold plunge pools would have been located nearby and the bathers would have dipped into the cold baths after soaking in the warm waters. The baths would have been filled to capacity during the day, as Romans took the medicinal as well as the spiritual values of the baths, very seriously. Public baths, like the one here on the hills of Rome, were common in all Roman cities and conquered lands.

Now, the ruins stood as a reminder of how far we have come, or how far we have fallen, Dominic thought. He wasn't sure in which direction man had gone. It was one of the prime reasons he had become a priest. Even as a young man he had questioned where man had been and where he was going, both in a spiritual sense and in a simple scientific sense. What more could man achieve? What more could man do to benefit man? What more would man do to kill off his fellow man? Those questions had plagued him and his lack of ability to answer them, had tormented him.

He'd entered seminary at Saint John Fisher in a quest to answer those questions and the many other questions that the answers to the first set of questions would bring about. He never got answers, only more questions.

Through the course of his lessons in seminary he had learned to remain silent, allowing the many questions he had to fester within him. He believed in God. At least at one time he did. Now, he wasn't sure. How could there be a loving God, as the church taught, if there was so much suffering? He'd nearly driven himself crazy with the unanswered barrage of questions that had continued to fill his head. He was at once a rebel— rebelling from the church—and the Templar—filling the Temple of God. He'd succeeded at being the rebel. But as for filling the temple, there he had failed.

And now, he was feeling completely alone. Abandoned. Utterly confused about his past, his present, and his future. There was no sense to it. If God had a plan for him, Dominic had absolutely no idea of what it was. He was completely lost. No star to guide him, no flock to follow...He laughed out loud at the ridiculousness of his thoughts turning to song lyrics and cliché.

A movement in the shadows caught his attention and he watched as Tonita stepped out from behind the tangle of fig branches. She moved slowly, methodically, her eyes sweeping the ruins and the hillside. Apparently, seeing no one, she moved away from the stand of trees.

Dominic began to step out of the crevice, then hesitated and sank back as far as he could. He needed to be sure that no one had followed her. He had not seen a single person in the area of the ruins for the past several hours. His body ached from the crouched position he had to take to fit into the crevice, and he desperately wanted to stand. But he remained. And waited.

Tonita too, had remained hidden in the stand of fig trees for more than several hours. She had waited and watched. No one had entered or exited the ruin of the baths while she waited. Except, that is, for Dominic.

Concealed within the dense mass of branches and leaves, Tonita had remained still and quiet, as Dominic slowly circled the walls and pools of the baths, stopping every few feet to check his surroundings. Once he was sure that no one was following, he climbed the walls, using the old bricks as a foothold.

A task, Tonita determined that Dominic must have completed before, as he easily made it to the top of the three-story wall in little time and with little effort. She'd held her breath as Dominic quickly skirted along a dangerously crumbling edge to the crevice, and once there, he had virtually disappeared.

Now she felt assured that she and Dominic had not been followed. "We're alone." Tonita kept her voice low, just in case. "Come down." She stared directly at the crevice high upon the wall.

Dominic couldn't believe that she knew where he was. He stepped out. "How the hell did you know I was up here?" His tone was both inquisitive and irritated.

"I watched you climb up there."

"How? There wasn't anyone around when I did," Dominic said as he made his way down the wall.

"Apparently there was." Tonita smiled at him.

Dominic jumped down the last few feet, landing softly on the damp soil. "And what spy school did you go to?" He smiled back at her.

"I knew that you would come here. It was just a matter of when."

Dominic stumbled as he came down the hill, closing the gap between them quickly. He reached for Tonita pulled her closer and hugged her tightly.

"We should get out of the open," Tonita said, breaking his hold on her.

Dominic leaned in and kissed her.

This time she reached around him, wrapping her arms tightly under his. She let him kiss her for a long moment. "I've missed you," she said pulling away from him. "I was scared. Confused."

"Join the crowd," Dominic said. Then smiled. "I'm just as scared and very confused." The moment was over, even though they still selfishly clung to one another. "But I knew that I would find you here."

"I couldn't think of anyplace else to go," Tonita said. "I was going to call that inspector and tell him that you'd been kidnapped."

"Kidnapped?"

"What was I to think?" Tonita took a step away. "You yell 'Don't follow me,' and the next thing I know you're gone."

"I knew the car had been sent by the Vatican."

"What the hell for?"

"That part I'm not too sure of. I thought it was for a scolding. But when I got there I panicked. I ran." He hesitated, then continued. "Tonita, I don't want you to get hurt. I don't think that it's a good idea for you to be with me."

"Are you nuts?" She turned taking the single step in his direction that now separated them. "You got me all involved in this...whatever the hell it is, and now I'm staying involved with this and you,"

He smiled. "I knew you'd say that."

"What else was I supposed to say?"

"You could have told me that I'm on my own. That you don't need this. That you don't need me."

"Then I would have been lying."

Dominic kissed her on the cheek. "Come on." He took her hand and led her through the ruined walls, following the same path out that he had taken on the way in, leading them back to the street.

EIGHTEEN

Dominic reached for the door to his apartment, pressed down on the tongue of the latch and heard the click of the release. It was unlocked. He shot Tonita a sideways glance.

"What?"

"It's unlocked." He gave her a look that said it all.

"Don't give me that look," Tonita's voice took on an edge. "You always forget to lock it."

Dominic raised an eyebrow and a boyish grin exaggerated his delight, "But this time you were the last one out."

Tonita raised her shoulders. "Sorry, what can I say? Don't run off and tell me not to follow, anymore. Then I won't run out of your apartment, wondering what the hell that was all about and forget to lock your door." She smiled at him.

Dominic pushed the door open. He was about to mount a defense to her criticism but hesitated as a loud thump echoed down the short hallway, reaching Dominic and Tonita at the door.

They froze.

"The cat?" Tonita asked, putting a hand on Dominic's arm.

"I don't have a cat."

"The neighbor's then?" Tonita lowered her voice to a whisper.

Dominic brought his index finger to his lips, giving Tonita the quiet sign. She obliged and moved closer to his side.

Inside, another thump was followed by the choked sounds of whispers. Dominic stepped inside, followed closely by Tonita.

The Third Hour

"Shouldn't we be going in the other direction? Tonita asked holding tight to Dominic's arm and matching his step.

Dominic stopped. Listened. "Stay here," he whispered into Tonita's ear.

Tonita backed off, ducking into the doorway of the hall bath.

Dominic watched her move into the hall bathroom. Then took a slow step forward. He wasn't sure if he should creep in and surprise the intruder or rush in and surprise whoever it was. He wasn't even sure if it was an intruder. But given the events of the last day and half, he was fairly sure that he could assume it was. He decided to go for it. He gave Tonita a quick glance, making sure that she was safe. He took a second longer allowing the adrenaline to build and then with a loud grunting roar, he rushed into the living room.

The room was fairly dark, lit only by the sunlight that eked its way through the grime and dirt that covered the outside of the windows. Rome was notorious for its air pollution, especially during the early nineteen seventy's, and evidently these windows had not had a proper cleaning since then and by the looks of them, long before, Dominic thought, as he pulled up short and entered the room. His intent was to scare off whoever was inside and avoid a confrontation. He hadn't thought about the fact that the door to apartment was behind him and so was Tonita. The intruder would have to make a dash for the hall and the door and hopefully not discover Tonita as he did. It really didn't matter, Dominic soon realized as the plan to scare off the intruder didn't work and instead he ran smack into the man.

The brown, cloak-covered man fell to the side as the force of Dominic's body hit him hard. He whimpered as he hit the wall, a crucifix falling from his hand.

Dominic pulled himself up, glanced at the man and the fallen crucifix. Then a sound caught his attention and he turned to see another man, older, lying on the floor, gasping for breath.

One man dressed in a monk's cloak. The older man gasping, dressed in..."Shit what the hell is this?" Dominic screamed, as he recognized the uniform of a Catholic Priest.

A monk, a priest and a crucifix, Dominic thought that it sounded like the set up to some barroom joke. But this was not a joke and that was not an ordinary crucifix that they monk had been holding. It was about six inches long, silver or some silver-looking metal, and protruding from the back of it was a long ice pick-like dagger.

Dominic hesitated a moment trying to figure out, in as few seconds as possible, if the crucifix-ice pick-dagger belonged to the monk or to the priest. He didn't have to wait long for the answer.

The monk lunged for the crucifix dagger.

Dominic lunged for the monk.

The monk reached the crucifix-ice pick before Dominic reached the monk. "You must die," the monk said in deliberately precise English, with an odd Italian accent, and heaved his body at Dominic.

Together, they fell over the older priest, crashing down hard on him. He let out a whimper, and Dominic had a brief thought of concern for the old priest, but it quickly passed as the crucifix dagger was pressed nearer to his chest.

Dominic reached out, grabbed hold of the monk's arm with both of his hands, and pushed. The monk was surprisingly strong, and despite Dominic's continued resistance, the crucifix dagger edged nearer.

***

Drool fell from the corner of the monk's mouth, as the anticipation of the Key's death filled him. *The Key is remarkably weak*, he thought. Not at all what he had considered, then he reconsidered. God of course was with him. Taking the strength away from the Key. It was his destiny to kill the Key. To preserve the secrets of the Pope and of the Church. The Jesuit and God had commanded him to act. "God will reward me in the afterlife for your death, and the Jesuit will reward me now, I am the destroyer of the Key. God bless me, Brother Salvatore, as your soldier," he said, as he pushed with surprising ease against Dominic's arms.

As if in slow motion, the crucifix dagger closed the gap between the sharp point of the crucifix and Dominic's heart.

***

Dominic grunted, gritted his teeth, and pushed back against the monks hand with everything that he had. It was not enough. The crucifix dagger closed the last few millimeters and Dominic could feel the pressure as the point of the crucifix dagger first pierced his shirt and then his skin, slipping easily through the muscles of his chest, growing nearer to his heart. As he watched the point slide into his chest he expected to feel a searing shock of pain, but instead, only felt the pressure of the point. An odd serenity slipped over Dominic. A strange curiosity kept his eyes glued to the crucifix as it slipped deeper into the pectoral muscles. Just as with a zebra, whose jugular was pierced by the canines of a lion, there was no pain, only panic followed by resolve.

The predator and the prey.

Dominic's strength was giving out, he considered relaxing his arms and letting the point of the crucifix pierce his heart, ending the struggle. He couldn't hold on much longer and the panic that had gripped him at first was now slipping away to the realization that this was going to be the death of him. He looked up into the sickly smile that spread across the monk's face and a resolve made its presence known. In his final seconds of life random thoughts crossed his mind. Maybe this was the end God had intended for him. He had abandoned God after all, and just as Inspector Carrola had said the day before, "I hope that God does not need some time away from you." Perhaps God did? He let his grip on the monk's arm slacken.

Dominic could see what could only be described as sheer glee in Brother Salvatore's eyes. The monk giggled, as he readied himself to plunge the crucifix dagger all the way into Dominic's rapidly beating heart. His smile grew and nearly beamed. Dominic struggled against him. But the monk was more than he could manage.

***

He could hardly contain himself. He was about to witness, no, partake in the death of the Key. All would be right when the Key was dead. All would be safe. No one would know of the truth and the deceptions that had been proclaimed or denied for decades. The church would continue. Brother Salvatore's eyes closed. He pulled his full weight up and prepare to bare it down on the crucifix dagger and into the Key's heart.

***

Dominic said a last silent prayer.

And just as the full weight of the monk's body was about to bear down on the crucifix, the monk slumped to the side, falling onto Dominic. His grip on the crucifix dagger released.

Dominic remained still for a moment, then pushed the monk off of him. The crucifix dagger, now embedded into Dominic's flesh, remained upright. Dominic followed the crucifix dagger protruding from his chest up to the nearly angelic face of Tonita, who stood with the heel of one of Dominic's dress shoes at the ready to strike again onto the head of the monk.

NINETEEN

February 1945
Roosevelt Aviation School
Roosevelt Field, Naval Air Facility

"Bill?" A crew cut, straight-laced, scientific looking man stood in the doorway of the classroom.

Bill looked up from his notes. He immediately recognized the man as one of the men from his class earlier that day. The man looked twenty-two, maybe twenty four. By his ridged stance and the way he held his arms at his side, he had certainly come from a military background.

"Mind if I ask you a couple of questions?"

"Sure." Bill stood up. "Come on in."

"Your class today was a..." he fought for the words, "...interesting. I actually had a few questions that I wanted to ask during your talk, but then the guys..." His voice trailed off.

Bill smiled. "I understand. The other guys kind of made it difficult."

"I'm really interested in the theory of time and space. I've studied up on it best I could. But you seem to have a better understanding of it all."

"Thanks...sorry, I've forgotten your name."

"Ray Scott."

Bill's expression gave away some shadow of skepticism.

"I know," Ray said, smiling. "I have two first names. Blame my parents." He chuckled, adjusting his black-rimmed glasses.

"Well, Ray. Shoot."

"What's that?" Ray's grin turned serious.

Richard Devin

"Ask away, shoot, what's your thoughts?" Bill said, watching the man and noting uneasiness about Ray, as though he was hiding something and not particularly well. *Maybe just nerves*, Bill considered, then dismissed the thought.

"Oh, OK." He paused briefly, then continued, "I have my own theories on the possibility of traveling through time and that's why I was so interested in hearing you speak." Ray sat down in one of the chairs.

"Great," Bill said, taking a chair alongside. "I may have taken the time travel element a bit too far. I meant to just mention it, but I think it got the better of me."

"So do you really believe it's possible? Or were you just trying to get some of the older guys here pissed off?"

"I wasn't trying to piss off anyone. It just happened. Then the argument got to me. And I don't like people who aren't willing to open themselves up to the possibilities and..." Bill stood and walked to the desk in the center of the room close to the blackboard. "What I had hoped to do was get a better understanding of the physics of flight from the guys who actually keep the planes up in the air. I've had plenty of talks with engineers and scientists, but I've never taken my studies down to ground level. That's why I'm here. It's just part of my studies." He paused taking a good look at Ray Scott. "To answer your question, I think time travel is possible. I know, looking at me, a nineteen year old kid..."

"Some say genius, nineteen year old kid," Ray tossed in.

Bill shook his head and arched his shoulders. "Some may. I don't."

"I picked up a bit of information about you: graduated high school at sixteen, moved on to study at Columbia University..." Ray pulled a piece of paper from his pants pocket and read, "Research into the atom with faculty members I. I. Rabi, Enrico Fermi, and Polykarp

Kusch. That's an impressive list for anyone." Ray folded the paper and returned it to his pocket.

"What's this all about, Ray?" Bill stared at the man.

"Physics. Time Travel." Ray took his glasses off. "Maybe even God."

An odd thought hit Bill, and he immediately questioned whether Ray needed eyeglasses at all or were they some cheap attempt at a disguise? Nothing more than a prop.

"Physics and time travel are right up my alley, Ray. As for the God business, I don't believe in God. I say I'm agnostic simply because it's easier on those who do believe. But I'm an atheist." Bill's eyebrow arched, "If you'd like the truth?" He waited. When no response came, he continued. "So, if you want to talk about the glorious powers of God? I'm not your man."

Ray stood, folded the glasses that he had just removed moments ago, and placed them in his shirt pocket. He walked the ten or so feet to the door.

Bill couldn't help but question the action, as apparently the need to see clearly was not a concern for Ray Scott, any longer.

Ray turned just before stepping through the doorway. "Thank you, Bill. You've been a tremendous help." He reached for the doorknob and pulled the door closed behind him. Ray Scott exited the building that housed the education hall, leaving Bill alone in the classroom.

***

Ray Scott crossed the hot pavement of the airfield without looking back toward the education hall, or the man he left in the classroom, although he was sure that he was being watched by him. He dodged a stream of utility vehicles, workmen, and airplanes, and headed toward a small, nondescript metal-sheathed building, that could only be described as a shed. Except for a crudely painted identification number, 773–H, on the otherwise faded, chipped, and worn paint that managed to cling to the rusted metal facade of the building, there were no distinguishing marks.

Ray's pace was deliberate, almost cautious. He circled around the small building once, then headed to the back, where he stopped. Here the line of sight to and from the other buildings, hangers, and people milling about the airfield, was completely blocked. There were no outbuildings behind the shed, securing the privacy of anyone standing behind it. What appeared to be hapless military planning was actually a perfect disguise. No one paid attention to a shed at an airfield. There were many of them scattered about, some large, others no bigger than an outhouse. Ray and the others could come and go with little concern of being spotted. Still, Ray glanced around the corner of the shed, making sure, one more time, that no one was in sight or watching him.

He pulled a half-inch by three inch magnet from the pocket of his pants, and held it up to the right side of the shed, moving it slowly up and down a one foot section near the top portion of the siding. He heard a click and the door popped open. What had moments ago appeared to be a seam in the sheet metal, now revealed a doorway.

He inserted his fingers into the small opening and pulled on the door. The sheet metal slid open, easily moving on well-oiled hinges. Ray Scott stepped inside, allowing the door to close silently on the spring mounted hinge.

He paused for a moment, allowing his eyes to adjust to the interior lighting. A narrow set of stairs led to a floor below. A string of bare bulbs, which had been hung precariously along the smooth cement walls of the hallway, dimly lit the way. Ray stepped down the stairs and immediately felt the cool damp air on his face and arms. He followed the lights along the zigzag of the corridor, going first right, then left, then repeating.

The Third Hour

Twenty five yards later, planted precisely under one of the large hangers topside, Ray slid open a glass door and entered what he and the other's had dubbed...The Time Room.

TWENTY

Tonita screamed, "Stop!" Her arms raised high above her head, with the heel of Dominic's dress shoe, once so carelessly tossed to a corner of the room, at the ready to strike. She had already leveled the heel of the shoe into the monk's head once, and she was prepared to do it again, both hands clenching the toe of the shoe—precisely aiming the heavy black heel.

The monk, however, did not move. He lay where he had fallen. The only movement was a thin steam of blood that flowed from his right ear, down his cheek and slowly dripped to the floor.

"Is he dead?" Tonita asked, with shoe still at the ready.

Dominic looked up at her from his prone position on the floor. "I don't know. You see, I've got this little problem of my own." He glanced to the crucifix dagger still embedded in his chest.

"Oh, Dom!" Tonita started to lower the shoe, then decided a quick kick into the monk's side wouldn't be uncalled for. She kept the heel of the shoe aimed at the monk, lifted one foot, and kicked, landing her foot powerfully into his side.

The monk moved and inch or so forward from the force of the kick, but did not make a sound.

Tonita slowly lowered the shoe, all the while keeping an eye on the slumped body of the monk.

The sound of a groan had the shoe back up over her head in an instant, ready to strike again. Still the monk did not move, and he made no sound.

Another groan of pain, followed by a cough, then the breathless sounds of someone desperately trying to catch their breath, then Dominic too, was on his feet. A slight dizzy feeling swirled in his brain and he closed his eyes until his legs steadied.

"Dom," Tonita whispered. "A priest?"

Dominic opened his eyes as the swirling motion in his brain, calmed. He stepped in the direction of the sounds, and winced. The crucifix dagger pierced into his pectoral muscles and sent a searing pain up his shoulder. When he stood still, the pain ceased. But once he stepped forward again and the muscles in his chest expanded and contracted, a white hot fire shot through his chest up to his shoulders, causing his entire left side to convulse. He steadied himself once again, sucked in a breath of air and held it. He pulled on the crucifix dagger, gritting his teeth at the feel of the metal dagger pulling through his skin. Once its length slid completely out of his chest, he allowed himself to breathe, letting air out slowly. The dagger left a small hole in his shirt and in the pectoral muscles underneath. Pumped once again with adrenaline, Dominic stepped forward. He turned the weapon around, intending to use it on whoever this older priest was.

Tonita kept the shoe and its deadly heel poised and ready, but let Dominic step around her.

The priest had pulled himself away from Dominic's struggle with the monk, taking a slight refuge by the old leather chair. His breath was returning and his voice rasped, "Dominic. Thank you," he said, between repeated coughs.

Tonita lowered the shoe, and after one quick glance to the monk, tossed it aside. "Who is he?" Tonita nodded in the priest's direction.

Dominic shrugged his shoulders. "I don't know."

"Well, he knows you." Tonita turned to the priest. "Apparently you know who he is. Mind if I ask who you are?"

The old priest used the arm of the chair to steady himself and pushed himself up to his feet. "My name is

Bill." He paused as he caught Dominic eyeing his clothing. "Bill, to my friends. William Celent is my proper name. "

Both Dominic and Tonita watched, studying the movements of the man as he struggled to gain his footing. Neither offered help.

Tonita turned to the monk on the floor. "Okay, we know your name. Now, who is he?"

"A brother of the Society." William Celent said.

"And what is he doing here? Dominic said with a bit of irritation. He held the crucifix dagger between his fingers ready to push it into the flesh of the old priest, should he need to.

"I'm afraid he was here to kill you."

"And you were here to help him do that?" Tonita moved slightly closer to Dominic.

"No." William Celent stood up straight. "I was here to protect you."

Dominic lowered the dagger to his side in a conscious effort to appear at ease. "Protect me from what?"

William Celent reached out a hand, "I'm afraid I have much to explain."

"All right," Tonita said, trying to take control of the situation. "We know your name, so, what do you want? What are you doing here?"

"As I said, protecting you."

And is that why this monk was trying to kill you?" She paused giving the priest a chance to respond.

"I have every intention of answering your questions, my dear, and I'm sure there are plenty more..."

"Oh, you're right about that," Tonita said, interrupting the man.

"But, I believe our good man here, needs some medical attention first." William Celent turned his gaze toward Dominic.

Tonita followed Celent's gaze to Dominic.

The Third Hour

Dominic's skin had grown pale in color. His eyes were glazed and the bloodstain from the wound to his chest had spread. He was losing blood quickly. Only the adrenaline that pulsed through his body had kept him standing.

And its effects were beginning to fade.

TWENTY ONE

February 1945
Roosevelt Aviation School
Roosevelt Field, Naval Air Facility
The Time Room

Unlike the damp, dimly lit hallway, the Time Room was state of the art. It was well lit and naturally cool, being well-below ground, with walls painted a clean white, leaving the drab government green and gray to those above ground. The floor was covered in a tapestry of area rugs, giving it a Caspian feel. Soft, big band music played static free over a radio in the corner.

Ray Scott slid the glass door closed behind him and stepped into the Time Room. He was greeted by a slight nod from a technician who barely looked up from the control panel he was tinkering with and a "Hey," from another technician on the other side of the room.

Ray traversed the room, going straight to a glass walled office on the far side. He could see a man inside the paper-strewn office in a rumpled shirt, sleeves rolled up, leaning unevenly onto his forearms. The man inside pushed one sleeve up higher in the unconscious movement of a habit. He continued to write, erase, and write again, onto a column of numbers on the sheet of paper in front of him.

Ray pushed on the door, sliding it on the tracks into a pocket in the wall. The man at the desk barely glanced up, and only minimally acknowledged Ray's entrance into the office. Ray closed the pocket door by pulling on it until it slid out of the space created for it within the wall. It moved smoothly along its track and clicked into the latch on the frame. With the door closed, the room was soundproof. "Don't you think it's ironic that in a secret room, well-below ground, filled with high security clearance men and women, there would still be need for a soundproofed office?" Ray said.

The man at the desk looked up, put his pencil down, and for the moment stopped his furious calculations. "There are secrets even among those who keep the secrets," the man punctuated the statement with a raised eyebrow.

"How right you are, Vern." Ray sat down in the chair on the opposite side of the desk from the man. "The young instructor will agree to join us. I just need to convince him."

"That is very good news," Vern said, as he attempted to refold the rolled up shirtsleeve of his left arm.

"Good in a way." Ray watched the man opposite him with curiosity. Ray stood. "We don't have much time, Vern."

"Time?" Vern said with a grin. "Not to worry, I'll make more."

Ray reached into the pocket of his suit coat and pulled out a thrice-folded sheet of paper. He tossed it onto the sea of papers already covering Vern's desk.

Ray watched Vern's face take on a concerned look as he reached for the paper, picked it up, unfolded it and read it aloud.

> *The Secretary of War has approved a project, whereby certain understanding German scientists and technicians are being brought to this country to ensure that we take full advantage of those significant developments which are deemed vital to our national security.*
>
> *Interrogation and examination of the documents, equipment, and facilities in the aggregate are but one means of exploiting German progress*

in science and technology. In order that this country may benefit fully from this resource, a number of carefully selected scientists and technologists are being brought to the United States on a voluntary basis. These individuals have been chosen from those fields where German progress is of significant importance to us and in which these specialists have played a dominant role.

Throughout their temporary stay in the United States, these German scientists and technical experts will be under the supervision of the War Department, but will be utilized for appropriate military projects of the Army and Navy.

War Department
Bureau of Public Relations
Press Branch
Tel. RE 6500
Brs.3425 and 4860

For Immediate Release
October 1, 1945

Vern looked up from the press release. "This date is wrong." He quickly dug out a small calendar from under the pile of papers. "It's February. This release is dated for October, seven months from now."

Ray pushed on the door to the office sliding it once again along its track into the pocket in the wall. "That should give you plenty of time to complete the project here, and then join your team from Germany." Ray stepped out of the office, then turned back to Vern.

"And, of course, to join your family." He traversed the room and exited through the same doorway he had entered.

A moment later, the technician that gave a "hey" to Ray Scott as he walked by, stepped into Vern's office. "Mr. Von Braun?" he said, then waited for the man to look up. When he did, the technician continued, "I could use your help."

TWENTY TWO

Dominic's pale color turned completely white as he attempted to remain standing.

"Dom!" Tonita screamed and lunged for him. She was too late to catch him and break his fall, and too small to be of any real help should she have made it in time.

His eyes rolled back into his head and he collapsed with a thud onto the old wooden floorboards. His head bounced as it hit the floor—a double thud. The red stain of blood on his shirt, where the crucifix dagger had pierced his flesh and muscle, was spreading rapidly.

And to make matters worse, the monk—Brother Salvatore, let out a long moan and began to move.

"Help me," Tonita looked quickly to Celent, then stole a glance back to the monk. She was afraid to take her eyes off the monk for too long, lest he spring back to life.

Celent, who was only now beginning to recover from his own struggle with the monk, stepped around the heap that was Brother Salvatore, and began tending to Dominic by pulling open Dominic's shirt, attempting to wipe away as much blood as he could with the tails of the shirt. "I'm not a doctor."

"Forget it." Tonita looked one again in the direction of the monk, then decided that the he wasn't going anywhere, and pushed her way between Celent and Dominic. "Let me," she said, as she slid her hands onto Dominic's chest and pushed, watching as the hole from the crucifix dagger opened and closed. "As far as I can tell, the dagger went in just above the heart. I think it only sank into the pectoral muscle. If it had gone any deeper, it would have caused some damage to a major organ or artery, and there would be more bleeding." She applied pressure to the wound with booth of her hands. "Watch what I'm doing." She gave Celent a moment to observe. "Now move your hands in, where mine are, and keep a steady pressure on his chest."

Celent leaned in and eased his hands in place of Tonita's, all the while maintaining pressure on the wound. He straightened up onto frail arms, pushing down as hard as he could. He could feel the beat of Dominic's heart, and despite the blood loss and the bumps to his head, it remained strong. Dominic may have a concussion, but his heart was in good shape. "His heart is beating strongly. I don't think that dagger did any damage to the heart or lungs," Celent said, as he looked up at Tonita.

Tears welled in Tonita's eyes as she looked from the Celent to Dominic.

"He'll be all right. We'll be all right," Celent said.

"What about him?" Tonita looked to where the monk had fallen.

A low guttural voice stopped her from further questions. "No! The Key must die!" Brother Salvatore jumped up from his prone position on the floor and rammed into Celent with surprising speed and strength, then fell once again to the floor.

Celent's hands, already covered in blood, gave way and he lost his balance, as his hands slipped on Dominic's torso.

"No! La chiave deve morire. The Key, the Key must die!" Brother Salvatore, still half dazed, adrenaline charged, dragged himself, like a wounded animal, toward Dominic, using the last bit of strength.

Celent struggled on the slippery, bloodied floor. He threw his body on top of Dominic's.

The monk pushed Celent away, then reversed the action and pulled at Celent's clothing, dragging him closer, until a piece tore away from Celent's jacket, throwing the monk off balance. Brother Salvatore fell forward, nearly dislodging himself from the position he had taken straddling Dominic.

Celent regained his balance and grabbed onto Dominic's arm, holding tightly, pulling Dominic toward him in a weak attempt to get Dominic's body away from the monk.

The monk grabbed on to Dominic's opposite arm and a human tug of war ensued, as both Brother Salvatore and Celent pulled in opposite directions on Dominic's arms.

Dominic's body stretched out like those hung on a cross.

Brother Salvatore smiled at the sight.

"Let him go or you will surly suffer the wrath of God," Celent said as he noticed a quick blur of movement from the corner of his eye.

"You fool! I am the wrath of God!" Brother Salvatore said. He stared into Celent's eyes, daring him.

For a moment the two stood with Dominic stretched between them. Neither one giving.

Then Brother Salvatore's eyes glazed over. The sick smile replaced by shock. His knees buckled and he fell to the floor. He tried to regain his stance, pushing up on arms that would not support him, and fell back again. His legs kicked out and his body shook.

Then a scream.

This time Celent heard the pop, and smelled the undeniable scent of sulfur.

Brother Salvatore slumped to his side, a slow wheezing sigh escaped through his lips.

The first shot had only grazed the monk, burning his flesh, as though coarse sandpaper had been rubbed vigorously against his skin. The second shot hit him hard. The bullet plunged into his side, tearing through his rib cage, cracking and shattering any bone that happened to be in its path, then continued through a lung before exiting Brother Salvatore's body through his back. The wheezing sound of escaping air continued, coming from both the monk's mouth and through the gaping hole in his side, as his bullet pierced lung discharged its once life giving breath into the room.

Celent raised his head, turning to Tonita. "You have a gun?"

It was a redundant question.

Tonita clearly had a gun. She was holding it, pointing it at the now dead body of Brother Salvatore. She lowered the gun to her side.

"I don't," she said, in answer to the Celent's question. "Dominic does."

TWENTY THREE

Trepuzzi, Lecce, Italy.

The Novice immediately shot upright, bending at the waist, looking as though a corpse had raised itself from a coffin. He had lapsed into a semi-conscious state, lying on the blood wetted, cold stone floor of the Oath Chamber, waiting for the Jesuit to return. Left alone and without direction, the Jesuit had administered the Oath of Induction, and then, vanished. Now, a deep stinging and penetrating burn to the Novice's shoulder roused him from his self-induced hypnotic trance.

For the past several hours the Novice had stood where he had been, unmoved by the cold and pain that crept up from his bare feet to his calves, creeping into his abdomen and finally to his back and neck. When he could bare it no longer, he begged forgiveness from God for his weakness and lay down on his back. He spread his arms out to his sides, then crossed his legs at his ankles in imitation of Christ on the cross, and began to pray.

"Show me the way, Lord. Show me the way," the Novice began in Aramaic, the language of his Savior. He had studied the language, now seldom spoken, and had become, like in all that he did, a master of it. Speaking in Aramaic, he was certain that his prayers would be heard first. "My life was given so that I may serve you, Lord. Show me the way. You have led me to the Jesuit and to the Order. I am ready. Show me the way."

The twenty-three years since his birth had been spent preparing his mind, soul and body for any task that the Lord might ask of him. The hours in the gym worked every muscle to perfection. He was ripped. Not a gram of fat on his body. Gluttony was not a sin of the

Novice. His body was God's work, and he worked it to perfection.

His mind too, had become taut and lean. He thought only about the work that the Lord has asked of him, and built his life around his calling. He spoke English, Italian, Spanish, Hebrew, German, and Russian flawlessly, and often carried on conversations with himself speaking in one language and responding in another. He studied the history of the Church to such detail that there was not a single Cardinal or scholar who could debate him and win. He knew the Church's strengths and weaknesses. And he would defend them both.

Since his early childhood he knew that he was different, that he had been chosen. He did not need, nor did he seek out the company of others. He was alone with God. When his parents were killed in a church bombing in Louisiana, it was a tragedy to some, a relief to him. He had taken it as a sure sign that he had been selected by God to serve the Church. And he would serve like no other before him, save his savior, Christ.

God had selected Christ to be his son.

God had selected the Novice to be the guardian. It was God's plan and he would fulfill it. And he would stop at nothing to serve God.

"God, I am yours. Show me the way." His breath caught and he gasped as a burst of searing pain sliced and burned into his side. He grew dizzy from the intense pain and his mind clouded. Then, in an instant the pain ceased and his mind cleared, and he knew without question what his task was. His God had heard his prayers, and they had been answered.

He stood. "All the power and the glory," he said, looking up to the heavens. He found his clothes—tossed to a side of the room earlier, when the Jesuit had directed him to stand naked before God—dressed quickly, then made his way down the dark cramped hallway, wet with seeping water. He went up several small flights of stairs to a doorway, paused, listening to the inner voice that chanted repeatedly in his head, *The Key is alive. The Key must die.* His lips moved, as he silently joined the inner voice, repeating, *The Key is alive. The Key must die.* He pulled the door open, exited the circular building that posed as a tomb, and stepped out onto the paved walkway of the cemetery.

TWENTY FOUR

Celent's face changed like the four seasons, as he stared at Tonita: first the bewilderment of spring, then the softening smile of summer, into the sharp chill of fall, and finally, the icy stare of winter.

Tonita had fired the second shot, hitting Brother Salvatore in the ribs, tearing through his chest, and exiting out his back. She still held the pistol at the ready, just in case the monk made a move.

He did not.

"Why don't you put that away?" Celent said, waving a hand at the pistol.

"What if he's not dead?" Tonita raised up her chin, pointing it in the direction of, what she hoped was, the dead monk.

Celent pulled himself up from the floor, using the back of the sofa as support. Even then, it was a struggle, and though he looked to Tonita for help, she wasn't about to move, until she was sure that the monk on the floor was not coming back to life.

Celent was on his own. Once up, he continued leaning against the sofa, gasping for breath, sweat beading on his brow and above his lip. The struggle earlier with Brother Salvatore, followed by another near death experience with the same crazed monk, was nearly all Celent could take. After a moment, when he had sufficient breath to speak, Celent took the few steps toward Brother Salvatore, knelt down and felt his neck for a pulse.

"I'm quite sure he's dead."

"I'm not taking any chances. Shake him or kick or something," Tonita said, moving slightly to her left so that she would have a straighter shot, should the monk prove to still be alive.

Celent put his fingers to Brother Salvatore's neck once again. "Really, I'm sure that he is dead." He stood slowly and went through the motions of making the sign of the cross over the dead monk's body, but abandoned the gesture half way through, as his hand reached what would have been the bottom of the cross.

Tonita not only lowered the gun, she dropped it on to the floor. The adrenaline jolt that had pushed her into pulling the trigger had now dissipated. She immediately turned her attention to Dominic who didn't look any better now than when he had fallen to the floor. "Listen," she said looking at Celent. "I don't know what you have to do with all of this or why you're in Dominic's apartment, or why, for that matter, this monk guy is in here, and what you two were doing? I don't know and I don't care right now. I saved your life and now you better help Dominic or..." she trailed off. She had apparently forgotten that she had just dropped the pistol to the floor and had nothing in her hand to threaten Celent with. She lowered her eyes to the pistol.

"You won't need that, I can assure you," Celent said. "I'm an old man and I've just taken quite a beating myself from this fellow." He kicked the dead monk's foot.

Tonita eyed him for a moment, her mind was whirling with questions about the monk, Celent and why they were after Dominic. For the moment, though, she could only hope that she had saved the good guy, if there was a good guy, and that he would now help her save Dominic. "All right. You help Dom and we'll figure the rest of this out later."

"Deal," Celent said, and immediately went back to Dominic's side.

Tonita joined him.

After a quick look Celent stood. "We've got to get him to a hospital."

"No." Tonita's tone was adamant. "No hospital."

The Third Hour

Celent took a long look at Tonita. She was young, innocent, and caught in a web from which she was unable to escape. No, he reconsidered the thought. She would never be allowed to escape. Her destiny would forever be tied to Dominic's. He wondered if she would have made the choices she had, if she'd known the truth at the time? Was she in love? In answer to his own question, he guessed yes.

Dominic's safety was of the utmost importance to the Church and to Celent. Dominic had been watched every moment of the day and was unaware of the great lengths that Celent had taken to hide the presence of the observers. There were many who watched. Always unseen, but always present. They reported Dominic's every move, including his contacts with Tonita.

When Celent had first been made aware of Tonita's growing feelings for Dominic, his impulse was to get rid of her. It was complicated enough trying to keep Dominic under surveillance. He did not need or want the intrusion of another. But as he thought it through, he came to a better understanding that Tonita could be an asset to him in his surveillance of Dominic. She slowed Dominic down and it was much easier to spot and follow two, rather than one. Instead of doing away with Tonita, Celent actually did what he could to enhance their relationship. Of course, his hand in their developing relationship could never be revealed. But a bouquet of flowers sent without a note to Tonita or a letter to a friend extolling the relationship that she was beginning with Dominic, allegedly from Tonita, left accidentally at Dominic's apartment, didn't hurt the relationship. If Dominic were to fall in love, it wouldn't be such a bad situation, Celent considered. But if the relationship between Dominic and Tonita ever threatened his plans, Tonita could easily be dealt with. As long as she kept Dominic where he could keep a close eye on him, she was an asset. But should she ever become a liability...*Well, no need to worry about that now,* Celent thought. "You're right, Tonita, we cannot take the chance of moving him now. We'll stay here and see to him, unless his condition worsens and we need a doctor. Agreed?"

Tonita eyed him. "Agreed."

TWENTY FIVE

December 5, 1945
East Coast of Florida
1545 Hours / 3:45 P.M.
Flight 19—Avenger Torpedo Bomber Squadron of Five

"Powers. Respond." Lieutenant Charles Taylor's voice carried with it an uncharacteristic hint of stress. "Powers? Powers? What is your reading?" the seasoned pilot continued. After one minute and thirteen seconds of radio static, Lieutenant Taylor brought the handset up to his mouth about to try again.

The static was broken. "I don't know where we are. We must have gotten lost after that last turn." Captain E.J. Powers, piloting FT–36, sounded frightened. "Coordinates unknown."

Taylor pushed the button on the side of the handset in, "Repeat. Repeat last transmission."

Communication between the two pilots was once again lost to static.

***

The radio transmissions were picked up by Lieutenant Cox flying FT-74. He adjusted the dials of the radio, trying to tune in to the last transmissions from the lost pilots. "This is Flight Instructor Lieutenant Robert Cox receiving on 4805 kilocycles. Please repeat." Lieutenant Cox released the button on the side of the microphone handset and listened. He had been searching the airwaves for the last hour in hopes that the group of five Avenger Torpedo Bombers in route from a bombing practice run at Hens and Chicken Shoals north of Bimini in the Bahamas, would once again be in communication.

Static.

"I repeat on 4805 kilocycles," Lieutenant Cox spoke slowly and clearly. "This is FT–74, plane or boat calling Powers. Please identify yourself so someone can help you."

Static.

"Do you read me?"

Static.

Then, suddenly, the hard Latin beat of percussion and horns, and the clear sounds of Musica Cubana filled FT–74's cockpit, a common occurrence when flying near the island nation of Cuba. Lieutenant Cox adjusted the dial on the radio, fading out the Cuban music station and then back into 4805 kilocycles and a hopeful response from Powers.

Static.

"This is FT-74. What is your trouble?" Lieutenant Cox hesitated then repeated, "This is FT–74. What is your trouble?"

This time the static was broken.

"This is FT–28," Lieutenant Taylor, piloting the aircraft flying in formation to Captain Powers, responded. "Both of my compasses are out and I'm trying to find Fort Lauderdale. I'm over land but it's broken. I'm sure I'm in the Keys but I don't know how far down and I don't know how to get to Fort Lauderdale." Lieutenant Taylor was clearly rattled. He had flown the area in and around Fort Lauderdale and Miami for the past six months. He knew the territory well from both on the land and above it.

"FT–28? This is FT–74," Lieutenant Cox said, trying to disguise the concern in his voice. "Put the sun on you port wing, if you are in the Keys, and fly up the coast until you come to Miami." He paused for a response, when none came he continued, "Fort Lauderdale is 20 miles further, your first port after Miami. The air station is directly on your left from the port." Lieutenant Cox

The Third Hour

waited for a response from the pilot of FT–28. After several minutes of silence, he radioed again. "What is your present altitude? I will fly south and meet you," he said hoping that Powers, Taylor or the pilots of the four Avengers that were flying with them, would pick up and respond to the broadcast.

"I know where I am now," Lieutenant Taylor radioed back. "I'm at 2300 feet. Don't come after me." The Lieutenant was beginning to sound more at ease.

"You're at 2300? I'm coming to meet you anyhow," Lieutenant Cox said, ignoring the request of Lieutenant Taylor and turned the Avenger Torpedo Bomber he was piloting south, fixing a course to meet up with the lost Avenger FT–28 and the squadron somewhere in the Florida Keys.

All seemed well. The lost squadron of Torpedo Bombers was heading north over the Florida Keys and Lieutenant Cox was heading south to meet them. The distance wasn't great and the aircraft should be in visual contact within a few minutes.

The radio remained silent.

Minutes later. "This is FT–28 calling FT–74," Lieutenant Taylor said, with the recent ease being replaced with intense fear. He didn't try to hide it from the squadron to the side of him or to Lieutenant Cox. "We have just passed over a small island." His voiced trembled. "We have no other land in sight."

Lieutenant Cox hesitated before responding, contemplating where the lost squadron--four of which had a crew of three and one with a crew of two—were. "No other land in sight," he repeated the words of Lieutenant Taylor aloud. If the Avenger had no other land in sight, they were far beyond the Keys, he thought. He was beginning to have serious doubts about the lost squadron.

"FT–74, this is FT–28. Can you have Miami...someone turn on their radar gear and pick us up? We don't seem to be getting far." Lieutenant Taylor fought to maintain control of his growing panic—he was losing. "We were out on a navigation hop and on the second leg I thought they were going wrong, so I took over and was flying them back to the right position. But I'm sure now, that neither of my compasses are working."

"You can't expect to get here in ten minutes. You have a 30 to 35 knot head or crosswind," Lieutenant Cox radioed in an attempt to calm the pilot and the crews listening in. "Turn on your emergency IFF gear. Or, do you have it on?"

"FT–74. We did not have the Identification Friend or Foe gear on," Captain E.J. Powers, piloting FT–36 to the side of Taylor's aircraft broke in. "I'm at angles three point five. Have on emergency IFF. Does anyone in the area have a radar screen that could pick us up?"

"This is Air Sea Rescue Task Unit Four at Fort Everglades." The land based rescue operations unit had picked up the transmission and radioed to the lost Avengers. "FT–28 we will notify NAS Miami." A moment later, Air Sea Rescue Task Unit Four continued, "FT–28, is there another plane in the flight with a good compass. Can they take over?"

"ASRTU-4, this is FT–28. No one can take over. We are all lost. Headings unknown." The transmission started to break up. "Position unknown. No help."

"FT–28, this is FT–74." Lieutenant Cox raised his voice to a shout, "Your transmissions are fading. Something is wrong. Something's wrong. What is you altitude?"

Through static, FT–28 responded, the signal growing faint and nearly lost, "I'm at 4500 feet. Visibility 10 miles..."

And then, silence.

***

The Third Hour

Three hours and forty-seven minutes later, "Training 49, Lieutenant Jeffrey, this is Navel Air Station Banana River, come in."

"NAS Banana River, this is Martin Mariner, Lt. Jeffrey, on Training 49, roger."

"Training 49 proceed to New Smyrna and track eastward," the radio attendant at NAS Banana River gave the coordinates in a clipped tone.

"NAS Banana River, this is Lt. Jeffrey on Training 49. Will head south, then track eastward and attempt to intercept Flight 19." Lieutenant Jeffrey was matter-of-fact. This was not the first air- sea search for him and his crew of thirteen aboard the Martin Mariner. The plane could fly all night, 12 hours or more on a full tank. It was powerful enough to take off and land on water, as well as on a runway. The Martin Mariner was a massive flying machine at well over 14,000 pounds. And this Mariner, Training 49, was the temporary home to the five pilots and eight crewmen aboard.

Like Lieutenant Jeffrey, the rest of the crew had anticipated an easy few days, until they would all be heading home for Christmas. Most in the Combat Air Training Program at Banana River hadn't been home since beginning the program in September of 1944. Now, as the end of 1945 grew near, the crew grew restless.

The seas below the Mariner—Training 49, had become very rough as the front moved in. The ceiling was overcast, visibility dropping from 1200 to 800 feet, winds picking up at 25 to 30 knots, west southwest. The crew strapped themselves into their seats, snapping the seat belt's fasteners into buckles and pulling them tight. The air around Training 49 became increasingly more turbulent.

NAS Fort Lauderdale, just over 150 miles to the south, the Navel Air Station that was home to the five Avenger Torpedo Bombers that made up the now lost Flight 19, was reporting weather calm and clear.

It was evident to Lieutenant Jeffrey that the weather front had not made it up to Fort Lauderdale. He checked his watch. With the front approaching, he didn't have much time to find the lost squadron. He and the crew had been airborne for approximately three minutes. He was just about to make a turn south and attempt an intercept with the missing five Avenger Torpedo Bombers. "NAS Banana River, this is Training 49 reporting."

"Training 49, this is NAS Banana River, come in."

No answer.

"Training 49, this is NAS Banana River, come in." The voice of the seaman at the Navel Air Station was steady. "Training 49, this is NAS Banana River, come in." His third attempt and still nothing.

Lieutenant Jeffrey in the Martin Mariner—Training 49, and his crew of thirteen, did not respond.

And there was no response from any of the five pilots or the crews of the five Avenger Torpedo Bombers.

There was only silence.

Six planes.

Twenty seven men.

Vanished.

No radio contact would ever come.

Not a trace of any plane would ever be found.

Not one body would ever be discovered.

They were there...and then...they were not.

TWENTY SIX

Rome
Dominic's Apartment
Several Hours Later

Dominic's color slowly returned. He was no longer a pale blue-white. Instead, a reddish peach color had filled his cheeks, giving him back the color of the living. His breathing had also steadied.

Tonita watched in an almost hypnotic movement. Dominic's chest rose, held its position, then fell. Rose then fell. Rose then fell. A rhythm that was threatening to send Tonita into a losing battle with sleep. She fought to keep her eyes from closing, and to keep her mind from drifting, concentrating on the monk, and Dominic, and Celent. The visions came back to her in a blurred collage:

The monk—dead on the floor.

Celent—who slept just feet away.

And Dominic.

Both she and the Celent had struggled to move Dominic to the sofa, where he was now resting. She watched again as his chest rose and fell.

A breath in.

A breath out.

She could leave right now, walk out the door of Dominic's flat, while the Celent slept, while Dominic recovered, and while the monk was still dead. Despite the fact that the monk had not moved in hours, she had her doubts about him. She cast a sideways glance at the body of the monk—just in case.

She diverted her gaze to the hallway and the door to the street at the end. She could easily get up and walk out the door and end all of this. Her feelings for Dominic had grown easily since their first encounter. He was troubled and just maybe—she had given this considerable thought—that's why she fell for him. She needed someone who needed. The sound of Barbara Streisand's voice singing about people who needed people, snuck into her thoughts. A cough startled her from the dream state and her eyes snapped open.

"Hi." Dominic's voice was raspy.

Tonita took a deep breath and let it out in long sigh. "I must have fallen asleep." She rubbed her hands on her face.

"You did," he said, struggling to sit up. "Ouch."

"Ouch?" Tonita rested a hand on his chest. "I'd be swearing my head off."

"I am, all in my head, where only God and I can hear it," Dominic said, and turned his head, looking around the room. He caught sight of Celent in the chair. "Is he..." he struggled with the words, "alive?"

Tonita laughed. "Yes."

"Well, you can't be too sure around here." Dominic's laugh turned into a bout of coughing. He brought his hands up to his chest, holding the muscles in place. "Boy, that hurts."

Tonita pushed herself up from the chair using the sides to steady herself. The day had taken a toll on her. "Here take these," Tonita said, handing him a glass of water and a handful of pills that she had set aside earlier. "They should help the pain. But what you really need is antibiotics. I looked around for some, but didn't find any. I don't suppose you have any lying around?"

"Sorry," Dominic replied between swallows of the water and the pills.

"I can get all the antibiotics and pain medication you need," Celent spoke from his assumed slumber on the brown leather chair.

"You're awake?" Dominic sat up.

"Don't assume that just because an old man closes his eyes, he isn't still paying attention. You will learn my son, that you learn most, when those around you forget that you are there."

"Okay, that's a little heavy for me." Tonita did not try to hide the sarcasm.

"Perhaps, but true none the less," Celent said, as he opened his eyes. He stood up using the wide leather covered arms of the chair as support. "If you are up to it, I say we leave now."

"And go where?" Tonita snapped.

"To a safer place."

"Where is that?"

"The Vatican. More precisely, my flat there," Celent said.

"You have an apartment at the Vatican?" Dominic eyed the man. "Why?"

"And why should we trust you? We don't know you. You just showed up here. We've never met you and..."

Dominic cut Tonita off. "I think what Tonita means is that we're a little scared."

"Hell, that's not what I was saying at all!" Tonita gestured with her hands wide apart. "I was saying that I don't trust your sorry ass. And I'll be damned if I'm going to go anywhere with you."

"You are quite right young lady." Celent looked directly into Tonita's eyes. "If you don't come along with me, and if I don't get you somewhere safe, you will be damned!"

***

His senses reeled. Bolts of electricity coursed through his veins, feeding his muscles until they were pumped, ready to snap.

The Novice continued on his course, distracted from his cause by no one. He did not know which direction to take, which block to turn on, or which street to follow. He had no map to guide him. There wasn't a need for one. God would lead him to the Key.

Richard Devin

People in his path stepped away. Cars and trucks, and those annoying idiots riding bicycles, parted as he approached. His mission was of Divine intent. And God, as he had done for the masses fleeing Egypt thousands of years ago by parting the waters of the Red Sea, had cleared a path for him.

The intense pain he felt earlier in his shoulder and his rib cage had subsided. His intuition led him to the knowledge that Brother Salvatore was dead and that the Key lived. But that would soon change.

TWENTY SEVEN

July 3rd, 1947
Corona, New Mexico
4:13 A. M.

The lightning struck the ground with such ferocity that the small boulders and rocks in its path shattered into pieces, spraying out like fireworks.

Mac Brazel had been sound asleep, until the thunderclap from the nearby strike of lightning jolted him awake. The old timbers of the small ranch house shook, causing mortar, long ago dried out, to fall into the cavity between the ceiling and the roof, scaring the rodents who took refuge there. He jumped out of the bed, quickly making his way to the open window. The frightened bleats from the several hundred sheep on the ranch, now huddled together in a tight undulating circle, assaulted Mac through the open window.

Water had splashed in, wetting the floor and window casings of the old ranch house. It wasn't the first time that windows in the house had remained opened during a rainstorm. Storms were so rare and lasted so short a time, that most in the area of the many ranches and few houses, didn't concern themselves with a bit of rain splashing in. As Mac reached up to pull down on the sash in an attempt to close the warped window, another strike of lightning hit with equal ferocity. He watched as sparks first flared up and then cascaded down to the point of impact.

Lightning again lit up the sky. This time it failed to reach the earth. Instead, the bolts crisscrossed through the clouds. Flashes of white backlit the dark gray masses of clouds, casting shadows of gray upon darker gray.

Richard Devin

Mac tightened the muscles of his weatherworn, ranch honed shoulders and began to pull down on the old sash, as a breeze swept into the dank room. He hesitated closing the window completely, breathing in the ozone-laden air, and feeling the rain-cooled breeze on his bare skin. It was a rare but appreciated sensation.

All was momentarily quiet, and it appeared as though the storm was about to blow over. Then, the ranch house shook again. Rocking. Shuddering. An explosion of light and sound hit the ground south of the ranch house. Rock and dirt burst into the sky, fanned out, and settled into a long path. Mac stood, half groggy still from sleep, half frightened to death, mesmerized by the lightning spectacle. For a moment, he considered that he might be dreaming and willed himself awake. A gust of wind pushed the spray of rain into Mac's face and he knew for certain that he was not dreaming.

The herd of sheep that would most often be far out in the acres upon acres of desert land, now poured into the nearby corral. Their wails grew in volume. Frightened to the point of panic by the last explosion of lightning, they jostled for position pushing into the small corral near the ranch house.

In the distance, the ground appeared to be glowing. And Mac surmised that the brush had caught on fire from the lightning strike, as it often did, after having baked in the desert sun for several weeks or months before a storm moved in. He continued to watch the glowing earth, internally debating whether to mount up now and ride out to the fire, or wait until morning. The rain continued to fall in ever increasing cloud bursts making his decision for him. He could safely wait until the storm passed, and for morning light. The fire wouldn't make it far if the rain continued and the southern pasture could use a good burn anyway, Mac convinced himself, as he pulled the window most of the way closed. He fell back into the bed and restlessly waited for sleep or morning's light, whichever came first.

TWENTY EIGHT

The drive to the Vatican from Dominic's apartment was uneventful. One quick call from Celent and a sleek black Mercedes Benz arrived at Dominic's apartment in little time. Tonita could not help but stare out the window as the driver maneuvered the Mercedes through the now clogged streets of Rome. She watched every passerby and every car that came alongside the vehicle analyzing the situation. She was prepared to scream out at any moment, should anything or anyone appear suspicious to her. But no danger, or presumed danger, presented itself. And she, Celent, Dominic, and the driver all arrived, passing through the gate to the Vatican without incident.

The driver stopped the car at the doorway to Celent's apartment, and after climbing the stairs to the second story flat, Dominic fell into the first chair he saw, nearly collapsing. Celent immediately picked up the telephone. It was a gilded and ivory handset with a dark mahogany base, which looked as though it belonged in the mansions of the Vanderbilt's or the Getty's or the royal palace of some old Italian aristocrat. Celent spoke in a direct tone into the telephone, as Tonita wandered about the apartment, she could clearly over hear the call. Just as he had promised, Celent had called the Vatican infirmary for supplies.

In short time, Tonita had Dominic patched up and resting comfortably. She, however, could not sit still, and kept bouncing from the chair to the settee to the sofa, in an endless migration around the room. She could barely restrain herself any longer. When Celent returned from the small kitchen of the apartment, rolling a serving table topped with tea and biscuits, she pounced. "All right, want a full explanation."

"I thought that perhaps you might be hungry after the events of the day and appreciate some tea." Tonita's long hard stare convinced Celent to abandon the ploy immediately. "I'm sorry, you're right, Tonita, you do deserve an explanation," Celent said, as he pushed the rolling cart to the side of the sofa and sat down. "Some tea?" He picked up the pot and poured a cup. The comforting smell of Earl Grey wafted up, as the steam rose from the cup and pot.

"No thank you," Tonita snapped.

"Dominic? It's my favorite." Celent held up a cup by the saucer.

"Yeah, sure, and Tonita will have a cup." Dominic shot a quick glance her way.

Tonita caught the look in Dominic's expression and reconsidered. "Yes, on second thought I will."

"Excellent." Celent filled two more cups, keeping one for himself and handing the others to Tonita and Dominic. "Sugar or milk?"

"Straight is fine for me," Dominic said, as he breathed in the aroma.

Tonita just shook her head, placing the cup of tea onto a side table.

"Charles Grey, the British Prime Minister and the 2nd Earl Grey, his father being the first, was given the recipe for this tea by a Chinese mandarin with whom he was friends, and whose life he had saved." Celent sipped the dark hot liquid. "Much as I am doing for you." He sipped again.

Dominic glanced to Tonita. "By bringing us here?"

"That is part of it. I can assure you that if you did not accompany me and you remained at your flat." He took another sip from the cup. "You would be dead by now."

"Enough of this." Tonita waved a hand in the air. "Dominic's injuries may be painful, but they were not life threatening. I could have fixed him up right there at his place. I just needed the supplies. We didn't need to move him."

"You could have applied the proper gauze and bandages to him, Tonita. In that, you're right. But you could not have saved his life." Celent paused, waiting for a response. When none came, he continued, "Even as we sit here enjoying the peaceful surroundings of the Vatican and the protection it affords us, you are being stalked."

Dominic set his cup of tea down onto the small, elegantly crafted, coffee table positioned in front of the chair, splashing some of the liquid onto the table, as his pectoral muscles pinched from the heavy tape covering the wound. "I'm being stalked?"

"Hasn't that been evident?" Celent cocked his head.

"There definitely have been some strange goings. But stalked?"

"You deny the obvious, Dominic? Just like you deny your religion?"

Dominic rose, a little too quickly, and clutched at the gauze-wrapped wound on his chest. "That is not true. And that was out of line."

"Dominic, ease up. You don't want to start bleeding again," Tonita said moving toward him.

"A couple of strange occurrences, and I'm being stalked," Dominic said as he moved away, stepping to the window.

"Nervous?" Celent spoke softly.

"No."

"Then why the sudden interest in the window?"

Dominic turned and stared into Celent's dark eyes. "You misread me. I'm angry. Not concerned."

"Well, son, I would advise you to remain concerned, and to come to terms with your anger."

"My anger is in control and meant for you."

Celent picked up the teapot and filled his cup. "Only because I state the truth."

Dominic bit his lip and ran his hand through his hair, pushing it off of his face. "Come on, Tonita. We're out of here." He moved toward the door. Tonita was at the door, just as Dominic reached it.

"Thanks for your help. We'll manage on our own." Dominic pulled down on the golden lever of the door handle. The door swung open.

"Leave if you must. It is your free will. But Dominic, I will not be able to save you a third time."

Dominic turned to the Celent.

"The monk that attacked you in your apartment acted once before. He was stopped. But the priest who saved you then, gave up his own life for yours."

Dominic paused reflecting back. "The man...the priest," he corrected "in my apartment?"

"He saved you." Celent struggled a bit as he stood, he took a step toward Dominic, "Imploratio Adiumentum. Ue Bonfjote. Tazor Li."

"You know what he said?"

"Of course." Cardinal Celent smiled. "I gave him those words. I sent him to watch over you and to warn you."

Dominic stood at the door for several minutes. Silent. Then he closed the door and stepped the few feet to where Celent sat. "You're not a priest?"

"Of course I am. I have been for quite a long time."

"A priest would not have an apartment, on the Vatican grounds," he glanced around the comfortable living quarters. "Not one like this. He would not have a driver and a car at and he would not be wearing that ring." He grasped Celent's hand and brought it up. His anger faded, replaced by resurgence of faith and the comfort it afforded. Dominic looked up from the ring and stared into Celent's eyes. For the moment he gave himself back to the church and holding Celent's hand he dropped to his knee. He kept his head down and brought the hand to his face, allowing his lips to lightly brush the rectangular gold ring, which was set with a large sapphire and worn on the fourth finger of the right hand.

A Cardinal's ring.

Cardinal Celent placed his other hand gently onto Dominic's head. "Stay. I have much to explain."

TWENTY NINE

There was not the slightest hint of hesitation in the Novice's actions as he pushed the door to Dominic's apartment open, slamming it against the old interior stucco wall. The doorknob smashed a hole into the wall, splattering the crumbling mortar, sending chunks and pieces of it into the air and onto the floor. He did not care if anyone heard him. He was not concerned with stealth. His task was at hand. And he would fulfill it.

His momentum never stopping, he stepped inside and boldly began his march down the short hallway, heading toward the interior of the apartment. He reached the living room, coming out of the hallway prepared to do battle, then stopped.

He listened, cocking his head as a coyote might to pick up the slightest sounds of hidden prey in the grass. There was nothing more than the filtered noises seeping in from the street, and the ever present hum of the electrical motor from the old refrigerator.

He sniffed the air. It had the heavy odor of the beginnings of sweet decay and blood.

The smell of death.

His body shook. Every muscle had been primed to fight. To kill. To do the Lords work. That energy now erupted from him. He tilted his head back, and from deep within a primordial scream welled up and spewed forth.

In one quick movement, The Novice picked up Brother Salvatore's limp, now bloating body and slammed it against the wall, shaking the interior of the apartment.

Brother Salvatore's head hit hard, denting the wall. The body fell back to the floor, knocking over a small table, sending a lamp to the floor, where it shattered.

The Novice watched as the body came to a rest against the wall. His rage momentarily quenched. All became quiet.

Suddenly, the crucifix that Dominic had secured to the wall several months before, gave way and fell, sliding straight down the wall, as though it were connected to a track that controlled its decent. The crucifix came to rest on Brother Salvatore's back. The figure of Christ nailed to the cross, facing up.

Brother Salvatore's body had landed on his stomach. His head however, had twisted, facing backwards, eyes looking over the shoulders of the limp, broken body staring blankly towards the heavens.

And then he saw.

Brother Salvatore's arms, bent slightly, were stretched out to either side of his body. His legs were crossed at the ankles. The body lay in perfect imitation to the crucifix that had just fallen onto his back.

THIRTY

July 3rd, 1947
Corona, New Mexico
8:27 A.M.

Mac Brazel wasn't a cowboy out of central casting, even if he looked like he was stepping up to the cameras in a western themed film, as he mounted the blood bay gelding. He was the real thing. Ranching had been his way of life for forty years. He loved the range, the solitude it afforded him, and the people who worked the land with him when he wanted company.

The storm earlier that night had kept him from sleep. After a quick cup of strong coffee—he had never mastered the art of coffee making, so strong was the only way he could brew it—he dressed, saddled his mount, and planned to follow the fences south, heading in the same direction that he had seen the immense flashes of lighting earlier that morning.

The herd of sheep that he tended on the ranch had settled down from the previous night's scare and were now spanning out among the unusually wet range. Puddles and ponds, that would disappear by midday, filled every low lying area attracting flocks of desert grouse and skittish antelope herds that hurried to the puddles taking advantage of the rare abundance of water.

Mac stood up in the stirrups and scanned the horizon, shielding his eyes with one hand. The sky was clear, not a trace of smoke, despite the flames and cascades of sparks from the lightning strikes the night before. Mac considered the lack of smoke, and then figured that the downpour of rain had done a sure job in dousing any lick of flame. It was good news for him. A fire would spread fast on the desert range and he wasn't looking forward to a day of driving sheep that were already frazzled from the night before, out of the line of fire. Sheep weren't very bright, and despite the scorching heat from desert brush alight with flames, they tended to flock in panic, too frightened to move out of the fire's path. The last thing that Mac wanted after a night of lost sleep was long day of rounding up and rescuing sheep.

Mac started off, urging the gelding into a steady walk. He had traveled about twenty yards down the southern fence when a faint voice behind him caught his attention. He pulled up on the reins and turned in his saddle as the horse came to a stop.

"Wait Mac. Wait up." The blurred image of a small horse and even smaller rider accompanied the voice. "Mac? Mac?" The small boy approached, holding tightly to a horse that moved at a considerable gallop. "I saw it too," Dee Proctor said, as he reined the little horse in alongside of Mac. "It was amazing wasn't it Mac? Amazing!" Dee could hardly contain his excitement.

"It certainly was." Mac squeezed his calf muscles, signaling his horse to move forward.

"What do you think it was, Mac?" Dee urged his horse to keep stride with Mac's mount. Dee Proctor rode like no other seven year old. He spent every free minute either on, under, or around horses. There was nothing Dee wanted more than to be with a horse and to ride. When Mac brought his own two children to stay at the ranch, from their home in Tularosa, where they stayed most of the time with their mother, Dee would ride with them for hours, covering every inch of the range. With Mac, the rides were more like work, finding and rounding up stray sheep, mending broken fences, clearing debris, and today, searching for lightning strikes. It didn't matter to Dee, riding was riding.

Dee's folks, Floyd and Loretta Proctor, had purchased the neighboring ranch several years earlier, and like most in the country had become quick friends to Mac, his children, and his wife. For the majority of the year Mac's wife and children remained in Tularosa, New Mexico. The schools were better there and the ranch life didn't suit his wife. So most of the time, Mac was on his own, except of course when Dee Proctor was around.

"I think it was lightning, Dee," Mac responded to Dee's question.

"But I bet you never saw lightning like that. Did ya' Mac?"

"You're right there, Dee."

"My ma and pop came and took me to their bed last night. I think they were scared. But not me. As soon as I could, I got out of bed and watched the lightning till morning."

Mac smiled at the young man's enthusiasm. In truth, it mirrored a bit of his own. "It was a sight all right."

"Where do you think it hit, Mac?" Dee didn't let him answer. "I think it struck up there." He pointed to a slight rise in the land.

"Could be," Mac responded. "Could be almost any place 'round here."

"We'll know soon enough, Mac," Dee said, then added, "What're the sheep doing up there, Mac? Look." He pushed his stubby legs up in the stirrups to get a better line of sight.

"I don't know," Mac said, as he and Dee set off at a gallop.

As they reached the rise, they pulled their mounts up to a walk, and curiously gazed at the herd of sheep standing uncharacteristically still. Their heads bobbed in an odd unison, all the while keeping the herds' collective eyes staring across a stretch of torn up land that could only be described as a debris field. The other half of the heard, stood opposite, divided by the scattered debris. And despite their thirst, neither side would cross to gain access to the water guzzler that remained undamaged but littered with debris.

Small shiny bits of metal foil, like autumn leaves, drifted in the hot breeze. They clumped, blown together under brush and rocks, decorating the landscape in glinting confetti.

As Mac and Dee moved in, they noticed a track that looked as though some huge flat rock had skipped off the land, as one would do on the still waters of a pond. At first Mac could make out one area of impact. It had flattened an area of the range. The brittle grasses and scrub brush around the impact area had been singed. Shiny metal pieces of foil littered the area in abundance.

Mac reined his horse to a stop and dismounted with a quick swing of his left leg over the saddle. Dee started to follow. "No Dee, you stay put." Mac handed him the reins to his horse. "You keep a tight hold there."

Dee took the reins and wrapped them around the horn of his saddle and watched as Mac moved cautiously toward the impact site.

The sheep on both sides of the debris field followed Mac, slowly matching his stride keeping pace and distance, as if in some hypnotic trance.

Mac stopped.

The sheep stopped, both herds, divided by some invisible field, but tied together in step.

Mac started forward.

The herds moved with him.

The water guzzler in the middle of the debris field had been spared any direct hit by the lightning, or whatever it was that struck there. Although the water guzzler had not been hit directly, dirt and the foil like metal pieces were scattered around it. Mac walked up to the guzzler, the sheep following in parallel rows.

The guzzler was not damaged and it continued to pump up the water from deep underground. Mac leaned in, bringing his face closer to the water. He smelled it, and with no suspicious odor present, he cupped a hand, dipped it into the cool water, and raised it to his lips. Just before taking a sip of the water, he breathed in the scent once again. Convinced that the water had no strange odor, other than the slightly sulfur smell common with well water. He tasted it. Nothing. It was, as far as he could tell, fine, untainted water. He let the water fall from his hand back into the basin of the guzzler. It splashed down onto several bits of the foil like metal that had landed, or had been blown into the water. Mac noticed that some of the pieces floated, while others, that looked to be the same or closely the same size, sank. He pulled out one piece that was floating on top of the water and fished out another from the bottom of the tank. He rubbed the pieces of foil with his fingers and thumb. The foil didn't tear or scuff. He held first one, then the other piece of debris up to the sun. Like a watermark on a fine piece of linen paper, Mac could clearly make out the design inside each piece of foil. He assumed the design was a series of numbers—not because they looked like numbers, to him they actually looked more like flowers—but because of the way they were arranged, in columns like a mathematician would arrange a complex formula. Mac dropped the foil pieces back into the water, where once again, one floated and the other immediately sank.

"What is it, Mac? Who left it here?

"I don't know." Mac took the reins from Dee and mounted his horse. "Come on Dee," Mac said, and moved on following the path of the debris.

Further ahead, just about twenty five yards from the first impact site, they came upon a second, and shortly after that, a third.

"I don't think it was lightning," Dee said.

"Pretty smart for a young'un, aren't you?" Mac said, then considered what the boy was saying. "Lightning would have caused the dirt and rock to fuse together causing a small crater. But whatever hit here flattened the land."

"Or bulldozed it." Dee pointed to the sides of the impact zone. "Did lightning do that?" Dee asked, giving voice to the same question that Mac had.

"Not sure."

"Did lightning leave all this shiny stuff on the ground?"

"Not sure about that either."

"Well, Mac, maybe they know?" Dee looked up to a distant hill.

Mac pulled his horse up to a sliding stop. He stood in his stirrups and followed Dee's line of sight to the top of the hill. There a figure, distorted by the rising heat waves, stood looking back at Dee and Mac.

Mac glanced around taking in the scope of the surrounding terrain. He allowed his eyes to linger over the rocks and scrub brush that covered the land, checking each for any other figures that may have moved into the area. He returned his gaze to the hilltop and the figure that was there, still looking at him. Mac glanced back to the water guzzler. "What the hell?"

"Mac, you swore," Dee chastised the man, then looked around to where Mac was looking. "Where'd they go, Mac?"

Mac snapped his head back and forth, from the figure on the mound of rocks back to the water guzzler, squinting his eyes as he scanned the land.

The sheep that had crowded each side of the impact zone, mimicking his every step, were nowhere to be seen. They had silently moved off. Disappearing as though a magician in a sideshow had snapped his fingers and commanded them to vanish.

Mac looked back to the mound and the figure still there. Only now it was moving toward them.

THIRTY ONE

Cardinal Celent pushed the now cool cup of Earl Grey tea to the side and leaned back into the cushions of the chair. He looked skyward, locking his gaze for a long while before closing his eyes.

Dominic glanced at Tonita and offered a silent gesture of confusion.

"I am not well. As you can see time is catching up with me," Cardinal Celent said, without opening his eyes. "I have seen much in my time, but my day's end is near." He opened his eyes and sat up, leaning forward, hands gripping the armrests of the chair, "That is why you must be told," he said, looking at Dominic.

Dominic turned in his seat. "Cardinal, you'll outlive us all." he said, fidgeting with a corner of a pillow.

Cardinal Celent laughed. "That may be true," he said wondering if Dominic could understand how true that statement was. "But I'm afraid only God knows that. The majority of my days are behind me. And there is little I can do about that." Cardinal Celent smiled. "Are you nervous?"

Dominic looked away and then back to the Cardinal. "No."

"Tense, perhaps?"

"No." There was a hint of irritation to Dominic's voice.

"My faith, like your own faith, has not always been unwavering. I doubted. I even spoke out against the Church and its teachings." Cardinal Celent allowed his eyes to drift off to a darkened arch in the room.

Dominic looked directly at the man sitting across from him. He opened his mouth to speak, then stopped.

"For many years, in my youth, I was without doubt about God."

"I'm confused. You just said that you were without doubt about God, but you spoke out against the church that you are a part of. Did you not believe in God?" Tonita asked.

"Oh, my dear, I believed. That is, I firmly believed that he never existed."

"You were an atheist?" Dominic squinted his eyes as he asked the question.

"I was a scientist," Cardinal Celent responded. "I was a man whose thoughts were based on fact, not belief. I found those who preoccupied themselves with tales of fancy and religion to be beneath me. Nothing more than mere fools who needed some reason, some explanation to their lives and to living."

Tonita interrupted, "Wait a second. I'm getting the atheist part, but turning from a scientist into a Cardinal? I'm a little stuck there."

Cardinal Celent smiled. "You do speak your mind."

"As, apparently, from what you're telling us, you did too."

"Touché."

"I know it is not the background one would normally think of for a priest."

"It does not seem to fit." Dominic said.

"You were a scientist of what?" Tonita's voice carried with it a hint of disbelief.

"Tonita, there's a flaw in your question." Cardinal Celent allowed a grin to spread on his face. "Your question assumes a past tense. I not only was a scientist—I prefer to say a student really—but I still am." Cardinal Celent laughed. "We do not always know why we do the things we do, or what there may be planned for us. And that is true for atheists, and scientists, and the devout."

"Planned for us?" Dominic raised an eyebrow and ran his hand through his hair. "That doesn't sound like the words of a scientist."

"And, of course, you are right. They are not words of a scientist. They are the words of a man." Cardinal Celent raised an eyebrow, mimicking Dominic's expressions.

Dominic turned away from the Cardinal, stood, and moved again to the window.

"So," Tonita spoke up. "A scientist of?" She let her voice trail off.

"Ah, yes. Your question," Cardinal Celent said, looking down and pulling on his shirt, brushing away an imagined piece of lint. "Rocket science. Propulsion."

Tonita stood up, a frown crossing her face.

"I guess one could say travel." Cardinal Celent continued

"Rocket science and travel? What, do you do, book airfare and cruises to ports unknown?"

"Tonita," Dominic admonished.

"It's quite all right." Cardinal Celent pushed himself up and out of the chair, a smile spreading across his face. "Yes. As a matter of fact, I did book travel to ports unknown. Although, my background is in rocket sciences and propulsion. My main field of study was travel." Cardinal Celent paused briefly. "Time Travel to be more precise."

Tonita and Dominic turned nearly simultaneously to one another.

"And since I'm being straight with you, Tonita, as I promised to do, I must tell you that I not only studied Time Travel," he paused again letting the anticipation build. "I was the first person to do so."

"Do what?" Tonita asked.

"To travel through time." Cardinal Celent waited, half expecting Tonita and Dominic to bolt for the door. When they did not, he continued, "Actually there were three of us. We all traveled back in time. Unfortunately for the others, only I have survived."

***

The Novice stormed from Dominic's apartment, knocking down a woman on the street as he exited the building. She screamed at him, but he paid no attention to her and the others who were looking at him. He had no time for her or for anyone. He had a task that needed to be executed and he was not going to disappoint the Jesuit or God.

Dominic could not hide from him for long, he thought, as his rage intensified. The Key's feeble attempts to circumvent the Lord would not go unpunished, and his escape from death was only for the moment. No matter how far the Key ran or who helped to hide him and his fornicating girlfriend, they could not change destiny or time.

The Novice smiled.

But he could.

THIRTY TWO

July 3rd, 1947
Corona, New Mexico
11:13 A. M.
90 minutes from Roswell

"Dee, let's head back," Mac Brazel said to the boy, as he turned his horse away from the figure on the hilltop, and back in the direction of the ranch house and main barn.

"Shouldn't we go and talk to 'em," Dee said, pointing to the distant figure.

"No," Mac said sharply. "We should just head home."

"But maybe he knows something?"

If there ever was a time for the term, 'shaking in your boots', Mac thought, this would be it. He tried to remain calm, and he gallantly fought the urge to charge away at a full gallop, and just get the hell out of there.

Dee Proctor was the calming factor that Mac had working for him. The seven year old boy did not fear the unknown. Instead, he questioned it. Mac wished he could do the same and briefly contemplated going toward the figure. But his instincts took hold and pushed him to turn and run, "I'll call the sheriff in Roswell when we get back, Dee. He'll know what's going on."

Before Dee could stall him with more questions, Mac dug his heels into the flanks of the horse and leaned forward, urging his mount into a lope, with Dee's little mare just behind, and a trail of dust behind him them.

Twenty-five yards down the fence, Mac peered over his shoulder to the hilltop where the figure stood. He half expected it to be gone...it was not. "Come on, Dee," Mac said. "We have to hurry up." He urged his horse into a full gallop and without looking back again, charged toward the ranch house.

THIRTY THREE

"What do you mean you went back in time?" Tonita was up and pacing. "Like, you went from one time zone to another? That kind of back in time?"

Cardinal Celent stood. "No, not like that at all." He walked to a stack of books and began to rummage through them, pulling books from the top of the stack, then stacking the removed books on top of the table. "We were not the first to try, you understand. Others had attempted many times, but not to any success. There were explosions in Siberia. Villages and forests destroyed. People killed. Planes and ships lost to sea or..." His voice trailed off, "well we don't know where." He found the book he was looking for, then neatly restacked the books he had just removed. He made his way back to the chair, sat down, placed the book he had just removed from the stack on his lap, and continued, "But we learned much from those early mistakes. And of course, we tried not to duplicate them. But this is a difficult science, you understand, and despite our best efforts, we occasionally failed." He paused, looking off into the distance, then continued. "We failed far too many times." There was a sudden sadness that overtook the Cardinal's face.

"We?" Dominic's voice was nearly a whisper. "Did you mean, the church?"

"Oh no. No. Not the church." Cardinal Celent looked slightly bewildered by the question. "The church had nothing to do with the experiments, at least not in the early days of the project. I was a scientist. We were all scientists. Most of my colleagues, myself, included, were not believers in the tales told by the church. Religious dogma had no effect on our experiments, especially those of the Roman Catholic Church, which I considered to be nothing more than an ancient ruling body. A government, that was, and perhaps still is, fighting to keep its power." He fiddled with the gold crucifix that hung from a chain around his neck. "No. The church had nothing to do with the projects. Only the governments."

Dominic waited a moment for the Cardinal to continue. When he did not, he asked, "The U.S?"

"Oh yes. The United States, and at the same time, the Soviets, were actively involved. The United States and the Soviet Union were the only two powers that had enough money and influence to carry out the experiments." He paused, lost for a moment in thought, then continued, "The Germans attempted, at one time, to build a device, but had to abandon the project once Hitler involved the country in war. Actually, if had not been for the Nazis, our own project may not have been possible and the Russians may have been the first. You see, the Nazis, put together an amazing team of scientists. Of course, the scientists didn't have much choice in the matter. They were told what to do and where to go if they wanted to live. Same with the Russians really. The U.S. didn't exactly use the threat of death, but we did...how should I say this? Pressure some scientists into working on the project. Especially the Germans."

"The U.S. was working with Hitler's scientists?" Dominic's voice was a bit on edge.

"Sorry to say that we would not have had the science that we needed if it had not been for the Nazis. So in a way, yes. But not with Hitler's consent, you understand. The U.S. government, in a covert action brought over many of Germany's top scientists to work on this and later other projects. You know of some of them quite well. Now they did not all come here willingly, as I have said, we did put some pressure on them. But, in the end, I'm sure that they would have all agreed that it was for the best. After all, we're still around and Hitler is not."

Cardinal Celent shook his head. "So much good could have been done, and instead it was wasted."

"So, let me get this straight." Tonita's voice carried a tone that already belied her feelings about the Cardinal's statements. "You traveled in time?"

Cardinal Celent smiled. "That is correct."

"So that means you went somewhere, right?"

"You are correct."

Tonita paused taking a turn from the Cardinal's penchant for dramatic pauses. "And, where did you go?"

Cardinal Celent shook his head. "A good question Tonita, and one that I am prepared to answer." He had both Tonita and Dominic's undivided attention. "But, I think, perhaps, it is better that we start not at the beginning, where we traveled to, but rather to where we returned." Cardinal Celent picked up the book from his lap and held it out to Dominic.

Dominic took the book from the Cardinal, glanced at Tonita, and turned the book so that the cover was face up. The leather binding on the spine and cover was loose and frayed. Only a hint of the gold-embossed lettering remained on the spine of the book. The cover was also worn and faded, but the gold lettering reflected enough light that Dominic could still make out the title. He frowned, puzzled. Then the expression on his face relaxed as he stared at the word embossed in gold.

And its full meaning hit him.

He looked first to the Cardinal, then back to Tonita, and read aloud, "Roswell."

THIRTY FOUR

He could see their shadows through the window, distorted images gliding along the walls of the Cardinal's apartment. Ghostly shapes danced, colliding, merging, forming new shapes that danced again. And then he was there. Dominic. The Key, standing at the window where he was in perfectly clear sight.

If he had had a gun, the Key would be dead by now. The Novice allowed the image of a bullet tearing through the Key's body, ripping into muscles and veins and organs, to form in his mind. But a gun and a bullet were so impersonal, he thought. Dominic was the Key, and death by a bullet was not what the Novice had in mind for him. He would not destroy the Key with gunpowder and lead. The Key would have to be killed properly. It would be slow process that would allow the Key's energy to be absorbed. The Novice, who would then put it to its rightful use within the Order and the Society.

The Novice crouched down slightly, leaning back onto the knee high stone wall. From this angle he watched as the Key gesticulated. The movements were that of an angry and confused man. He laughed as he read into Dominic's movements, noting how Dominic could not control his emotions, letting them spew out in hand gestures.

The Novice allowed his mind's eye to conjure up an image of Dominic and the slut that clung to him. His thoughts slowly unfolded the pictures of Dominic's death and hers. He did not hate the Key, just as the predator does not hate his prey. Each understands their role in life and death. And while the prey may not die willingly, it does in the end cease its struggle and allow the predator to take its energy. The Key and The Novice had their callings. Only one would succeed. No remorse. No regrets. Just destiny. He understood and respected the Key. The Key too had been called, not by God, as the Order and The Novice had been, but by man. That was the Key's downfall. He served man and not God. He would have to be killed properly, with dignity. The Novice had formulated his plan for the Key's death, in preparation for Brother Salvatore's unsuccessful attempt. The good Brother had not failed, he realized, instead it was clearly in God's plan that he should be the one to slay the Key. He would take his time with the Key, and he would kill him, respectfully, allowing the Key to give up his life's energy willingly.

But the slut could die the way a slut should. A smile spread across The Novice's face. He would not need to be gentle with her. Instead, he could take great pleasure in her death and enjoy himself. He convulsed slightly, blood flowing to his penis, expanding it. She would be punished for serving man and betraying God. He convulsed again at the thought of what he must do. His penis had grown hard and erect and he fought to keep control of himself.

Tonita skirted by the window and his rage, both, internally and in his groin, grew to near bursting.

The Novice closed his eyes and prayed. *Give me control to do what is right. Give me the power to do what I must. I will give you the glory.* He repeated the prayer in Aramaic to himself several times, until his rage and his penis went flaccid, and his control returned, a sure sign that God had heard him. He opened his eyes and glanced back to the window.

There, Cardinal Celent stood, perfectly backlit by the interior lights. A halo surrounded him, like a scene from a DaVinci painting of some angel or saint. The Cardinal's back was to the room and a sliver of light reflected off of the windowpane, casting a glow on Cardinal Celent's face.

Richard Devin

The Novice flushed. His face reddened and bumps rose on his arms. He stood, no longer concerned about concealing himself in the shadows of the wall, as he could clearly see that Cardinal Celent was staring directly at him.

THIRTY FIVE

June 16th, 1948
Kapustin Yar
Soviet Air Base
U.S.S.R

Soviet Air Force fighter pilot Arkadii Ivanovich Apraksin was a highly decorated, knowledgeable, and honorable man. Having flown for years with the Soviet Air Force, he was completely respected and admired by the rank and file, as well as by the commanders at the Kapustin Yar airfield. Test missile launches, space shuttle deployments, as well as experimental aircraft runs, were common occurrences at Kapustin Yar, and Apraksin's expertise in the fields were well noted.

Apraksin could clearly see the airfield located on the banks of the Volga River and the city of Stalingrad, just about 75 miles east from his vantage point at twenty seven hundred feet. The horizon was mostly clear with just a few scattered clouds that only added to the picturesque drama, as the fighter buzzed through a cloud, made a turn to the left and began to circle the airfield.

The base commander radioed to Apraksin, "Repeat. Repeat transmission." He lowered the mouthpiece to his side. "Go to speaker," he ordered the radio technician.

"Speaker open, sir."

"Apraksin, repeat transmission."

"There is a cucumber-shaped object flying directly in my path." The static that had garbled the last transmission was gone, and the pilot's voice came in loud and clear. "There are lights all around it," Apraksin radioed back, "And the object echoes on my radar."

"Confirm radar," the base commander shouted out to a nearby radar technician.

"Commander," the technician answered. "Object confirmed.

"The aircraft is not responding to my signals."

"Apraksin, you have my order to close in on the aircraft. The pilot is in violation of Soviet airspace." The base commander stood over the radar screen, watching as the dot representing the jet fighter and the dot of the unknown aircraft moved. "Circle unknown aircraft and report."

"I cannot, Commander," Apraksin radioed. "The aircraft counters every turn. I will try to close in."

"You are to order the aircraft to land."

"Yes, sir," Apraksin responded, "closing airspace with unknown aircraft." He maneuvered the Soviet fighter into a direct collision course with the unknown aircraft. Apraksin radioed back to the base commander, "Nine point seven kilometers and closing."

All in the control room remained silent, listening. The base commander stood behind the radar technician looking over him to the radar screen, watching.

"Now within..." Apraksin started to transmit then hesitated. "The unidentified aircraft is descending."

Static.

Followed by silence.

"Waiting on orders, Commander." Apraksin remained calm, his voice steady.

"Apraksin, you are to destroy the unknown aircraft." In contrast to Apraksin, the base commander's voice rose.

"Decent confirmed," the radar technician shouted before his commander had a chance to ask.

"I am ordered to destroy unknown aircraft, Commander?"

"Shoot it down. Shoot the object down now." The base commander's voice trembled. "You are ordered to shoot the craft down."

"There are lights surrounding the object, Commander," Apraksin radioed. "Landing lights. The aircraft is landing..." Static cut him off.

"Apraksin, say again," the base Commander ordered, as he released the control button on the microphone.

"No. No!" Apraksin shouted. "It is not landing! The lights...the lights! I have lost control of my engines and all technical systems are out. All systems are down. Engines down. Altimeter down. Compass is spinning. The lights are directly on me. I cannot see the aircraft." Apraksin was nearly hysterical. "Blinded. I'm going down. Going down."

The radio went dead.

"Sir, the unknown aircraft is gone," the radar technician said. "Only one echo remains.

"That cannot be."

"Sir, it is no longer on radar."

The base commander picked up a telephone handset from the bracket on the wall. All eyes in the room turned and watched as he gestured, speaking in hushed tones.

Moments later, Apraksin managed to glide the fighter to a rough landing on an air strip on the far outer edge of the Kapustin Yar airfield, away from other aircraft and buildings.

When the fighter had rolled to a stop, Apraksin popped the cockpit canopy open and breathed in deeply, allowing the stress of the flight to dissipate. As soon as he pulled off the headphones, he heard the unmistakable clicking of chambers being armed. He looked down, half smiling. The aircraft was completely surrounded by service men, weapons at the ready, all aimed at the cockpit. Apraksin's smile faded. He was held in the cockpit, ordered not to exit. An hour later experts from Moscow and the local Stalingrad KGB arrived.

The fighter aircraft was immediately hauled off and impounded—to be studied—the KGB said. Apraksin was removed from the area sedated—for his own comfort—and taken to KGB headquarters in Moscow—for safekeeping.

Apraksin woke in the hospital at Saratov where he gave a detailed statement of his encounter with the oddly shaped, unknown aircraft. After several days of observation, he was presented to a special medical board comprised of top KGB doctors. The doctors determined that additional treatment was necessary and sent Apraksin to a psycho-neurological institute for further observation and study. There he was given shock treatment and psychotherapy. 'Despite their best efforts,' as the newspapers would later report, Apraksin was declared 'disabled' to further duty.

All personnel on duty at the base that day were reassigned and relocated to far off bases in Siberia or to headquarters in Moscow, where they could be watched for any signs of trauma—so the KGB reported.

No trace of the unknown flying object was ever found, and most records of the occurrence vanished.

THIRTY SIX

"I thought aliens landed at Roswell?" Tonita took the book from Dominic's hands and began flipping the pages.

Cardinal Celent laughed, looking through the window, his back still to Dominic and Tonita. "Isn't that great? The story that has grown around Roswell, and the landing there has taken on a life of its own." He continued to stare at the Novice, who stood motionless on the street below. "Have you ever been there?"

"Roswell?" Dominic questioned.

"Yes." Cardinal Celent shook his head in positive motion, not so much in affirmation to Dominic's question, but as an acknowledgement to the Novice that the game was on.

"I haven't." Tonita tossed the book to the sofa. "I'm not into this, aliens invading us thing, and all this UFO nonsense."

"It's a fascinating place really. Roswell." Cardinal Celent turned his back to the window and to the Novice. "So much built up on nothing more than rumor."

"So, there was never a spaceship crash in Roswell?" Dominic picked the book up from the sofa and slowly turned the pages.

"Oh I didn't say that. Yes, there was a crash in Roswell. Well, close to Roswell anyway. But it wasn't a space ship," Cardinal Celent spoke, keeping his place with his back to the window. He did not want to relinquish his position, afraid that either Dominic or Tonita would take his place and discover the Novice standing, waiting, outside. "The crash outside of Roswell was real. Of course, the government covered it up with stories of balloons and luckily for us the local police and newspapers printed the story, which of course grew into the story of Roswell as we know it today. Fascinating. But the crash was real."

Tonita wrapped her arms around herself. "This is just too much."

"Please sit down," Cardinal Celent said to Tonita, then added, "Both of you." Cardinal Celent waited a moment. When neither Tonita nor Dominic moved to the sofa, he continued, "Please."

Dominic stopped flipping the pages of the book and took a long look into the Cardinal's eyes. "Tonita," he gestured to the sofa taking a seat there.

Tonita uncrossed her arms and reluctantly joined Dominic on the sofa. She looked up at Cardinal Celent. "Well?"

"We chose Roswell for several reasons. One, because of its remoteness. Two, because of the air force base not far from the city. And three..." He chuckled. "Because of the name."

"Why the name?" Dominic looked to Tonita, who shrugged.

Cardinal Celent held his hand out. "The book, please."

Dominic reached across the sofa and handed the book to the Cardinal.

Cardinal Celent fingered the worn cover. "In 1873 Roswell was named in honor of the founder's father. That is the real story. Still, the name bore some significance to our mission." He continued to finger the torn leather binding on the book, then continued, "We took the name of Roswell, to be a sign."

"A sign from the aliens?" Tonita said, sarcasm pouring out of every word.

Cardinal Celent laughed. "Not aliens. God."

"You don't," Dominic started, then caught himself. "You didn't believe in God."

"True. I may not have, but there were others who did. It was their sign. I dismissed it. It didn't have any bearing on our mission—or so I thought at the time."

"What changed your mind?" Tonita said, sitting forward.

"There are Artesian wells in the area surrounding the town. The wells gave life to the area, and without them the town would not have been able to succeed. It would have died and turned to dust, becoming a ghost town, like so many in the deserts of the western United States. Perhaps, we would never have heard of Roswell." Cardinal Celent shifted his position, taking hold of the end of the table near the window, easing his discomfort from standing for so long.

"Here, sit down." Dominic said, noting the slightly pained look on the Cardinal's face.

Cardinal Celent smiled, replacing the grimace. "I'm fine. Really." He did not dare leave the space in front of the window. Even with his back to the window, he sensed that the Novice was below and had not moved. He was still there, watching.

Cardinal Celent kept his composure, continuing despite the pain in his joints and the burning sensation at his back. "Roswell is a common spelling and combination of two words. Rose—a flower and Well—life. The flower of life."

"Rose Well?" Tonita asked.

"We know this in the Catholic Church by another name." Cardinal Celent said, and watched as the expression on Dominic's face registered the meaning.

"The mother of Jesus," Dominic spoke the words softly.

"That is right, Dominic. The well of life—the Virgin Mary." Cardinal Celent said.

The quiet sound of glass slowly cracking caught Cardinal Celent's attention. Dominic and Tonita, seated on the sofa, looked to him as he cocked his head trying to place the noise. He raised a finger to his lips in a gesture of quiet.

Without further warning, the window behind Cardinal Celent exploded inward. Shards of glass sprayed into the room. Large triangles of glass cleavers lodged themselves into Cardinal Celent's back. He fell forward taking the brunt of the assault.

Smaller pieces of glass, as though they had been perfectly aimed, headed directly toward Tonita. She flinched at the explosion, covering her head with her arms, throwing herself into Dominic's lap.

Dominic recoiled and instinctively fell over Tonita, shielding her further. His head, shoulders, and arms became dotted with small shards of imbedded glass.

Tonita screamed, as other small slivers of glass penetrated her skin at her unprotected back.

Within seconds, the storm of glass subsided and an unnerving silence from the peaceful Vatican grounds floated in through the now glass-less window.

Dominic pulled himself upright, wincing as his skin and muscles twisted the glass imbedded into his body. Droplets of blood began to ooze out where the glass shards had lodged.

Tonita slowly lifted her head. "Is it over?"

"I think so." Dominic put his hand on her back. She winced. "Sorry. Don't move." He looked at her shard embedded back. "You've got glass all over you."

"What the hell happened?" Tonita asked, slowly rising to her feet. "Oh God, Dominic, you're bleeding."

"I'll be fine." He stood and looked to the where the window once was. "A bird or something must have hit the window."

"Some bird." Tonita started toward the window. "Dominic!" She nodded toward the window.

On the floor in front of them, Cardinal Celent had fallen. His back was badly torn by the glass. Large dagger like pieces of the window protruded from his back. His clothes were torn and, in places, shredded by the blast. He stirred, struggling to move.

"Cardinal, don't move. We'll get help." Dominic gestured to Tonita to get the phone. "Stay still."

Cardinal Celent raised his head slightly off of the floor. "It is all right, my son. I will not be fine." He coughed, spitting out blood. "My death has come."

"We're getting help." Dominic looked back at Tonita on the telephone. "Tonita's calling now. Someone will be here."

"I'm afraid they'll be too late for me." The Cardinal struggled to keep his eyes open.

Tonita set the telephone handset down onto the cradle. "An ambulance is on the way." She joined Dominic at Cardinal Celent's side, broken glass crunching under her footsteps. She kicked away some of the glass with the side of her foot, clearing a path.

"There is more that you must know." Cardinal Celent's voice grew considerably weaker. "I am sorry that you will have to learn without me. I had hoped that we would have more time. But time is not ours to keep or to manipulate. That I have learned." Cardinal Celent reached out with one hand and grabbed hold of the leg of the nearby table. He pulled on it. "Help me to stand."

"You shouldn't move," Tonita began.

Cardinal Celent offered, "I must." He held his hand out to Dominic, "Help me."

Dominic glanced quickly at Tonita, then reached forward, taking hold of the Cardinal's hand, and nearly slipping on the glass covered floor, he pulled the Cardinal to his feet.

The glass cut deep into the Cardinal's back, as he took a step and then another toward the sofa. Steadying himself on one the arm of the sofa, he leaned forward and picked up the book on Roswell that he had thrown when the window behind him had shattered. The book had landed on the sofa, narrowly missing Tonita's head.

"Here take this. Keep it safely with you. And you will understand."

Dominic took the book from the Cardinal.

"There is more to be said by the shortest chapter in the Bible, than in all the words in the whole book." Cardinal Celent pointed to the book.

Dominic noticed how shaky the Cardinal's hand had become. "You need to rest..." Dominic's words were cut short as a wheezing breath escaped from the Cardinal's mouth.

"You have been chosen. You wear the crown," Cardinal Celent said. And then collapsed.

Dominic turned to Tonita. As he did so, her hand went to her mouth covering a gasp. "Dominic."

Dominic looked into the gilded mirror that hung neatly on a small space on the far wall. His reflection revealed that bits and pieces of glass had become embedded in his skull, circling from his forehead and around to the back. With the light of the room glinting off of the shards of glass and the droplets of blood, that were now running down his face, the reflection was clear.

Dominic's head was covered by a crown of thorns.

THIRTY SEVEN

Inspector Carrola pushed by the old nurse, and despite her objections, pulled back on the cream colored curtain, sliding it along the metal rail on chrome rings. It made a kind of bell sound as the rings clinked together along the rail.

Dominic turned his head as did the young doctor tending to him.

"Aspeta," the young doctor, not more than twenty-five said, shooting a look of anger at the Inspector. "Aspeta, nessun ospiti."

"I am not a tourist and I do not wait." Inspector Carrola flashed a badge at the young doctor. "Tourist? That is correct?" He looked to Dominic

"Visitor. Tourist is okay," Dominic answered the inspector.

"You would say tourist?"

"No, visitor."

Inspector Carrola looked at the young doctor. "I am no a visitor."

The young doctor shook his head at the Inspector, then turned his attention back to the embedded glass shards in Dominic's head.

"He's only an intern and he thinks he's a doctor." "I didn't think that I'd see you." Dominic winced as a piece of glass was pulled out of the flesh surrounding his skull.

"That is the difference. I knew that I would see you again."

"Unfortunate."

"For those who surround you, yes," Inspector Carrola said, watching as the doctor pulled several pieces of glass from Dominic's flesh. "You have a way, signore, of...how do you say...making the tide?"

"Making waves."

"Ah, yes. Making waves." Inspector Carrola moved around the bed, coming up behind the doctor. "I don't understand this saying really. It doesn't make sense to me."

"It means churning things up. Making a mess of a situation.

"And that you do. Am I not right, Dominic?"

"Lately."

"Finito," the doctor said, dropping the surgical tweezers onto a stainless steel tray. He grabbed a roll of white sterile gauze from the stand and began to wrap it around Dominic's head.

"Tell me. What happened tonight?" The inspector watched as the doctor manipulated the gauze around Dominic's head.

"The window broke."

"How did this happen? The window broking?"

"Breaking, not broking."

"How did this happen then?"

"Something broke the window."

"A bird maybe?" Inspector Carrola picked up some of the instruments on the stand inspecting them.

"Per favore, Ispettore." The doctor glanced at the inspector and the surgical tool in his hand.

Inspector Carrola dropped the tool.

"Maybe? I didn't see a bird." Dominic tried to keep his head still, but failed.

"Non si muova," the doctor ordered.

"Sorry, spiacente," Dominic apologized and tried to remain still.

"Someone put a rock into the window?"

"Maybe? I told you I didn't see anything."

"Perhaps, that is because there was no rock, Signore. And also, there was no bird."

"I can't help you then. We were just talking..."

"Talking about what then? I can ask you?"

Dominic barely missed a beat. "Books and travel."

Inspector Carrola picked up a set of tweezers. "Are you going somewhere?"

"No, Inspector. I'm not planning on it."

"And your girlfriend? Is she going somewhere?"

"She is not my girlfriend."

"Did I use the wrong word?"

"Per favore, Ispettore!" The doctor's tone was sharp.

The inspector put down the tweezers. "I'm sorry. But sometimes my English is no so good."

"The word is correct, Inspector. It's the implication that's wrong."

"Ah, I forgot. You are a priest. No girlfriend then."

"If you don't mind Inspector?" Dominic jumped down from the surgery table, waving off the doctor. "I would like to see Tonita and the Cardinal."

"Yes, yes. I am sorry to be keeping you."

"If there is nothing more then?" Dominic headed toward the door, not waiting for an answer.

"No. That is it. You go to see your girlfriend." Inspector Carrola waved a hand animatedly in front of his face, shaking his head. "I'm sorry. I use the words wrong again. Go see your friend."

"Scusilo. Dove posso trovare Tonita e Cardinale?" Dominic said to a passing nurse.

"I can help you there," Inspector Carrola said, waving the nurse off. "Tonita is in the room just across the hall. And the Cardinal Celent...you will find him in the morgue."

THIRTY EIGHT

The Novice pushed on the door to Cardinal Celent's flat, expecting it to be locked. It was not. The door swung open a few inches, then stopped.

He had been waiting on the street, staring up at the window to the Cardinal's flat, with the tourists, Vatican employees and priests, nuns and passersby, while the police and Vatican officials inspected the flat, looking for something they could never find. He had covered himself in a tunic, taken from the closet of an office on the ground floor of the same building that housed the Cardinal's flat, he blended in perfectly.

He pushed on the door again and it completed its arch, opening widely. The Novice stepped inside. The glass from the shattered window had been swept from the floor, and the opening of the window was now covered with a sheet of clear plastic. It bellowed inward like the sail on ship. But this sail could not move a ship across the seas. It would barely hold back the cold of the night air.

Small shards of glass, missed by the cleaning crew, glinted off of the light of the sun. There was an eerie stillness to the apartment. He stepped away from the door, coming fully inside the apartment. There was a sudden chill to the air and in his veins. He was at once cold and began to sweat. His calm was replaced by a nervousness that penetrated his every cell. He started to shake. He was disorientated. Confused.

It was just moments ago, as he climbed the stairs to the Cardinal's flat, that he had been reveling in the feeling of his power and control. He had only just focused his energy and thoughts on the pane of glass at the window, and then watched as it cracked and shattered. It was more than he had anticipated. But then,

God's power was under no man's control, he thought, as a smile spread across his face, and he quickly made the sign of the cross.

He moved around the room, taking note of the teacups and the still heavy fragrance of Earl Grey that lingered about them. He allowed his hand to glide along the back of the sofa and the chair to the table and the abundance of books piled upon it. He touched as many of the books as he could, hoping to sense something. But there was nothing from any of the books, only a growing, gnawing nervousness inside him.

Get out.

It was as if someone had just spoken it aloud to him.

Get out.

A threat? A warning? He contemplated the words of the unspoken voice.

A car door closed on the street below, just below the plastic covered window. He pulled at the covering, tearing a small section from the white duct tape holding it to the wall, and peered through.

Two people stepped out of a police patrol car. A man and a woman. The patrol car pulled away slowly, leaving the man and woman on the street. The man glanced up to the window.

The Novice quickly released the plastic covering, letting it fall back to the wall. He smiled as he watched the man take hold of the woman's hand. The Key and his slut had returned.

Get out.

The warning echoed again within his thoughts.

He took a step forward, unconsciously obeying the order, then stopped, flicking away the thoughts of leaving from his mind.

"Stay," he commanded to himself out loud. Stay and kill the slut and make the Key watch. Then the Key too, would die.

Get out.

"What are you asking of me?" The Novice turned his face skyward and spoke aloud.

He heard the street level door at the bottom of the stairs open. Hushed voices swept up the stairway into the flat.

The Novice took a step toward the open apartment door, intending to close it. As he moved toward the door, his hand fell upon a book left on the corner of the table by the window. A book on Roswell. A searing flash of pain coursed its way from his fingertips, up his arm and deep into his brain. His hand recoiled instinctively from the book and the pain ceased. He held his hand just above the cover of the book and feeling nothing, let his fingers drop down so that they were lightly touching the tattered cover. In an instant, an intense pain shot from his fingertips directly into his brain. He pulled his hand away, momentarily dazed. He shook off the effects, just as Dominic and Tonita stepped into the flat.

Sheer panic, a feeling that the Novice was not accustomed to, overwhelmed him. His muscles tensed. His body ready to react, to spring in any direction that his mind asked of him. But his mind would not act. His thoughts were frozen, scattered at best, unclear, and in turmoil. His flesh reddened. Sweat broke out on his brow and trickled down the side of his face. He urged a hand to wipe it away, but the hand remained hovering above the book.

Tonita was the first to step into the apartment. "Are you sure this is alright?" She turned her head to Dominic, who was just a stair step behind her.

"No one else is staying here and we've..." Dominic came to a stop mid-stride. He reached out, grabbing Tonita around her stomach with his arm and pulled her quickly to him.

"Dom? What the hell?" she said, pulling at his arm.

"Hello." The Novice smiled, finally gaining control of his thoughts and body.

The Third Hour

Tonita turned in the Novice's direction, startled, "Hello," she sucked in a breath and then let it out. "You scared the hell out of me."

The Novice fought the urge to grin broadly at Tonita's statement, reveling in the hint of fear that he had caused her. "I'm sorry to have startled you," he spoke in the soft quiet tone and manner that he imagined a Vatican emissary would use. "I've been sent by Vatican security to insure that everything here is in order. Well, the best that it can be given the circumstances." He paused for moment eyeing Dominic and Tonita with a smile remaining on his face. "Are you looking for something?"

"No. We were just checking to see that the apartment was secure," Dominic said, without taking his eyes off the man.

"I can assure you that it is well protected." The Novice moved toward the doorway and the stairs. "You are not with the police?"

"Oh, no, we are...we're friends of the Cardinal" Tonita pushed herself closer into Dominic as the Novice approached.

"Are you..." He looked into Dominic's eyes, "... all right?" He allowed his eyes to drift up to the bandage covering Dominic's head.

"Yes," Dominic said, dropping his arm from Tonita's waist and bringing it up to touch the gauze wrapped around his head. "Just an accident."

"They seem to be happening quite frequently, Accidents." He waited for a response, when none came, he continued, "Won't you come in? I'm nearly finished here."

The Novice reached forward taking a hold of the door. "I understand if you wish to have some time alone with your thoughts."

Tonita smiled at the man. "Thank you. That is very kind of you."

"No. We'll be on our way," Dominic said, as he pushed Tonita around him, so that she now stood at the top of the stairs, behind him. Dominic stepped into the doorway blocking it.

The smile on the Novice's face spread. "If you wish. But the offer stands."

Dominic placed an arm behind his back and using his fingers, motioned for Tonita to move aside. "I'm sorry," he said to the Novice, "but I didn't get your name?"

The Novice's smile faded then returned. *He's digging,* he thought.

***

Dominic extended his hand forward. "I'm Dominic," he said to the man before him, who hesitated, then slowly extend his own hand.

The hands of the men met.

Dominic could feel the man's flesh slide over his own. The hand was rough, calloused, and not at all as smooth as Dominic had expected it to be. Dominic wrapped his fingers around the man's palm and began to move his hand up in the gentlemanly motion of the traditional Western greeting. The moment that Dominic had a secure handshake, he pulled the Novice toward him with all the strength he could muster.

The Novice, caught off guard, fell toward Dominic. Off balance, he stumbled. The plastic smile on his face replaced by shock.

Dominic did not let the momentum slow, and he pulled harder, allowing his arm to cock back completely.

The Novice reached out with his left hand, crossing his own body, grabbing for the door to steady himself and missed. His hand slid along the door panel and he dug his fingernails into the wood in an instinctive effort to grasp something. But he only managed to scratch a curving trail into the wood. He flayed his arm, twisting his body as he did, throwing himself further off balance.

Dominic held tight to the Novice's right hand, and yanked one more time on his arm, pulling him through the doorway, past Dominic, and narrowly missing Tonita. At the last moment possible, Dominic released his grip on the Novice's hand and sent him free falling, head first down the stars.

Tonita screamed, "Dominic!"

Before the Novice completed his tumbling, bone-cracking, flesh-tearing fall down the worn steps, Dominic had taken hold of Tonita's hand, pulling her with him, taking the steps two at a time.

***

Blood splattered onto the walls of the stairway from a gash in the Novice's head. He grunted as the air in his lungs was forced out with every hard landing. The Novice attempted to gain control, reaching for the old railing. Missing. Trying again, before his head smashed into the stone wall at the bottom of the stairs. His eyes closed as the blur of, walls and stairs, arms and hands, legs and feet, were replaced by darkness.

Dominic and Tonita had made it halfway down the stairs, following the thuds, grunts and groans of the Novice, when Dominic stopped, turned and retreated back up the stairway.

***

"Dominic, wait."

Tonita was near frantic. Confused about the course of events that had just taken place, she wasn't sure if she should follow Dominic or make a run for the street. She didn't know if he was crazy and just attacked some priest unprovoked, or if he was protecting her. She glanced at the Novice lying twisted at the bottom of the stairs. She turned and started back up the stairs after Dominic. Two stairs later, she stopped. She screamed. Then turned around and headed down.

Before she had taken three steps down, Dominic rejoined her.

They reached the bottom of the stairs together, and jumping over the Novice's crumpled body, they made their way out of the door onto the Vatican streets.

Dominic did not let up. He pulled Tonita toward the Museum Gate.

She almost tripped, briefly losing her balance. She steadied herself, regained her footing, and followed Dominic once again onto the streets of Rome.

THIRTY NINE

"Dominic. Wait. What are you doing?" Tonita was breathless, sweating; her hair clung to her forehead. "Dom, stop!" She pulled away from him and leaned her exhausted body against a wall of peeling yellow paint. She wiped the hair from her eyes and screamed, "What is this? Why are we running? Why did you push that priest down the stairs? Dominic? What's wrong with you?" She concluded the rant of questions in tears.

Dominic leaned in close to her. He was breathing heavily and his words came out in short strains. "That priest, brother, or whatever he said he was," he took a deep breath, "believe me, Tonita. He wasn't." He took in another breath and blew it out slowly. "That man was going to kill us."

"Dom? He was there watching over the place."

"I know that's what he said. But, he wasn't. There was something about him. Evil."

"Dom. He was just standing there."

"Tonita. He wasn't just standing there watching out for the Cardinal's possessions or his apartment. I don't even think the Vatican knows that he was there. They certainly did not send him." Dominic spoke breathlessly.

"And how, Dom? How do you know this?"

He stepped back from the wall, pulled off a thick piece of the paint, and examined it. There was layer upon layer of paints in that little piece. Red first, then brown, with a deeper brown, over tan and then the yellows. Different layers of yellows, one under the other, from bright to faded, to the last layer of pollution covered and stained yellow. "I don't know it." Dominic let the paint chip drop from his hand. "All right, let me ask you a question. How did he know to speak to us in English and not Italian?"

"Maybe he heard us coming up the stairs? And we were speaking in English, so he spoke to us in English."

"Possible." Dominic went silent. His eyes wandered over the faded yellow layer of paint, stained with years of pollution. "He knew that we were with the Cardinal. He didn't even ask us if the Cardinal was all right."

"Dom, he's with the Vatican. Of course he knew that the Cardinal had died. And he must have known that we were with him when the window blew out. I'm sure everyone knows, thanks to Inspector Carrola." Tonita sighed, extending her hand to him. "So, now what? What do we do now?" Tonita stared into his eyes.

"I don't know."

"You have to know, Dom. You can't continue not knowing."

"Unfair." Dominic stepped away from her. "I didn't ask for any of this. It just happened."

"Unfair is what you're doing to me."

"I didn't ask you to come along, Tonita."

"No, you just yanked me along." She took a step toward him, reached out, placed her hand under his chin, and turned his face to her. "Dominic, that man could be dead back there. We've got to call someone. Send him help. We just can't leave him lying at the bottom of the stairs."

"Tonita, trust me. We don't want to help him."

"Why?"

"Because he's part of this. He's part of whatever 'this' is..." He turned away from her. "Nothing is right anymore."

"Thanks. I'll assume that present company is included."

Dominic looked backed at her, shook his head and walked away.

"Now what? Where are you going?" Tonita called after Dominic. "What? Are you just going to leave me like you did that priest and the church?"

Dominic stopped mid-stride. "Nice Tonita. Thanks," he said without turning around.

A long silence covered the distance between them.

Finally, Tonita broke the silence and the distance. "All right." She took several steps to close the gap between them. "Dominic? Meet me half way."

Dominic turned around, breathed out a heavy sigh, and moved to her.

"That wasn't too hard was it?"

Dominic leaned into her and kissed her. His arms wrapped around her body and drew her close to him. He held her there tightly, not letting his mouth and hers part.

Tonita responded in kind and her arms became twisted in his. After a moment, she pulled back. "Well, big boy, is that a gun in your pocket or are you just happy to see me?" she said in her best Mae West accent.

Dominic smiled at her. "Neither." He lifted up his shirt revealing half of a book tucked into the waistband of his pants.

Tonita grabbed the book and pulled it out of Dominic's pants. "You went back into the Cardinal's apartment to get this."

"Hey." Dominic flinched instinctively.

"Let me get this straight. You push a priest down a flight of stairs, maybe killing him because he's going to hurt us, although he never made a move to do so. Then, you grab me, push me out of the apartment, all because of this unseen danger, and..."

"It's not..." Dominic tried to interject.

Tonita held up her hand, placing it in front of Dominic's face. "Oh, I'm not finished. You grab me. Rush me out. But then, in spite of this murdering priest who may be waiting for us at the bottom of the stairs playing dead with blood splattered everywhere, you rush back into the apartment to get this." She presented the book to Dominic's face. "A travel book?"

"Well...yeah!"

"You've got to be kidding me?" Tonita shook her head.

"Was that a question or a statement?"

"A book?" Tonita asked. Then added, "That was a question."

"Can I?" Dominic reached for the book.

Tonita rolled her eyes and handed him the book.

Dominic took it, letting his fingers touch hers.

She shook her head, turning away.

Dominic turned the cover back inspecting the first few pages, then using his thumb flipped through the remaining pages, fanning the book. He paused, held the book by the spine, and turned it upside down. He shook it. Then, turning the book face up, flipped the pages again. And then once more.

"Are you hot?" Tonita could not conceal the sarcasm in her voice

Dominic didn't respond. Instead, he flipped through the pages again. This time he stopped at a page. Watching. Studying. He bent the spine back and held the book open on the page. Then he looked up at Tonita and smiled.

"What's that grin for?" Tonita's eyebrow raised and her head cocked to the side.

"This." Dominic let the book fall open to page seventeen, chapter three. *Getting to Roswell.*

Tonita glanced down at the opened book; she mouthed the words of the chapter title and then looked up at Dominic. "Please tell me you're not thinking of going there?"

"I'm not."

"Thank God."

"But we are." Dominic nearly broke the spine on the book by folding the pages back as far as he could. Then, methodically, he began to tear page seventeen from the old binding glue. The page came away easily. "Here." He handed the book to Tonita, keeping only the page he had just removed. He read the words printed onto the first side of the page. Considering them. Then he turned the paper over to page eighteen and read each of the words printed there.

"You found something?" Tonita asked.

"Not sure." He took the page and held it at arms' length to the sky, letting the cloud filtered sunlight pass through it.

"Well what are you looking for?"

"Not sure of that either."

"Okay. Let me try this another way."

"Shoot." Dominic continued to turn, twist, and flip the torn page seventeen.

"You tore the page from the book for a reason, right?"

"Yes," Dominic answered without looking at Tonita. His eyes swept the page as he turned it over and upside down and up to the sun again.

"What was that reason?"

"This page is different."

"How so?"

"I noticed it before," he said.

Tonita's expression begged for further explanation.

"When Cardinal Celent handed me the book back in his apartment. I noticed that a page or two seemed different...thicker maybe. I dismissed it then as just a fluke."

"And now you think that page has some information hidden on it?"

"Yes, my dear Doctor Watson. You are correct."

"That's weird."

"Maybe. But I'm sure that Cardinal Celent was trying to tell us something."

"Why didn't he just say it?"

"I don't know. But then that fits in with the way my life," he paused and looked directly into Tonita's eyes, "our lives have been going. I don't know what to expect next."

"Can I take a look?"

Dominic eyed the page again. "Sure," he said and handed to Tonita.

She turned the page around.

"I did that already," Dominic said, as she performed her inspection.

"Yes, I know. But you may have missed something.

Then concentrating, she read every word.

"I did that, too," Dominic said.

"You're not helping," Tonita chastised, then held the page up to the sun.

"And I did that."

"But you didn't do this," Tonita said, then spat onto the page.

"Tonita!" Dominic shouted, then added, "That was gross."

Tonita rubbed the saliva into the fabric of the page. She glanced up at Dominic with a big smile and showed him the page. Where the saliva had dampened the page, a new image of crisscrossing lines had partially appeared.

"You're brilliant."

"Hey, all those days of candy-striping at the hospital were not lost."

"Oh? They teach Candy stripers to spit on things?"

"Didn't you ever do a litmus test, where the paper reacts to something that's alkaline or acidic and turns it different colors? When I was a kid I got this really cool, well, I thought it was really cool at the time, science kit."

Dominic didn't let her finish. "Come on. We've got to find some water."

Tonita glared at him. "Dom, we're in Rome. There's a freakin' fountain on every corner."

FORTY

Dominic led the way to Plazza del Quiriti near the small church of Saint Gioacch. The Plaza's small fountain, extruding from the corner of an unnamed building, spat out water from the mouth of lion. Dominic eased the page that he had torn out of the book on Roswell into the cool water.

"Careful. Don't soak it," Tonita said, as she watched.

Dominic looked at her. "Do you want to do it?"

"No way. If it gets ruined, I don't want to be blamed for it."

"Then let me," he said, as he touched the page onto the surface of the water. He watched as the liquid followed the fibers of the paper, drawing up from the underside of the page to the top side of the paper. It now revealed fully, the crisscrossing image that Dominic and Tonita had glimpsed earlier.

"A map?" Tonita said, leaning over Dominic's shoulder.

"Just as I thought." Dominic pulled the page gently from the surface tension of the water and held it against the smooth surface of the building. "It could be a map. But to where?"

"Lots of lines. No names," Tonita mentioned the obvious.

"Thanks for pointing that out. I kinda noticed it myself."

"Just making an observation."

"Well then, what would you say to this?" Dominic paused for a moment, squinted his eyes, and stared at the page. "Where did the page come from?"

"A book," Tonita said. Then quickly added excitedly as though she had just won a prize, "On Roswell. A book on Roswell, New Mexico."

Dominic shot her a sideways glance. "And you think I'm weird?"

"I do," she said, nodding her head.

"This is a map of Roswell. It has to be. Or at least someplace in or near Roswell."

"But isn't New Mexico like a big desert?"

"We're going to find out." Dominic removed the page from the wall of the building and waved it gently in the air, drying it. He quickly stopped waving the paper, and brought the page up close. "Oh shit. For a minute I thought the map wasn't there." He looked back to Tonita and held up the page. "It's still there."

"Good thing. What if it disappeared and it wouldn't come back?"

"We'd be in trouble."

"You're lucky it didn't," Tonita scolded him, smacking his shoulder for good measure.

"We need to get on a flight to the states."

"How? I don't have my passport. You don't have yours. And we don't have cash to pay for it."

Dominic winked. "Let me take care of that."

FORTY ONE

Tonita pulled the Tumi tri-folding garment bag up close to her, resting her arm on it. She had taken a taxi from the Plaza del Quiriti to her apartment and packed, (per Dominic's orders, "Only one small carry-on bag.") then reported to the airport two hours and forty-five minutes later.

She was there.

He was not.

She found a seat just inside. She was in luck, she thought. The chair was close to the door and it didn't have an armrest in between it and the chair attached to it. She stretched out, allowing her legs to rest on the one seat and leaned back on the other. The soft "swoosh, swoosh," of the revolving door at the airport terminal's entrance, coaxed her eyes into closing. Immediately, the past day flashed in silent vignettes in her mind. Confusion wormed its way in, bringing with it doubt and wonder. For a moment she considered getting up and leaving, walking out of the ever circling airport door, heading for the taxi line, and then disappearing back to her cloistered life.

"Right where I asked you to be," Dominic's voice was distant, clouded, muted.

A softly faded vision of Dominic's face and ruffled good looks appeared in her mind. She couldn't leave him. Loving him had nothing to do with it. Then, she corrected herself. It had everything to do with it.

"Tonita."

She heard him speak her name. Softly. And then his touch.

"To-ni-ta." He sang her name

Tonita opened her eyes. "Oh, I must have fallen asleep. I didn't see you coming."

"You must be exhausted. I'm sorry. But you'll have plenty of time to sleep on the plane." Dominic pushed her legs off of the chair and sat next to her.

"And how, exactly, am I getting on the plane?" She rubbed her hands over her face and stood up.

"Come on. I'll show you on the way." He jumped up excitedly.

Fiumicino was very busy and crowds lingered near the airport's shops and restaurants. Long lines of passengers snaked around security check points and at the ticket counters. Dominic led the way to a small, unmarked office just to the side of the B Terminal security checkpoint.

"In here." He took hold of Tonita's arm and guided her into the office.

A short woman dressed in a dark suit looked up at Dominic and smiled. "Padre di buon pomeriggio, come posso aiutarlo?"

"Good day to you too," Dominic said. "I need two tickets on the next flight out to New Mexico in the United States."

"Pronto," the clerk replied, and then stepped into a back room.

"What do you think? They're just going to give them to you? No money, no questions?" Tonita whispered.

"Yep. Just that. When you have these." Dominic handed Tonita an envelope.

Tonita opened the envelope and pulled out a Vatican Diplomatic pass. "Why do you have this?"

"Many of us do."

"Many of who?" Tonita said, as she inspected the pass. "This is real?"

"Sure is." Dominic took the pass from her. "Many people travel for the Vatican and most of them have one. I never actually traveled as a diplomatic emissary for the Vatican. But most of us don't. It's just a little perk you get with the job."

"Perk? You're priests for Christ's sake."

"Well put."

Tonita flushed. "Sorry. But you know what I mean."

"I know that it means we get to skip around security."

"You're kidding?"

"How many priests do you see standing in line?" Dominic winked. "And I can ask for tickets on any flight. Even if it's sold out."

"Who pays for the tickets?"

"It goes to a Vatican diplomatic account for sanctioned travel," Dominic said just as the door behind the desk opened and the clerk returned.

"Il vostro passaggio diplomatico, per favore?" The clerk smiled as she asked.

Dominic handed her the pass. She glanced at it and handed it back to him with two tickets.

Dominic smiled at the clerk and nodded his head. He pulled the tickets out of the ticket packet and examined them: Swiss International Airlines to New York with a connection on Continental Airlines making two stops, one in Houston and one more in Albuquerque, where they would have to change planes for the final segment on a small turboprop to Roswell. "There's going to be plenty of time to catch up on sleep," he said to Tonita and turned to the clerk. "Grazie." He smiled at her.

The clerk smiled at him again and gestured to a door behind the desk. Dominic pulled the door open, gave Tonita a nod, and stepped into a back office. It was crowded with the usual office equipment: a printer, fax machine, two copiers, telephones, a coat rack, coffee maker, and another door.

The clerk, still smiling, looked at the door in the back of the office and then to Dominic.

He stepped to the door, squeezing between the copier and the fax machine, pushed opened the door, and stepped into a long dimly lit hallway. "Grazie," he said, waiving to the clerk.

She nodded, turned, and returned to the front office, closing the door on Tonita and Dominic.

"Come on." Dominic held out a hand to Tonita.

She took it, letting her fingers linger as they slid along his skin.

He glanced sideways at her and smiled, as he folded his fingers between hers.

They walked down the long corridor that ran parallel to the hundreds of people waiting at the security checkpoint. After a flight of stairs that took them up, they came upon a doorway marked on their side of the hallway with the word...Gates. They exited through the door into the boarding area.

A Swiss International ticketing agent, blond, blue-eyed, thin and pretty, was standing just outside the door. Her smile and polite composure never waning as she said, "Welcome, please follow me." Then escorted Dominic and Tonita to the jet-way.

Dominic handed the little "Swiss Miss" agent the tickets.

She sent the tickets flying through the ticket validator, retrieved them from the other end, and handed the boarding passes to Dominic. "Padre di molti ringraziamenti."

"Thank you," Dominic said, and added. "Grazie."

Tonita followed as they walked down the jet-way to the aircraft door. Stepping in, Tonita turned to the right heading into the coach section of the plane.

"Tonita?"

She stopped and turned back to Dominic.

"This way," Dominic said, gesturing with his head.

Tonita looked at him puzzled. Then her expression softened and she rolled her eyes. She smacked him on the back and followed Dominic into first class.

FORTY TWO

The Jesuit continued to circle the hard backed wood chair in the center of the room as he had for been for the many hours previous. He moved without speaking, simply circling, eyes planted firmly on the chair and its occupant.

The Novice sat in the chair, silent, still. He pressed his back against the carved ornate wood of the chair back, allowing the relief of Christ's crucifixion to dig into his skin. He had failed the Jesuit and his church. The self-inflicted pain was a reminder to him of that failure.

The Jesuit kept circling, as though he were a caged animal in a zoo exhibit. Circling. Circling.

The Novice wanted to speak, but dared not. He kept his eyes straight ahead, catching sight of the Jesuit only when he came around from the back of the chair. Like the hands of a clock in a counter-clockwise motion, the Jesuit circled. Circled. And The Novice watched.

He had been so close to the Key and the slut. He could have killed them both. It would have been so easy and so poignant to do so there. They would have died in the same flat as the Cardinal. A Cardinal, a priest and a slut. A trinity of death. He almost smirked at the thought, but caught himself. He had underestimated the cunningness of the Key. His mind had been clouded. Confusion had set in and he could not focus his thoughts. It must have been that the Key had come knowing that, he thought, and took advantage of it. He would have to be more careful or simply act more quickly in the future. He would not allow the Key to have the upper hand again.

Their next meeting would be their last.

When he came to, at the bottom of the stairs, his head throbbed and his body was torn and bruised. It ached. Still, he came willingly to the Jesuit to confess his failure and to receive his punishment for that failure. He expected to be punished. His failure demanded it. His body and muscles as hard as the wood of the chair that he pressed himself into. It tingled with anticipation of the punishment. And again he had to repress a smirk and an engorged cock.

The Novice concentrated on his muscles working from his heel up to his calf, then on to his groin. Willing, demanding each set of muscles to relax. To become numb to the pain or excitement. His muscles responded, blocking the nerve receptors from processing the pain and sending that energy to the brain. Soon his entire body was relaxed, despite the hours he had been sitting upright and ridged in the chair. His thoughts came back to the room and the Jesuit. He listened, waiting for the counter clockwise walk of The Jesuit to pass in front of his face, as he had for hours. The Jesuit's steady pace, ticked off the moments, then hours. But now there was no movement. The Novice turned his head slightly and listened. His senses heightened. He heard only the air that seeped in under and around the uneven seal between the door and the doorjamb. No other movement, no other sounds...not even that of man breathing.

The Jesuit was no longer in the room.

FORTY THREE

The office was like that of any high ranking political figure in Washington, D.C.: sleek, dark polished wood, thick heavy drapery, big white crown and base moldings and a fireplace, complete with an ivory marble surround and pillars. Gilt framed pictures of the Senator standing, sitting, or laughing, and the ubiquitous handshaking with U.S. Presidents and leaders from around the globe, hung in specific locations around the office. Precise thought and consideration had gone into the exact location of each of the pictures. A person entering the office would view the most powerful, or the current politically correct, picture first at the apex, followed by those of less important celebrities, politicians, and business leaders, fanned out around the office. The office was a study in picture geography. The thought and design strategy had taken the art out of picture hanging and replaced it with science. Like most sciences, the science of picture hanging had an unexplained glitch. Out of place among the gilded frames, paintings, and photographs, and hung in the most prominent location just above the fireplace, was a large Crucifix.

The Senator replaced the telephone handset onto the receiver. He took hold of his cane and pushed himself up and out of the high-backed, leather desk chair. Despite his age and the cane, his step was lively and sure-footed as he made his way to the door of his inner office. He opened the door slightly and peered through the narrow opening. "My car, Michelle," the Senator said to his sixty-something receptionist.

"Right away, Senator," the Beverly Hills plastic surgery enhanced, pretty woman said, as she pressed a button on the console.

The Senator headed out of his office, closing the door behind him and locking it. He pocketed the key and walked through the reception area then out into the public hallway of the building. He walked carefully along the smooth, marble tiled floor of the hallway to the elevator. He touched the heat-activated button located on a panel between the two golden doors of the elevator bank. Just a touch of a fingertip and the button lit up, confirming that the elevator had been called. He smiled, grinned really, at the little button, recalling the moment of that little device's creation.

They were working on the command console for the experimental equipment panel and needed a switch or toggle that would turn on and off the components of the command module. The console was coming together, except that a toggle switched proved to be too dangerous to use, as it could easily be knocked by an errant elbow or head during the experiment, and disaster could result. A small cover had been placed over the toggle switches to prevent an accidental change in the position of the toggle. But the cover itself proved to be a problem. In the end there were just too many toggles and too many covers to fit on the console and to be operated by the pilot.

A dial that turned clockwise assembled with dials that turned counter clockwise was too complicated. If the pilot or co-pilot was blacking out, or semi-conscious, or injured and had to react instantaneously, remembering which direction a dial needed to be turned would be deadly. The same problem existed for a button that had to be depressed or left in the up position. There were far too many opportunities for disaster.

The group of scientists from Germany, who had volunteered to work with the United States' War Department on the project, were an inventive group of men and proved their worth in short order. The heat sensitive, touch control device that summoned the elevator was the direct descendant of their imaginations.

A softly chiming "ding–ding" alerted the Senator to the elevator's arrival. The doors slid open and he stepped in. He leaned forward to touch another heat-activated button on the panel inside the elevator, as the doors began to slide closed.

"Senator. Senator. Wait." A young male aid shouted, as he came sprinting down the hall toward the elevator.

The Senator extended his cane breaking, the invisible beam sensor, stopping the elevator doors from closing.

"Senator. This just came in for you. I thought you may need it," The young man gasped.

"Thank you Mister Trembowitz" The Senator said, taking the page from the panting teenager.

"Sean sir. I'm too young to be a mister."

"You're never too young to accept respect Mister Trembowtz," The Senator said as he unfolded the page and read; *Confirmed arrival, JFK*. The Senator folded the paper back up and handed it to Sean. "Shred that."

"Yes, sir," Sean said, taking the folded paper from the Senator's hand. He slid it into the pocket of his pants. "I'll see to it right away, Senator." He stepped away from the elevator doorway allowing them to begin to close. "Have a nice day, Senator Scott." And the doors slid closed.

FORTY FOUR

The flight had been, thankfully, uneventful, Dominic thought. He felt rested, but anxious. "At least we're in the states," he said to Tonita, as they exited the aircraft.

"Thank you for flying with us." The words came from a perky little flight attendant with a plastic smile molded securely onto her face and a name tag that read Carly, pinned to her navy blue uniform.

"You too," Tonita said back, mimicking the smile.

Dominic glared at Tonita.

"What?"

"You thanked the flight attendant for flying with us? What do you think? The airline gives them a choice?"

"Dominic?" Tonita raised one eyebrow. "Shut up."

He knew that was coming.

They headed down the jet-way, joining in with the rest of the passengers that formed the human river moving downstream.

John F. Kennedy airport is a good fifteen miles distance from midtown Manhattan. But even here on Jamaica Bay, on the edge of the city of New York, the uplift in energy was noticeable. People moved faster, talked faster, ate faster, lived faster. Dominic could not help but feel the urge to join that current of energy, and his step quickened.

"Dom? Slow down. We've been sitting for five hours." Tonita raised her voice to be heard over the ambient noise of the airport. "I need to stretch."

The human river of passengers turned to the right, following the commands of both the signs and the Immigration Agents, and headed down a set of stairs. Then they followed along a cold sterile marble hallway, devoid of any atmosphere, and one that could only have been designed by a government architect practicing the minimalist gray-green color scheme.

Dominic took hold of Tonita's elbow, yanked her from the flow of human bodies and walked to the left. A narrow hallway, just off of the main hall, led them to an area that was clearly marked with signs, stating in several different languages that the area was off limits. Dominic looked behind him. He saw that no one else was around and proceeded to push on the bar of door that warned, in big red letters: *Doorway Alarmed. No Passengers Permitted. Alarm Will Sound.* The mechanism clicked, as the horizontal bar was completely depressed, releasing the latch on the door. Dominic pushed on the door. It swung open. No alarm. "That was tricky," Tonita said, as the door closed behind them.

"You forget. I'm a Vatican diplomat," Dominic said, as he turned the corner and walked right into two heavily armed soldiers.

FORTY FIVE

"Father Renzi?"

"Yes," Dominic said, clearly flustered. "I'm Dominic Renzi."

"Come with us."

Tonita and Dominic glanced quickly at one another.

"Move forward," one of the soldiers urged, then added, "Please."

There was the clicking sound of metal on metal as the two soldiers swung the MP5 automatic weapons onto their shoulders and took up position behind Tonita and Dominic. "Proceed straight ahead," the same soldier ordered.

"This gets better all the time," Tonita smirked as she spoke.

"Tonita?" Dominic raised an eyebrow. "Hush up!"

Tonita and Dominic, with the two soldiers closely behind them, continued on course following the unpainted cement walls and floor of the hallway. Dominic noted that the hall remained quite straight with only an occasional bend or curve, no sharp corners. Instead of the hard edged ninety degree corners found in most corridors, this had none.

"No one can hide in here," Dominic said.

"Why would they?"

"No corners." Dominic kept his voice to a whisper, and ignored her question as he continued. "Nowhere to hide."

"Where are they taking us?"

"I'm not sure. I've never been down this far. The couple of times that I've been here, I exited through the first door and then up the stairs. Just where we met our friends here."

"Why were you even here?"

"Vatican Diplomat. I told you."

"Yeah, you did. But I didn't believe you."

"Should have." Dominic winked at her. "I've never had a problem with the Secret Service before. There's never been anyone inside the hall."

"And you know that they're Secret Service because...?" Tonita glanced at Dominic.

"Because they're carrying MP5's and they're letting us talk."

"MP5's?"

"The weapon over their shoulders. You know...that big gun!"

"I would have called it a rifle."

"But then you didn't serve in the military."

"And you did?" Tonita kept step with Dominic, edging a bit closer. Her arm brushed his.

"I did."

Tonita stopped. One of the soldiers almost smacked right into the back of her.

"Keep walking," he grumbled.

She turned to the soldier, "Sorry," and then back to Dominic, "My, my, the secrets you have."

"It's not a secret. It just never came up."

"If we weren't being escorted down this hall to...I don't know where, and we were alone, we'd be having a long discussion right now. You should be thankful we're under arrest." She turned forward, refusing to look at him.

Dominic turned his head and shouted over his shoulder, "Thanks, guys."

Having walked past the usual doors that he and other Vatican officials used to expedite their travel by circumventing security and customs and now in a section of the hallway that he was completely unfamiliar with, his attempts at remaining calm were only succeeding on the exterior. Internally his stomach was churning.

The foursome turned round a bend in the hallway that extended for another fifty feet, then ended abruptly, coming to a dead end with no exit in sight.

Tonita must have sensed Dominic's uneasiness and let her hand brush his. She glanced at him. "No door."

"I see that," he said, whispering back.

Their pace slowed as the end of the hall grew closer.

Dominic expected an order to stop them at any moment. Yet none came. And having received no orders from the Secret Service agents behind them to stop, they continued.

Now, ten yards from the end of the hallway, they kept walking.

Five yards. Still no order.

Tonita couldn't take it any longer. "Guys? There's a wall here." She stopped and turned around facing the soldiers. "We can't exactly walk through walls."

"Tonita?" Dominic pulled on her shoulder.

"Well, what? She pulled away from Dominic staring into at the agents. "What are they going to do? Shoot us?"

"No," Dominic said.

Tonita turned back to Dominic. "Then are you going to walk through that wall..." She didn't need to finish.

The wall had slid open.

FORTY SIX

The Novice remained steadfastly seated in the hard-backed, carved wooden chair. He had not moved. Hours upon hours passed after he had discovered that The Jesuit had left him there, alone. Hours spent seated in pain.

The Jesuit had imposed the worst punishment upon the Novice that there could be. That was no punishment at all. He had left the Novice to wallow in his own self-pity and regrets. He had allowed the Novice to sit undisturbed, lost to his thoughts and doubts.

Without guidance from the Jesuit, the Novice had turned to self-mutilation as his punishment for his failure and to redeem his sins. Tears slid down the Novice's face as he silently repented his failure to God. He never let his thoughts deviate from his failure. "Forgive me," his voice dry and rough repeated the words aloud, begging God to hear him. He pressed the muscles of his back and shoulders deeper into the carved crucifix on the chair back. The pain was intense and the wooden carving left a deep impression into his muscles. He grunted as he pushed down as hard as he possibly could onto the armrests of the chair, forcing his back into the carved wood, so much so that it touched bone. He cried out in pain. Blood began to form in droplets around the edges of the impression in his back.

"Forgive me, God. For I desecrate your church!" The Novice screamed out, as he pushed his body back. Suddenly, the back of the chair snapped. The wood splintered, sending the carved relief of the crucifix tearing into his flesh and muscle. Blood oozed from the red swollen skin surrounding the wound and the Novice tilted backwards. Steadying himself, he pushed down onto the armrests of the chair, forcing the stiff muscles of his legs and back to allow him rise. His legs failed him and he began to fall forward. In an attempt to slow the fall, he pushed out with his arms and hands, but they, too, had atrophied from the pressure of his own weight, having sat motionless for many hours.

He collapsed.

His elbows and shoulders hit the floor hard. "My God. My God. Why has thou forsaken me?" he cried out with all the volume his vocal chords could summon, quoting Jesus from his final hours. "Show me no mercy Lord, as I am not worthy." His body heaved, as he gasped for breath, crying. He gained control of his emotions and pulled himself up, arms shaking, sweat glistening from his body. And then on unsteady legs, he tried to stand. He managed to get to his knees. Then, using the seat of the chair, he pushed up. His legs would not support his weight and again he began to crumble.

Out of the darkness, an arm wrapped around the Novice's waist. And then another wrapped around his chest, supporting him, pulling him up. "You have been forgiven," the Jesuit's soft voice whispered into the Novice's ear.

The Novice turned his head to the side and laid it on the Jesuit's shoulder. "Why did you leave me?"

The Jesuit pulled the Novice in closer to his body, using his own body as support to help the Novice stand. He turned the Novice around so that they were face to face. "My son, I have born witness to your punishment. I did not leave you. You were never alone in this room." His voice remained soft and low. He stared into the eyes of the Novice, "I have been here all along."

FORTY SEVEN

It wasn't quite what he had expected, Dominic thought, as he looked into the room beyond the sliding wall. But on second thought, he didn't really know what to expect. He glanced around the once hidden, now exposed, room. It was nothing more than a room. No fancy or high-tech equipment. Not a map, nor a "Mission Impossible" style wall of glass that one could wave an arm about and bring up maps and schematics. No blinking diodes and screens. No bars or bunk beds. No sink, toilet, or drain. Not even a chair. As he took in the contents, or rather the lack of contents of the room, he readied himself, waiting for something to pop out at him.

He looked over his shoulder at the soldiers. They had not moved and offered no advice, no orders. As inconspicuously as he possibly could, he took inventory of the soldiers, noting the earpiece wires hanging from the backs of one ear on each of the men. Both were dressed in the same manner as those who manned the security lines in the public areas of the airport terminal. They had TSA badges sewn onto the black baseball caps covering their short cropped hair. The same badge was displayed on their shirtsleeves and onto the fronts of the crisp, white shirts that fit tightly to their bodies. The shirts were tucked neatly into black pants that fell to a cuff at the top of black-laced, rubber soled shoes. No military boots here. To the casual observer walking through the maze of walkways, halls, and corridors of the old airport, and with the exception of starched white shirts, as opposed to the wrinkled, untucked and unkempt white shirts of the generally talkative Transportation Security Administration agents who manned the lines, these agents would fit in completely, going unnoticed as anything different. Dominic noted that the agents had remained on the outside of the sliding wall, while he and Tonita had been prodded to cross the track that the wall slid on, and they now were on the inside.

"Sorta anticlimactic, don't you think?" Tonita asked as she looked around the room.

"I like it that way." Dominic moved his gaze around the room and up to the ceiling. "Doesn't look like much happens here."

The clicking sound of metal on metal caused both Dominic and Tonita to turn around and come face to face with the barrels of MP5's, raised to shoulder level and pointed directly at them.

"I think I've figured out why the room is empty," Dominic said, as he intertwined his fingers with Tonita's, gripping them tightly. He tried to smile, but it quickly faded. "They obviously don't want us to leave."

***

Tonita moved closer to Dominic, pressing her shoulder against his. She opened her mouth to speak, then closed it when she could not find the words. She closed her eyes as a strange thought crossed her mind, asking if she would hear the shot first or feel the bullet rip into her body first, followed by the sound of the bullet exploding from the gun? She tried to dismiss the gruesome thought and concentrate on something else—like the sound of something scraping and sliding. Stone over...She opened her eyes to the real not imagined-sounds of stone sliding over stone, as the wall, that had slid open to reveal the room inside, was now slowly closing.

"I don't think they're going to shoot," Dominic said, releasing Tonita's hand from his grip. He wiped his sweaty palm on the leg of his pants.

The Third Hour

The wall continued sliding easily on the narrow track.

Once the wall had finally closed completely, Tonita breathed again. "That was fun. What more do you have in store for us?"

"Like I knew that was going to happen." Dominic moved to the sliding wall, inspecting it. "This is ingenious really. Walking down that hallway, I doubt anyone would realize that it can move." He lay face down onto the floor, peering into the slight crack between the floor, the track, and the wall. "Look, whoever designed this even put in base molding that slides along with the wall."

"Remind me to tell Bob Villa."

"I'm just saying that it's really pretty ingenious."

"Oh. And so is being trapped in a room with no window and no doors."

"There's a door."

"Well then, go ahead and open it...if you think the soldiers and those big guns on the other side are gone." Tonita walked around the room letting her hand slide over the marble tiled walls. "What the hell is this?"

"I think someone is trying to keep us and does not want us to discover something."

Tonita stopped, turned around, and stared at Dominic. "What? Please tell me that you not telling me the obvious?"

"Look. Sorry. But I'm just as scared as you are. And I'm just talking out loud to calm our nerves."

"Well, actually, you're getting on mine," Tonita said, as she turned back and continued to slide her hand over the marble walls.

"All right. Let's look at this logically," Dominic said. "The soldiers or secret service, or whatever they are, could have just shot us. But they didn't. They could have searched us for weapons. They didn't. They could have taken away our documents."

Richard Devin

"They didn't," Tonita repeated for him. "I get the picture. Someone wants to detain us and knows that we're no threat to them."

"Right."

"So this someone could be a friend?"

"Right."

"We're just being held here while this friend is where?"

"I don't know."

"Waiting for what?"

"I don't know."

"But you think that this friend is on his way?"

"That's what I'm thinking." Dominic leaned against the wall. "Either that or we could die here and no one would ever know?"

FORTY EIGHT

"They have been contained." Inspector Carrola stepped into the cool room and closed the door behind him.

"There has been no harm done to them, I trust?" The question came from the weak old man lying face down on the bed. He struggled to raise his head from the pillow and face the inspector. "Come closer. I cannot see you."

Inspector Carrola stepped around the intravenous stand and the beeping machinery full of lines and tubing running to and from the man, and came alongside of the bed. "We expected the Jesuit to prevent them from leaving, but the Key is resourceful."

"They will not stop until he is dead." The patient coughed. "It has taken us many years, my friend, to build the trust of the few, and now we are nearly able to expose the truth."

"If God be willing."

"And the church."

"We have friends." Inspector Carrola placed his hand on the old man's arm.

"We are old and weak."

"But we have God. He is on our side."

"That is what the other side thinks too." The old man coughed several times. He placed his face into the pillow. When the coughing stopped, he continued, "Do we know after these sixty years whose side God is on? I am nearly defeated and yet the Jesuit appears strong. If it is he who is strongest, who will win? Then where is our God?" He coughed again, arching in pain.

"Cardinal, you must rest," Inspector Carrola said, while pushing a small button on the tip of a long cord, silently summoning the nurse.

The door to the hospital room opened even before Inspector Carrola had released his finger from the button. "Inspector? Cardinal Celent?" The stout nurse asked as she glanced at the beeping machinery and the zigzagging lines on the monitors.

"I will be leaving now." He looked to Cardinal Celent then back to the nurse. "Someone must be with him always."

"I will be here, Inspector," the nurse said nodding.

"Good," he said a little too sharply, then added. "And thank you, nurse."

"Cardinal, are you in pain?" The nurse adjusted a dial on the heart monitor and watched the lines spike up and down. "Maybe some medicine to ease that?"

"There is no medicine that can ease the pain of my deceit," Cardinal Celent said.

"It was necessary. Dominic will understand when this is done," Inspector Carrola said from the doorway.

"You are right, of course."

"If we had not told him that you had died, he would have remained here looking for answers."

"The answers were buried sixty years ago."

"And he will succeed in finding them."

Cardinal Celent raised his head from the pillow. "Go. I will be fine," he said, as the pain medication took control and he drifted into sleep and the memories of long ago.

Bill Celent hit the ground hard. He rolled, fell two feet down an embankment, landed on top of a rock the size of a basketball, slid off of the rock, scraped a knee, and finally came to a stop on his back. He gasped as the air was forced out of his lungs and into the atmosphere. He sucked in as much air as he could, but his diaphragm and lungs would not cooperate and he could not catch his breath. His arm, scratched by the dry, sunbaked desert crust, bled from his shoulder to his elbow. His head throbbed and his ribs ached. He touched his side, applying the slightest amount of pressure, and a searing pain shot through him. He closed his eyes, allowing the haze in his mind to disappear and waited out the pain. Slowly the pain in his side faded, as his lungs began to fill and an even rhythm to his breathing returned. Cautiously he sucked in oxygen with quick shallow breaths, allowing his lungs to fill. Then exhaled slowly. He repeated the processes of quick breaths and long exhales until his body relaxed and his muscles responded. Then he opened his eyes.

A sky, slightly darkened and overcast with scattered clouds, filled the panorama of his sight. He blinked away the slight dizziness behind his eyes and fought back the nausea gnawing at his stomach. Bill slowly raised an arm up to his head, running a hand through his hair and lightly massaged his scalp. He brought his hand to his face. No blood. Then he moved his arm back down to his side, anticipating the pain at his rib cage to return. It didn't. Good. Bruised, a little bloodied, but not broken, he thought.

He pushed off of the small rocks and stones that covered the ground he had landed on and raised up slightly. "Oow!" he spoke out loud. "That hurt." He brushed the dirt and small embedded pebbles from his skin and clothes, and took in his surroundings. The desert, just like it should be, Bill thought.

He stood, pushing up on shaky knees and dusted off the fabric of the thin gray jump suit meant to protect him from possible radiation exposure and heat. The suit may very well have done a great job on the heat and radiation, but it was terrible at stopping rocks. The legs of the jump-suit were torn, allowing bare bloody skin to show through.

A flap of the gray shiny material at his chest was nearly gone. He finished brushing away the dust and picked at the desert thorn brush that had become attached to the torn and frayed fabric. He stretched, and feeling only a slight ache in his side, started off toward a high outcropping of gray brown stone.

The loose stone and gravel slipped under his weight, creating small avalanches that tumbled down the side of the embankment as he scrambled up. Bill fell to one knee, and slid down several feet. He cursed the pain in his side that had been growing, aggravated by the climb, and regained his footing. A few well-placed steps and he reached the top.

Bill stood looking north. The land in the distance was arid desert, covered with brown, shrub brushes, low growing trees with snarled snake like branches, and dry washes, that would fill during a storm and flow like a river for several hours after a downpour. They were now empty of water, filled only with desert debris. A hot breeze kicked up, scented with the slight briny smell of salt.

Odd, he thought.

He turned around slowly, carefully, taking in the vast open land. His foot loosened a stone and it tumbled down the hill, hitting others on the way, scaring up a large-eared fox from its den. The fox darted down the hill into a nearby ravine. Bill watched as the fox, with its large oversized ears, disappeared from sight. Then a moment later, popped its head up from behind a brush and stared back at Bill. When he seemed secure that Bill was no threat, the fox darted back to his den.

Bill steadied himself on his precarious perch, checked his footing, and continued to turn around. "Oh my God," he said out loud knowing that it would be only himself and to the heavens that would hear. And then there were no words. He stood dumbfounded, opened mouthed. What he saw before him could not be. He closed his eyes for a moment, thinking that he may have hit his head harder than he had thought. When he opened his eyes again, the vision remained. He believed *that he had returned to the desert just as he was meant to. That the experiment had gone as planned. But now he realized that it did not. He was not where he was supposed to be. What lie before him could not be. And yet it was.*

Not fifty yards in the distance, a mass of people chanting, screaming, crying out, mixed into others that were laughing and dancing gleefully, all flowing from an arched gate in a large stone wall. They surrounded a group of soldiers surging around and in between them. Scuffles broke out among the crowd as some of the soldiers pushed at them, shoving some to the ground, chasing and hauling others away, as they cleared a path for the object of their furor and ridicule. In the center of rock strewn, dirt roadway, a small thin man carrying his burden walked slowly and deliberately on the path in the space created for him by the soldiers. His body bent forward under the weight of the heavy timber upon his shoulder. He stumbled, losing his balance briefly, paused, then regained his footing and continued on, only to fall to his knee two steps later. The crowd of onlookers spat at the man when he stumbled, pelting him with stones and whipping him with palm fronds as he struggled to rise again. A dark-skinned man standing along the side of the roadway where the road met a steep cliff, stepped forward to aid the fallen man with his burden. Before the dark-skinned man could reach him, other angry men in the crowd rushed forward and shoved him back away from the man who remained on his knees, pushing and shoving until the dark-skinned man was at the edge of the road and too near the steep sides, to fight back. The dark-skinned man brushed his hand over his torn clothing and looked back to the pained figure lying upon the roadway. The fallen man regained his strength and took to his feet pulling himself up and hosting the wooden beam back upon his shoulders. The masses, that had only moments ago jeered and spat upon the man, kicking at him and throwing stones at him, now cheered and urged that same man forward.

Bill studied the path, taking in the entire route from the large arched gate in the stone wall to the crowd and the place where the man had stumbled, risen and was now walking. He looked beyond the man and the onlookers, following the well-worn road to a small hill that rose up from the roadway and leveled off to a plateau. An outcropping of rock on the side of the hill jutted out becoming rounded along the top of the hill and came together at odd angles toward the bottom before falling off to a valley below. The sun, now hanging above the horizon, but not yet near its pinnacle, cast light and shadows upon the rock. It highlighted the ridges and deepened the pockets and the shadows where the sun's light could not reach. Bill gasped as his eyes and mind transformed the light and shadows, the ridges and the pockets, into that of a face upon the rock. Then with sudden realization, Bill saw that the wind and water carved face was not a face at all. It was a skull.

He quickly turned his gaze back to the crowd. He took in the soldiers and the man with the heavy wooden beam hoisted upon his shoulder, now struggling to make his way up the path to the top of the hill and the plateau above the skull-faced rock.

And then he saw them. Not slim trees as he had first thought them to be. But stakes. Three stakes standing tall, firmly planted into the ground above the skull rock, two were complete.

And the third stood empty.

Waiting.

FORTY NINE

Tonita woke to the hushed sounds of a male voice whispering. Her cramped arm lay under her and the cold marble tiles of the secret room's floor chilled her entire right side. She pulled her arm out from beneath her body's weight, raised herself up and leaned back against the wall.

Dominic stood in the center of the room, his back to Tonita. His hands were pressed together and his head bowed down. He spoke quietly, "Oh Saint Joseph, whose protection is so great, so strong, so prompt before the throne of God, I place in you all my interest and desires. Oh Saint Joseph, do assist me by your powerful intercession and obtain for me from your divine Son all spiritual blessings through Jesus Christ, our Lord. So that, having engaged here below your heavenly power, I may offer my thanksgiving and homage to the most Loving of Fathers." Dominic raised his head to the ceiling of the room, reflected, and then continued, "Oh Saint Joseph, I never weary contemplating you, and Jesus asleep in your arms; I dare not approach while He reposes near your heart. Press Him in my name and kiss His fine head for me, and ask Him to return the kiss when I draw my dying breath." Dominic moved his hand to his forehead, then his chest, then to his left shoulder, finishing the sign of the cross at his right shoulder. "Saint Joseph, Patron of departed souls, pray for me."

Tonita shuffled in her position in a subtle attempt to alert Dominic that she was awake. "Are you praying?" Tonita stood up, sliding her back against the wall, while pushing against the floor with her legs.

"I was. Habits of a priest are hard to break."

And you're a priest again?" She walked toward Dominic.

Dominic glared at her. "I've never stopped."

"It's funny how people find salvation when they have no other choice."

"I've always been a priest."

"Hey, you don't have to convince me." Tonita turned away from him slowly, walking in a circle around the room.

"I'm not trying to. And the prayer was not one of salvation. It was a prayer to Saint Joseph asking for strength," he paused and cocked his head, raising his chin up. "Strength in battle."

Tonita looked at him, massaged her still aching arm, and said, "Oh? Battle? As in a battle with our inner demons?" She contemplated pushing him harder, conjuring up those inner demons that Dominic kept so deeply confined, then backed off. Time for revelations later, she thought.

"As in," Dominic sarcastically mocked. "The Pope sent the prayer to the Holy Roman Emperor Charles V in the early fifteen hundreds. It was said that anyone who reads, says, or hears the prayer shall never die by drowning, poison, fire, or be captured by the enemy." Dominic let the words set in, then continued, "I thought we could use it."

"Well, we certainly fit into the 'captured by the enemy' part of that prayer."

Dominic paused. "Were you listening?"

"Kind of."

"Good then. We're both covered." He raised an eyebrow and smiled. "I would hate for you to remain 'captured by the enemy,' when I'm protected by the prayer and get to go free."

"You wouldn't rescue me?"

"Maybe?"

"I get a maybe?"

"Since I got an 'oh, you're a priest again,' yeah. You get a maybe."

"I'm only testing your resolve."

"Dominic, not Abraham."

Tonita shook her head. "What?"

"I'm Dominic, not Abraham."

"I still don't get it."

"Abraham and Isaac. It's the biblical story of Abraham and how he was tested by God, so that God would see what was truly in his heart. God ordered Abraham to take his son Isaac, his only son, to a mountain and slit his throat, then burn him as a sacrifice."

"And you are not like Abraham?"

"Not in the—I would do whatever God commanded without question, area. You should know that by now. Abraham did not question God's words and set out to sacrifice his beloved son. I, on the other hand, question everything that God asks of me." Dominic paused, looked up. "Is there not room for both; those who obey without question and those who question before they obey? Isn't God testing us all in different ways to see what is truly in each of our hearts?"

"Spoken like a true priest." Tonita moved closer to Dominic and stared into his eyes.

"Maybe?" he said.

She smiled, then wrapped her arms around him, burying her face in his chest. "Dominic, I'm scared."

Dominic engulfed her with his arms and pulled her in as close as he could. "I would be lying if I said that I wasn't."

"Let's just get out of this room and go someplace where no one will bother us. Where we won't be looking for something, and no one will be looking for us. We could live in a nice quiet little town in the country somewhere. Where there are woods and fields...and a canal."

"A canal?"

"We could move to Perinton," Tonita said, clapping her hands together.

"Where the hell is Perinton?"

"In western New York somewhere. I saw an article on it in a magazine on the plane. It's a quiet town in the hills with creeks and trains and..."

"And I know...a canal."

"Right."

"And we're just going to move there? Run away?"

Tonita let her arms fall away from Dominic and took a step back. "Isn't that what you've been doing all along?"

Dominic closed his eyes and breathed in and out deeply. He opened his eyes and looked into Tonita's. "Is that what you think?"

Tonita began to step toward him, then stopped. "Dominic, you left the states after seminary, moved to Italy, joined a church, left a church, and hid in Rome from yourself and from the church. Now, you're running again, this time chasing after some mystery."

"I didn't ask to get involved in this."

Tonita took that step toward him. "I'm not saying it's wrong, what you're doing. But you've got to admit that..." She let her voice trail off.

"Admit what?"

"It's just kind of strange that Cardinal Celent and the church wanted you."

Dominic laughed. "Why is that strange? Am I such a bad choice?"

"Dominic? You don't even believe in God."

"Why would you say that?" Dominic turned away from her. "I believe in ..." he began, then stopped. He walked to a corner of the room, leaned his head against the wall, and remained silent for several minutes. Dominic turned back to Tonita.

"I've always had my doubts. That's why I joined the church." He paused, sighed then let the words out. "And that's why I took a sabbatical from the church. I think God is there. Sometimes, I know he's there. When I look at all the church has. All the wealth, the power—hell, the church was a government for the longest time and maybe still is. That's when I doubt God exists. That's when I think that God is just an invention of man to keep other men in their place. To keep me in my place."

"And where is that, Dom? Where is your place?"

Dominic ran a hand through his hair, pushing it off his face. "I don't know," he said, his voice choking. "Maybe I have no place. Maybe it's me they're afraid of. Tonita, did you ever think that I might be the bad guy here. And that the good guys are trying to kill me. And that I'm the one being protected by evil?"

"No, Dom. I've never thought that."

"Do you mean that?"

"Of course I mean it. If anyone would know, I would know if you were one of the bad guys."

"How? How could you know?"

Tonita remained silent. The smile on her face faded and she turned away from him.

"You don't know," he said, walking away from Tonita. He faced a corner of the room, his back to her and hers to him. "You don't know and neither do I." He turned around staring at the back of her. "And you know what Tonita? God doesn't know either."

FIFTY

"Golgotha." Bill said the word aloud. "Golgotha," he said it again, as if he didn't believe it the first time.

Something was wrong. Very wrong. He wasn't supposed to be here. Bill thought back, retracing his actions and the course of events that led up to the countdown.

All systems were a go. There were no warning signals. All fail-safes were green and working. The crew had been locked in and the capsule was set.

He clearly remembered hearing the end of the countdown through the small speaker mounted inside the capsule. Seven...six...five...four...three...two. Odd, he thought. He couldn't recall hearing the countdown to one. But he must have as he was here, near the rock at Golgotha, he considered. Not where he was supposed to be in the desert of New Mexico, but here.

He rubbed his hands over his face and shook his head and body. But the result was the same. He could not deny that he was standing outside of the Damascus Gate of old Jerusalem, some two thousand years in the past. And he was now witnessing the procession that would bring a man to the cross. As the reality of the time and place hit him, he whispered, "Oh my God. Oh my God. What have we done?" And for an instant, he thought he saw the man burdened by the heavy wooden beam, mocked and spat upon, bleeding and tired, pause in his steps.

No one else. Not a Roman centurion, not a priest or peasant or pilgrim or child had taken notice of Bill standing upon a desert embankment beyond the ridge from the path that led in and out of the gate. Not one in the crowd had noticed him, except the one man that all others' eyes were upon. This one man, who could not *have heard the words that Bill spoke above the chanting, scolding rants of the crowd, and the distance, yet he turned. He raised his head and this one man those in the crowd were calling Jesus Christ, looked directly in Bill's direction.*

FIFTY ONE

The muffled click of an electric motor starting up caught Dominic's attention. He cocked his head to the side to listen.

"Dom? What?" Tonita took a step toward him.

He held up his hand. "Wait."

A second later the sliding wall began to move.

Tonita moved quickly to Dominic's side, allowing her hand to slide into his as she did so. She looked to him, "They're back," she said, using the same tone as the little girl in the "Poltergeist" movie.

Dominic shook his head and squeezed her fingers together in his hand, "Quiet."

The wall slid, nearly silent, along the track embedded in the floor. Only the faint "hum" of the electric motor hidden behind the thick masonry walls gave away the wall's pending motion.

The wall was midpoint along the track, revealing half of the dimly lit hallway and a portion of an arm. A moment later, the wall had cleared the figure. A lone man stood.

"I'm sorry to have kept you waiting. My old legs do not move as fast as they once did," Senator Scott said, turning around and taking a step back down the long hallway. He turned back to Dominic and Tonita. "Do you wish to remain in that room or will you be coming along?"

A moment of indecision, and then Tonita spoke up, "No. We're coming," she said, pushing ahead of Dominic. She high-stepped over the track as if the wall might come suddenly slamming back.

Dominic laughed, stepping out of the room as the wall reversed direction and started to close.

Tonita glared at him. "Not so funny now."

"Yeah, if I were a snail."

Dominic and Tonita caught up easily to Senator Scott who had continued down the hallway.

"The traffic on the way in was just horrendous. And then the airport in D.C. was a mess. You've been to Washington before haven't you?" He turned to Dominic.

"No, I'm afraid not," Dominic said, shooting a quick glare to Tonita behind the Senator's back.

"Well, you really must come sometime. Be my guest. Both of you. I'll take you on a tour of the place personally," Senator Scott continued, "I have a bit of experience in the D.C. area, you know."

Tonita glanced quickly at Dominic. "Well honestly sir, we don't know."

Senator Scott stopped. "I'm sorry. That was foolish of me. Of course you don't." He moved the cane in his right hand to his left. Then, completing the switch, he extended his right hand. "My name is Ray Scott. Senator Scott."

"Well, Senator, thank you for coming to get us." Dominic extended his hand to the Senator. Were you sent by the Vatican?"

Senator Scott motioned forward with his cane. "No, my boy. It wasn't the Vatican. No not the Vatican." He stepped forward, continuing the long walk down the hall. "Let me just say that it was a friend."

"A friend of mine, Senator?"

"Of course."

"Or would I be off saying a friend of yours?"

"You are very smart to draw the distinction." Senator Scott picked up the pace. "There are many times in my career that I wish I had asked the same question. Perhaps, then we would not be in the position we are today."

"And that position?"

"I'm here to give you aid, my son. I am both the friend of your friend's and a friend of yours."

"I am sure that you are..." Dominic began.

"But you doubt," Senator Scott cut him off. "As I'm sure that I would if I were in your place. You are here and I am here...to help you. Just as I'm sure your friend," he glanced at Tonita, "is here to do."

Tonita smiled at the Senator.

A smile that caused Dominic to hesitate.

"I'm sorry about the room back there, but we needed to keep you until I arrived. I hope that you were not too uncomfortable. We don't use that holding cell..." Senator Scott looked quickly in the direction of Tonita and Dominic. "I mean room, much. It's practically forgotten. I hope that the Secret Service did not frighten you?"

"Secret Service, Tonita," Dominic gloated.

Senator Scott stopped at a door about fifty yards from the hidden room. He looked back down the hallway toward the hidden room noting that the wall has closed completely. And once again, the hall looked as though it came to an abrupt end. "We go through here," he said, gesturing to the door.

Dominic looked in the opposite direction of the hidden room, scanning the length of the hall, then turned his gaze down the hallway following the Senator's. He returned to the door that they were now standing in front of. The metal encased door was void of any markings. No red painted warnings of impending alarms and arrest were apparent, should anyone venture through, and no numbers. Dominic thought back and could not remember the door when he and Tonita had been prodded along by the Secret Service. There were several others along the hallway that he did remember seeing. They were all clearly marked with warnings. Perhaps, that's why he missed this one. It just was not as noticeable, he concluded.

"Shall we?" Senator Scott motioned in the direction of the door.

The Third Hour

Dominic pushed on the bar that was bolted into the door, running perpendicular to the floor. The protruding bar slid into the base and the latch clicked. With the door open only an inch or two, the acrid smell of jet fuel gusted in and the roaring sound of jet engines assaulted their ears.

Senator Scott raised his voice above the noise of the revving aircraft engine, "Our ride."

FIFTY TWO

Cardinal Celent's eyes popped open. For a moment, he wasn't sure where he was. The peep of the nearby cardiac monitor and the intravenous tube running from the back of his hand up to the clear liquid filled bag, brought him back fully awake. The lighting in the room had been dimmed. The curtains drawn. He looked around for a clock, but found none. He checked the LCD windows on each of the many pieces of electronic equipment in the room for a digital display of the time. And again, found none.

He closed his eyes, took in a deep breath and then exhaled. His heart was racing with the memories that filled his dreams. He fought to slow his pulse and gain control of his thoughts and emotions, just as he had done that Wednesday so many years ago.

***

The air was clear that July day in 1947. A fierce storm was brewing in the distance and threatened to delay the experiment. The desert smelled clean with just a hint of ozone lingering on the breeze.

"How are you feeling?" Ray Scott came up alongside of Bill. The young director of the experiment dressed in a crisp white shirt, black rimmed glasses, and slicked back dark hair, looked every bit the part of a government employee.

"Nervous. Anxious. Scared." Bill listed.

"Don't be," Ray said in response, patting Bill on the back. "We've got it all under control."

Bill raised an eyebrow, smiled, and said, "Would you like to trade places?"

Ray slapped Bill on the back again. "Sure would like to. But you know I'm not the man for this job." He looked at the jumpsuit Bill was wearing. "I'm not much for shiny gray jumpsuits either." He laughed.

"How's it looking?"

"Like a man wrapped in tin foil."

Bill shook his head, then motioned toward the four large generators surrounding the thick metal building. "The experiment. How's that looking? Not me."

"All's a go."

The two men circled the small building, carefully stepping over and around the multitude of cables that ran from the generators about twenty five yards away from the building. Thick metal walls surrounded a small inner chamber that severed as the cockpit.

"Gentlemen," air force pilot, Lynda Lee said, as she stepped out of the cockpit.

"Well, I must say that you look better in shiny gray than this old man does." Ray jabbed his fist at Bill.

Bill ignored him, as did Lynda.

"All is well?" Bill took control of the situation turning his attention to the experiment about to take place. "Ray says 'all is go.'" He looked quickly in Ray's direction for confirmation. Ray shook his head. "You're all set then?" He turned back to Lynda.

"I'm ready. Everything's locked up and secure."

Bill picked up one of the three-inch thick cables and traced its length back to the generators. He tugged on it, then let it drop back to the ground.

"We've learned a lot from the Eldridge," Lynda said. "We'll have more control with a land based experiment. The ocean waters and the salinity levels were just too unpredictable and unstable." She nodded in the direction of a large tanker truck heading their way. "We better get out of his way."

Lynda, Bill, and Ray took several steps back as the tanker pulled along one side of the building, while another tanker stopped along the back. A trench forty feet in circumference and three feet in depth had been

Richard Devin

dug around the metal building and lined with a thin glossy metal-like plastic film.

"Lynda is right," Albert Einstein came up behind the group, and continued with the explanation. "We have learned from the tragic mistakes of the past. But that is science. We must fail many times before we succeed. But this will work, I am sure of it. You see, in order to conduct the proper amounts of electrical current to and through the building, the trench will be filled with salt water trucked in from the Great Salt Lake in Utah. The salinity content of the ocean is maintained at 3.5%, and that is where we failed with the Eldridge. The water from the Great Salt Lake has salinity content at 26% or better. The greater salinity is needed to conduct the proper amount of electrical current." Einstein's German accent gave the explanation a tone of authority.

"And we closely monitored the thickness and content of the metal here," Lynda picked up the explanation. "We didn't build the Eldridge so we had no control ..."

"Or knowledge, actually," Einstein interjected.

"True," Lynda continued. "Of the strength or nature of the metal used in the ship."

"Here we had total control." Einstein gave a nod to Ray. "And it will work."

"Still, all in all, the Eldridge was a worthy experiment, even if we did not get the results we had hoped for," Ray added.

"Let's just hope that we are better with this than with the Eldridge," Bill said. "I'll be in that thing."

"No need to hope, sir," Einstein said. "We are." Without another word he moved off to the control station set up inside a metal plate-fronted flatbed truck.

"Lynda? Bill? We're ready," U.S. Air Force Commander, Kupovits said as he joined them.

"Well then," Ray raised his voice giving it a carnival barker's tone. "Good luck." He stuck his hand out.

Bill took his hand, shaking it. "Thanks."

"Good luck, Lynda. Keep these two in line." Ray wrapped an arm around her.

"I will."

Ray stepped back. "Commander, it's all yours now." Ray nodded to the metal building.

"I'll take good care of it."

"You better. It cost us a pretty penny." Ray laughed.

"Is that what small, brown metal buildings in the middle of the desert run now a days? A penny?" Commander Kupovits extended his hand.

The two men shook hands, then Ray moved several yards away from the building and watched as Bill Celent, air force pilot, Lynda Lee and air force Commander Kupovits entered the building.

Bill turned and gave a wave as two men pushed on the door. It swung slowly on three, foot long metal hinges, closing with a soft whimper. One man put his weight against the door, while the other spun a two foot, diameter wheel attached to the outside of the thick metal door, causing the inner latch to seal the door tight.

The men moved away and an instant later the two tanker trucks began to dump the water from the Great Salt Lake into the trench. Almost immediately, the salt water began to react with the metallic plastic film, etching geometric lines, like crystallized snowflakes, onto the surface.

Ray Scott climbed up the four steps of the ladder to the flatbed truck, taking a position alongside Einstein.

Once the tanker trucks were emptied, the drivers moved the trucks off and the area around the brown metal building was clear.

"We are clear," an airman standing behind Einstein and Ray said, as he placed the binoculars he was looking through down on a table.

"Power up on one," Einstein said, *as he flipped a toggle switch and the first generator powered up. Once the first generator had come online, and had completely powered up, he flipped the switch to the second generator, waited until it had completely powered up and then continued the same process with the third, and finally the fourth generators.*

Once online, the current from each of the generators was sent to a coil of copper tubing that transferred the power to thin copper wire that had been wrapped around a six-inch diameter, ten-foot long magnet. As the current surged through the copper tubing and wiring, an immense magnetic force built around the lead core.

Einstein pulled on a lever, transferring a portion of the electrical current from the number one generator, into the cables attached. The cables led on, connecting to the metallic plastic film that lined the pit, and was now submerged in the salt water. Then, he pulled another lever transferring power from the second generator to the film and continued until the current from all four generators coursed from the copper coils into the metallic film. The salt water filled basin began to churn, and the same greenish fog that had surrounded the Eldridge began to build at the surface of the basin.

Then, without a moment's notice, the green fog expanded from the surface of the churning water, rising up and swirling around the building, as if a stationary tornado had come down from storm clouds above. The fog whipped around the building in frenzy, becoming so thick that the outline of the building was lost. Then, in a blinding flash the sky, lit up, followed by a loud crack that split the air, as if lightning had struck only inches away. Just as suddenly as it had begun, the fog dissipated and fell back to the surface of the water.

The Third Hour

The air around the basin cleared, revealing an empty space where the experimental building with its three occupants had been.

Einstein was left with only one word. "Gone."

FIFTY THREE

Within moments of boarding the SAAB 350B turbo prop, the aircraft was taxiing down the runway, picking up speed.

Dominic and Tonita had just snapped the seatbelt latch into the metal holder, when the plane lifted off at an angle toward the heavens.

Unlike commercial flights, there was no announcement offering safety instructions and the reminder to bring seat backs and tray tables upright and into the fully locked position. The interior of the aircraft was more like that of an executive office than that of an airplane.

"This plane reminds me of Air Force One," Tonita said, taking in the opulent interior of the aircraft.

"Really." Dominic looked about the plane. "And you've been on Air Force One?"

Tonita glared at him. "Pictures, stupid."

"Oh," Dominic said, a bit embarrassed.

"Dom, I really wonder about you." Tonita shook her head.

Senator Scott pushed down on the lever attached to the side of his seat and swiveled the cream colored, leather chair around, coming face to face with Dominic and Tonita. "We have been experimenting for a very long time," he began, without any preamble. "You have no doubt heard about many of the experiments that we have conducted into time travel."

"Well, honestly, Senator, no." Dominic shrugged. "I don't know much about any experiments." He turned his head counting the rows from the front of the plane to the nearest emergency exit, a habit he had when flying, and then to the back of the plane, making a mental note of the dark teak stained door marked 'lavatory' behind the last few seats. "Cardinal Celent did say something about Roswell and an experiment there, but that's it. And everyone has heard of Roswell." Dominic immediately felt foolish and internally chastised himself for the comment.

Senator Scott cocked his head and squinted his eyes slightly, looking at Dominic. "Yes, well, that is not quite true. Everyone may have heard about Roswell and the aliens who crashed there, but they don't know the truth behind it. You see, Roswell was the result of an experiment, not exactly the experiment itself."

"Result?" Dominic glanced at Tonita.

"So Roswell is not a crash site?" Tonita asked shrugging her shoulders.

"Then why go there?" Dominic's tone was matter of fact. "I'm sure you know, Senator, that Cardinal Celent had shown us a book on Roswell before he died."

"I did not know that."

"I'm confused, Senator. Forgive me, but if a friend has sent you...?"

"You have every right Dominic," Senator Scott said cutting Dominic off. "You don't know me and you should question why I'm here." He inhaled heavily. "We are people of secrets, you see. I have secrets that I have kept, even from those closest to me. Like Bill," he hesitated, "I mean of course, Cardinal Celent. I can assure you that he has secrets he too must keep even from me. It is safer that way. The truth is a terrible burden when you must keep it all. We share in keeping parts of the truth so that no one will bear the entire burden."

"And what is that truth?" Dominic leaned forward in his seat.

"I'm afraid that I am only able to help you find it. I cannot tell you of it."

"Why?"

"Because you would not believe me. No one would. The truth cannot be told—it must be learned." Senator

Scott stared into Dominic's eyes. "I am here to help you find that truth, but you must trust in me, as Cardinal Celent and God have done for more than sixty years."

"We found a page in the book on Roswell that we believe is a map." Dominic looked back at Tonita and was confronted with a look of confusion. Maybe, he thought, that he had been too quick to trust the man.

"I am aware of the book that Cardinal Celent spoke to you about, I have read it. But I must confess that I was not aware of a map hidden inside that the book."

Tonita cleared her throat, causing Dominic to look at her again. "I don't think that the map was placed in all the books printed."

"Tonita's right. I think Cardinal Celent put the map there." Dominic sat back and glanced out the window at the moisture laden clouds below.

"Well, it's not really much of map, Senator," Tonita offered.

Tonita was being cautious, Dominic thought deciding that it might be a better course for the moment. "Yes, more of a drawing..." Dominic began.

"May I see it?" Senator Scott did not wait for Dominic to finish speaking. He extended his hand to neither Tonita nor Dominic, but instead, between them.

Dominic's face registered the internal battle. He looked quickly to the sky, "I am Abraham," he said.

Tonita placed a hand gently onto Dominic's and smiled reassuringly.

Dominic reached inside his pocket and pulled out the page that he had removed from the book. He looked at it briefly, before handing it to the Senator.

Senator Scott took the page and carefully inspected one side. He held it up to the light and then turned it over, giving the other side the same attention.

"The lines were not there when we found the page in the book that Cardinal Celent had given us."

"Shown to us really," Tonita added. "He didn't give us the book. We took it," she said, knowing very well that she was not being honest with the Senator as Cardinal Celent was very clear on their taking the book with them.

"I'm sure that the Cardinal wanted us to have the book, or at least this page from it. He made of point of finding the book and showing it to us," Dominic offered in explanation, giving Tonita a quizzical look.

"I'm sure you are correct Dominic," Senator Scott spoke without taking his eyes from the page. "Cardinal Celent wanted you to know of the importance of this book. This page. It must have been very important to him to have kept the secret even from me."

"The page was no different than the others in the book, just another page of text, a little thicker than the other pages. That's all. But that's what caught my attention."

Senator Scott shook his head up and down, continuing with his examination of the page. "Why do you call it a map?" After several minutes of close scrutiny, Senator Scott asked, "It does not have any notations or landmarks on it. And I can find no key to explain the lines."

"We don't honestly know that it is a map," Tonita said.

"It just looks like it should be," Dominic added.

Senator Scott exhaled heavily. "A map to where?"

"Or what?" Tonita said.

Both Dominic and Senator Scott turned in her direction.

"Very good, Tonita," Senator Scott said. "This could be a map of something not to something." He turned the page around and over, inspecting the lines for some other clue. "You said that this was in the book on Roswell and that the page did not look like this when you found it."

"Right. It was in the book, looking like just one of the pages of the book. Text was the same. The history of Roswell was written on the page continuing the story from the page before." Dominic mimed the book in his hand. "As I flipped through the book in Cardinal Celent's apartment, I noticed that the page, well, a page, I wasn't sure which at the time, felt different."

"And you tore it out?"

"Not then, in the Cardinal's apartment. But, yes. I tore it out," Dominic answered the Senator's question.

"But you said it did not look like this." Senator Scott manipulated the page between his fingers.

"Right."

"And how did it..." Senator Scott hesitated. "Change?"

Dominic looked to Tonita to answer when she didn't—he spoke, "We put it in water."

"So then the ink washed from the page?"

"Yes."

Senator Scott let out a small laugh. "My friend, the Cardinal is using some old tricks," he said, continuing to laugh. "We used that ink many times during our experiments to hide pertinent information from those around us. There were many involved in the experiments that we did not want to know the truth about what we were doing. It was a simple enough way to cover up the documents. After all, no one would dare place a document stamped, "Top Secret," into water. We were fairly secure in the deception." He unsnapped the seatbelt and adjusted his position in the chair. "As a matter of fact, no one ever discovered it."

"What were you hiding?" Tonita sat up in her chair and like the Senator, unsnapped the seatbelt.

"Hiding isn't exactly the word I'd use. More like protecting. But whatever words you choose to describe the act, we did not want many to know." Senator Scott stared at Dominic, then directly into Tonita's eyes. "We still don't. You are among the very few who will know the truth."

FIFTY FOUR

Bill Celent was stunned. He felt his face flush, sweat beaded above his lips and down his back. His stomach churned. His legs threatened to give.

The procession before him continued on. The man, Christ, carrying the large wooden beam faltered, tumbled forward, regained his balance, and then fell again. The gathered crowd chanted in mockery of him. They surrounded him before the centurions pushed at them with shields and muscled arms, forcing them away. Christ tried to rise to his feet, but his legs were too weak and he fell to the side. The wood beam slipped from his shoulder, landing at the feet of a Roman guard. Christ slowly pulled himself up, first to his knees, then to his feet. He was panting, bleeding, nearly drained of life, but he found the strength to take another strained step. The Roman guard picked the wooden beam up and placed it gently upon Christ's shoulder. Christ looked into the eyes of the man then turned back to the street and the path before him. The Roman guard backed away and was lost to the crowd.

A scream of agony caught Bill's attention and he turned from the procession, looking to the top of the hill. Three stakes had been positioned in close proximity to one another at the pinnacle. Two had already been assembled with the six-foot wooden beam secured in place, and upon them each, a man was bound. One of the men screamed out again, words Bill could not make out, but the man's anger and vehemence was evident.

Bill was drawn to the crowd, to the spectacle, and to the man he believed was Jesus Christ. He took a step, moving down the small embankment toward the hill, the crowd, and the crucifixion. Then he caught himself and stopped. His mind raced with thoughts about the time space continuum, the time ripple effect, and the effect his being at the crucifixion of Christ would have upon time and history. He contemplated his next move. His head grew light, and he sat down as his breathing quickened.

Bill closed his eyes, relaxed, and breathed in and out slowly, until he felt in control once again. Now, he had to make some choices. It was clear that the experiment in the desert of New Mexico had not gone as planned.

Once the generators had been powered up, the electrical charge would cycle, magnetize the metal-sheathed building, and like the Eldridge a time warp would open. That was what was hoped for anyway. Apparently, that did not happen, and Bill stood quickly, turning on his feet, staring out at the horizon and to the place he had...well, landed. He couldn't think of a better word. Slowly, he allowed his eyes to follow the ridges, ravines and rock outcroppings, searching the shadows and the hills.

It wasn't there.

The experimental building, the capsule, was nowhere in sight. Perhaps, he thought, that it did not travel with him and had remained in New Mexico. Only he, Lynda, and Commander Kupovits were propelled through time. It didn't make sense, he thought, for him to be here. The capsule and the others must be here as well. Of course, the metal building had been camouflaged with splashes of dark brown, sandy brown, and light green paint to keep it hidden in the New Mexico desert from overhead low flying aircraft and the occasional rancher that might stumble by in pursuit of a lost calf or sheep. Now, that camouflage of paint and color made it impossible to locate the building in the desert of ancient Israel.

If it was here at all.

"Ancient Israel," Bill whispered, and he felt almost giddy. He was caught between extreme fear, overwhelming joy, and absolute confusion. Would time now be changed forever because he was where he should not be? Or is time only justified by the memory of humans? Would the donkeys that were ridden upon or the sheep that followed, being led to a slaughter as sacrifice know any different end now that Bill had stumbled into time? He could not shake the thought that his being here, at the crucifixion of Christ, would only change time if people in his time knew that he had traveled back in time. Bill thought of the saying of the falling tree in the woods making a sound or no sound if no one was there to hear it, and reformatted the question to suit himself. If a man travels in time and no one knows of it, did he really move back or forward in time? Could he change time that does not yet exist? What if time only exists in our minds, and thus, can only be changed by our own thoughts and perceptions?

The chant of the distant crowd echoed throughout the desert ravines and caught Bill's attention, pulling him from his thoughts. He looked back to the crowd and saw that many had now made their way to the hill and had begun climbing the steep path to the top. Christ languished behind, prodded on by Roman soldiers, priests, and peasants.

Bill put aside all thoughts of space, time, the whereabouts of Commander Kupovits, and Lynda. He could not now begin to contemplate what had happened to them, or to the building, or to how he was to return. His only thought now was that he must bear witness to one of the greatest events in recorded history. He would be the only living witness to this event and he would be the only man alive who could tell the world that Christ was a man, just a man, put to death with two others who were also, just men. Not gods, not prophets, not divine...only men. Once he returned to his place in time, he would be able to spread the truth and dispel the stories, myths, and fantasies of the many men who would later write of this event, and of their relationship with Christ. Men who wrote to satisfy their own desire for eternity. Once he returned, the world would know the truth.

Then the thought struck him.

If he returned.

FIFTY FIVE

"I'm afraid that we are on our own for this flight. No attendants, you see," Senator Scott continued, "so if there is anything you'd like, we'll have to help ourselves."

"I'm parched," Dominic said, rising. "Want something?" He turned to Tonita.

"Water would be fine."

"You'll find bottles in the refrigerator in the galley." Senator Scott pointed to the box structure, walled off from the rest of the aircraft located by the cockpit door, in the front of the plane.

Dominic hesitated, looked at Tonita. Waited. Then said, "Right. Tonita won't you help me?"

"For a few of bottles of water?" Senator Scott shook his head. "Come on, boy. You can do it."

Dominic made his way to the galley and retrieved several bottles of water from the refrigerator, noting that it was stocked with several bottles of Veuve Clicquot, Guinness beer, and Genesee Cream Ale—an ale he had never heard of. He reached in picked up two bottles of water and a can of the cream ale. He returned to his seat, handing off two of the bottles of water to Tonita and the Senator, keeping the cream ale for himself.

"Ah, a wise choice." Senator Scott nodded in the direction of the cream ale. "A unique beer I discovered somewhere along the way. You'll let me know what you think?"

"In just a minute." Dominic smiled as he popped the tab on the top of the can.

"You have heard of Bermuda Triangle?" Senator Scott said, turning the cap on the bottle of water, breaking the seal.

"Of course." Both Dominic and Tonita spoke.

"Then you have an idea of what our experiments are capable of?"

"I don't follow," Dominic said, after downing nearly half the contents of the can in his hand.

"The Bermuda Triangle is another direct result of the time travel experiments that we've been conducting these many years.

"Those experiments made planes and ships disappear?" Dominic took another swallow from the can. "This is great by the way."

"I thought you might like it. Not easy to find though." Senator Scott watched as the water condensation on the side of the bottle in his hand collected and began to run down the side. "The Triangle is a cover. Well, let me say that the legend of the Bermuda Triangle is a cover story propagated by the governments to cover up the truth."

"Governments?" Tonita wondered aloud.

"At first it was the Russians, masters, you know, of manipulation. We learned how to weave plausible stories around our experiments to hide them from the public." He paused, lost for a moment. "Rasputin was the first. In June of 1908 there was a large explosion over Siberia that destroyed a huge area of land and several villages. No one knows for sure how many people died. But the ground in the impact zone is still contaminated to this day."

"I remember reading that a meteor or an asteroid hit in that area," Dominic interrupted.

"Well, yes, that is the common story. The cover story, if you will. Rasputin was really much ahead of his time, as was Albert Einstein and Werner Von Braun. Rasputin had the ear, and dare I say, more, of the Tsarina Alexandra, and she would do anything for him. She did do anything for him. He convinced her that time travel was possible and that Russia should be the first to recognize this great new technology. And that he was the one who should oversee the experiments. The Tsar Nicholas was less than enthusiastic. At the time there were many troubles brewing in the country and he did not trust Rasputin. Alexandra convinced Tsar Nicholas that the experiments Rasputin was conducting would turn the sentiment of the country in favor of the Tsar, and the people would then rally around her husband. That, as we all know, did not happen."

"They were all assassinated. The entire family, even the children," Dominic added.

"Yes, that is true, but that would not happen for some years after the 1908 experiment. Perhaps, Alexandra was right in thinking that the country needed some great invention—the color-slide projector had been making its rounds in Russia and it was all the talk. Just think what an announcement that the Russians had conducted the first successful time travel experiment would have done?" Senator Scott contemplated his own question. "I don't believe the Russian people of the day would have accepted it, even if the experiment had succeeded. Rasputin built a simple, by today's standards, generator to turn magnetic energy into electricity. We used the same approach, but Einstein was the master at improving the Rasputin method. Rasputin was right on track. But with the vast amounts of unstable nitroglycerin and coal he used to produce the energy needed...well, hindsight is twenty-twenty, they say. If Rasputin could have controlled the detonation of the nitro, burning the coal and turning the combines, he may very well have succeeded. Unfortunately, the nitro could not be controlled and the resulting explosion killed many and scarred the land. Alexandra was devastated when Rasputin returned from Siberia and told her of the failure. It was she who devised a cover story for the destruction. Obviously, Rasputin had his hand in the cover up, as I doubt sincerely that Alexandra would have come up with the meteorite story on her own. That was brilliant really. Ask anyone in the old Soviet Union about the blast in 1908 and you'll hear the same response. A meteorite." Senator Scott sipped from the bottle.

Dominic took the opportunity to ask, "What does the Bermuda Triangle and the ships and planes that have been lost have to do with Rasputin's experiment?"

"Good question," Senator Scott continued, "The ships and planes lost to the Bermuda Triangle were the results of much later experiments."

"By the Russians?" Tonita asked.

"No, no. The Russians have their own missing aircraft and ships in an area they call Kapustin Yar. The Bermuda Triangle legend, however, is a direct result of the experiments carried out by the U.S. government."

"So, the Russians and the U.S. were working together?" Dominic leaned forward in his seat.

"The Russians were the first to experiment with time travel. Rasputin's experiment in the forests of Siberia was the very first large-scale experiment. Of course, as far as we know, both the U.S. and the Soviet Union, including early Tsarist Russia, may have been conducting laboratory experiments. I know for certain that we were."

"So, the Russians weren't involved with the U.S.?"

"In the Bermuda Triangle? No." Senator Scott paused for moment. "You must remember that the U.S. and the Russians both, under the Tsar, and later under the Soviets, were in competition with one another. The Russians were the first in space. That was a huge blow to all of us in both the space program here in the U.S and in..." he paused once again, "Let's just say other travel exploration programs."

"Time Travel exploration." Tonita said bluntly.

"Yes, time travel. I have kept too many secrets and it's not easy for me to tell you all the things I must tell and all that you must know."

Richard Devin

"The U.S. wasn't really much of a power in the early nineteen hundreds. How was it possible for the U.S. to compete with the Russians?" Dominic sat back.

"It wasn't. And in the early stages, the U.S. could not keep up. Rasputin's experiment was funded by the Tsarina, which meant that it had unlimited funds. The U.S. was shocked that Rasputin and the Tsarina had attempted such an expensive and technologically advanced experiment, but could do little at the time to invest the huge amount of funds needed to conduct our own experiments. If the Soviets and the U.S. had worked together in the early years, we could have saved many lives and billions of dollars. As it was, the U.S. couldn't commit the resources to the experiments until after World War One when we began to toy with the idea of time travel. By World War Two, however, we were totally committed. Then, we had a new rival and enemy. Germany was moving closer to a successful experiment. Although, as we understand it, on small scale. The Nazis concentrated on a plan they called, Schrittrückseite— Step Back. It was not the huge undertaking that we and the Soviets had become immersed in. Instead, Germany put all of its many scientists on the Schrittrückseite program, concentrating on stepping back only moments in time, not the decades and centuries we had been concentrating on. It seemed minute. But just think of what havoc the Nazis could have imposed on all mankind if they were able to go back in time. Not a year or a day, but for only a moment. That is when the U.S. government turned to a new ally and vast source of money."

"The Brits?" Dominic asked.

"The British were far too small and had far too little power. No, the U.S. turned to another government, a much more powerful government, one with unlimited wealth and one with the ability to control information and propaganda like no other government on Earth." He paused, breathing in deeply. "The Holy Roman Catholic Church." Senator Scott looked up to the heavens. "The Vatican became our co-conspirator and our benefactor."

FIFTY SIX

Bill Celent crept through the ravines and hid behind the rocks and boulders within the thorny scrub bushes that dotted the desert landscape. He had made his way down the embankment and was moving toward the hill where most of the procession had now settled.

He was standing at the bottom of the rock called Golgotha. The face of the skull, carved by millennia of wind, and rain, deep into the stone, was less evident from his vantage point. The pockets and holes in the rock looked simply, like a rock. The skull face had vanished.

Torn, scattered, pieces of cloth that had fallen, or were thrown over the cliff by the Romans and the peasants, had caught on the thorny scrub bushes, decorating them like, what Bill could only think of as, Christmas Trees. He gathered as many pieces of cloth as he could find, and quickly fashioned a covering by tying and weaving the pieces together. When he had finished, the cloth covered his head, shoulders, and torso. He took off his shoes and wedged them between two pieces of stone jutting out from the face of Golgotha. He rolled up the legs of his pants as high as his thighs, so only the bare skin from his knees down was visible. Unsnapping the rivets from the suspenders, he let the top of the gray shiny coveralls fall down at the front and back. And rolling the top down, he tucked it into the waist of the pants. He covered his body and head in the tied rags and stepped out from his hiding place. He circled around the skull-faced rock and began to climb the hill following the path that Christ and the others had taken.

He came around the side of the rock, climbed a few feet up, and despite using a trail that was fairly well-

worn, began to limp, as the sharp desert stone and scrub cut into the flesh of feet that were not accustomed to walking without coverings. Bill stopped, considered covering his feet with more the scattered rags, then realized that the limp in his stride would only add to the believability of his disguise. He stepped forward, limping heavily on his right leg, looking about, concerned that many eyes would be upon him. They were not. Jerusalem was crowded with hundreds of pilgrims that had come to town with sacrificial animals in tow for the Passover holiday, and Bill fit in perfectly between the beggars and the priests.

A man walked by him, holding out a hand and speaking in a language he couldn't understand. Instinctively, Bill raised a hand to his lips in gesture of one who could not speak and the man mumbled again as he walked off. Bill quickly decided that he needed to enhance his disguise by hiding his face beneath the cloth. By keeping his head and faced covered the entire time, allowing only his eyes to show. Hoping that this disguise would allow him to blend in and go unnoticed and undiscovered.

A keen observer, he thought, might notice that the skin on his legs and his feet was not rough and worn, like those of someone who had actually lived the life of a peasant. But he hoped the Romans and priests would be too preoccupied with the crucifixions to take notice of him. If he were discovered, there would be more written about this day in history than simply the crucifixion of Christ and two others. Bill wanted to know the truth, but he did not intend to change the course of history by revealing himself to Christ and the Romans gathered here.

He reached the dirt roadway that led from the gate in the city wall to the top of the hill, following the same path that the soldiers, priests, peasants, and Christ had taken just moments ago. He paused at a place in the road were Christ had stumbled. Bill noted a spot in the dirt where the end of the wooden beam that Christ was carrying had dug into the road when it had fallen. It had pushed up dirt and moved several small stones. He stared at the spot, feeling a cold chill sweep through him as he let the enormity of what he was doing seep in. He almost turned around, convinced that he should stop now, retrace his footsteps, find the capsule and return. But instead, fought the urge to run and began to take another step forward. As he did, he noticed a handprint in the sandy soil in the exact spot where Christ had fallen for the second time. Small specks of blood colored the sand and the pebbles on the road. Broken palm fronds were scattered about. Some had been used to cushion the way as Christ walked and others used to slap him upon his already scourged back and sides. Bill reached down and picked up one of the palm fronds. It too was smeared with blood. He let it fall back to the ground not wanting to garner the attention of a Roman soldier heading in his direction. The centurion walked by without the slightest hesitation. As soon as he had passed, Bill looked down to the roadway peering through the narrow opening in the hooded covering.

And that's when he saw it. What had once been covered by the palm frond, lay now uncovered and clearly visible. Directly below the imprint of the hand of Christ were several small lines scratched into the earth. At first, Bill could not clearly make the lines out. He repositioned himself, blocking out part of the sun and the symbol became instantly clear.

Where Christ had fallen, amongst the blood-spattered stone and sand, and broken palm fronds, and at the exact place were Christ's hand had pushed into the sand, two curving lines intersected one up and the other down, forming a symbol scratched into the dirt. A symbol that would not be used as in recognition of Christianity for years to come. And yet it was there, clearly drawn by Christ at the place where he had fallen. And at the same spot where the Roman guard had assisted him. The curving lines merged, forming the symbol of the Ichthys...the fish.

FIFTY SEVEN

"The Vatican?" Dominic asked, shaking his head.

Senator Scott looked directly into Dominic's eyes. "They had no choice. If the Nazis had succeeded, there would have been total chaos not only in Europe, but everywhere. The thousand year reign of the Third Reich would have been not a possibility, but a fact. Once the church was convinced of this, we had their complete support."

Dominic stood up and walked a few feet toward the rear of the plane. "What about the Russians? Was the church backing them?"

"Good question." Senator Scott smiled. "It shows me that you're thinking, my boy. But no. To answer your question. No. We do not have any proof that the Vatican supported the Russians and later the Soviets. Of course, we don't have any proof that they didn't either." Senator Scott continued, "My personal belief is that they must have, in some way, supported the Russians. The reality was that the Vatican became involved in the project to protect their own, and if the Soviets could lead them to that end faster than the United States could..." he paused. "Well, it just makes sense that they would have covered all their bases."

"And in truth, the Soviets were much further along in their space program than the U.S. was." Tonita swiveled in the chair from the window to where Dominic was standing.

"If that's the case then, that the church supported us and the Russians, why don't we hear of ships and planes missing from Russia, like we have here at the Bermuda Triangle?" Dominic asked. And the Russians had their own, Triangle of sorts to contend with.

"First, the Soviets were very secretive, even more so than we were. The U.S. let more information out, or allowed it to be in the public knowledge. The Soviets simply denied any reports and locked up anyone who tried to disseminate the information. In the U.S. the information was spun."

"Spun?"

"Yes. Turned into something more manageable," Senator Scott said, and raised an eyebrow. "Like the Bermuda Triangle. We couldn't keep the knowledge of planes and ships missing a complete secret. So, instead, we developed hypotheses to possibly explain what had happened, and then we started a legend. The Bermuda Triangle is one of those legends. There actually was no Bermuda Triangle before nineteen forty-five. We were conducting a pulse energy conversion experiment off the east coast of Florida. The hope was that we could better control the electrical energy field needed to create the power to send someone or something back in time. We had assembled a small team in the waters off of Miami on a couple of Navy destroyer escorts, disguised, not very well I might add, as fishing boats. The experiment went as well as we could have expected. The generators produced a significant amount of magnetic energy and we were able to control it. A pulse of that energy was aimed at a buoy set afloat in the ocean, and then nothing happened. That was exactly what we wanted. With past experiments, the energy created was too great to be controlled and things blew up, or disintegrated, or melded into one another. This time, there was nothing. We had controlled the power and directed it where we wanted it to be. And the end result was that nothing happened." Senator Scott looked to Tonita and then swung his eyes in the direction of Dominic. "Or so we thought."

FIFTY EIGHT

Bill was startled, nearly dumbfounded by the presence of the symbol. He knew the symbol well; Christians had begun to use the sign of the fish as a proclamation of their belief in Jesus Christ as the Son of God during the early Roman Empire.

Early Christian churches were little more than meetings held in a believer's house, later known as a house of worship. The devoted would come to the home, draw or signal with their hands the sign of the fish, and gain entrance. In many cases, only one of the curved lines would be drawn by a believer. The other would be filled in by another and then the eye of the fish would be drawn in by both, a gesture of their brotherhood and unity. But that practice was not initiated until years after the death of Christ. Hundreds of years later the Masons would take the eye symbol from the fish and incorporate it into their own symbol, weaving together ancient Christianity with modern politics, money, and war and passing on to unsuspecting millions the symbol of Christ the living God.

Bill stared at the simple symbol of two parallel lines drawn by Christ into the sand. He traced each line, one curving up the other curving down, intersecting at what would be the tail of the fish. As he traced the lines with his finger, one thought kept tracing its way through his mind. Christ could not have known of the symbol as a reference to him. History would not record its use for a decade or more after Christ's death. Why then, was the symbol here? Who was Christ drawing this for? And one answer kept screaming back.

It could only be for me!

He stepped around the handprint and the Ichthys, surprising himself at the reverence he gave them both.

The Third Hour

He did not believe in the Christ or in God stories. He never had. His parents were Christians, and, although, church was not a mainstay of the family's practices, they did occasionally attend a mass during the usual holidays when suddenly everybody found religion, Bill and his parents included. He didn't mind going to church. He had always enjoyed the pageantry of the services and there was the often good advice espoused by some priest from the pulpit. But in the end, it always led back to the same idea that those in the church were to be saved and those outside were to be converted in order to be saved.

Soon, Bill became one of those needing to be saved, those on the outside. He did not believe in Christ as God, or anyone else as God. He did not believe in God. Odd, he thought, that even though he was very secure in his belief that there was no supreme being, no creator, he hesitated calling himself an atheist and preferred instead to label himself agnostic. It left open the possibilities, he convinced himself, and like any good scientist, he should always be open to the possibilities.

Still, as he took another labored step up the rocky path to the hilltop, he could not help but feel there was something more here than the deaths of three men. He glanced back down the hill and the path, as the noise of several Roman guards laughing at some crude comment made its way to him. The guards' leather clad feet trampled over the spot where Christ had fallen, obliterating the Ichthys and the handprint erasing them from history. Bill kept himself from calling out to stop them. Instead, he watched as they stirred up the dust leaving the images only in Bill's memory. The guards pushed passed him, one saying something in Latin that Bill could barely make out as, "Move out of the way."

Bill followed the same path as the guards who had just passed and climbed the few yards to the hilltop. At the top, where the hill came to a small plateau, he found himself among a mass of people. Several hundred, he quickly guessed, mostly peasants, but some wealthy merchants on horseback rode about the crowd. The Roman Tribuni mounted on strongly muscled horses, shouted orders to the many more centurions that accompanied them, on foot. There were: priests and clergy, dressed in long flowing, darkly stained cloth with ornately decorated headwear, several robed government officials, and in the slight distance, one man, perched upon a rocky outcropping, lifting him slightly above the crowd. That one man was surrounded by a Cohort of Roman centurions and hung on stanchions to either side of him, ensigns bearing the silhouette of a Roman leader.

Pilate, Bill thought. Pontius Pilate.

Bill stared off at the man who ruled Judea, the Roman governor who history would record as the man who offered Jesus of Nazareth up to the crowds for forgiveness or death. And those crowds had responded with a cry of death to the man called Jesus of Nazareth.

The same Jesus that was now heaped onto the dry earth, bloodied and torn, exhausted to the point where he could barely lift his head or arm. His hair twisted and knotted into the roughly braided branch of thorns that was now imbedded into the flesh of his skull.

Bill circled the crowd. He was at once, dazed, confused, excited and anxious. So many sights, sounds, and smells intertwined. He tried to recognize words in languages that would be dead or seldom spoken in two thousand years. And again the realization struck him; he was in a time and place that was impossible to be in.

The experiment in the desert some two thousand years to the future of where he was now, had succeeded beyond his expectations. It dawned on him that Lynda and Commander Kupovits who were with him in the metal building that served as their capsule, may also be here or hiding nearby. He looked about at the weather-

worn faces surrounding him. Most of the men were bearded and dark skinned with long shaggy curls to their hair. Most of the women ran barefoot, as did the children.

Bill stopped, taking in the scene and the spectacle that was unlike any he had ever imagined. Where paintings and drawings by master artists in the centuries to come would show the scene of Christ's crucifixion as a solemn, dark, and foreboding ceremony, here there were children running and clamoring about, some playing what looked to Bill to be games of tag. Several groups of children moved slowly, heads down, sweeping the ground with their eyes in a search for dropped articles of cloth, food, or coin.

Bill closed his eyes, allowing his sense of smell and hearing to paint a mental picture of the scene before him without the distraction of sight. Immediately, he was taken back to a field that had been mown short only a week before. It was the second cutting of wheat straw and the clean fresh smell of mown grass lofted in the air. The late summer air, warm and humid, was pierced by lights strung along high poles, and neon so bright it lit the clouds above with hues of green and yellow. He was there once again, among the country carnivals of his childhood. The sounds, smells, and cacophony of images came back to him. And beneath his hooded head, he smiled.

Bill opened his eyes and confirmed what his senses were telling him. Most among the crowd were not acting in despair. There were few that carried the pain of sadness in their eyes. No tears fell streaming down the faces of those who stood and watched, and there were no wailing women beating their heads and chests with clenched fists crying out. Vendors, abounded, hawking their wares from the backs of small donkeys or ramshackle wooden carts pulled by men and beasts. Beggars of all sorts held out cupped hands, flat boards, or chipped wooden bowls to all who passed closely by seeking a coin or crumb. Religious men walked about chatting animatedly, ignoring the two men that already hung from the crosses just a short distance away and occasionally pointed to or nodded in the direction of the one man who awaited his fate. It was not unlike the carnivals of Bill's country youth. Except that this was a carnival of death.

He had to fight to keep his tongue silent. He wanted to scream out, to make the priests and peasants and Romans understand the gravity of what they were about to do. Their act would change the years to come in ways they could never imagine or understand. It occurred to Bill that the people who were here upon this hilltop did not care if the man, who still lay on the ground panting heavily, was the Son of God or simply a lunatic. The gathered crowds didn't understand and they didn't care to. What they did know was that the man called Jesus Christ was not good for them and their lives. He made times difficult in many ways, agitating the Romans and the priests by disrupting the long established beliefs and the daily practices of life. He put them all at risk. To the many congregated here, the crucifixion of Jesus would make their lives simpler. Crucifixion was not an unusual event during Roman rule of Judea and many other lands. The death of Christ and the two others, especially now, only days before Passover, was, to most in Jerusalem, a celebration of order and the end of a heretic's ranting.

There was a quick parting of the crowd, as several Roman soldiers rushed from their station—near the man Bill believed to be Pilate—toward the man Bill knew to be Christ.

Four centurions surrounded Christ, picking him up by the arms and dragging him toward the upright timber post that had already been secured and sunk several feet into the ground. Christ did not struggle or argue with the centurions. His body was limp, unresponsive. Bill watched the man, waiting for some sign of struggle, of resistance, that would prove that Christ was still alive. He suspected that Christ may have died while on the ground long before being tied and nailed to the cross, and watched the man for signs of life.

He turned his attention to the many gathered here. Some eyes looked away as Christ was dragged to the base of the stake. Some had tears. Most did not. Those that dared to cry did so silently, as they feared the wrath of the Romans more than that of a man who called himself the Son of God.

Bill studied their faces and that of Christ. His hair fell upon his face, knotted and twisted, caked with the dried blood and entwined into the twigs of thorn placed upon his head. He remained silent and still, despite the jeers and tormenting spat upon him by the crowd.

The crossbeam that Christ had carried through the city and on the path up to Golgotha had been placed in front of the longer, stationary post. The centurions stopped a few feet in front of the crossbeam and dropped Christ on his side.

A commotion behind him caught Bill's attention and he turned to see the man he thought to be Pilate circling through the crowd in a small chariot. He screamed at them, then charged off, making his way down the hill toward the gate, following the same path Christ and the crowd had on their way up to the sight of crucifixion. The man in the chariot yelled out in a gruff voice at the crowd, in Latin, "Illic is exsisto jesus talea abbas. Vos certus!" There he should be. Jesus bar Abbas. Bar Abbas. You decided! "Vos certus!

You decided!" Pilate entered the city through the gate and was soon out of sight. Only a bit of dust, kicked up by the horse and wheels of the chariot remained.

A moment later the centurions were back at their task, working together, as they had done many times before, with hundreds of others condemned to the cross. The centurions laid Christ onto his back. They pulled his arms upward, above his head, and stretched them out to the sides. Christ's hands were set atop the wooden crossbeam and bound into place with strips of animal skin that had been tanned into leather. One of the centurions reached into a satchel that was strapped around his shoulder and removed from it an iron spike about seven inches in length, and an iron headed hammer. He felt with his fingers for the position between the bones on Christ's wrists and readied the spike. He glanced toward Christ, who did not turn and recoil to the pending pain that was sure to sear through him, but, instead, looked directly to the sky.

Bill watched in silent horror as the centurion raised the hammer above his shoulder and brought it down with force. He struck the spike, two...three...four times, before it was firmly implanted through the wrist and into the crossbeam of olive wood.

Some in the crowd turned from the scene unable to bear witness to the gruesome task, but most watched, mesmerized. Bill closed his eyes briefly, but the sound of cracking bone and wood, and metal against metal, as the hammer was brought down again and again, was more horrific without sight, than it was with. He quickly opened his eyes.

The two thieves, that had already been placed upon the crosses, spat at the crowd, ridiculing them and the centurions. A sign had been nailed into the wood post of the cross above the head of each man that read: "Brigand"—thief. A few among the crowd spat back at the thieves. And a group of children, none more than ten years of age, tormented the thieves by throwing small stones and sticks at them, until a centurion took a step in their direction and ordered them to stop.

The Third Hour

Bill moved in as closely as he dared, examining the body of Christ from a distance. He was still unsure if Christ was drugged, dead, or unconscious. He stared at the blood-streaked, scratched, and cut chest of the man, looking for movement. But he turned away after a moment concerned that someone in the mob would notice him. Despite the covering of torn cloth and rags, he was concerned that his curiosity made him stand out, and that those around him would see that he was a man not of their own, and that he would end up like the two thieves and Christ—hung upon a cross.

The centurion finished the task of nailing Christ's wrist to the crossbeam, then moved to the other side to repeat the process with the other wrist. The sound of cracking bone and splitting wood assaulted Bill and he almost lost the contents of his stomach. He fought back the urge to throw up, and the urge to turn his head from the scene that no one in his time could imagine. He did neither.

Having secured Christ by the arms to the crossbeam, the four centurions lifted the crossbeam, together with the man upon it, and placed it on top of the post that had been seated into the ground.

Bill moved his eyes from the top of Christ's head, down his torso to his legs and the earth below them. He was suddenly taken aback as he realized that the crosses were not set high above the ground, but were, instead, not much more than six feet tall in total. He had always imagined, and had seen paintings and drawings depicting Christ hanging high above the ground, towering above the heads of those who gathered to witness the crucifixion. But here the three crosses were only slightly taller than a man's height, and one was certainly shorter, as the thief's feet barely missed touching the ground.

The same centurion, who had nailed Christ's wrists to the crossbeam, mounted a small ladder that he had leaned against the back of the post. The centurion climbed to the top rung and nailed the crossbeam into the post, forming an upper case "T". Christ's body and weight were supported by a small wood, shelf-like seat as the crossbeam was secured. But that could not stop the jolt of every hammering blow from pulsing through the stake. Christ's body shook with each strike, causing his head to fall to one side.

Bill was nearly certain now that Christ had already died long before being hung from the cross. He couldn't get close enough to see if he was breathing, or to feel for a pulse. But from his casual observation of the man, he was coming to the conclusion that what history had recorded was truly just a story told by a few men who were themselves seeking glory and fame.

Having secured the crossbeam to the post, the centurion nailed into place the titulus cruces bearing the crime of Jesus Christ, Iesus nazarenvs rex ivdaeorvm, in Latin, followed by the same wording in Greek, and then one more line, the last line, in Hebrew. They read: This is Jesus, King of the Jews.

At once there was a roar among the crowd. Bill could not make out the words, as most spoke in Aramaic, but he could understand the words in Latin and the tone of all the voices. The crowd was clearly unhappy with the titulus and railed against Jesus for the crime of calling himself the King of the Jews. The crowd turned on the centurions, taunting them, demanding that the titulus come down, that the words King of the Jews, be scratched away and replaced with "He said that he was King of the Jews."

The centurions pushed back at the crowd and threatened to strike any who ventured too close. There was a task to be finished, and by their demeanor, the centurions clearly intended to complete it.

The centurion who had just nailed the titulus above Christ's head stepped down from the small ladder and *came around to the front of the stake. He pulled from his satchel another long iron spike, and with the assistance of two other centurions, pulled the legs of Christ to one side of the stake, bending them at the knees. One centurion held Christ's legs in position, gripping them at the calf of each leg, while the other swung back and hammered a spike through the heels of both feet and deep into the wood of the post.*

The thieves to the sides of Christ had now been hanging from their crosses for several hours and the strain of the crucifixion was beginning to show. In panting breaths they taunted Christ to save himself and them, if was truly the Son of God. They mocked him, cursed him, and then in desperation, begged him. Christ paid no heed to the thieves, the crowd, or to the centurions. He remained silent, head bowed.

With their task complete, the centurions gathered the clothing they had torn away from Christ as he lay upon the ground, and made their way through the crowd toward the rocky point that Pilate had occupied.

Bill followed them for a short distance, eager to catch any of the words that history could never have recorded, staying as close to them as he dared. The centurions came to rest on the rocky point, they tossed off the satchels of tools and picked up skins of wine to quench their thirst, and then tore into stacks of bread and fruit.

Bill stood at a distance halfway between the centurions and the crosses, mesmerized by all that was taking place. He turned back to the three crosses staggered only feet apart in a crude line, just as Christ brought his head up. Christ stared at the centurions as they drank the wine and ate the bread. A slight smile formed at the edges of Christ's lips. Then, he turned his gaze away from the centurions and looked through the crowd. His eyes swept and touched upon every face that had gathered here. And every man, woman and child grew silent. All tormenting had stopped. The children laughing and playing on the outskirts of the rocky hill ceased in their antics. The vendors hawking wares shuttered their cries. The Roman centurions put down the skins of wine and loafs of bread. All turned their eyes to the crosses. On the hilltop, above the rock called Golgotha, there was silence. Not even the breeze dared to rustle a branch. And the ravens' ever-present call went silent. Christ's gaze hesitated on each face of every man, woman and child. Until there was only one man left. One man whose eyes the gaze of Christ had not touched.

His eyes met Bill's. The intensity of Christ's gaze made Bill want to turn away, but he could not. He was transfixed.

It was the third hour when Christ spoke, still staring directly into the eyes of Bill and no other. "Abbas, indulgeo lemma; pro haud non quis operor." His voice was soft and dry. His words in Latin, not Aramaic, and they were directed to one man and one man only. "Father, forgive them; for they know not what they do."

FIFTY NINE

"An entire squadron disappeared." Senator Scott raised his hands into the air, then snapped his fingers. "Gone. Just gone."

"And none were ever found?" Dominic cocked his head.

"Not a trace. Not one. There were radio transmissions from the flight leader to the bases in Miami and Fort Lauderdale. Search and rescue ships and planes were sent out, but nothing from any of the missing planes was ever located."

Tonita sighed. "Completely vanished?"

"Too many people were involved to try to cover the missing squadron up, so the Defense department—the Department of War at the time—began to plant misleading information about the strange happenings in the waters off Florida and the Bermuda Islands. They did a pretty good job of it, too, wouldn't you say?" The Senator concluded.

"So, how does Roswell fit into all of this?" Dominic took a seat directly across from the Senator.

"As I mentioned before, Roswell is not the beginning of something. It was actually the end."

"It is really a crash site?" Tonita asked, disbelief evident in her tone.

"Yes," Senator Scott started, "It was a crash site. But not a crash of what you may think. No it was not aliens or beings from another planet," he said with a bit of a laugh. "It is a crash site for an experiment in time travel, one that we thought had gone terribly wrong. But one that we found out later, may have gone just the way He wanted it."

Richard Devin

Dominic looked to Tonita who shook her head. Then he turned his quizzical gaze to the Senator. "He? Senator?"

Senator Scott shrugged his shoulders, "God." Senator Scott leaned forward nearly whispering, "It was the way God wanted it to be."

SIXTY

Suddenly, the air split, as a crack of lightning struck so close that Bill instinctively covered his head with his arms. The night sky was intermittently lit by the lightning, and then plunged back into total blackness, just as a wave of thunder-pulsed air hit, shaking the ground and rocks that Bill was cowering under.

He wasn't sure where he was. It was only moments ago that Christ had uttered the words, *Father, forgive them; for they know not what they do,* directly to him. In a crowd of hundreds, Christ had sought out each face, each set of eyes, until Christ's own eyes had fallen upon Bill and the remained. Unmoving, not blinking and the words had been spoken. Words that now repeated in his mind in Christ's own voice, pitched low, dry and gruff, with an odd accent unknown to Bill's ears. *Father, forgive them; for they know not what they do.* A statement recorded in the Bible by Luke, but said not to the Roman centurions, or the priests, or those gathered as Luke would have us believe. But said to one man and one man only.

Bill.

Bill stood up as the sky above lit with a bolt of lightning that fingered out as though it was searching the land, feeling its way around. "He knew. He knew. He knew!" Bill screamed out to the pouring rain.

And as if in confirmation to his statement, the sky split apart again, as a bolt of electrically charged current hit the ground not three feet to the side of him. Dirt and small pebbles, picked up from the impact, pelted him, and then the sound of thunder, low at first, then, rumbling so much so, that the bones in Bill's body shook. It hit him hard and he fell back, crumbling to the *ground, losing all conscious thought. His eyes closed and his body went limp, as the rain in the desert continued to fall...that night in Roswell.*

SIXTY ONE

The landing was so smooth Dominic hardly noticed they had touched down. His eyes opened and closed in that sleepy, slow motion movement that starts to awake the senses. His sleep had been heavy. After learning from Senator Scott of Roswell and the Bermuda Triangle...and God only knows what other experiments that the government had conducted and that the Senator had not talked about. He laughed at the unintended pun.

Yes. God only knows, he thought, and opened his eyes fully, as the engines revved down and the plane slowed, nearing the end of the runway.

Tonita and the Senator were up and walking toward the door to the aircraft as soon as the plane had come to a complete stop. Well ingrained, commercial flight rules of remaining seated with your seat belt fastened until the plane has come to a complete stop, were obeyed even in secret government planes with no one on board to enforce them.

A grounds crewmember knocked on the outside of the aircraft, and a moment later the airplane's cockpit side door popped open. It slid on hydraulic hinges with a slight hissing sound until it stopped, clicking into a latch on the side of the plane.

The scent of jet fuel and burning rubber swept into the cabin, rousing Dominic from the final moments of slumber.

"Welcome to Roswell," Senator Scott said, looking back at Dominic, still slouched in the leather, swivel chair.

Dominic stood, rubbed his face, brushed back his hair, grabbed a bottle of water and headed for the door. "Let's go," he said, as he stepped between Tonita and the

Senator and out onto the stairs leading to the tarmac below.

"The Senator won't be joining us," Tonita said, stopping Dominic in his tracks about halfway down the rolling stairs that had been butted up against the plane.

Dominic took hold of the handrail and turned back. "Why? You've come this far?"

"I'm an old man, Dominic. I'm good for a story or two, but I wouldn't do you any good out there." The Senator gestured to the desert that lay beyond the Industrial Air Center.

Dominic opened his mouth ready to debate the Senator on the merits of coming along with Tonita and himself, then, dismissed the thought. "Thanks for the ride, Senator." Dominic had to shout over the engines of the aircraft that were now revving up. Then he turned away and continued down the steps to the hot pavement below. He and Tonita had barely made it to the shadow of the terminal building, when the aircraft they had just arrived in began to taxi away.

"What now?" Tonita asked, quickening her pace to keep up with Dominic.

Dominic held the door to the terminal open, allowing Tonita to enter first. "Rent a car and head out to the desert, I guess," he said, stepping into the building just behind Tonita. Despite the one hundred plus degrees outside, he shivered as he hit the wall of cooled air inside the terminal that contrasted sharply with the hot dry air from the tarmac.

He looked around at the few people who lingered inside the compact Industrial Air Center terminal, safe from the scorching sun outside. Waiting, he assumed, for their flight, or the arrival of someone, or maybe they were just here to get out of the heat, his thoughts concluded. A twenty something-woman wearing an unrecognizable airline uniform stood at a counter that looked more like it belonged to a fast-food restaurant than the ticketing counter of an airline.

"Excuse me." Dominic stepped up to the counter. "Could you please tell me where I might go to rent a car?"

The twenty-something woman looked up at Dominic, smiled. "Sure. Just follow the signs." She pointed to the overhead signage that had arrows embossed upon them, pointing in every direction with captions that read: Restroom, Ticketing, Ground Transportation, Baggage Claim, Auto Rental.

"Oh." Dominic shrugged. "Thanks."

He glanced at Tonita, who had remained by the door, shaking her head at him

"So, you saw the signs?"

"Yeah." Tonita said the word as though it was a verse to a song. "I've seen them all along." She paused, giving Dominic an odd look. "A little hard to miss, I'd say."

"Really?" Dominic said, and walked away. "Come on," he shouted over his shoulder.

Tonita looked back at the twenty-something airline agent, rolled her eyes, and followed after Dominic.

"Thank you for flying with us," the twenty-something woman called out and waved.

Tonita smiled back, nodding.

Twenty minutes later, Dominic and Tonita were pulling out of the airport connector road in the rented automobile, following the signs that would lead them to route 285 north. "After this road, we need to take 54 south. It's not the most expeditious route," Tonita noted. "But this map from the car rental agency doesn't give much detail."

Out of Roswell, the highway followed a flat, arid landscape. Only the occasional small rocky bumps in the land or washes gave the land texture. Several signs along the highway pointed to the alleged location of an Unidentified Flying Object crash site.

"I had no idea that so many UFO's had crashed in Roswell," Dominic said, then added, "and they're not even in Roswell. Wasn't that where it all was supposed to have happened?"

"Here, listen to this." Tonita flipped the map over. "There are actually six alleged UFO crash sites in and around Roswell, New Mexico," she said, reading from the text on the back of the map.

"Six?"

"Six," Tonita continued reading. "The most popular of crash site legends is the ranch site outside of Corona, New Mexico." Tonita looked up. "Not Roswell. Corona is about ninety miles from here." She pointed to a spot on the map, then flipped back to the text and continued to read, "It is from there, that rancher Mac Brazel reported a crash to the authorities on July 6, 1947. Brazel told the sheriff in Roswell that he heard a loud explosion on the night of July 2, and found thin, shiny, metal-like foil scattered around the ranch land near where he suspected the explosion or crash took place. The next day, while exploring the area, he said that he had come across a figure on a hilltop near what he believed was a crash site. He told authorities that the sheep on the ranch would not go anywhere near the crash site, and asked them to come out and see the area for themselves. Brazel returned to the ranch and on the 8th of July," Tonita paused, "He was taken into custody..."

"They arrested him?" Dominic said, as he passed a semi-truck crawling in the left lane of the highway.

"Not by the police." Tonita turned back to the story printed on the reverse of the map, and finding her place continued, "The military arrested him or took him into custody, if that's any different?"

Dominic eased back into the left lane, leaving the semi far behind. He glanced quickly at Tonita. "The military took a civilian into custody because he thought he heard an explosion?" Dominic asked. "That doesn't seem right."

"And get this," Tonita traced a finger along the text on the back of the map. "When Brazel returned to the ranch after the military had taken him into custody, he told a newspaper reporter that the debris he had seen scattered all over the crash site was gone. Every bit of it had been picked up, and not a trace of the crash remained. He's reported as saying. And then, years later when Brazel was interviewed by a television reporter for a story on the Roswell incident, he said, 'After they took me away and held me for a couple of days, they brought me back to the ranch. When I got back to the ranch, it looked like no one and no animal had ever stepped foot on that land where the crash was. It had been swept clean. I even think they planted new scrub brush just to cover this crash up.'"

SIXTY TWO

An odd sound greeted Bill as he began to come to. His first thought was that he was dreaming...dreaming he was awake and that the noise was part of that dream, or some hallucinogenic side effect of time travel. He opened his eyes fully, then immediately closed them again, as the full burst of light caused his pupils to dilate too rapidly. He could feel the heat of the sun on his arm and began to take note of the aching pain in his legs and the small of his back. He wasn't dreaming, he thought, and opened his eyes again, more slowly this time, allowing his sight to adjust to the light of morning.

Then the noise again. The sound came intermittently and then together, as though a choir director had singled out a voice or two and then had the whole choir join in.

Fully awake, his brain clicked in and gave the sound an identity. He jumped up.

Baying.

All around him sheep stood huddled in groups, baying at him. Bill took a cautious step toward the herd, concerned that there might have been a wolf or coyote nearby. The sheep made no attempt to turn and run from him, or from any looming predator. Instead they stood their ground, watching him. In the distance, just beyond the flock of sheep, he could see what looked like a well. It was just twenty or thirty yards off, but the sheep were nowhere near it. They stood off to either side and along...Bill froze.

Directly in front of him, stretching for many yards, was, what he could only think of as, an impact zone. His senses alerted, he turned slowly, looking beyond the sheep, taking in the whole area. Bits and pieces of the foil lay scattered all around. Foil that Bill immediately recognized as the same foil that had once lined the manmade ravine dug around the small metal building. Or more precisely—the capsule that transported him into time. A slight breeze kicked up and that same foil that had at one time, held back the water from the Great Salt Lake, and conducted the electromagnetic power from the generators to and through the metal building, now blew in the slight breeze. Like confetti after a parade had passed, Bill thought. The foil stuck to the brush and gathered in piles pushed up by the wind, and against the rocks and large chunks of metal that lay tossed about. They looked as though they had been torn, ripped in pieces and then bent into odd angles by some delusionary artist, creating an apocalyptic landscape.

Bill took a few steps toward the impact zone, picked up a piece of the metal and examined it. It was lighter than he had expected. Smooth and even to the touch, where it had been ripped and torn by the impact. He ran a finger cautiously on the perimeter of the metal; it too remained smooth, despite its jagged edge. It took only a moment more before he placed the origins of the metal. Like the foil, the metal pieces had come from the small brown, camouflaged building that he, Lynda and Commander Kupovits had been in. The same building that Einstein and Von Braun, along with teams of scientists, had developed to serve as a time capsule. The metal was a combination of iron, copper, gold and platinum mixed in a perfect amalgamation that would conduct electromagnetic energy, while transporting and protecting the occupants. Einstein and Von Braun had worked together with a select team that could be trusted, or blackmailed, as in Von Braun's case, into secrecy. It was evident, since the Eldridge disaster, that steel and iron were not the correct conductors for the massive amounts of electromagnetic energy that was

required to boost the ship or capsule through time. Steel
and iron too easily failed. Their molecular structure—
under the tremendous pressures of time and energy—
warped and melded together or disintegrated. The four
metals of time, as Einstein dubbed it, were supposed to
solve the problems incurred by the Eldridge and Project
Rainbow. That did not appear to happen, Bill thought,
as he tossed the piece of metal to the ground.

He started off toward the circular metal well,
calling out to Lynda and the commander. His voice was
rough, dry, and he could not produce the volume he
thought he needed. After a futile attempt, he abandoned
the idea. Bill covered his eyes, using one hand as a
visor, and scanned the horizon. There was nothing in
the distance, except more horizon and more desert. He
took another step toward the well. Thirst and survival
were fast becoming his main concern. He could do
without food, but without water, in the dry heat of the
desert, he knew he wouldn't last long.

He took another step and winced in pain as a sharp
rock cut into his foot. That's when he noticed he was
barefoot. His eyes followed his body from his feet up to
the calves of his legs, and to the torn strips of cloth that
covered him. The worn rags he had found tangled in the
brush of Golgotha, still clung to him. If he had had any
doubt about Golgotha and the crucifixion being a real
or a dream, it disappeared in a flash of stark reality.

The sheep began to bay again, this time louder.
Their voices joined together in a song of unison. Their
attention turned to the distance, opposite Bill.

Bill turned quickly, peering off in the same direction
as the sheep. Two people mounted on horseback were
slowly approaching him. They were still far off, but Bill
thought he could make out one figure as a man, and the
other, a child. He started to bring both of his hands up
to his mouth to cup it and channel his voice in their
direction, when he noticed that one hand was empty.

The Third Hour

He had used it to shield his eyes only a moment ago, but the other hand remained clenched. He moved his arm up, bringing his hand closer to his face, and willed the clenched had to open. Slowly, Bill's fingers splayed back, revealing his palm and the contents of his hand. What he saw there caused him to suck in his breath so quickly, that his lungs threatened to burst.

Bill immediately turned to run back to the spot by the rocks and the small bump in the desert landscape that he had just moved from. But he stopped dead in his tracks. Lynda and Commander Kupovits' bodies lay atop the rocks, just above the spot where he had been when he came to. Even from this distance, Bill could see that the bodies were contorted. The muscles in their faces had been stretched and pulled, looking much like the painting of The Scream by the Norwegian painter, Edward Munch, which he had seen once on a slide in a required undergraduate course. He had found the painting to be an odd mix of emotion and texture. Even then, he had wanted to look away, but the painting would not allow him to. Just as now, the grotesque faces of Lynda and Commander Kupovits stretched into a silent scream, with eyes wide open, looking skyward and mouths agape, would not allow his eyes or his thoughts to drift away.

There was but one thought, and one thought only, that repeated over and over in Bill's mind, without regard for the insanity it was nearly causing him. If he had just traveled back in time and born witness to the crucifixion of Christ...

Where had they gone?

And, what had they seen?

SIXTY THREE

Dominic eased off the gas pedal, allowing the rental car to slow down. He pulled off of NM247, carefully maneuvering the car from the pavement onto the dirt road, just past mile marker 17. "Are you sure this is right?" He put his foot on the brake, bringing the vehicle to a complete stop.

"It's on the map," Tonita said, feeling a bit nervous.

The dirt road stretched out over the desert, running for miles ahead of them. They could see that it ran straight, then turned, climbing up a small hill, then twisted again and vanished into the distant desert.

"Wow! Kinda like the 'Yellow Brick Road.'" Dominic pursed his lips and whistled a few notes. "This is it?" Dominic asked once again.

Tonita quickly turned back to the map. "This is it. But where is it?" she said, as she attempted to fold the map back up.

"That is a very good question." Dominic stepped on the gas and slowly moved the rental forward. "There's only one direction, so I guess we head that way."

"And how do we know when we get to...wherever, there is?"

"You know, Tonita? I don't know. I've never been here and you've never been here, and I don't know anything more than you do," Dominic snapped.

Tonita shook her head and turned away, staring out the window, watching as dust picked up and clouded behind them. "Okay. That was a little 'Jekyll and Hyde' of you."

Dominic breathed out a long sigh. "I'm sorry. That was unnecessary...I'm sorry. Really."

Tonita turned back to him. "I'm sorry, too, Dom. I'm sorry that I got pulled into this scheme and that I don't know where I'm going, or what I'm doing or who I'm doing it with...Really!"

Dominic slammed on the brakes, sliding the rental to a dusty stop. He jammed the gearshift lever forward, threw off his seat belt, grabbed Tonita by the shoulders, and kissed her.

He kissed her...and she responded.

She struggled with her seat belt. Tossed the map to the floor. And wrapped her arms around Dominic's neck. Returning the kiss.

Dominic leaned into her and she fell back against the passenger door.

She could feel the sun beating down through the tinted glass, contrasting with the cool air blowing out of the vent in the dash of the car.

A moment later, his hands found her breasts, and through her clothes, he caressed them.

She pulled him in tighter to her. Her hands ran up and down his back, along his sides, and into his hair. She felt as though the earth below her was moving. She opened her eyes briefly, and saw that the sky above was moving. There were no clouds to speak of, only small wisps of white punctuating the vast openness of blue. But the white wisps streaking the sky, were in motion. "Dom?" Tonita started, then paused.

Dominic breathed out heavily and said, "I know. I want you, too. Just as badly."

"No, Dom." She brought her arms underneath him and pushed him up a few inches. "We're moving."

"What?"

"The car. It's moving."

Dominic pushed up, and then scrambled to get back into the driver's seat, while Tonita tried to right herself. "Oh shit," he said, as he pushed his foot down onto the brake, stopping the car. Then slid the gearshift into park. He looked at Tonita and grinned. "I thought I put it in park?" He laughed. "Guess I got a little ahead of myself."

"Guess you did." Tonita laughed with him.

"Look, we don't know where we're going out here anyway, so why don't we just head back into town, grab a bite and a room." He paused a moment, grinning at Tonita.

"You were saying," she said, without a hint in her voice that she had picked up on his line.

"Then we can do some research and head back out here tomorrow," Dominic concluded.

"Best plan I've heard in a long time."

Dominic put the car in gear, turned it around, and headed back out to route 247. Leaving the dirt road behind him, he turned left on a heading into Corona.

"What was that you said about a room?" Tonita placed her hand on Dominic's leg.

He floored it.

SIXTY FOUR

Bill looked over his shoulder, turning from the horrific open-mouthed, silent screams plastered onto the faces of Lynda and Commander Kupovits. The two horsemen were still approaching. Their horses moved slowly at a steady walk, kicking up little puffs of desert dust as each of the horses' hooves were picked up and then placed back onto the dry earth. Nature's choreographer had done a fine job here, moving the wind and the dust, and the beat of the horses' hooves in perfect time. Step, dust, step, dust, step, dust.

Lost for a moment in the mirage like vision of the horses, warped by the heat rising from the desert and their macabre dance, Bill snapped back to the reality of the moment. He moved quickly over to the mound of rocks. He carefully emptied the contents of his hand—brought with him through eons of time—onto a large piece of the metal foil he found stuck under the scrub brush. He began to dig. He pushed rocks aside and dug into the earth with his bare hands. Soil, which had been baking in the heat of the sun for millennia, formed a sharp desert crust that bit into his hands. But once he had broken through, the sandy soil was remarkably soft. He dug furiously, without regard to his now cut and bleeding fingers.

Bill stood, wiping the sweat from his face, and looked back to the horsemen who had reached the water guzzler, stopping just several yards shy of it. Bill wasn't sure if they had seen him, but he held out hope that they had not. He waited. Watching.

The riders stood up in their stirrups using their vantage point atop the horses to see all around them. Bill countered by crouching down behind the rocks. He struggled in an awkward bent position to quickly shed the rags of torn cloth from his body, revealing the shiny metallic jump-suite once again. He pulled down the pant legs and rolled down the sleeves of the jump-suit. His shoes were gone, but there was nothing he could do about that, short of taking the ones off Commander Kupovits' body. He gave it a quick thought, then dismissed it, and decided there wasn't time and that it would be best to stay barefooted.

He bundled the rags of cloth together quickly. Then he took the large piece of foil that held the contents of his hand and placed it together with the rags and cloth. He lined the hole that he had just dug with more of the metal, then placed everything into the hole and filled it in. He covered it with rock and dirt in a chaotic arrangement that he hoped mimicked nature.

Moments later, after covering the hole and giving the site a quick inspection, Bill climbed up on top of the rocks. He steadied himself and waved his arms in the direction of the horsemen. He yelled, trying to push his voice past the rough, dry sound that his vocal chords produced. But he was quite sure that the horsemen could not hear him over the din of the baying sheep. He continued to wave his arms and yell, until one of the horsemen turned his eyes from what he considered to be a well and the sheep to Bill.

The smaller of the two horsemen pointed in Bill's direction. The other turned, stared for a moment at Bill, and then, with a quick jolt on the reins of the bridle, whipped the horse's head around and took off, heading back in the direction that he had come. The smaller horseman spurred his horse into a lope, catching up quickly with the other rider, who looked over his shoulder toward Bill. Then, he leaned forward in the saddle, urging his mount forward into a full gallop.

SIXTY FIVE

After a breakfast of alien waffles, UFO sausage and flying saucer eggs at the Alien Café, Dominic and Tonita headed for the car. The day, like most in Corona, New Mexico, was hot, dry, and bright. The sun, unimpeded by clouds of any sort, beat down upon the desert and the asphalt.

"You know those eggs we just ate?" Dominic asked Tonita, as they walked across the street, leaving the relative comfort of the Alien Café to the parking area of the motel.

"What about them?"

"We're going to be fried in no time. Just like 'em."

"Just be sure that I'm sunny side up." Tonita sent a wry grin in Dominic's direction.

"Oh, you're gonna be in trouble." Dominic smiled. "Big trouble."

There was little traffic on the street and only an occasional tourist or local walked the sweltering sidewalks. Still, the Alien, UFO, and Of Another World kiosks that lined the sidewalk outside of the motel were open and ready to sucker in any one who could not possibly leave Corona without a memento of their investigation. In Corona, one could purchase every known and unknown alien souvenir imaginable. Vials of Crash Site Dirt sat next to: plastic flying saucers, alien-head flashlights, T-shirts, flip-flops, saucer caps, rings, pins, bracelets, and necklaces, all fashioned in the shape of a spacecraft or alien.

Dominic smiled, nodding politely at a young man hawking the "Strange But True" souvenirs from a tented kiosk. Senator Scott was right, he thought, invent a story that was completely false, based on events that really happened, and a whole subculture will sprout. And it did. Not only about Roswell and the alien craft that crashed there, but also around Nevada's Area 51 where the aliens from the Roswell crash were taken. The same was also true of Project Rainbow and the Eldridge—the ship that disappeared and reappeared miles away. According to Senator Scott, these stories, fables, and now legends were all true, or somewhat true. These events had now been clouded over by rumor and innuendo, and manipulated into folklore and legends. Thanks to the United States government.

Dominic walked quickly by the kiosks, ignoring the calls of the vendors to stop and shop. He turned to hurry Tonita along. "Let's get out of ..." he stopped in mid-sentence. She wasn't with him. He looked quickly around, but did not see her. "Tonita," he shouted in the direction of the motel. When she did not answer, he started back. He looked into each of the souvenir stands he passed, calling out her name several times to blank stares and no answers.

Dominic looked back, following the curve of the street in the direction he had just come. The street was beginning to come alive. Several families with their kids in tow were making their way down the obstacle course of vendors and stalls. He noticed one little girl talking to someone hidden by the shadows of the overhang and the T-shirts swaying easily in the slight breeze. He waited a moment for the assumed parent or sibling to step out of the shadows. When he or she did not, he made his way up to the stall.

"Oh Dom?" Tonita said. "Where did you head off to?"

"Me? I was right there, and then you disappeared."

"Dom? I haven't left this place." Tonita looked at him cocking her head. "You kept walking. I thought that you would stop and wait for me."

"Sorry, I got a bit distracted."

"Easy enough to do around here." Tonita smiled at him. "Look at what this little girl ..."

"I'm not a little girl. I'm Annabel. I told you," the child said.

"Yes, I'm sorry you did tell me your name." Tonita placed her hand gently on the child's brunette curls. "Annabel was just showing me her puzzle."

"Wow. That's nice, Annabel." Dominic reached for Tonita's other hand. "We've got to go now." He smiled at Annabel. "Be careful. And go back to your parents now." He took a step out of the kiosk.

Tonita held tight to Dominic's hand. "We should wait with her until her mom and dad come looking for her."

"It's just my dad," Annabel said, playing with a folded piece of paper.

"Well then, we'll wait until your dad comes to find you."

"He's always getting lost." Annabel grinned.

"Annabel was just showing me her puzzle. Isn't that right Annabel?"

"Daddy made it. He's good at making puzzles."

Dominic looked at Tonita and at the little girl, taking the hint. "Okay, where's the puzzle," he said, taking a step closer.

"Right here, silly." Annabel held up her hands, the forefingers and thumbs of each hand were pressed together holding what looked like a paper pyramid.

"That's a great little puzzle you got there, Annabel." Dominic glanced back to Tonita.

"Watch," Annabel said, as she manipulated her fingers and thumbs and the puzzle changed shape.

"Wow! You made it go from a pyramid to boat." Dominic gave the little girl a wink. "That was great."

"Annabel? Annabel?" A tall thin man with shoulder length brown hair, slicked back, revealing strands of grey, stepped into the kiosk. "Annabel, what did I say about staying with us?"

"Sorry, Daddy." The little girl's sheepish grin belied her true feelings.

"She was just showing us her puzzle," Tonita said, then added, "Hi, I'm Tonita and this is Dominic." She extended her hand to the man. "Sorry if we kept your little girl."

"No, no. It's not your fault. Jeff by the way." He took Tonita's hand. "I'm Jeff."

"Well, you have a wonderful little girl here."

Jeff rubbed his hand through the little girl's hair. "We certainly do."

"I was showing them the puzzle you made Daddy."

"You really made that?" Dominic said, and reached out to the little girl. "May I see your puzzle?"

"Sure," Annabel said. "Daddy can make you one too."

"I use them in my class," Jeff said. "I'm a school teacher, and I use these to get the kids motivated. They're great for teaching math."

Dominic took the puzzle from Annabel and inserted his forefingers and thumbs into the small openings formed by the folded paper. "Like this?" He showed his hands to Annabel.

"Now move them," Annabel said, and squealed in delight as Dominic struggled with the puzzle.

"You can make all kinds of these puzzles," Jeff said. "Flexagons, are what they're really called, and they can get pretty involved."

"This simple one is involved enough for me." Dominic tried to manipulate the puzzle once again.

"There you go," Jeff said, as Dominic got the puzzle to change shape. "Now you have it. Doesn't he Annabel?"

"You did it, Mister. You did it." Annabel clapped her hands together.

The Third Hour

Jeff pulled his daughter in close to him. "Hey, we better get going. Mommy's going to wonder where we are."

"Well, it was very nice to have met you, Annabel." Tonita extended her hand to the little girl.

Annabel smacked it with her own little hand. "High five," she shouted, laughing.

Dominic handed the paper puzzle back to Annabel.

She quickly placed it back on her fingers and began moving the puzzle and her fingers in time to a song that she apparently was making up as she went along.

"Thanks, Jeff. It was nice talking to you," Dominic said.

"You too," Jeff said, as he and Annabel walked away.

"You ready?" Dominic looked at Tonita. "Or do you have some more alien souvenir shopping to do?" He smiled.

"No, I'm done."

"Then let's head out to the desert." Dominic started in the direction of the rental. "Got the map?"

"It's right here." Tonita patted the back pocket of her jeans.

"Good."

The parking lot adjacent to the motel was nearly empty, there were a couple of old pickup trucks with faded paint that seemed to last forever in the dryness of the desert, a motorcycle, and the rented Oldsmobile Alero. Dominic tossed the backpack into the driver's seat and quickly unzipped it. He pulled the page from the book on Roswell out of the pocket stitched into the inside of the bag. "Tonita, you think that this is some sort of map, right?" he asked, holding up the page.

"That was my first thought."

"I did, too, and so did the Senator." He moved around to the passenger side of the car, coming alongside of Tonita. "But if it is a map, we don't know how to read it."

Richard Devin

"Right. Look at it. The lines don't make any sense. They don't line up to form a roadway or a landmark. It's just squiggles drawn onto a page."

A slow grin grew across Dominic's face. "Come on," he said, grabbing Tonita by the hand, yanking her in his direction. Together, they headed back out to the street, now slightly more crowded with both foot and auto traffic.

"What are we doing?" Tonita hesitated, "And you left the car door open."

"Don't worry about it." Dominic pulled her along, keeping a tight hold on her hand as they dashed, then stumbled, in and around the kiosks and stalls. "There!" He pointed up the block, then let go of Tonita's hand, and took off. "Jeff! Hey Jeff!" he yelled in the direction of the man, his wife, and their daughter. "Jeff! Hold up a minute!"

SIXTY SIX

Cardinal Celent's eyes fluttered open, and for a moment he was lost in between his memories of Roswell, Golgatha and the experiment, and the reality of the hospital room. He blinked his eyes, then again. Was he dreaming now? Or had he just awakened from dreaming? The thoughts battled one another internally, until the harsh disinfectant smells of the hospital contrasted sharply with the sense-memory smells of the ancient desert of Judea, and brought him back to the present.

He sat up as best he could, pushing against the thin mattress of the hospital bed. He fumbled around for the remote control, tangling the intravenous lines with the cord to the remote. He struggled for a moment to untangle the cord and IV line, then pushed the button on the front panel of the remote that would bring the back of the bed upright. After a moment he had the back of the bed up, supporting him. He tucked the remote under his leg and leaned back into the, not so comfortable, bedding that covered the tight springs and mechanical devices hidden underneath. He let his mind wander around the storm of thoughts and memories that swirled inside.

Even after the nearly seventy years since the experiments in the New Mexico desert, his thoughts remained sharp and focused, recalling all of the events with detail. He had made a point, throughout the years, to never allow his memories to cloud or gloss over each of the moments of that day. What had happened that day, happened exactly as he had remembered. His thoughts and memories of the day he stepped into the time capsule, and the day he returned, were cataloged in his mind. Documented and annotated. He was a scientist first, and a theologian reluctantly.

After standing on the pile of rocks, in what he would later learn to have been the New Mexico desert outside of Corona, watching the two horsemen gallop away, he could do little to combat the feeling of being abandoned and alone.

He was well aware that working with the government on experiments in time travel was always a lonely and risky venture. Working with the government on any secret experiment was at best a risky venture, especially during times of war. Those involved in time travel experimentation, or those involved in the cover up of time travel experimentation, never knew the whole story. That's the way government works best, Ray Scott told him, weeks before the trip into the desert. Secrets layered upon secrets. So many layers that no one was ever sure what was truth and what was propaganda. Cardinal Celent smiled and shook his head slightly, as he wondered if anyone would ever know the complete truth. Then, he asked out loud to no one in particular, "Could they even understand if they did know the truth?"

He had been living a life of secrets and lies—covert was the way the government directors described it—ever since being recruited so long ago by Ray Scott. He corrected himself—Senator Ray Scott. They both had titles now; one had been rewarded by the United States government for services outstanding, and one by another government, the Holy Roman Catholic Church: for secrets well kept.

It was during the initial experiments, when he had first been recruited, that he found himself unsure of his talents and those of the other scientists that had been brought onboard. And there were many moments of doubt about what he and they were trying to do. Not in whether time travel could be accomplished, but rather in whether it should be accomplished? In theory, time travel was not impossible. It was definitely highly improbable, but so were many of the conveniences of modern man. But that did not stop the world from embracing the new technology, whether it became a benefit to man or was proven to be detrimental to man.

He remembered asking himself many times over, would time travel be good for mankind or would it prove to be the ultimate evil? As many times as he had asked himself the question, it would remain throughout his life: A question that he could not answer. But he didn't have to, as it was a question that had been answered for him.

Father, forgive them for they know not what they do.

***

The bodies of Lynda and Commander Kupovits with their distorted, grotesque faces had started to bloat. Bill noticed that the jumpsuits they were wearing had become decidedly more snug, especially around the abdomens of each. He contemplated burying them, but decided against it, as he did not have anything with which he could move the earth and rocks that would be required for the task. And even if he did bury them, he knew that the government would want the bodies for an autopsy and research, and they would only have to dig them up again. So, he just moved them out of the direct sun into a fairly shaded area.

After pulling the bodies around to the other side of the rocky mound and out of the direct sunlight, Bill headed off toward the well. He was exhausted and in desperate need of water. He made it halfway to the iron structure, when he realized that the desert was filled with an eerie silence. The sheep that had stood on parallel sides of the well were gone. They had moved off quietly into the desert, leaving Bill alone with only the sound of a whimpering breeze rustling dry, snarled tumbleweed.

He turned slowly around, just as he had done in the ancient desert of Israel when he had first glimpsed the walls of Jerusalem, not expecting to see anything, but knowing something was there. When he had completed a one hundred and eighty degree turn, and now had the well to his back, and was facing the rocky mound, he saw them.

Three figures stood atop the rocks, looking directly at him. The heat of the sun bounced off of the desert rock and baked earth, causing the images to ripple. Bill stood for a moment waiting for the mirage to disappear. It did not. Instead, the figures began to move. And stepping down from the rocks, they moved in his direction.

Bill contemplated both running away and running toward them.

He did neither.

SIXTY SEVEN

"Jeff! Jeff. Wait up!" Dominic shouted as he ran toward the man.

Jeff turned around, saw Dominic coming towards him, and pulled his daughter in close to him in the unconscious movement of a parent protecting their child.

"Hey, I'm sorry to run up on you like this," Dominic said, slightly out of breath. "But you were telling me about the paper puzzles that you use in your classes."

Jeff stared at Dominic, then diverted his gaze over Dominic's shoulder as Tonita came up behind him. Jeff relaxed as Tonita reached them, stopped, and smiled. "Yes. What about them?"

"I have a map, or at least that's what I think it is, that I can't figure out, and I was hoping that maybe you could take a look at it?"

Jeff nodded. "Well, sure. I don't know that it'll do any good, but I'll look at it."

"Thanks. Anything would help." Dominic gave Tonita a quick nod, and then handed the map to Jeff.

"My daddy can make an airplane for you or even a fish," Annabel said, displaying her paper puzzle. "Show 'em, Daddy."

"Sure. Weeble, in just a minute." Jeff took the page torn from the book on Roswell from Dominic, looked at one side, then turned it over, studying the opposite side. After a few minutes of concentrated thought, he turned it around again. "I think," Jeff started, then went silent again as he flipped the page from horizontal to vertical, turning it over and quickly back. "It's a tri-hexa-flexagon."

Dominic cocked his head, brushed the hair from his face, and asked, "Is that good?"

Richard Devin

Jeff laughed. "Oh, sure. It's a fun puzzle. Not all that easy to make. But once you get the hang of it, not all that hard either."

"Can you do it? I mean, can you turn the page into that tri hexa thing?"

"Tri-hexa-flexagon," Jeff stated. "Three sides and six faces. And sure I can."

Dominic pointed to a table with an umbrella covering it, offering a canopy of shade a short distance away. "Let's sit over there."

Tonita and Dominic took a seat opposite Jeff and Annabel at the partially shaded table. There was just a touch of movement to the air as a breeze picked up momentarily and then faded away.

"Now, how do we know that this is a tri-hexa-flexagon?" Jeff asked, as though he were instructing a high school class in mathematics. He handed the page—map—to Dominic.

Dominic turned the map over, looked at both sides intently, and handed the page to Tonita. "I don't know. Do you?"

Tonita took the page, and without so much as a nano-second of thought, handed it directly back to Jeff. "No. But he does."

Jeff smiled and reached out for the map. "I do."

"Daddy knows everything. Don't you, Daddy?" Annabel said, giggling.

"No, Weeble. Daddy just thinks he does." Jeff leaned over and kissed his daughter on the head. His eyes moved from his daughter to Dominic. "But this," he waved the page in the air, "a tri-hexa-flexagon, I do know." He looked into Dominic's eyes. "Trust me?"

"Sure, we trust you." Dominic said.

"Okay, then."

Dominic and Tonita watched as Jeff creased the page into a folded strip. Then, beginning on one end, folded a corner down, creating a triangle into the paper.

The Third Hour

He repeated the process, folding each triangle into another. When he had reached the end, he turned the page over and repeated the processes until the page resembled a strip of paper, that when standing on its side, zigzagged. Jeff, took the strip of paper, laid it out onto the flat surface of the table, and smoothed out the page so that it would lie flat. "I'm going to need some glue or tape. Double-sided is best."

"Let me check with one of the souvenir stands," Tonita said as she jumped up from the table. A moment later she was back with double-sided tape. "Just what the doctor ordered," she said, handing the tape to Jeff.

"Perfect." Jeff took the page, refolded it into the zigzag shape and, snapping off a small section of tape, applied it to one end of the strip of folded paper. Then he twisted the strip around and attached the other end of the paper, pressing the two pieces into the double-sided tape, until they were held firmly together. He picked up the completed puzzle and showed it to Dominic and Tonita.

"Daddy, you made a stop sign," Annabel said, again giggling. "A stop sign."

"Not quite, but close. A stop sign has eight edges to it." Jeff showed the tri-hexa-flexagon map to his daughter, and then displayed it to Dominic in a movement reminiscent of a game show host. "This only has six sides, see?" He counted them out. "One, two three, four, five, and six."

"You're right, Daddy."

Dominic nodded in agreement with the little girl.

"Now watch what happens if I push two of the edges together and hold them, while I pull another corner apart." Jeff manipulated the form and the crisscrossing lines that had made absolutely no sense when presented on the original paper. Now, came together, converging and continuing at points leading off to the edge of the flexagon.

"And if I hold two other edges together," Jeff said, as he held two of the other edges together and pulled at the corners of another. A new design came together and the map continued. "See?"

"Very good, Daddy." Annabel's voice rose in excitement.

Dominic again nodded in agreement.

"Whoever thought this through really put some time into it. This is complicated." Jeff handed the map to Dominic.

Dominic cradled the map in his hands, as one would an egg that had the yolk blown out from it, leaving only the shell.

"It won't break," Jeff said. "It's pretty secure."

"I'm not sure how to use it." Dominic squeezed together two of the corners.

"That's right. Now hold them tight and pull at another corner."

Dominic did, and when nothing happened looked up at Jeff. "What's wrong?"

"Nothing. Some corners will work and some won't." Jeff pointed to another corner of the map. "Try that one."

Dominic pulled on the corners that Jeff had indicated, and the map moved into a new configuration. The lines that had ended on one side connected and continued on another.

"That's it," Jeff said with a hint of congratulation in his voice. "You have to play with them to figure out which side leads to another. Even though it doesn't look like it, every flexagon, whether it is a simple puzzle or a complicated design like this one, has a front or beginning, and an end. Let me show you." Jeff held out his hand.

Dominic handed the map to him and leaned in as Jeff demonstrated.

The Third Hour

Jeff went through the design sequence of the map once, then hesitated, and ran it one more time. "Okay. You see here?" He held out the map to Dominic and Tonita. "This is side one." He manipulated the paper. "This is side two." Then he continued the sequence until he had cycled completely through. "And side six." Jeff concluded the demonstration and handed the map back to Dominic. "Whoever designed this made it easy for you to recognize the sides."

"Oh, really?" Dominic's sarcasm was evident in his tone. "How's that?"

"Look here." Jeff placed his finger near the edge of the first side of the map, "This." Just at the tip of his finger a lone symbol in the far corner of the page stood out. --A--. "That's the..."

"Greek letter A," Dominic finished the sentence for him. He glanced back at Tonita, then again to Jeff.

Jeff manipulated the page once again and moved the map to the next sequence. "And there's the B." The Greek letter --B-- appeared in the same place on the new page as the A had on the previous. Jeff folded the map once again revealing another side. "Now, here's where I figured this out." Jeff pointed to the corner of the third page where the alphabet continued. "See here. The designer of this flexagon uses the --Γ-- gamma symbol here, just where our letter --C-- would be. And on the next page you'll find the delta symbol --Δ-- followed by the epsilon, which to most would look just like our --E--."

"So, to a casual observer, there is no pattern," Dominic stated.

"Right. Unless of course you're into math or you're a Greek scholar."

Dominic reached out and took the flexagon map from Jeff, stared at it for moment, then looked up at the others and smiled. "Or...you're a believer in divine intervention."

SIXTY EIGHT

Dominic turned the rented Oldsmobile Alero off of route 247 just past mile marker 17, as he had a day ago, skidding on the dirt road, and then heading out into the desert. "Are you sure you're on the first page of that..." He hesitated.

"Flexagon," Tonita finished for him.

"Map," Dominic added.

"Yes, I'm on the first page." Tonita held the flexagon in one hand and the map from the car rental company in the other. "I've compared the flexagon map with the map from the car rental, and I'm sure that this is the road we just turned off of." Tonita showed the flexagon map and the car rental map to Dominic.

Dominic slowed the car down to a near stop, and looked back and forth between the two maps. "I think you're right. This looks like the same road that we turned off of." He pointed to the line on the car rental map. "See? This is Route 247 and it sort of squiggles around here. And so does this." He pointed to the flexagon. "If we use route 247 as a landmark, then we can follow the markings on the flexagon to ..." He glanced up at Tonita. "Well, to somewhere."

"Somewhere? That scares me."

"It's the best answer I have." Dominic stepped on the gas and the Alero moved forward, bouncing on the dirt road.

"I hope this car makes it." Tonita reached up and grabbed the support bar attached to the frame of the car, just above the passenger door. "I'm not sure, but I seriously doubt that an Alero was made to trek into the desert."

The dirt road ran straight before them, following the natural lay of the land, for the most part, but occasionally cut counter to the grain of the desert. It was a seldom-used roadway. No tires had left the imprint of their treads in the sandy dirt, or if they had, the wind had smoothed them all away a long time ago.

Tonita followed the dirt road on the flexagon map, occasionally glancing out of the rear window to check their position against the paved roadway of Route 247, now far behind them. Every now and then a side road branched off of the main road and Tonita checked them off as they progressed deeper into the dessert. "Okay, we just passed this little road here off to the side, and we're at the edge of the first page of the flexagon."

Dominic adjusted the air conditioning vent of the Alero to blow directly on him. The vehicle was working overtime, and the fan of the air conditioner was blowing out more of a breeze of cooled air than a blast of cold. Dominic began to feel the heat, both from the sun beating down on the car and from the stress of being out in the middle of the desert with a folded paper map that may lead them nowhere, and without so much as a gallon of water with them. He hadn't thought about the drive into the desert in terms of survival, but now he wished he had. There had been plenty of opportunity to secure food and water to bring along, but the thought had not occurred to him until this moment. Not too bright for an ex-service man, he thought.

The adventure that the flexagon had promised clouded his mind and filled his thoughts with the possibilities of what may lie ahead, so much so, that the dangers of the trek were lost. He chastised himself for not being prepared, and contemplated turning back and beginning again the next day better prepared.

"It works!" Tonita nearly shouted. "I moved the flexagon from the -- A --page to the -- B -- page and look." She held up the flexagon so that Dominic could see it without diverting his eyes from the dirt road ahead. "The lines match perfectly."

Now, with their destiny clearly laid out before them, Dominic dismissed the thought of turning around and beginning again tomorrow. He pushed down onto the gas pedal of the Alero and urged its little engine forward.

Just over 16 miles into the desert, Tonita maneuvered the flexagon to the fifth page of the map. Near the far edge of the map, the lines of the road curved around a small circle that could not be seen when the page was at its original size and before it had been folded into the flexagon. The circle was formed by an arch in one fold and an arch in another fold that curved in the opposite direction of the first. Separately, they formed part of the lines that squiggled around the page. But once the map had been folded, only a small portion of the lines remained visible. Two portions of the lines formed the circle.

"Do you see anything? Tonita asked, squinting her eyes.

"Like something alive?"

"Well, that too. But there's a circle on the map and the road curves around it, so I'm thinking that we should see something."

"That circle could mean anything. An old building. A rock. A hole."

"Or that!"

Dominic looked in the direction that Tonita was pointing. Her arm stretched out, her index finger extended, crossing his line of sight. Diagonal to their heading less than a half a mile ahead, the rusted remains of a metal structure lay crumbled in the desert.

SIXTY NINE

Bill Celent stood between the well, gurgling with the sounds of life preserving water, and the rocks on which the three figures had been standing. The same three figures that were now moving slowly, almost cinematically, as if directed by some great silver screen mogul. They moved between the ripples of heat. Their outlines against the backdrop of the darkening desert sky were distorting, almost melting, in and out of human form. Their silent march continued in Bill's direction without hesitation.

In the distance, far behind the slowly moving figures, great clouds of dust lofted, then fell back to the earth following the direction of the breeze. The dust clouds rose, fell off, and then rose again. Like a game of dominos, the dust tumbled in order. A quiet rumbling, that Bill felt more than heard, as it welled up from the soles of his bare feet, accompanied the distant dust clouds.

The three distant figures continued their approach, either not hearing or not caring about the dust clouds and the rumbling to their backs. A flash of recognition sparked in Bill's mind as he watched their steady movement. The delirium of traveling in time and the scorching heat of the desert gave way to scientific deduction. Soldiers.

Behind the soldiers, three military transport trucks, canopied in a darker green canvas, reminded Bill of the covered wagons, of the not so distant past, as they traveled these same desert paths. The transport trucks broke through the veil of dust that had kicked up when the thick-treaded rubber tires tore through the desert crust. The rumbling of the trucks' engines now clearly heard, as well as felt, scared a flock of grey desert grouse into the air. They circled over Bill's head and he turned and following the flock, watching as they landed not far off, and immediately took cover under the scrub brush.

The military transport trucks came to a halt in a chevron pattern, just behind the three soldiers. Cab doors popped open and the driver and passenger in each of the trucks jumped down. They ran to the rear of the trucks, and in moments the gates of the trucks had come down, and an area of earth, that may not have ever been creased by the footsteps of man, was crowded with solders.

"Bill Celent?" One of the three foot soldiers glanced at a photograph then repeated, "Bill Celent?"

Bill cocked his head, somewhat confused that they would know his name, and somewhat relieved. He answered, "Yes, I'm Bill Celent."

"If you wouldn't mind, sir." The soldier with the photograph stepped forward, "Come with us."

As if he had a choice, Bill nodded and fell in alongside the three soldiers.

The other soldiers, who had arrived on the military transport trucks, were lined up in perfect military fashion, and as Bill passed, he heard orders shouted out to them by a clipboard carrying sergeant. "Every piece of debris will be removed from this area. I don't want so much as to find a bolt or nut. If I do, I'll have yours." The sergeant raised his voice and his blood pressure. "Do you understand me?"

A rousing, enthusiastic, "Yes, sir!" in near perfect unison was the reply.

"No questions," the sergeant continued, shouting at his men. "There are to be no questions. Every piece of everything that does not belong in this desert will be removed. We will not leave a trace of this..." the Sergeant glanced down at the clipboard in his hand and read from a printed page, "This Air Force experimental *weather balloon, behind." He looked up. "That is what crashed here. An experimental weather balloon. Do not deviate from that. Do you understand me?"*

Again, in unison, a choir of, "Yes, sir!"

Bill was ushered to the back of the nearest transport. He peered around the truck and watched as the soldiers obeyed the sergeant's orders and spread out, moving like an ocean wave and using their bare hands to pick up anything that was foreign to the desert. One of the soldiers grabbed Bill by the arm. He along with the other foot soldiers, moved to the back of the transport parked farthest away from the wave of troops, stepping carefully through the scrub, and climbed in. The engine came to life as the driver backed the truck up and turned it, heading back in the same direction that the trucks had come.

As the truck pulled away, Bill could see a group of soldiers push the bodies of Commander Kupovits and Lynda into black body bags and carry them off, placing the bodies under the canvas cover of one of the other transports. He sighed with a long breath and relaxed, as the other soldiers moved away from the rocks, leaving what he had buried there, undiscovered.

"It's all right now. You'll be fine," The lead foot soldier said, misunderstanding the sigh as a sign of relief at being rescued.

Bill smiled and nodded his head. "Thank you." He leaned back, resting his head on the canopy support bar that curved above him, and closed his eyes. A moment later, he opened his eyes, sat up, and looked at the lead foot soldier. "I was trying recall in detail everything that has happened since the ..." He hesitated, "the crash. I'm afraid that I may leave some important details out when I speak to your commander." He over emphasized the last words. "Might you have some paper so I can make a note or two?"

The soldier looked around the bed of the transport. Then, with a snap of his fingers, he grabbed a clipboard that had been stuck between a canopy support beam and the back of the bench seat. "Sure, here." He handed Bill the clipboard.

"Thank you." Bill pulled the pencil from the spring-mounted clip and made note of the soldier's name, "Corporal." He leaned toward the soldier and read from his name badge, "Stolt. Corporal Stolt." He wrote the name down on the paper clipped to the board. "I'll make sure to mention your services Corporal. You and your men have been very kind."

Corporal Stolt smiled. "Just doing as I'm told."

"Never the less, worth mentioning," Bill said, then turned his attention to the page on the clipboard and the view out of the back of the transport. He began to work feverishly on the notes. Concentrating. Glancing out of the back of the transport. Then writing, moving the pencil over the page.

An hour and twenty minutes later, as the transport turned off of the dirt trail on to a paved road, Bill placed the pencil behind his ear, rested the clipboard on his lap, and closed his eyes nearly drifting off to sleep immediately.

Within a minute the transport fell into a pothole in the paved road and then lurched up, stretching the shocks to their limits.

Corporal Stolt and the two other soldiers grabbed on to the bench seat for support.

Bill, caught off guard, bounced hard onto the bench and flayed his arms in an effort to grab onto something. The clipboard flew from his lap. Bill reached for it, but lost his balance as the transport fought to right itself. The clipboard continued through the air, hitting the knee of Corporal Stolt before falling to the ribbed metal floor of the transport bed. It landed face side down.

The Third Hour

Corporal Stolt picked up the clipboard and turned it over. He looked at the page, squinted his eyes, and then looked up to Bill. He examined the page closely, bringing it up nearer to his eyes. His face contorted into confusion as he turned the clipboard and the page of paper to Bill and the other soldiers. Lines. The page was filled with lines. Lines that ran in no particular order—zigzagging in every direction—running parallel, perpendicular, and curving all over the page.

SEVENTY

Dominic steered the rented Alero around what had been built as a well, but was now ruins of steel and iron. What had once been filled with water, now tumbled over with sage and desert brush.

A small burrow had been dug into the earth by a desert tortoise or owl, along one side of the rusted ruin that now gave refuge to a rattlesnake that slipped into the hole as Dominic came around the side of the car. "Be careful of that," Dominic said, pointing to the burrow.

Tonita stopped, looked in the direction of the hole, and immediately changed course walking in the other direction. "This was for water?"

Dominic walked the perimeter of the structure coming alongside Tonita. "It had to be a water source. I'm sure that they grazed sheep on this land, and they would have needed a close supply of water. So wells like this were dug. Guzzlers, the locales call them." He walked about ten yards out into the desert and kicked at the earth with the heel of his foot. "It doesn't look like there's been much grazing out here lately."

"I hope not," Tonita said, kicking at the rusted outer ring of the well.

Dominic did not respond. He brushed the hair from his face and slowly scanned the horizon. A small ravine ran off to the left, carved out by water from rain that had fallen long ago onto the scorched desert crust in sufficient quantities to cause a flow. It ran for few yards down slope and then ebbed out into a larger flow plane. But that was long ago, and any moisture now lay hidden deep underground. The surrounding earth appeared, at first glance, to be flat, almost void of dimension. But as Dominic continued to scrutinize the area, he noticed that the land did have shape. He could clearly see small hills, nothing more really than little bumps in the earth, and small depressions carved out by wind and water over eons of time.

"Come on," Dominic said, then began to walk away.

Tonita followed leaving the well and the car to their backs. "Where are we going?"

"I don't see much out here, and I don't know what we're looking for. So, let's just walk around," Dominic called over his shoulder.

"Can you wait up for a second?"

Dominic stopped, and without turning around, waited for Tonita to come up alongside of him. Once she joined him, they moved forward. "I don't know what we're doing here." His voice carried an evident irritation to it. "And I don't know what we're looking for." He shifted his eyes to the ground.

"We're looking for something."

"Thank you." Irritation replaced by sarcasm.

Tonita stopped, grabbed Dominic's arm turning him around. "All right, the map brought us this far and we know we followed it correctly," she spoke matter-of-factly. "So, we are where we are supposed to be." Her eyebrows raised, and a grin spread across her reddened cheeks, "Now, we just need to figure out why we're where we are supposed to be." Tonita laughed.

"Was that one of those tongue twisters, like...say sun shine city real fast five times?" Dominic smiled.

"No." Tonita pouted. "I was just summarizing why we are where we are."

"And so concisely, too."

"I'm only trying to help."

"Do me a favor." Dominic looked directly at her. "Stop then."

"Look, there was a circle on the map and we found that." Tonita held the map up pointing to the circle and then to the ruins of the well behind them.

"We hope."

"Stop being a doubting Thomas."

Dominic stared at her. "No one says that anymore."

She glared at him, "The road, or the line that we think is the road, stops at the circle. The circle is the water thing over there, and there is nothing else here or on the map." She pointed to the ground. "The map stops here. I think that we should look around that old well. Something has to be there, because there is nothing between there and that rock." She pointed up to a pile of rocks that had at one time been a mound covered with sand and dirt. After millennia of wind and rain, the dried earth had been eroded away, leaving what looked like a pile of boulders.

Dominic raised his eyes skyward, then turned to Tonita. "What did you just say?"

"I was pointing out the obvious, Dom. There is a well that doesn't work anymore, and who knows when it last did, and nothing more between it and that pile of rocks. That's it."

"Upon this rock," Dominic whispered. "Upon this rock," he said loudly. "Come on." He grabbed hold of Tonita's hand and took off running, pulling Tonita with him.

With the old well to their backs, Dominic and Tonita headed for the pile of rocks and small boulders fifty yards ahead of them. The sun, now high overhead, cast a shadow that fell slightly in front of them as they ran. Dominic glanced down at his shadow and that of Tonita's just behind him. The shadows glided over the land and brush; silhouettes warping and conforming to the land, rocks and plants, transforming from two shadows to one as Dominic and Tonita's bodies adjusted to the terrain.

The rocks were now just a short distance away and Dominic shouted, "Upon this rock, I will build my church!" As he said this, Tonita moved off to his right, still trailing behind him. He countered and moved to the left, their shadows fell together. And for a moment, in the shadows, having become one, the silhouette of a man, with a long flowing robe and outstretched arms welcomed them forward. They followed. At the foot of the rocks, Dominic and Tonita came to a stop as the shadow of the man, his arms wide apart, continued to flow up the face of the rocks, and held there. "And the gates of hell shall not prevail against it," Dominic said breathlessly, then let go of Tonita's hand. The shadow figure on the rock dissolved from one robed figure back into the silhouettes of Dominic and Tonita.

Dominic quickly climbed up on the rocks. He surveyed the area in every direction. The rental car sat baking by the old well, rippling waves of heat emanating from it. High mountain ridges, many miles away, sloped down to the valley floor and opened up to the great vastness of the desert. An occasional insect's buzz broke the silence that, until then, had only been broken by their pounding footsteps and gasping breaths. "This is the spot," he said, looking down from his rocky perch at Tonita.

"This is the spot?" Tonita asked. "The spot for what?"

"Whatever it is that we're supposed to find."

"But we don't know what we're supposed to find or where to look for it."

"I do," Dominic said, raising his hand to his heart. "Upon this rock, I shall build my Church and the gates of hell shall not prevail against it." Jesus said that to Cephas, a man who joined Jesus and the Apostles. Cephas was also called Simon. But he is better known as Saint Peter the Apostle. Jesus renamed Cephas giving him the name of Peter when he came to Jesus and fell in with the Apostles. Peter!" Dominic exclaimed. "The name means rock!"

"So it's here?"

"It must be. Whatever Cardinal Celent did, or found, or saw that day in the desert, must be here." Dominic surveyed the area again, turning in a complete circle. "If we're supposed to see something from here, I'm not finding it. There's nothing more than just the same scrub and dirt and dust," Dominic said, as he bent his knees to jump down. He hesitated, contemplating the ten foot plunge, then pushed his weight down onto his lower legs and feet and began to spring off the rocks. Then, one foot slipped on the blackened desert baked surface of a boulder. His arms flew out to steady himself but there was nothing there to grab hold of. He fell onto his butt and slid down the surface of the rocks, half landing and half falling to the smaller stones below. His feet dug into the stones, pushing them forward. His back scraped against the edge of the rock. He arched backwards as the skin was peeled away from his back in a steady line crossing his shoulder blades to his ribs. His shirt tore, his hand bruised and his ankle twisted, as he finally came to a stop.

Tonita covered her face with her hands as Dominic slipped on the rocks and fell, releasing only a slight gasp from her covered mouth. "Are you okay?" She leaned forward extending her hands to Dominic.

"I think so." Dominic tried to stand, slipped again on the stones loosened from the fall, but caught himself. "That hurt." He hobbled away from the rock.

"You tore your shirt."

"I don't think that's all I tore," Dominic said, turning around and raising his shirttails. "Here look."

"Oh, Dom you've got a nasty scratch. You might even need stitches."

"Well then, I hope you brought a sewing kit? 'Cause I didn't."

"When we get back into town, I'll have a closer look," Tonita said, letting the shirttail fall gently. "Dom, do you think we should just go and come back? You're hurt. We didn't bring any supplies. We're not very good at treasure hunting..."

"Tonita?" Dominic whispered.

Her voice trailed off, "What is it?"

Dominic didn't respond. He raised his arm, letting his index finger slowly uncurl from his fist, and pointed to the glint of sunlight off the foil protruding from the stones at his feet.

SEVENTY ONE

Two days later, an Alitalia 767 touched down at Fiumicino Airport outside of Rome. As the plane rolled to a stop and the "ding-ding" signal from the cockpit alerted the flight attendants and the passengers that it was safe to stand, Dominic reached down and patted the backpack that he had kept his legs around for the length of the flight. Reassured that the backpack and its contents were safe, he unbuckled the seatbelt and stood. The man on the other side of the isle in 17 C also stood, and for a moment the two men jostled for the free space of the plane's left aisle.

"Dom? Just sit down and relax." Tonita patted the seat next to her that Dominic had just vacated. "No one is going anywhere, and we'll have to wait at baggage claim anyway."

Dominic sighed, stood his ground, half in and half out of the aisle for a moment, longer, and then relented, taking the seat next to Tonita. He placed the backpack on his lap and waited for the other passengers on the plane to begin moving forward.

A voice on the intercom announced they had arrived in Rome, and that it was now safe to deplane the aircraft.

"Who made up that word?" Dominic turned to Tonita not really expecting an answer. "I hate it. We are not deplaning. We're disembarking. We're exiting. We're getting off."

"Okay, Dom. I get it." Tonita rested her hand on Dom's arm. "You're a little edgy?" It wasn't really a question.

Dominic sighed, brushed the hair from his face, and waited as the front rows of passengers started to move out.

***

Twenty minutes later, Tonita emerged from the rest room, stationed along the corridor of gates. She hesitated in the hallway, looking around for Dominic. A moment later, she saw him in a bookstore, just across from the restrooms. She'd just started off in his direction, when she banged into the side of something hard.

"Oh, excuse me," the voice came from a man.

"No. I'm so sorry," Tonita responded, and reached out to the man's shoulder. It was as hard as muscle could get, and as Tonita took in more of the young man, she realized how handsome he was. No, she thought, gorgeous. He wasn't just handsome; he was a hunk.

"I should have been watching where I was going. Did I hurt you?" the hunk said, beaming bright white teeth at her, through perfectly parted lips.

"No. No." Tonita stared into his almost hypnotic eyes. "I'm fine."

"Va Bene," he said in Italian, belying his native tongue.

"Yes. All is well," Tonita translated into the English.

He arched an eyebrow. "Well, then I hope the rest of your journey is uneventful." The man turned and walked off.

Tonita stood and watched the young hunk walk away, and just as she was about to look away and attempt to relocate Dominic, the young man turned back to her. He winked and smiled. Tonita glanced away, looking past him, and then quickly moved her eyes back to the man. She smiled back to him.

He nodded, turned, and continued moving down the corridor toward baggage claim and the airport terminal exits.

Tonita found Dominic still browsing the aisles of books and book related gadgets. "Ready?"

Dom looked up from the back cover of a newly released book on Jack the Ripper and the woman who loved him. "This is interesting." He held out the book to Tonita.

She took it, looked at the front cover, examining the raised letters in blood red and the beautiful girl below them. She turned to the back of the cover and read the blurb.

"I never thought about it," Dominic continued. "But, even Jack the Ripper could have had someone who loved him."

Tonita finished reading the back cover blurb and flipped through the pages, as if she could judge the contents of the writing by the weight of the page. "Looks intriguing. I'll have to read it." She placed the book back onto the shelf. "I love a good story."

***

They walked out of the small bookstore and headed toward customs and baggage claim. The lines at customs snaked around a series of handrails, designed to keep everyone in order and moving forward. Constant announcements from the overhead public address system, warned all, that cell phone use in this area was prohibited, and to please wait for the agents to call you forward. The PA repeated in Italian, English, Spanish, and Japanese, before Dominic lost interest and stopped paying attention. He took Tonita's hand. "Come on," he said, leading her to one of the available customs agents. Dominic pulled out the Vatican diplomatic cards and waved them in front of the agent.

The bored looking man hardly glanced at the documents before saying, "Benvenuto a Roma, goda il vostro soggiorno."

Dominic smiled at the agent, then responded, "I live here. But, of course, I'll enjoy my stay." He continued ahead, walking past lines of tourists awaiting their passport inspections. When he reached the doorway leading to baggage claim, he stopped and waited for Tonita to catch up.

She was standing just past the customs desk, speaking animatedly with a man that looked like he had just stepped off of the covers of high-end fashion magazine.

The man was casually dressed in low cut jeans and a button-down shirt that was mostly unbuttoned. He had the shirt untucked in the back and partially tucked into the jeans in the front. His deep-red hair was brushed back off his face, and hung over his ears, as though each strand had been perfectly arranged. There was a familiarity about the man that Dominic could not immediately place, and he thought that the man may have been a model or actor that he had seen on television or in a magazine. Whoever he was, Tonita appeared to know him. Dominic swept the room with his eyes. Odd, he thought. If the man was an actor or some supermodel, no one else recognized him. Hundreds of people just deplaned, and were now lined up against the rails slowly making their way through customs. Not one of them took notice of the man. Dominic concentrated on the man's face. He had seen him before. That he was sure of. He called out to Tonita, "Hey, come on." A touch of jealousy surged up from his stomach as Tonita turned in his direction, smiled at him, and held up her index finger in the "just a minute" gesture.

Dominic leaned back on the wall and, trying to act as uninterested as possible, stared down at the floor. Every half a minute or so, he pushed the hair from his face in an attempt to disguise the fact that he was watching Tonita's engrossed conversation with this man. A moment later, he abandoned the hair in his face ploy and just stared out into the crowd, unconcerned.

Tonita laughed a laugh that distance prevented Dominic from hearing. She covered her mouth like a silent film star, sweeping the air in a grand gesture with her other hand, then bringing it back to her waist, as though she had been choreographed in the art of seduction.

The man reached out with one hand and rested it gently on Tonita's arm. He cocked his head, completely absorbed by Tonita's conversation. Then, he turned in Dominic's direction, diverting his gaze from Tonita to him, and a slow smile that could only be described as pure evil, spread across his face.

In a flash of recognition, Dominic realized that the man Tonita was standing with, was the same man, dark haired at the time, head partially covered by a hood, and body robed, that they'd discovered in Cardinal Celent's apartment. The man who claimed he was in the apartment at the behest of Vatican officials to watch over and protect Cardinal Celent's belongings. The man who had tumbled down the flight of stairs leading to Cardinal Celent's apartment, landing in a crumpled heap. And the same man that Dominic and Tonita had left for dead. Without a moment of hesitation, Dominic burst into a full run, charging straight at the man.

Too late. The Novice had contemplated Dominic's every possible move, and moved his hand from Tonita's arm up to her throat in a split second.

Tonita was caught completely off guard, and could barely get out a muted scream, before The Novice's hand closed around her throat.

With incredible speed and strength, the Novice moved behind Tonita, replacing his hand with his forearm, planting it precisely against her trachea. He pulled back onto her body and she could do nothing more than give in and fall back onto him. His smile grew.

"Let go of her," Dominic was yelling as loudly as he could, still racing forward.

The commotion attracted the attention of the customs guards, who ordered people down, and then rushed toward the trio, rifles raised.

"Aiutila. Help her!" Dominic shouted to the guards, obeying their command to stop.

"Sono un Novice. Questa donna è un whore e deve essere delt con!" The Novice raised his voice to a shrill. "Deve morire!" His words were followed by a heinous laugh. "She must die priest. And so will you!" he spit out in English.

Dominic took a cautious step toward the Novice.

The Novice countered with a jerk on Tonita's neck. Her eyes fluttered, as her face began to turn a deep red, going to blue, as the trachea was sealed and her breath was cut off. The Novice moved, dragging Tonita with him as he headed toward baggage claim. He made his way quickly through the glass enclosed security door separating customs from baggage claim, easily slipping by the guards and security agents there, who were just as ineffectual as the guards and agents in the customs hall.

A baggage carousel that snaked, rather than circled, filled the area around baggage claim number seven. The track, weighed down with hordes of overstuffed bags, entered the public area of baggage claim through a black, heavy vinyl flapped door on one side of the track, and after snaking around the loop exited out another black vinyl flapped doorway on the far end. If a bag remained on the track, in several minutes it would come out the first doorway again, snaking around the track until claimed, or back out the into the maze of belts, risers, and rollers to start the trek again.

The Novice pulled Tonita up to the snaking baggage track and quickly flipped her over his body, slamming her onto the moving beltway. He jumped on top of her, and like a kid in a carnival thrill ride, waved as he and Tonita exited through the flapped door into the bowels of the airport.

Richard Devin

A tremendous amount of shouting and commotion accompanied the rush of guards, security, and police as they scurried about the customs and baggage claim areas. All rushing about, but accomplishing little.

Dominic jumped onto the moving belt and began to ride it into the unseen baggage loading area of the airport, following the same path that the Novice had just taken. Suddenly, he was thrust forward, tumbling off the belt, hitting his head on the metal edge of the beltway platform, and falling onto the hard, tiled floor. He pulled himself up and saw that a security agent had pressed the emergency button and stopped the belt. He cursed at the guard, "Va Funguila!" checked the backpack on his shoulder, and threw himself through the door, leaving the public area of baggage claim behind.

Once through the thick black, vinyl flaps and into the interior maze of the baggage transit area, Dominic's eyes had to adjust to the stark difference in lighting from the harsh florescence of the public area to the poorly lit inner workings. Only luggage generally traveled through this inhospitable maze of belts and rollers that took the overstuffed bags from hundreds of travelers from the holds of hundreds of aircrafts, and routed them to the correct baggage claim area. It was a place that few ventured into, except on the rare occasions to dislodge a bag that had become stuck on a curve or a loose rail.

Tonita's scream echoed among the clanging, moving bridges of metal-wheeled rollers and thumps of the heavily stitched seams of the rubber belts spinning rapidly around tension pins.

Dominic looked up. He scanned the upper reaches of the crisscrossing belts and rollers. Luggage and boxes of every sort and size passed around and in front of him, confusing and camouflaging any movement that the Novice might make. Dominic noticed a two foot-wide catwalk that followed the path of most of the belts and rollers. In some places it extended above a set of rollers, and in other spots, crept below. If a piece of luggage slipped into a support brace or jammed on a curve, the blockage would cause a collision and a pile up of luggage just like a jackknifed rig on a four lane highway in fog. A maintenance worker would be summoned and have to crawl, stoop, and hurdle the belts and rollers following the catwalk to find the area that needed clearing. The design was certainly drawn out by a crazed person, as no normal mind could have come up with such configurations.

"Dom!" Tonita yelled. This time clearly.

Maybe she had gotten away, was Dominic's first thought, and he responded, "Tonita? Tonita?" He whirled around, looking up and down, searching the area on either side of him. In between the thumps of belts and clangs of rollers, he heard the quick sound of leather shoes pounding on metal-ridged grating. He quickly turned and caught the movement of the Novice with the limp body of Tonita slung over his shoulder.

She had been able to scream out his name only a moment ago, and now she lay flung over the Novice's shoulder, unconscious...or worse. An image of her face, contorted, gasping unsuccessfully for breath with the Novice's hands wrapped around her throat, flashed in Dominic's mind. He forced the image out of his thoughts, then scrambled up the catwalk. He jumped over the belt and slid down a roller, riding a piece of luggage, like a raft down a waterslide, but again the Novice was too fast.

Distant voices and the crackling of radios let Dominic know that security and the police were inside. He called to them, "Sono Dominic Renzi, Padre Renzi. L'uomo biondo ha..." He almost said that the man they were hunting for had his girlfriend, but after just announcing that he was a priest, decided that would not be the correct wording, and just said girl. "Una ragazza chiamata, Tonita. È dentro qui."

"Come out. Uscito—lasci la polizia prendere la cura di questa situazione and, let the police handle this." A gruff voice made its way to Dominic.

Slightly below Dominic, and off to the right a good twenty yards, a blast of light flooded the interior of the baggage area. A door had opened and closed quickly, letting in the blinding burst of sunlight and the unmistakable sounds and smells of a roaring jet engine.

Dominic leapt down to the ground, secured the backpack to him and hurried in the direction of the door. Several police officers, mixed with a couple of airport security agents, had also decided to make a run for the door. The pack met there almost simultaneously and pushed on each other to get through. If Tonita's life had not been in danger, Dominic thought that this scene would have been laughable. But now, it only spurred him to anger. He burst through the guards and police, and found himself on the tarmac face to face with the Novice.

Tonita lay at his feet. Her body limp. Her color becoming blue. Dominic wasn't sure if she was dead or alive. He raised his eyes from Tonita's body to the Novice.

"Don't be so concerned priest. Your whore is not dead." The Novice grinned. "Not yet." He raised his foot and placed it on Tonita's neck. "But she can be, if you'd like."

"Leave her." Dominic knew that the words were meaningless, but the urge to say something, anything, to the deranged man, overcame his senses. "Take me. That's what you want."

"Oh, I will take you." The Novice laughed. "As if you have a choice, you offer yourself up to me. What about God? Did you offer yourself up to him in the same way? You are a fake. You are no priest, and you do not deserve the Lord's blessing. So there is no need for you to offer yourself as a sacrifice. Your life is mine. And you will die." The Novice leaned his weight forward allowing the toe of his shoe to come down on Tonita's neck. "Just like your whore."

Dominic diverted his eyes from Tonita's neck and the Novice's foot firmly planted on it, to the distance over the Novice's shoulder. He noticed a jet taxiing toward the gate that he, the Novice, the police, and security, were standing around. Apparently, no one in ground control noticed that there was a crowd of people gathered on the tarmac at the gate, and apparently, none of the guards or police considered calling in it in.

Instead, they stood, rifles and pistols raised, some pointing at the Novice and others pointing at Dominic. He hoped that the Novice might turn and look in the same direction, giving the police and security a clear shot. When he did not, Dominic spoke up, "It's not safe here. Let Tonita go and take me. I can get us out of here."

The Novice considered the words for a moment. "You are right that it is not safe here...for you and the whore. If I am to die with you, that is what God has planned for me. I am his servant, and unlike you, priest, I have not disavowed him. I have not chosen to leave him after he has placed such faith in me. I am his soldier, a novice with the Jesuit order. I will fulfill my commitment to my oath and my God, and I will protect the Pope, even if it means giving up my life."

Dominic shifted his feet in an attempt to disguise the slight forward movement. He shuffled a bit to one side and then the other, inching forward.

The Novice's foot still lay angled onto Tonita's throat, with the heel of his shoe on the tarmac and the upper portion at the toe on her jugular. He looked as though he was demonstrating the use of a fuel pedal in an automobile. "That's right. Come closer, priest. I want you to see her die."

Dominic went ridged.

"You fear death." The Novice shouted. "You fear your death and her death. Yet you live because God gave up the life of his only son. He did not fear death as you do. He willingly gave into it. You are not worthy." The Novice shifted his body putting one leg behind him, then leaning back.

The taxiing jet had closed in on the gate and was now making a final turn, following the painted lines leading directly to the gate and jet way. The groundscrew, that would normally accompany an inbound aircraft, was nowhere in sight. They had abandoned the pilot to steer the jet clear of other aircraft and into the gate on his own.

Tonita stirred. One arm lifted slowly up, and then it fell again.

An immediate wave of relief flushed through Dominic's body. She was alive, he thought. Then the gnawing fear came flooding back, replacing the relief and the realization that he had to act soon.

And, as if he could read Dominic's thoughts, the Novice shouted, "Not much longer priest. Repent and I may let this whore live. Explain to God why you left him, and why you continue to hide in his church. Why is it, priest, that you use him so?"

"I do not hide in the church. And I have not left God or the Church."

"I doubt God would agree."

Dominic pushed the hair out of his face. "He has a path for all of us."

"Then his will—will be done through me."

"No!" Dominic shouted. "You're right. You have been sent by God and he has a message. And you are the bearer of that message."

The jet began to swing around toward the gate, slowly, closing the gap between it and the jet way.

Dominic sucked in his breath, as he traced the painted line from the two parallel wheels at the front of the jet to the gate. The line curved, then ran straight, ending in a short 'T' at the jet way. Tonita had been carefully laid out so that her body ran perpendicular to the painted line. If the Novice did not kill her, the jet would.

The pilot perfectly executed the turn, and revving the engines slightly, the jet moved forward.

"It is time." The Novice stared into Dominic's eyes, as the jet's engines surged. He arched his back letting his head fall back.

Dominic shouted, "No!" and rushed forward.

The jet moved within a few feet of the Novice and Tonita's limp body on the tarmac.

Dominic's heart pounded as adrenaline poured into his veins. His eyes bounced from the oncoming jet to the Novice's foot at Tonita's throat, then back again. He calculated the distance, and with growing dread, knew he could not make it in time.

The Novice stood his ground. He watched as Dominic raced forward, ready to sacrifice his life for the whore. "You are a fool," he shouted over the revving engine of the jet. "You will both die." Suddenly, the Novice's face went blank. His eyes opened wide. And then his whole expression turned to shock. He stumbled, falling backwards, fighting to maintain his balance. His right hand came up to his left shoulder, cupping it.

Dominic continued forward without letting his eyes move from the Novice. He scooped up Tonita, half lifting, half dragging her body off the painted line, out of the path of the oncoming jet and the twin wheels rolling along the line. He pulled her back toward the terminal.

The Novice pulled his hand away from his shoulder, revealing a growing scarlet stain. He looked directly at Dominic. Then, his eyes drifted over Dominic's head, allowing his gaze to linger there.

The jet came to a stop, just feet from the Novice and the end 'T' of the painted line.

The Novice averted his gaze from behind Dominic to the jet in back of him. He turned back to Dominic and smiled.

Then suddenly, the pilot revved the jet's engines. The turbines sprang to life and spun with ferocity, roaring and whining in a cacophony of noise, propelling the aircraft forward as it closed the gap between the front wheels of the plane and the painted "T" at the end of the line.

The Novice's eyes grew wide and the sudden realization hit him, as he first stumbled, then was picked up by the tremendous force of the spinning turbines and sucked backwards into the engines, folding in half, face to foot, as the fan cut him into pieces and thrust him out the rear of the engine in a scarlet spray.

Dominic stared at the unfathomable sight of a man blended by the jet's turbines into little more than liquefied flesh and blood. The awestruck disgust at the horrific sight turned quickly to relief, as a moan escaped from Tonita's lips. Her eyes opened, fluttered, and closed. Dominic turned, looking over his shoulder to the same spot behind him. The place the Novice had been looking.

Inspector Carrola stood atop a small set of stairs that led from the terminal to the tarmac, pistol raised.

SEVENTY TWO

"Dominic?" Inspector Carrola spoke softly, respectful of the chapel and the prayers recited here.

Dominic lifted his head from his hands and shifted his knees on the thick padding of the pew's knee rest. He didn't turn around. He didn't have to. The voice was instantly recognized. He had been waiting these past few hours for him to come. The hours spent here in the chapel had been a welcome relief from the minutes spent on the tarmac at the airport. The flow of adrenaline pumping through his veins, as he watched the Novice toy with Tonita's life, and his own, had faded soon after the events unfolded, and had left him feeling empty, sad, depressed and exhausted.

The Novice got what he deserved, Dominic thought and then immediately tried to erase the thoughts and the vision from his consciousness of the final moments. Instead every detail grew sharper, words and sounds unheard, as he stood upon the tarmac, were now clearly heard and left to repeat in his mind. Sights and smells came rushing back as he contemplated the moments. He had, just in the nick of time, as the saying goes, he thought, pulled Tonita to safety. But the vision of two-foot diameter wheels rolling over her torso, with the hundreds of tons of aircraft above them flattening her body—kept playing out in his mind. Dominic shook his head trying to dislodge the vision.

The medical team at the airport pounced on Tonita once the area was cleared. They swarmed around her, shouting in Italian for medical equipment and supplies. They pumped and pounded on her frail body. Jabbing syringes of clear liquid into her veins. Her body remained limp. And despite the comforting words of the medics, Dominic could not help but wonder and worry and draw the only conclusion that he could.

Until that moment in the customs area of the airport, when the image of the Novice, disguised in a hooded robe at Cardinal Celent's apartment, flashed back, he had all but forgotten about the man he now knew as the Novice of the Jesuit order. A Novice to the Society. He had believed that the man—the Novice—was dead, or at least seriously injured after the fall down the long set of stairs that led to Cardinal Celent's apartment. He never expected to see the man again, and when he saw him at the airport with his hair deep red and his strength intact the images of the man in Cardinal Celent's apartment and the man in customs, did not immediately come together. He consoled himself with the thought that he didn't even know of the man and his determination to kill both Tonita and himself.

At Cardinal Celent's apartment, he had acted on instinct. There was a clear sense of evil and Dominic had acted almost without thought, pulling the Novice forward, causing him to lose his balance and tumble down the stairs. All of his actions—reactions, he reconsidered—were that of prey. It was instinctive. It was an act of self-preservation.

It was all coming together as he laid out the events of the last few days. The monk who attacked him and Cardinal Celent in his apartment. The priest who died there. The Novice. Cardinal Celent. Senator Scott. The Vatican. Each had a role in the events. Each participated to do what they thought or were told that God wanted them to do. And then a thought struck him with an emotional sledgehammer.

Tonita?

His doubts played on him. He pushed them away with prayer. *Our Father who art in heaven...*he began the silent prayer, but before he could finish the first line, the words of the Novice came back to him. *I have not*

chosen to leave him after he has placed such faith in me.
He started the prayer again, *Our Father who art in heaven...*and the doubts intruded once again. Dominic raised his eyes upward, looking to the one stained glass window high above the Nave of the chapel. The blue, red, yellow, and purple glass reflected the light, not cast from the sun, but from the LED lighting framing the window. Dominic shook his head in dismay.

The Novice had spoken the truth. Dominic had chosen to leave the church. He had given up on God and the church, but still lived in the shadows of Vatican, taking refuge there. And he did this while denying the church and God. *How had the Novice known?* The question dogged him.

Had he become a modern version of Judas, betraying God, and all the while taking comfort and refuge in his church? He hid there, just as Judas had.

Dominic had left the church because of the lingering doubts in his belief. He had convinced himself that those were doubts about God, and whether He existed. And if He did, whether He cared about man or not. Now, head raised to the heavens, he realized the cloud of doubt was not about whether God existed, but, instead, whether Dominic existed. He was secure in the existence of the shell that others called Dominic—in his body of flesh and blood. He could feel it, taste it, and abuse it. It was his to do as he wished. But there was more. Or, he thought, should be more, and that is where his true doubt lie. He could not commit to the spirit of himself. *Self-preservation or divine intervention?* The question rose up in his thoughts.

A hand touched Dominic's shoulder, lingering lightly there. "Chi più meglio per indicare che il dio esiste, il credi o non—il credi? Who better to learn that God does exist? The believer or the non-believer?"

Dominic turned toward the softly spoken voice.

Richard Devin

Cardinal Celent took hold of the pew rail and lowered himself to the bench. He carefully slid forward, placing his knees on the knee rest. He brought his hands together, then, making the sign of the cross, he said, "In the name of the Father, and of the Son and ..." he paused, turning to Dominic, "in the name of the Holy Spirit." Completing the sign of the cross, Cardinal Celent raised his hand, moving it to Dominic's face. He wiped away a tear that had slowly formed in the corner of Dominic's eye. He stared for a long moment, looking past the surface of Dominic's eyes and into his soul. "And Jesus wept," he said, repeating the words from the shortest verse in the Bible.

Dominic leaned his head on Cardinal Celent's shoulder. Then, turning to the large cross that hung from the ceiling of the chapel at the front of the nave, he spoke, "Lord, I am not worthy, but only say the words and I shall be healed." He repeated the words falling into a chant, "Lord, I am not worthy, but only say the words and I shall be healed. Lord, I am not worthy..."

And Cardinal Celent joined in, "... But only say the words and I shall be healed."

SEVENTY THREE

Cardinal Celent brought the ancient bits of torn cloth and rags to his face and breathed in the stale, raw aroma of the two thousand year old fabric. The dry desert air of New Mexico had kept the cloth from mildewing and rotting, and despite the more than sixty years that the cloth of ancient Judea had remained buried under the stones and rocks outside of Corona, the material had little deterioration. He carefully placed the bundle of cloth down onto the altar of the small chapel.

Dominic and Inspector Carrola each stood to one side of Cardinal Celent, like altar boys at mass, watching Cardinal Celent as he unwrapped the metal-like foil that had once lined the water pit surrounding the small brown building. It was the same foil that he had gathered from the brush of the desert after his return from ancient Jerusalem. He carefully pulled it back, piece by piece, revealing more of the rags of cloth. He set the cloth aside, then removed a small bundle of tightly twisted foil that had been hidden underneath. He slowly untwisted the end of the foil and poured out the contents onto the altar. A handful of pebbles and sand fell onto the polished wooden top of the altar, forming a tiny pile. Cardinal Celent looked up to the cross, then turned to Dominic and said, "The blood of Christ." He reached out and picked up one of the rust colored, blood stained pebbles, took Dominic's hand, and placed the pebble in the center of his palm. Cardinal Celent wrapped his own hand around Dominic's, closing them both.

Dominic's eyes closed, and his head fell back as his body shuddered. After a moment he opened his eyes and smiled.

Cardinal Celent unfolded his hand from Dominic's and turned back to the altar and the bundle of foil and cloth. Removing another layer of foil, revealed a final wrapped object; he pulled the last piece from the foil and, with great care, began to fold back the layer upon layer of foil that had encased the object for more than sixty years. The last piece of foil was peeled back, revealing a folded square of papyrus paper. Cardinal Celent touched the papyrus with the tip of his first two fingers and was immediately taken back to the scene of the crucifixion. In his mind, he replayed the moments.

A commotion behind him caught his attention, and he turned to see the man he thought to be Pilate standing in a small chariot pulled by a team of heavily breathing horses. Several Centurions followed the chariot on foot, keeping up the best they could, as Pilate circled the plateau of Golgotha, screaming at the crowd, "Illic is exsisto jesus talea abbas. Vos certus!"

The crowd of thieves, peasants, and clergy parted in the wake of the chariot, and then, like a great ocean wave, folded back together as the charging horses and crazed man passed.

Pilate circled again, nearly trampling an older woman who could barely move quickly enough, and would have certainly been hacked to death by the pounding hooves, if a man hadn't grabbed her by the waist pulling her out of the path of the oncoming chariot. Pilate passed her, with only inches separating the woman and the chariot's wheels. He gave her no notice and continued shouting his rant, "Illic is exsisto jesus talea abbas. Vos certus!" His face red, veins pulsing in his neck, Pilate snapped the reins onto the haunches of the horses and urged them on into a frenzy. He circled again raising up the dust and throwing the crowd into a near panic as they tried to project the path of the chariot and clear a route. The centurions, who had been following the chariot on foot, had now given up the chase and stopped near the pathway, panting and sweating under the heavy cloth and armor of their rank. They watched in dismay as their commander screamed again to the crowd, and then turned the chariot in their direction.

Pilate headed directly for the centurions and the spot where William "Bill" Celent, the young scientist, who would someday be Cardinal, now stood. The crowd ahead of the chariot scurried out of the way of the galloping horses and the bouncing, nearly out of control, chariot. Pilate grabbed the reins with one hand and steadied himself with the other, taking hold of the rail mounted to the side of the chariot. He pulled the reins to the right, and the horse responded by turning onto the pathway and headed down the hill, following the same path Christ did on his way up to the sight of crucifixion. The chariot's wheels hit a rut in the worn path as it turned, sending Pilate and the cart into the air. It landed hard. Pilate fell forward. The chariot skidded to the side, then righted itself. Pilate pulled back on the reins, leaning his body back as he did. The horses slowed and Pilate turned back to the crowd. And again, in a voice now rough and dry, yelled out in Latin, "Illic is exsisto jesus talea abbas. Vos certus!" There he should be. Jesus bar Abbas. Bar Abbas. You decided! "Vos certus! Vos certus!"

Pilate, with the Roman centurions, again in quick pursuit, continued down the path back through the gate and into the city of Jerusalem. The now crazed crowd turned their attention to the remaining centurions and the task at hand. The crucifixion.

Bill Celent adjusted the rags and bits of cloth around his face, making sure that only his eyes could be seen. He took a step forward, glancing down to check his footing, and there, not a foot and half in front of him, he saw the rolled sheet of papyrus. As the chariot that Pilot was commanding hit the rut in the path and jostled the cart into the air, the papyrus roll had also gone airborne and had landed there at the feet of Bill

Richard Devin

Celent. Unseen by others in the crowd, who were too concerned with their own wellbeing and the man who lay in a crumpled heap on the ground before them, Bill picked up the papyrus roll and tucked it into a fold in the jumpsuit, well camouflaged beneath the rags.

On the altar, unwrapped from the foil and exposed, the papyrus that had once been rolled, was now a flattened square, compressed by the years hidden beneath desert rock, but still remained quite supple. The edges had frayed and one corner had broken away, crumbling into near dust and collected at the bottom of the foil wrapping.

Cardinal Celent pulled gently on the edge of the papyrus. The sheet came away from the underlying sheet. Even though the papyrus had been folded, it did not bond into the sheet below. Now, using both of his hands, Cardinal Celent held the top of the scroll with one hand, pressed firmly down on it, and with the other hand pulled the sheets apart. As the sheet uncoiled, letters became visible: IES. The lines of text were not written left to write, but ran from the top to the bottom of the scroll. Cardinal Celent unfolded another, the center piece of the papyrus roll, and now a more of the text could be seen: IESUS.

Cardinal Celent looked into Dominic's eyes and smiled. He continued to watch Dominic's expression as he unrolled the scroll completely, pressing it flat to the altar, revealing the complete text.

IESUS NAZARENVS REX IVDAEORVM

היהודים מלך והמתנזרת ישו

Ο Ιησούς του βασιλιά των Εβραίων

Dominic's eyes grew wide. He brushed the hair from his forehead, glanced at Cardinal Celent, then traced the letters of the first line of the text with his finger, and read the words aloud, "Jesus Nazarene King Jews." He looked back to Cardinal Celent, then back to the papyrus scroll, as the understanding of what he was reading—what he was looking at and what he was touching—struck him with as much force as a bolt of lightning surging from the clouds above could have. He read the line again, "Jesus the Nazarene King of the Jews."

Cardinal Celent smiled as he watched the man next to him; the Key had just come to the understanding of the task that God had handed him. Just like himself, God had chosen a non-believer to carry the truth and the unimaginable burden that knowing the truth would bring. He had, with the aid of only the trusted few, been able to shoulder this holy burden for the past sixty years. And now, he was just a moment away from passing it on. An odd sense of loss, tremendous freedom mixed with regret, welled up within him. It had been an unexpected journey. His life had been in science, not the occult, and religion had little effect upon him. Yet, God had taken him from the books of fact to a book of faith. He had learned that he did not need faith to carry this burden. He had been shown the truth. A truth that he quickly learned, that must be kept for the few. It was a truth too dangerous to reveal to the world. Governments and people had set up their lives around their systems of beliefs and faiths. And the revelation to the world of what had happened in the New Mexican desert sixty years ago would have caused the world,—that had at the time just come out of a war that involved to many governments, countries and people—to slip back into chaos.

Cardinal Celent fought to release the information. He wanted to show the world what he had found. Show them that God did exist. He was convinced that it would heal the wounds of war. Other's, however didn't agree. The Soviets would never have accepted the church or Jesus, nor would the Japanese, the Chinese, or any other country and government that had already established its power and authority. There were far too many who would rise up against the truth. "My numbers are legion." The words of Satan crept into his thoughts. Cardinal Celent had come to understand what the consequences of revealing the truth to the world would mean. And when the Vatican had ruled on the matter, in a secret synod chosen by the Pope, and had decided that the time was not right. Cardinal Celent had then, reluctantly, obliged to be of the few to bear the burden of this truth. It was his hope that during his lifetime, that truth could be revealed and the world would come together in it. But as he now knew, there had not been, nor would there ever be a time when the truth could be told.

Cardinal Celent let his hand slide away from the bottom of the papyrus scroll that he had pressed flat against the altar, revealing the few remaining inches of the papyrus and the wax seal there.

"Pontius Pilate," Dominic said the words a loud. He touched the cracked darkened wax lightly with the tip of his finger. He could feel the rounded, smooth edges and the indentation of the seal into the wax. The profile of a man and the words Pontius Pilatus had been pressed into the wax while it was molten over two thousand years ago. The impression remained clean and clear. The wax seal was encircled by a legend that read in Latin: Praefectus Judea. "This is the seal of Pontius Pilate?"

"When the Governor of Judea rode through the crowd, excitedly screaming that he had offered Barabas to them in order to spare Jesus' life, this scroll fell to where I was standing. I picked it up, but did not know at the time what it was. And when I returned to the desert in New Mexico, I was surprised that I had it. But, like everything that happened that day in Roswell, we were not in control," Cardinal Celent said, then looked into Dominic's eyes. "These are the words that Pilate wrote," he said, then added. "What I have written I have written," quoting the words of John from the New

Testament. "Pilate responded with those words when the chief priest's made a request to him to change the titilum, 'What I have written I have written.'"

Dominic touched each line of the text on the scroll and spoke, quoting John further, "Pilate also had an inscription written and put on the cross. It read: 'Jesus of Nazareth, the King of the Jews.' Many of the Jews read this inscription, because the place where Jesus was crucified was near the city; and it was written in Hebrew, in Latin, and in Greek."

SEVENTY FOUR

Dominic carefully folded the papyrus scroll back onto itself, then, securely wrapped the metal foil around it. He repeated the process with the blood stained pebbles, securing them tightly by twisting the ends of the metal foil, so that the small package resembled a piece of wrapped candy. He laid out the pieces of cloth, one on top of the other. Then, he put the metal foil wrapped papyrus scroll and pebbles into the middle of the cloth and folded the material, drawing the bottom portion up and then folding down the top. He folded the ends together creating an envelope of the cloth. He took the bundled artifacts, wrapped them in the remaining metal foil, and placed that into his backpack, zipping the compartment closed. He flung the backpack over his shoulder and turned to Cardinal Celent. He opened his mouth slightly, as if there were words for this moment, hesitated, then closed his mouth and simply stared into the eyes of the Cardinal.

A moment later, he reached out taking hold of the Cardinal's hand, placing his own within it.

The men shook hands, each lost for words.

Dominic stepped away from Cardinal Celent and headed up the main aisle of the small chapel.

Inspector Carrola stood at the door. He had remained a silent guard and witness, and Dominic realized in that brief moment in between the steps in his stride, that Inspector Carrola's involvement had, all along, been a part of the design. Dominic stopped in front of the Inspector, smiled, and held out his hand. The Inspector had been right of course, questioning Dominic's faith and loyalty. Hard words that stung at the time. But now, words that rang true, he thought, as he took the Inspector's extended hand and shook it.

"She is okay, Dominic," Inspector Carrola said, releasing Dominic's hand. "Tonita is okay, and she will recover completely."

Dominic sighed, let his smile slip for a moment, and then nodded. He pushed through the doors leading from the small chapel back into the brightly lit, sterile hallways of the hospital.

***

"The peace of the Lord, be with you."

"And also with you," a near unison response welled up from the seated congregation.

"The mass has ended. Go in peace."

The congregation rose to its feet as the organ high up in the balcony above began to sound a low brassy note. "Amen," they chanted back.

Father Dominic Renzi stepped down from the altar, turned back to the cross, and the image of Christ hanging, arms stretched, head looking skyward, intricately carved into the wood. He bowed, made the sign of the cross, and turned back to the waiting congregation, now singing out to the vibrations of the organ. He walked to the back of the church. He waited there as the song ended and the congregation exited past him, shaking hands, kissing babies, and blessing many.

"You seem to have found your calling."

Dominic looked up. "Yes, I believe I have."

"Well done. We are very proud of you." Inspector Carrola slapped Dominic on the side of the arm. "You will never be alone, you know that. We will always be here."

"Thank you, Inspector." Dominic smiled. "I am sure that I can count on you. But it will be many years before I will need to pass on the truth."

"I may not be here then, and certainly Cardinal Celent will not, but there will always be someone. Someone you can trust." Inspector Carrola paused as a congregant passed by. "It is our destiny." Inspector Carrola slapped Dominic once again upon the shoulder and exited the church.

Fifteen minutes later, after the last of the congregants had filed by and the doors to the church had been closed, Dominic stepped into the sacristy—the room that connects to the nave of the church, just beyond the altar. There, he removed the chasuble, lifting up the garment from over his head and carefully hanging it in the closet. He reflected momentarily on the large cross embroidered into the fabric, the symbolic representation of the purple robe worn by Christ when he went before Pilate. He untied the stole and hung it next to the chasuble, then the cincture, and let the alb— the long tunic—fall loosely to the floor.

There was a knock at the sacristy door, followed by, "May I come in?" and Tonita stuck her head into the room.

"Sure," Dominic waved her in.

Tonita stepped in. She cocked her head and looked at Dominic, who, dressed in the long hanging white tunic, with his dark hair and deep, black eyes, and the bit of shadow caused by the dark hairs of his shaven face, looked as though he had just stepped out of painting by Rubens.

Tonita sighed.

"I'm glad you came by. I was hoping you would."

"I can't stay long, the others are waiting." Tonita gestured out the open door.

Dominic stared at her, smiled, raised an eyebrow, and said, "You look beautiful."

"In this?" Tonita frowned. "You've got to be kidding?"

"No. I'm serious."

"Well then," Tonita laughed when she spoke, "so do you."

Dominic looked into her eyes. "I'm going to miss you." He wanted her, and he was sure that she wanted him. They loved one another. Truly loved one another. Yet, both had chosen paths that would lead them away from each other. *A higher calling*, he joked internally, as he fought the urge to grab her, kiss her, and have his way with her.

"Sister? We will be departing shortly," An Italian accented voice echoed in from the hall.

Tonita smiled, then let the smile slip as she fought back tears. "I'm sorry, Dom."

"No need to be."

"I didn't want to deceive you. I didn't want to hurt you." Tears began to slip down her face. "And I didn't mean to fall in love with you." She rushed forward and flung her arms around Dominic's neck.

Dominic returned the embrace, holding on to her tightly, pulling her close, feeling the coarse fabric of the Habit she was wearing. After a moment, he gently pushed her back.

Tonita raised a hand and brushed the hair from his forehead. She stepped back from him. She looked at him. The expression on her face changed from sad to smiles and back again.

"I have something for you," Dominic said, pulling the book of Roswell, that Cardinal Celent had given him, off of a shelf and handing it to her. "Just a way to remind you."

Tonita took the book and brought it up close to her heart. "I don't think that I'll need any mementos to remind me. But thank you."

"Sister? You are coming now?" The older woman's voice carried a tone of concern.

Dominic leaned in and kissed Tonita on the cheek. "Goodbye."

She turned and walked out the door. "Yes, Mother Superior. I am on my way."

***

Minutes later, the other sisters in the Order had all settled into their seats on the motor coach. Most were now in silent prayer, reading passages from the Bible. Some eyes were closed, asleep, or genuflecting. Tonita sat alone in the seat. Since her return, the others had given her the space they thought she needed. None of them knew for certain the reason that she had been gone for so long. "Personal time to find herself and to reaffirm her calling with God," Mother Superior had told the sisters when they asked about Tonita's absence from the Order. She had deceived them also, and she told herself that she would make that up to them. And that someday, they might understand.

Tonita looked out of the large, tinted window of the bus as the driver carefully maneuvered the coach slowly through the narrow and crowded streets of Rome. The drive back to the convent at Abbazia di Santa Maria in Farfa would take little more than an hour. But in that hour, the Sisters of Santa Maria would virtually be transported back to the middle ages and to a sanctuary of great importance to the papacy of old. Today, the former great abbey of the papacy has given way to time and the elements, and few reside there. The sisters of Tonita's order preside over the small guesthouse, taking in and caring for the few tourists who venture to the medieval city.

Tonita glanced at the book on Roswell she had tucked into the flap on the backside of the seat in front of her. Cardinal Celent had come to her personally, visiting the abbey on an historical tour from the Vatican. He had arranged, prior to the trip with the Mother Superior, to meet with Sister Maria a Sunta, the divine name that Tonita had taken on when she had joined the order. It was then, that Cardinal Celent had recruited her. She sighed heavily, regretting and celebrating her decision at once. She reached out and lifted the book from the pocket of the seat in front of her. She flipped through one page and then another. Then, taking her thumb, fanned the pages of the book, taking in the dusty, worn smell of the paper and ink. She fanned the pages again, then once more. It wasn't the smell of the dried up paper that had caught her attention. There was something else. Tonita opened the book so that it was flat on her lap. The pages quickly fell to the right and to the left, parting at the approximate center of the book. All the pages fell to one side or the other.

Except one.

The page that Dominic had torn out. The page that contained the hidden map. That one page now stood alone. It had been placed back in the book.

Tonita lifted the parted book and closely examined the page. It had been carefully pasted directly into the center fold of the book, just where the binders glue would have been, holding the page tight into the bind. She turned her eyes to the lines of text on the previous page tracing the last line into the next. The text flowed perfectly from the previous page, onto the new page and then onto the page after. There were no revealing marks that the page had ever gone missing. No new text. No torn text. And no missing text. The page fit perfectly with the other pages of the book. And except for the fact that it was almost unnoticeably thicker, no one could ever know that it held the map to the truth.

SEVENTY FIVE

The cloisters at Abbazia di Santa Maria, built during the Middle Ages, surrounded a library. The sisters of Tonita's order, in addition to seeing to the needs of visiting guests at the guesthouse and helping to care for the few Monks who lived at the abbey, they were also in charge of the upkeep of the magnificent collection of over twenty thousand rare volumes.

Tonita searched the row upon row of near capacity shelves that lined the walls. Ancient, painstakingly hand printed and painted gospels, and rare tattered books on Greek and Roman history, the Crusades, and works by Albrecht Durer, the German master printer of the 16th century, were tucked into every conceivable place. Some stacked upon others, some rested on shelves in front of books, lined in perfect little rows. It was an amalgam of chaos and order. She stopped toward the end of the long row of shelves and climbed upon a chair that doubled as a ladder. She pulled out a small book that had been tucked in between two others, leaving an inch gap in the row of tightly compacted books. She reached into the cincture of the habit she had gone back to wearing, giving away the street clothes that she had worn for so many months, and took out the book on Roswell that had been securely tucked into the cincture. She slid the book on Roswell into the inch wide opening between the two books. She then took the book that had originally occupied the space and pushed it into the same space, making it look as though only one book filled the slim area between the book on the right and the book on the left. She hopped down from the chair and left the library, closing the door on a room filled with millions of words...and the silent truth.

EPILOGUE

Senator Scott stepped spryly up onto the stage. Cameras were rolling. Photographers snapped shots and reporters crowded the room. He did not want to look feeble and aging to the press corps —despite his advanced age—so he grinned as though he moved without the soreness and stiffness in his muscles that accompanied his age. He moved to the podium situated center stage. The round seal of the United States with the symbolic eagle, shield, olive branch, arrows, stars and stripes, like the great seals of ancient Judea and Rome, was attached to the front of the podium. "Ladies and Gentlemen, honored guests, and members of the press, thank you for your attention. My name is Senator Ray Scott. I have been a member of the United States Senate for a great number of years now, thanks to my constituency and God. It gives me great pleasure, after many hard won battles in congress, to announce to you today that the funding for the Atlas Pulsed Power Experimental Facility, which has been moved from Los Alamos in New Mexico to the Nevada Test Site, has been appropriated." Senator Scott moved his eyes around the room, glancing quickly at each of the military guests and reporters in the room. His eyes held for a moment, caught in the gaze of a man standing against the back wall of the room.

The man nodded slightly, almost unnoticeably.

Senator Scott retuned the nod, then quickly moved his eyes, sweeping the room again, and continued with his speech. "The $49 million dollar Atlas Pulsed Power machine will be a great asset to our scientific community and will serve the United States well. Its ability to generate massive electromagnetic..." he paused, "Well, let me bring Doctor Joseph Bechtel to the podium to explain the significant accomplishments that this machine is capable of. Doctor Bechtel."

"Thank you, ladies and gentlemen. I wasn't prepared to speak. I'm really just here to support the Senator, who I can assure you knows every detail of the Atlas Pulsed Power Machine. But let me give it a try." He adjusted the glasses on his nose, just as one would have expected of a scientist of physics to do, then continued, "The Atlas Pulse Powered Machine is really just a big magnet. The machine is a circle of twenty-four meters of approximately seventy nine feet in diameter, and has the ability to produce an electrical output that is equal to four times the world's total electrical power production. The way it works is like this: the amperage of Atlas is very near, if not over, thirty million amps. The machine stores the built up electrical energy slowly, over a period of time, and then releases it in a jolt that is massive. The jolt of electrical energy is caught within the magnetic field and funneled into a thin beam that can project a plane from New York to Los Angeles in just a few seconds. It is a remarkable machine. You might say that it is a machine capable of permitting time travel..."

Senator Scott moved quickly, stepping in close to the Doctor, and gently eased him away from the microphone. "Thank you, Doctor Bechtel for that information. I know you weren't prepared to speak, so we will keep any questions for Doctor Bechtel until after the press conference. I would also like to mention that our technical exchange with the Russian scientists on the Atlas project will also continue as planned. The exchange with Russia on pulse-powered science has been a great achievement for both of our countries. After all, it was with Rasputin that this journey all began. And it is with God's blessing that we will continue."

The man at the back of the room looked directly into Senator Scott's eyes, a gaze that the Senator could not pull himself away from. The man raised his right hand

and moved it to his forehead. He touched his forehead, then moved his hand to his chest, then his left shoulder and completed the gesticulation at his right shoulder. He brought his hand up to his lips and kissed the curled fingers and mouthed the words, "Father forgive them for they know not what they do."

Both men, locked in each other's gaze, glanced up to the round, black trimmed, plastic covered office clock, as the minute hand moved precisely into place. Ticking off the last second...to the third hour.

About the Author

Richard Devin has facilitated negotiating seminars and workshops and served as an advisor and mediator to Fortune 500 Company Executives in the United States, Canada, and Mexico and hundreds of smaller "Mom and Pop" establishments throughout the country. As a Theatrical Talent Agent and Talent Manger in Los Angeles, his client list included Academy Award, Grammy Award and Emmy Award winning and nominated actors and performers. He now lives in Las Vegas and spends his days with his Oldenburg mare, Immerjoy – in the pursuit of dressage perfection (we're a far way off).

Devin was a contributing writer for Envy Man magazine as well as Southern Nevada Equestrian and is the published author of Ripper – A Love Story (13Thirty Books) two business books to the showbiz trade: Actors' Resumes: The Definitive Guidebook (Players Press, 2002) and Do You Want To Be An Actor? 101 Answers to Your Questions About Breaking Into the Biz (Players Press, 2002) and Stop Saying Yes – Negotiate! (13Thirty Books) He contributed to two anthologies: Tales from the Casting Couch (Dove, 1995) and Glory (Sands Publishing, 2001). He is an award winning playwright, having received the Foundation for the Vital Arts Award for his plays, Deceptive Peace and My Mother's Coming (produced by Money Shot Productions, Hollywood CA) and is an optioned screenwriter.

Check out some of the other titles from

13Thirty Books

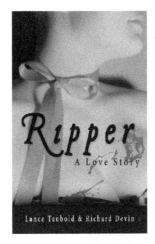